Also by Jennifer Vanderbes

Easter Island

Strangers at the Feast

A NOVEL

Jennifer Vanderbes

SCRIBNER

New York London Toronto Sydney

Scribner
A Division of Simon & Schuster, Inc.
1230 Avenue of the Americas
New York, NY 10020

First Scribner hardcover edition August 2010

SCRIBNER and design are registered trademarks of The Gale Group, Inc., used under license by Simon & Schuster, Inc., the publisher of this work.

For information about special discounts for bulk purchases, please contact Simon & Schuster Special Sales at 1-866-506-1949 or business@simonandschuster.com.

The Simon & Schuster Speakers Bureau can bring authors to your live event. For more information or to book an event contact the Simon & Schuster Speakers Bureau at 1-866-248-3049 or visit our website at www.simonspeakers.com.

Manufactured in the United States of America

10 9 8 7 6 5 4 3 2

Library of Congress Control Number: 2009049756

ISBN 978-1-4391-6695-6
ISBN 978-1-4391-6699-4 (ebook)

In memory of Jim Higgins
(1973–2009)

Strangers at the Feast

Prologue

ELEANOR

*T*hey had been happy people, thought Eleanor.

When others spoke of what happened to her family, they shook their heads. *But the Olsons were so happy!*

Happy, and peaceful.

Eleanor believed she had been a good mother, teaching her children not only to say please and thank you, not only to keep in their elbows while cutting food, but also, when the roast was burned, to compliment Mrs. Murchison on a magnificently cooked meal. When they received gifts, her children wrote detailed notes. *Dearest grandma, we had our furst snowfall last thursday, and I wore that eggskwisit blue skarf you gave me. . . .* Photos were sent—Douglas and Ginny squinting in strategic feverishness at the Monopoly set from her husband's boss, Jeremiah Reynolds; pink-faced and tangled in their room playing Twister, a gift from the mournfully barren wife of their longtime accountant. Because politeness indicated good breeding. And Eleanor believed that small gestures of consideration—a door held open, a dinner plate cleared—cultivated a mind-set of good citizenship.

So, when the time came, her children helped blind men at crosswalks. They hauled Ms. Henderson's groceries from Safeway to her clapboard house. Many times, at the end of dinner parties, Douglas, a mere thirteen, came downstairs to help Pamela Strouse into her thick mink coat, smiling through her Glenlivet kisses, offering his elbow to steady her. *How courteous your children are!* people had always said. *How well you have raised them!* When the Westport library burned down, the children sold lemonade to raise money for the reconstruction. Once, on her way home from college, Ginny pulled off I-95 to help a woman with a blown-out tire and nearly got struck by an eighteen-wheeler. At this Eleanor put her foot down. For the sake of your mother's heart, she had said, do me the courtesy of staying alive.

Being a parent wasn't easy.

First came the breastfeeding and burping, then frantically intercepting every coin, paper clip, and rusted battery in a ten-block radius. Horrid images kept you up: fingers and fan blades, foreheads and marble floors, necks and venetian-blind cords. When your children made it safely to grade school, every finger and toe accounted for, you had to steer them away from the kids who spoke out of turn, who set tacks on the teacher's chair and whiled away afternoons in detention.

The reward for all this, of course, was the adolescent protest perfected over the centuries: the silent treatment.

When you suggested to Douglas that his college girlfriend wasn't an appropriate guest for a family holiday, he might scowl as you lay the silver on the Christmas table. Such sights were needles in a mother's heart. Had you misjudged? Had you gone too far? But you endured the difficult moments because, in the long run, your children would be thankful.

Eleanor's own mother knew this.

"Let him go," she had said when Eleanor fell in love with Howard Brinkmeyer her senior year of high school. Her mother said his parents would want him to find a nice Jewish girl. He was not going to marry a blond girl named Eleanor Haggarty; she might as well wait for John Glenn to invite her to picnic on the moon. She was an experiment for him, a shiksa hors d'oeuvre to cut his hunger before the main course. Having married at seventeen, her mother worried that Eleanor was wasting time. Did Eleanor want to turn out like Alice Freeman? Or worse, like old Miss Barksdale? Being alone—they had lost Eleanor's father to cirrhosis—was no easy life for a woman. Still

Eleanor sulked for months. By flashlight she read *Romeo and Juliet* and soaked her pillow with tears; she cut her hair in a bob and declared she would join a convent. But when, a couple of years later, Howard proposed to a girl from his synagogue, and Eleanor met Gavin on Cape Cod, she knew—though she certainly didn't admit it—that her mother had been right.

It was 1968 and Gavin had just graduated from Yale. From her raft in the ocean Eleanor had seen him running on the beach, kicking up sand. He seemed led by his chin, his blond hair blown back in the breeze. A while later, when she came splashing out of the water, he lay sideways on the sand, reading. He set down his book and smiled.

"Someone pinch me."

"I'm not falling for that," she said.

"Ah, the mermaid speaks. But does she go to restaurants?"

That night, over lobster rolls and fried clams, they squeezed lemon wedges and licked their sour fingertips and spoke about what they wanted to do with their lives. Or Gavin spoke, and Eleanor listened. She didn't know what she wanted to do, but she loved the way he talked—about his heroes, people like John Kenneth Galbraith, John F. Kennedy, and his own father, who had been a two-term mayor of their Massachusetts town. He confessed to funny habits, like keeping track of the votes of Supreme Court Justices. He said he had his best ideas when he was running long distances, that the world became crystal clear in the sixth mile, that he could see his future. He said he either wanted to be a public defender or a professor. He hated hypocrisy and laziness.

Eleanor said she didn't really hate anything.

Afterward they drove to the beach and Gavin pulled apart pieces of saltwater taffy, which they each chewed in a giggling race to name the flavor: cinnamon, bubble gum, peach. The smell of barnacles and wooden docks and sea foam brushed warmly over Eleanor's face. From the trunk Gavin pulled out a violin and played Bach's *Arioso* and people in nearby cars turned off their engines and climbed onto their hoods to listen. He seemed the most passionate and dazzling man she had ever met.

This, of course, was before the war.

"Stick it out," her mother said after they had married and Gavin returned from Vietnam, sullen and withdrawn. A lot of war wives were whispering about divorce. A classmate from Wellesley had paid a week's typing-pool wages to talk to a lawyer, then slipped Eleanor his business card, insisting she wasn't going to spend the rest of her life married to some nut job who threw kitchen knives at the sofa: "The foam is popping out everywhere!"

Would that be Eleanor's life? No, her mother said. Make the coffee and iron his shirts. Serve him steak au poivre with baked potatoes and kiss him before bed. Say yes if he wants to touch you, even if you are sleeping. Don't ask what's wrong. Pretend everything is fine and soon enough, it will be. There were few marital problems, she added, that couldn't be cured with a baby.

Eleanor said she didn't think Gavin wanted a baby.

Her mother said, "That's why God made safety pins."

Her mother was dying, and Eleanor feared the dual blows of being orphaned *and* divorced.

She got pregnant. They had Douglas, then Ginny. They moved to Westport, Connecticut.

Their life progressed with a deliberate contentment. She tended their new house, raised the children—but Gavin remained remote. There were no violin serenades, few compliments. He spent his mornings jogging miles in the dark, before the sun was up, and in the evenings he pressed his eye to his large black telescope and gaped at the moon.

"There better not be a naked lady up there," she'd joke.

He brought home a solid paycheck from Reynolds Insurance, along with an annual sales bonus that allowed them a modest one-week vacation in Newport, and on her birthday each year, a bouquet of pink roses. He never threw knives at the furniture, never stumbled home sour-mouthed from scotch, never leapt to the ground at the bang of a backfiring car, and for this Eleanor counted herself lucky.

"As you get older, Ellie, there are few things you want in life but for your children to be safe and healthy," her mother said the morning she passed away.

Eleanor would later understand what she meant.

As she sat on the sofa at night with her *Reader's Digest,* waiting for her husband to come home, she would take stock. What did she have? What had she accomplished? She would look around at the photographs from family trips; Douglas's high school lacrosse trophies; Ginny's first published academic article; the crayoned artwork of Douglas's twins; and she would think—My children are grown and healthy adults. I have beautiful grandchildren. She would thank the Lord that everyone was at peace, everything was in order.

She could happily buy the groceries and weed the garden because everyone she cared about was well.

But if someone were to try to threaten that? Was there a length to which a mother wouldn't go?

Part I

GINNY

Ginny flicked on the kitchen light. The stuffed brown grocery bags sat exactly where she'd left them the night before when her department chair called. Distracted by another one of Priya's tantrums, she'd forgotten about them entirely.

It was still dark out, and as Ginny leaned close to the window to glance outside she felt a draft; mental note: get some kind of insulation, or putty, or a whole new window. She made lots of mental notes lately, though she suspected that *actual* notes would be better, since after two months her bathroom faucet still went drip, drip, drip and she had nothing resembling a doorbell or a dead bolt. She'd spent so many years in Manhattan passing her super in the hallway—at which point her mental Post-its magically came to life—she was having a hard time remembering that this suburban house was hers, and if anything needed fixing, she'd be the one wielding the wrench.

Switching on the space heater at her feet, she let out a long yawn. She was never up this early. Early risers bragged about the start of the day, getting a jump on things. What was the big deal? It was just like late at night, her favorite time. Only she hadn't had any coffee yet and her face—the windows over the sink unkindly moonlighted as mirrors—was shockingly puffy.

She turned the radio on, softly—an NPR broadcast explaining the history of Thanksgiving. *And the grateful Plymouth Pilgrims . . .* No, no, no. Off! They always prettied up the story.

Ginny appreciated that Thanksgiving still got people elbowing

9

onto airplanes and trains, piling into minivans and driving hundreds of miles to see family; it was one of the few times she saw her brother and his kids. But she could never get over the wild historical inaccuracy of the thing.

Most people knew only the Pilgrim and Indian prologue: how the newly landed Plymouth colonists couldn't make heads or tails of the local flora, how they had the fishing skills of desert nomads, how they couldn't track an animal to save their own skin. Only half survived the first New World winter. Enter Squanto of the Wampanoag tribe. He taught the Puritans to catch eel and grow corn, introduced them to squash. With his help, 1621 brought a massive harvest, so Plymouth's governor invited Squanto's entire tribe for a three-day feast of wild duck, boiled pumpkin, fish, berries, lobster, and plums.

But this festival of thanks wasn't repeated for another fifty-five years, by which time the Wampanoag were gone. The pudgy Pilgrims were now thanking God Almighty for their victory over the heathen natives.

Ginny had seen the original 1676 First Thanksgiving Proclamation, the crisp yellowed vellum on which a beautiful calligraphic script complained that the Almighty Lord had "brought to pass bitter things against his own Covenant people in this wilderness." Still, he *was* almighty, so the Pilgrims didn't overdo the whining. "It certainly bespeaks our positive Thankfulness, when our Enemies are in any measure disappointed or destroyed."

Pass the cranberry sauce! Another slice of sweet-potato pie in honor of the slaughtered Pequots! The day was a celebration of *genocide,* which was why modern descendants of the few Native American survivors, Ginny occasionally noted over dinner, did not gather on the last Thursday of November to happily devour turkey.

But she'd promised herself this year not to say *genocide,* or get into any lectures on Colonial history. Actually, she'd promised her brother. He called it a buzzkill. And the truth was—was this a sign of age? A dawning conservatism?—the actual *buzz* of being a buzzkill was wearing off. She had mortgage payments. She had a daughter.

Ginny tiptoed to the bottom of the stairs and listened to hear if Priya was moving around yet. Nothing.

And it wasn't as though Ginny couldn't rally feelings of patriotism. She knew enough of world history to realize that if she'd lived in any other era, in another culture or country, there was a chance that at thirteen she'd have been left to die on a mountaintop, an Aztec sacrifice to fend off drought. Or she might have been stoned for promiscuity; she had gotten around. It was lose-lose with primitive cultures—they got you for being a virgin *or* for being a whore. At best, an unmarried thirty-four-year-old woman who couldn't cook a proper stew would be sent to live on the community fringes with the widows. Yes, her country had committed sins, but in the context of human civilization, Ginny cut it some slack.

Anyway, it was too early to be thinking like this. Today was going to be an unprecedented event in the Olson family!

She got the French press started: grinds, water, stir, wait. She'd learned this from her father. Making coffee was the only time he set foot in the kitchen, because he was particular about its strength. So at age fourteen Ginny started drinking coffee, standing beside him early in the morning while he carefully rolled up the sleeve of his gray suit, his spoon clinking the glass exactly ten times. Percolators are for peasants, he would say with a wink. That was his saying when he didn't like something. Salad, paper napkins, Christmas cards—all for peasants.

And then she grew up and spent her college years studying the habits of, well, peasants. It struck her now that that might have been her sad attempt to get closer to her father: *Dad talks about peasants. Sign me up for peasant studies! Call it anthropology!* Of course, they rarely talked about her work. They rarely talked. When she called, her mother always picked up, practically before the phone rang, like some Wild West pistol draw. *Oh, your father's off doing something . . .* Ginny sometimes imagined her father tied to a chair, gagged, desperately inching closer to the telephone while her mother declared he was fine, fine, fine.

Her fantasy, of course, was that he wanted to talk but that circumstances prevented him from doing so. Which was not true. Her father was simply quiet, aloof. He liked his telescope, his newspaper, his morning runs. He barely read her dissertation when it was published. But there were advantages to that. She knew—thank God—he'd never lay eyes on her most recent article, "The Emasculation of the American Warrior," in the *Journal of American Cultural Studies*. Not pleasant reading for a Vietnam vet.

Ginny poured her coffee and looked at the counter. In between a bag of apples—were you supposed to refrigerate apples?—and a red mesh sack of potatoes lay the frayed notebook pages on which she had scribbled notes for her speech.

The night before, Mark Stevens, the department chair, had called from the airport to invite—or actually persuade—her to give the keynote address at a feminist geography conference being held in March. The Twenty-first Century: Putting Women in their Place. The only thing Ginny hated more than conferences billed as feminist were conferences with clever titles. But Mark was throwing her a bone. The stipend was good, and after her emergency sabbatical that fall, she needed to pad her résumé for her tenure review.

Her department was on her side, but there were still university reviewers to contend with. Her work had become dangerously interdisciplinary; integrating paleontology and anthropology into American studies was seen as stepping on other people's toes. (Academics, Ginny knew, had colossal toes.) She'd published a book of poetry on Colonial themes, which had garnered her attention that could work against tenure. Also, some people did not appreciate the irony of their popular lecture course—The History of the American Family—being taught by a woman who showed up at every university function with a different date, one of them, regrettably, a graduate student.

Perhaps because she was a bit of a loner, social networks had always fascinated her. After majoring in anthropology, she spent two years in Sudan and Nigeria studying the family structures and social mores of the Dinka and Yoruba. She lived in a grass hut and sipped Nescafé from a tin cup every morning. She strung beads and wove grass baskets and herded cattle, and at night, by the soft glow of an oil lamp, scribbled data and observations in her notebook. It was a mind-opening and spiritually stimulating experience that ended unfortunately with an affair with Dr. Blaise Langley, her married field advisor, whose ideas about his own family structure and mores were, in the end, a bit too open-minded for Ginny's taste.

Back home, American cultural geography won her over for graduate school. She was done with ringworm and mosquito nets and advisors who thought they were Indiana Jones. For the first ten years, she was consumed with research and teaching. Migration maps were thumbtacked to her apartment walls; encyclopedic census reports barricaded her bed. She skipped out of parties early and smuggled thermoses of coffee into the special collections division, reading through the night about life on the frontier.

The early settlers amazed her—they had pluck, they led lives of sweaty drama. Theirs was a world of corsets and whipping posts and indentured servitude. People worked the land and died in ungainly ways. Modern life, in comparison, seemed a cinch.

As the smallest political unit of society, the family struck Ginny as the perfect microcosm for examining social change. Alimony, social security, domestic architecture, medicine, child care, war—they were all products, to some degree, of the evolving family. Ginny had once spent countless nights fervently debating other PhD candidates as to whether industrialization caused or reflected the shift from extended to nuclear family.

Now, at thirty-four, she didn't care so much. Like those college dorm-room debates about the meaning of life, the conversations were like bubble gum or gobstoppers—junk you eventually lost the taste for, or feared you'd choke on.

Her first years teaching—when she watched her students shuffle into class in their Puma sneakers and Diesel jeans, slinging overstuffed North Face backpacks onto their desks—she went off on passionate tangents about the Dinka and the Yoruba, pleading against capitalism and urban individualism (God, she hoped they didn't know she lived alone in a high-rise), and their eyes would collectively roll. They liked their lives. They liked their gizmos. And now, though she hid her cell phone and iPod when she approached the room where she gave her Primitive Utopias lecture, as soon as she was clear of campus, Ginny pawed through her purse and rescued her electronic friends and then, like her students, lost herself in a private sea of sound waves.

At least she listened to *world* music.

But Ginny had recently curtailed her tirades against consumer culture, her outrage over the societal ramifications of industrialism. She worried it sounded like the misery of a single woman with too much time on her hands. Also, her classes were beginning to bore her. Semester after semester her lectures were the same—the curse of history, you had nothing new to talk about. Once in a while, just to spice things up, to see some faint shock on her students' faces, she'd dim the lights and throw on a slide show of Colonial birth-control methods.

Here we have a very leathery-looking pig-intestine condom. Notice the ties on the end to fasten it. These were extremely expensive, thus reused dozens of times.

Next slide . . .

Mainly, she sat in her small campus office, waiting for students who rarely showed, amusing herself by inventing fake historical movements and academic jargon.

I am diarrhetically opposed to the diabetic polemic on the Combustible revolution. Revisionist hysteriography!

Clearly, a massive paradigmatic shit has occurred here.

What do you call an obvious case of tuberculosis? Conspicuous consumption!

Or she put her feet up on her desk and threw darts at the bull's-eye she'd covered with a photograph of John Wilkes Booth.

Squirrels scurrying up a tree outside caught her attention. The rising sun cast a soft light on the square patch of grass outside her house. She couldn't properly call it a lawn, didn't want it to be a lawn. She had never seen the point of landscaping and lawn mowers. All that work to have a patch of nature that looked entirely unnatural? Ginny would have preferred a bit of jungle out front, a touch of rain forest, a thick vine her guests could swing in on.

Guests! She looked at her watch and surveyed the room to see what she could do quietly. Scrub the potatoes, peel the apples? Open the cans of pumpkin?

She opened the eight cans, orange goop plunking into a large glass bowl, then tossed them into the trash. She was religious about recycling newspapers, printer paper, cereal boxes—anything to do with saving trees—but she loathed washing dishes, and so the empty cans and jars of marinara sauce went zip!, straight to the garbage.

Ginny rinsed her hands and assembled her cookbooks. The coffee was finally doing its work, her synapses firing at normal speed. She couldn't believe she was doing this—hosting a family event.

How her mother had protested when Ginny called to explain that she wanted everyone to come to her new house in Mamaroneck for Thanksgiving.

"Oh, dear. I'll make up an itinerary for you: when to start the stuffing, the turkey, because nothing's worse than a bunch of guests angrily waiting to be fed. They will practically—"

"Mom," Ginny had cut her off, "all you need to do is finally meet Priya. Just come."

Her mother went silent, having been chastened many times—perhaps unfairly—for her bossiness, a tendency that by this age Ginny knew her mother could not control. Then she whispered, in what almost seemed the voice of a child, "I'm excited."

DOUGLAS

*D*ouglas was getting ready to load the car as Denise skipped down the stairs in her aerobics-class way, wearing pink velour sweat-pants and an old sweater. Her bright blond hair was pulled into the tight, high ponytail she wore for yard work. The twins, Brian and Brandon, and his youngest, Laura, followed sluggishly in their play clothes.

Denise clapped. "We're leaving in T minus ten, everybody, okay?"

"That's what you're wearing?" Douglas asked.

"I didn't want to make Ginny feel like we're expecting something fancy."

"You look like you're expecting hot dogs."

"I'm allowed to be comfortable."

"You wear a cocktail dress for Arbor Day."

"Suddenly you're Mr. Fashion? This meal will not involve sipping from china, I guarantee you."

"Denise, would you rather visit your own family?"

This, as always, silenced her. Douglas did not want to engage in the all-too-familiar argument that would end with Denise storming his cluttered desk to pull out unpaid bills. This was the first day in months he was going to be able to spend with his children and he was feeling festive. He was also eager to see Ginny's "phenomenal deal." She'd bought just after the bubble burst, snagging a preforeclosed three-bed, two-bath. The listing she had e-mailed three months ear-lier—subject line, To Buy or Not to Buy?—had said oak floors, a sun-

17

porch, and a buildable acre, under $350K. Not to mention a good school district. All just thirty minutes north of Manhattan. *Buy! Buy! Buy!* For a person who didn't know the first thing about finance or real estate or even a credit report, Ginny had snagged a bargain. At least someone was benefiting from the 2007 market massacre.

Denise was clearly miffed, though. If anyone other than Douglas's mother was going to cook a family feast, she thought it should be her.

"Well, I'm putting on a tie. My sister is not serving us Schlitz."

"Put on a tuxedo if you want, Doug. I don't care." Which wasn't quite true. Denise liked to pick out his clothes: blues and grays that she said brought out his eyes, loose-fitting sweaters that hid the spare tire he'd recently developed.

Denise, on the other hand, had maintained her figure, as well as her year-round tanning-bed glow. His wife had a stunning ability to keep herself together, to stay fit, better than most women her age with three children. In fact, she looked almost identical to the twenty-four-year-old version of herself he'd married, except for her eyebrows. Over the past year her eyebrows had been plucked to near invisibility. At night, he'd see her leaning into the bathroom mirror, tweezers glinting from her hand. It was frightening to watch, but even when she climbed into bed, the crescents above her eyes red and swollen, Douglas politely pretended not to notice. It was stress. And he, alone, was the cause.

One of her balding eyebrows arched at him now:

"Would you at least first hand me the juice boxes," she said, "and the disinfectant towelettes and help me get ready for this unnecessary drive?"

They packed up the Lincoln Navigator, loaded the dolls and the Game Boys, an array of antibacterial gels and wipes, the car seat, the GPS, and his present for Priya. Over the years their trip preparations had become militaristic: checklists and double checks; a final inventory. If push came to shove, they could survive an ice age in that car. Denise had set her watch alarm to a five-minute departure warning, and when the alarm beeped, they herded the kids in—chop, chop, chop—programmed Ginny's address, and started the engine.

So later that night, when the detective asked, Douglas knew with certainty that it was 11:00 a.m. when they left the house.

GINNY

I said I was doing the cooking, Mom."

Her mother had arrived early, alone, hugging a pyramid of gravy and cranberry-sauce vats.

"Don't be silly! These are just little tidbits. Nibbles."

From her purse she pulled an apron and fastened it over her Thanksgiving sweater. "Put me to work!" She planted a noisy kiss on Ginny's cheek. Ginny thumbed off the parentheses of her mother's Maybelline Pink Peony lipstick, a vibrant fuchsia she had worn religiously since Easter brunch 1996, when Ginny's father looked up from his lamb roast and said, "You know, Eleanor, that pinkish stuff brings out the green in your eyes."

Her Shalimar, as usual, nearly knocked Ginny down. Her mother was a potpourri of consumer scents: Oil of Olay, Listerine, Woolite, the sulfuric bite of her Loving Care. If her mother ever abandoned her array of chemicals, Ginny doubted she would recognize her.

"Well, when do I get to meet my new granddaughter?"

"She's napping," Ginny said.

"I've been waiting months!"

"Wine, Mom?"

"It's much too early for wine, dear."

Her mother began unpacking her elaborate collection of dishes in the shapes of the items served in them. Then she unloaded a plastic-wrapped tart. "It wouldn't be Thanksgiving without my pear tart with the graham-cracker crust." Her mother opened the refrigerator and gaped at the disarray. "Goodness, let's just leave it out."

Ginny uncorked a bottle of Chardonnay and poured a glass. She took a long sip and scanned the kitchen: an assembly line of bowls and pots and cutting boards.

"I did come early so I could be the first to meet her." In fact, Ginny's mother arrived early for everything—dentists and doctors appointments, of which there were many; movies, so she could get an aisle seat in case of a fire; her own surprise fiftieth birthday party, which she had sniffed out, arriving early to set up the proper cups and napkins and plates rather than endure a noisy chorus of *Surprise!*

"You want to go shake her awake, Mom?"

Her mother waved away the suggestion. "Listen, sleeping can be a sign of illness. I raised two children. I have expertise. All my lady friends are bombarded with questions by their daughters. Does my daughter even ask me about which bedtime stories to read? What to do for a runny nose? You must turn to somebody with questions."

"God bless Google," said Ginny.

"And you trust these strangers on the Internet?"

"You make them sound like child predators."

Her mother's eyes flared and she shook her head vigorously, as though shaking away the image of a man in a dark van offering a lollipop to a girl on the street. Then, as though remembering the times Ginny had chided her anxiety, her mother collected herself and smiled brightly.

"Well, it won't do to have you drinking alone. I'll have a little sip. Just a taste to keep you company. Oh, that's way too much. Ginny, it'll go to waste!" Ginny and her brother called this their mother's refuse-and-booze strategy. By initially refusing alcohol, in her mind, she never actually drank it. "Well, okay, yum, that is lovely. Zip dee do, straight to my head!" She touched her cheeks. "You know, you look very good, Ginny. You're rosy. Like an Eskimo."

"Mom, you're always assessing me."

"Arrest me for paying my daughter a compliment."

Her mother couldn't help herself. Ginny was *her* product. Like an apple in the supermarket she was inspecting for wormholes.

Ginny dumped the potatoes into the sink, let the faucet hiccup on. "Look, there's a recipe on my laptop screen out in the living room. Would you print it?"

Her mother sipped her wine, adjusted her bulbous gold clip-on earrings. "I hope those aren't *russet* potatoes. Please, if you love your family at all, you must use red potatoes, red creamer potatoes. And honestly, I cannot go mucking around with people's printers. Don't you think someone should set the table?"

Her mother looked at her watch, eyes widening with alarm, and dramatically tightened her lips, making it clear she was extending the maternal munificence of keeping them zipped. She grabbed a fistful of utensils and strode to the table.

God knows why I thought she could click *print,* mused Ginny. Her mother couldn't change a tire or a lightbulb. She didn't know the difference between a flat head and a Phillips screwdriver. Remote controls? VCR? It's not that she was stupid. She went to Wellesley. But she grew up having things done for her, first by her father, then by her husband. She would sooner stare at a broken television for hours than crouch down to see if it was plugged in.

Suggest she jiggle a cable, and she'd say, "Ginny, do I look like an electrician?" Or, Ginny's favorite response, "My hair is wet." Her mother didn't want to be electrocuted.

If anyone lacked the frontier spirit, the desire to meet a challenge, it was Ginny's mother. *Excuse me, but how long before we get to Oregon? I was told this was a trail. This doesn't feel at all like a trail.* Ten miles out of Missouri her mother would have been shoved from the wagon.

She wanted to *feel* useful, but not be useful.

When Ginny's mother came of age, housework could eat up the week. But in the last twenty years, the world had belched out an array of machines and services that allowed women to squeeze chores into one day. Microwaves and laundry machines. Wrinkle-free fabrics, frozen dinners, Cuisinarts, nonstick pans—Febreze! As far as Ginny was concerned, nothing in world history had done more for women's liberation than Chinese takeout. A piping-hot, tasty meal for four in little white cartons! For under twenty-five dollars! That had been the subject of Ginny's first published paper: "How General Tso Liberated American Women."

These changes should have given Ginny's mother time to learn Spanish, or yoga. But new activities frightened her. So cleaning house turned into a tea ceremony. She stretched out errands as though she were paid by the hour, by the number of times she opened and closed the trunk of her powder blue Lexus. One day she needed milk, the next day she had to *carpe* the sale on red seedless grapes. Dry cleaning was picked up and dropped off on entirely different trips. It would have taken a team of Nobel Prize–winning physicists a month to calculate her carbon footprint.

Like the work of tollbooth collectors and movie-ticket sellers, her services were being rendered obsolete by technology.

But what happened to people when the world made their sacrifices unnecessary?

"*I* could have gone to Columbia graduate school," her mother sometimes reminded her children, stressing how their grandmother advised her to forsake a master's degree and instead start a family when their father returned from Vietnam. She said it with a demure but self-righteous smile, or with laughter—as though she couldn't believe she would ever have done such a crazy thing! But who mentioned a thing so frequently unless it bothered her?

If her mother had more than one glass of wine, she would bring it up several times at dinner. "Children, do you know where I could have gone after Wellesley?" and Ginny's father would say, "Since we're on the subject, Eleanor, do you know where *I* could have gone?"

Then she simply asked someone to pass the spinach.

DOUGLAS

Good, his father's car wasn't at Ginny's house yet. The last thing Douglas wanted was extra time with his father, who would no doubt grill him about the latest round of subprime write-offs. Once they got the game on, they'd be fine. They'd talk sports. He just had to stall until then.

His mother's car had already claimed the only patch of blacktop, so Douglas parked on the street. Even at a distance, he could tell her tires were low. It irked him that his mother, a woman terrified of car accidents—she religiously read the police blotter to identify dangerous local roads—was so lax about car maintenance. He'd have to check her engine oil, ask her when she'd replaced her brake pads. The last time he'd been in the car with her it had rained, and her windshield wipers merely smeared the water around. Worse, she had contentedly leaned forward, her nose virtually to the glass, squinting through the blur as though she had no idea wipers existed that would allow her to see the road.

"Welcome, welcome!"

A storm door slammed as Ginny stepped out of the house in flip-flops and blue jeans. She hugged herself in a long, rust-colored cardigan. Her red hair was pinned in its usual loose bun, her freckled face happy and glowing. She wore her signature purple cat-eye glasses. Douglas always felt a momentary shock when he saw this carelessly glamorous woman who was his sister. A far cry from the pudgy child whose doughy face was scaffolded with braces and bifocals.

Douglas threw open the door of his Navigator. "We bring hungry mouths, Gin!"

"God, you all look like you just stepped out of a William Merritt Chase painting!"

Denise shot Douglas a glance. She found Ginny's compliments pretentious. But Ginny was an academic; it was to be expected.

Stepping from the car, Douglas took in the yellow colonial salt-box—a post-and-beam construction with a flat front and center chimney. Ginny had explained that the layout was a holdover from the time when houses were taxed on the number of stories: the front was two stories, but the back roof sloped down to one. All Douglas cared about was that home buyers paid 10 percent more for anything quaint: developers had started building saltboxes again.

"So you went colonial," he said.

She grinned. "It did seem fitting."

The place desperately needed a paint job and new shutters, the yard was strewn with yellow and red leaves that needed to be raked, but it was set back nicely on a level, buildable one-acre lot. Normally, it would have sold for a good half million. His sister had done well.

Ginny stepped forward to help unload the car. "Don't tell me you got another SUV?"

His sister's social conscience was a gland that never stopped salivating.

"Denise wanted red instead. I aim to make my wife happy."

"Two SUVs!" sneered Denise. "Fat chance." She made straight for the trunk, and Ginny froze for a moment, registering the tension. Fortunately for Douglas, the twins, who had just turned nine, exploded from the backseat.

"Well, look how enormous you've gotten!" said Ginny. "How will you ever fit in my house? Dougie, what are you feeding these kids? Camel cannelloni? Hippopotamus burgers?"

"Our favorite new food is Worcestershire sauce."

"Oh, good, 'cause I've got a barrelful inside!" They charged the door, and Ginny leaned into Douglas. "What's that?"

Denise was unloading a pile of foil-covered plates.

"Hummus and Wheat Thins," said Denise. "For the twins. They always get hummus and Wheat Thins before dinner."

Ginny sulked at her flip-flops. "Great. Excellent."

Douglas lifted Laura out of the car, careful not to separate her from her tablecloth. This was a red and green tablecloth, from Christmas three years earlier, that his daughter had grown attached to. Now, at age five, if anyone tried to take it from her, she screamed. Douglas thought the glittery gold thread attracted her. Sometimes, Laura begged the twins to mummify her in the tablecloth and parade her through the house. Which Douglas found impossibly cute.

One of the shocks of fatherhood had been how much more enamored he was of his daughter than of his sons. He played catch with his boys and took them to action films, but he was so absurdly mesmerized by Laura that he could sit on the lawn with her for hours just picking blades of grass. She was happy and magical and the way she whispered "Daddy" with her licorice breath made him feel like a king. The high-wire act of his domestic life was masking this favoritism.

Ginny swept her arm into a purple foyer, which smelled of incense. "You like?"

"Nice casa, Sis."

The foyer, despite the purple, had a pleasant arch that made it seem more spacious than it was. It flowed nicely into the living room, which had been painted mauve with white baseboard. As they all started in, Ginny raised her palm: "Shoes, guys!"

Douglas set Laura down, heeled off his shoes. The oak floorboards needed refinishing. He gave a good knock to the foyer wall. "Plaster, huh. When was the place built?"

"Oh, 1950, or maybe 1960. Pre–civil rights."

"Basement?"

"A messy one."

"Then it was probably the forties or the fifties. By the sixties it was all concrete-slab foundation."

Denise marched the kids into the living room and began unloading bags. Douglas could see her rapidly scan the space like an auctioneer, trying to figure out how to erect a play area for Laura in what was barely a quarter of their own living room. He figured the ground floor was about twenty-six by twenty-four feet, the upstairs half that. On a full acre, most people would have bought the place for a teardown.

Douglas knocked another spot and heard the hollow thud of drywall. "Someone's done renovations. Does it still have the original fusebox?"

"Probably."

"Gin, you need to know these things. You at least had an inspection?"

Between her chaotic romantic life and her teaching and writing, his sister had little interest in life's necessities. She paid bills months late, forgot to file taxes. She could explain, in tireless detail, the medical-insurance practices of seventeenth-century Dutch immigrants in Pennsylvania but forgot to pay her own premiums. Adopting a child and buying a house within a three-month period was a lot to bite off, especially for Ginny.

"Yes, yes, yes, Doug." Her chin dipped with affectionate pity, always sorry for her businessman brother's obsession with paperwork. "I have a tome on this house and you're welcome to read through it if that's your idea of a fun Thanksgiving."

"I'll say two things and then I'll stop: if they found even a hint of Radon you need to get an abatement system in here pronto, and for the love of Allah, make sure the electrical system is up-to-date. You've got two-prong outlets. I don't want you turning on a light and going up in a bonfire."

"What about meteorites?" She shook his shoulder in mock terror. "Have you seen my roof?"

"I'm not kidding, Gin. Look, I have an Estonian guy who'll rewire this house for fifteen hundred dollars."

"How much for meteorite proofing?"

"You got ibuprofen? I'm starting to feel a big pain in my ass."

"Aw, Dougie, I'm just being careful."

"You know, Ginny, if you do some rewiring and fix the roof, maybe get a paint job on the outside, you could probably flip this place in a year and make good money."

"No flipping!" Denise called from the living-room floor, flanked by the children. "Do not get your sister started on flipping."

He wished his wife wouldn't act like as if his ventures had all been failures. Negative energy, too much negative energy. He wanted to remind her that she hadn't complained when flipping made them a hundred grand in two years, or when he used the cash to fly them to Acapulco and to Disney World. She certainly hadn't complained when he bought her a double-strand diamond bracelet. But he wasn't going to argue; no, today was all about recharging his battery.

"Now, Ginny, I'm giving you the benefit of the doubt, assuming that I don't need to explain the dangers of lead paint."

Ginny threaded her arm through his. "How about a drink, Dougie?"

"First things first. Where's my new niece?"

ELEANOR

*E*leanor stood alone in the kitchen, examining the mess her daughter had made: potatoes and parsnips splayed all over the counter. Soiled cutting boards, balled-up plastic bags, and—well, Eleanor would have to rinse this out—a mug of coffee that appeared to be hours old.

Eleanor was not surprised. For years Ginny had bristled at the idea of women in the kitchen, as though roasting a pork loin and baking raisin bread were acts of degradation. Also, Ginny had never much *liked* Thanksgiving, offering an almost undetectable rolling of the eyes each year as she arrived, which Eleanor thought stemmed from her daughter's experience in Westport Elementary's Thanksgiving play. Cast as the turkey at age nine (through no fault of Eleanor's, Ginny was a plump child), Ginny wore a brown leotard with feathers and a red paper beak, and was required to squat onstage for the play's full second act as the little Pilgrims and Indians circled her, singing "Oh, What a Harvest, What a Friendship!" As the curtain fell, several mischievous Pilgrim girls plucked the feathers Eleanor had spent hours gluing. Tucking her in that night, she braced for Ginny's tearful query as to why *she* hadn't been cast as a Pilgrim, preparing a full explanation of the inevitable misdeeds of ill-bred children and the importance of forgiveness. But Ginny merely lay beneath her blanket, working something through her head; finally she declared that during her time onstage she had thought long and hard about what it was like to be a turkey, to think turkey thoughts, to feel turkey feelings, and that henceforth (this was the year Ginny used "henceforth"), she would no longer eat animals.

It delighted Eleanor that now her daughter was at least *trying* to cook.

For there had been a time—years ago, admittedly—when Eleanor had thought Ginny would grow up to be exactly like her.

The young Ginny would patter into Eleanor's room, storm her closets, and then parade about, lost in the fabric of Eleanor's beige housedresses and seersucker suits. For her grand finale, Ginny stepped into Eleanor's sequined black dress, and tottered around in her high heels, her neck hung with pearls.

"How on earth do you doooo?" Ginny exclaimed. "I'm Mrs. Olson, and the pleasure is all mine."

At the grocery store, if Eleanor smelled a melon, Ginny would sniff it, too, and at the checkout register, she demanded to put the items on the counter herself and to hand over the coupons. As a treat, Eleanor would sometimes hand Ginny her wallet and let her count out the money.

At school, her daughter made her cards with drawings of a small bunny rabbit—Eleanor called Ginny "Bunny"—beside a mommy bunny rabbit; inside they said: *I miss you, Mama Rabbit*.

Ginny studied photo albums of Eleanor and said, "Mama Rabbit was so pretty."

Once, in Bloomingdales, Ginny wanted to look at the Hello Kitty section. But Eleanor's attention had been caught by an end-of-season outerwear sale. That year, with Gavin's promotion to junior sales broker, he had raised her allowance, which meant she could afford a new winter coat. She slipped excitedly into a green cashmere double-breasted one, fastened her purse on her shoulder, and spun around.

"Does Mommy look elegant?"

But Ginny was nowhere in sight. Tearing through the coat racks, Eleanor shouted her name. Finally she spotted a young woman riding the escalator down toward her, Ginny at her side.

"Good God. Where was she?"

The woman shook her head slowly, remembering something awful. "I saw her with a man. He was holding her hand and something didn't feel right, you get that queasy feeling in your gut."

"What man?!"

"That creep is probably in Poughkeepsie by now. I asked your daughter, 'Do you know that man?' and he ran like the cops were coming."

Eleanor tugged off the green coat and threw it on the floor.

That afternoon, on the train back to Westport, Eleanor felt a headache coming on. Her brain seemed to be pressing into her eyeballs. She had lost her father and her mother, as well as her younger sister; Eleanor was no stranger to grief. But to lose her own child? She felt she had glimpsed a black chasm. She had seen, for a moment, how merciless the world might be; there were no limits to what could be taken from you. Yes, she could return to her white clapboard house, but on the periphery, on buses and subways, on sidewalks and in cinemas, in deep and distant forests, dark forces lurked. A strong passion stirred within her: She would defend her children with sticks and stones; with her fingernails, her naked fists.

"I have never been so furious with you," she said, climbing into bed with Ginny. "How could you have gone off with that man? It is simply not the behavior of a child who cares one iota about her mother."

Ginny's eyes were red. "I just wanted the Hello Kitty. All the girls have it."

"And do all the girls wander off with strange men?"

Eleanor patted her hair, the heat of her daughter's scalp rising through her fingers. She kissed Ginny's forehead, more forcefully than she intended.

"Ouch. I'm sorry, Mom."

"Now this headache won't go away. I'll have to take an aspirin, I think. Maybe two. Do you think I should take two?"

"If it hurts bad."

"Yes, I think so." Eleanor laid her head on her daughter's shoulder. "Whatever happens, Ginny, don't tell your father or Douglas about this. They simply will not understand and it will upset them. You won't tell them, right?"

And her daughter, who even as a child understood loyalty, never told.

They shared other secrets. One afternoon, years later, Ginny left a note on her mother's dresser.

Dear Mom,

Maybe you think it's too soon, and maybe you'll say no, but I think the time is absolutely right for me to start wearing a brassiere. Many other girls in school are wearing them, as I am made to see every day in the locker room. And I am one of the only girls without one. Do not get the wrong idea please because I do not think I have big boobs. But sometimes when I wear a t-shirt now and there are boys around, I am uncomfortable. If you do not think I am ready I will understand but I do think I am ready and it would be sad if you didn't think so too. Also, I read in a magazine that there are health benefits to wearing a brassiere for your spine. I lost the magazine but I could go to the library and see if they have it. Anyway, I will be in my room, waiting for your answer.

> *Love,*
> *Ginny*

Eleanor arranged a shopping expedition for the next day. She set her hair and put on her best dress and plaid coat. She dressed Ginny in her burgundy gingham smock, and when the saleslady asked, "Is this your lovely daughter? So grown-up!" Eleanor beamed with pride.

Lavender, pink, ivory, white—they bought four brassieres with adjustable straps. That night, Ginny locked herself in her room for hours, finally emerging as Eleanor was preparing dinner.

"Do I look like Dolly Parton?" Ginny giggled, twirling into the kitchen.

"You look positively lovely."

At dinner, Ginny eyed her chest, shifting the shoulder straps and scratching at the clasp. She entirely ignored the casserole on her plate, an act for which Eleanor normally would have admonished her, except that Eleanor felt herself the guardian of a magnificent secret. Her daughter was becoming a woman.

A month later, when Ginny's menstruation began, they locked themselves in the upstairs bathroom while Eleanor explained the various sanitary options, and the responsibilities of a woman to store these well out of sight, and to dispose of them discreetly.

This would be the last time Ginny sought her advice.

If only Eleanor could have pinpointed the day Ginny slid away from her. But no unpleasant incident prompted the change. It was merely, as the parenting books had warned, an adolescent withdrawal.

"Ginny, would you like to come to the store?"

Her daughter was busy, she was tired, she found the glare of the store's white lights oppressive.

If Eleanor happened to mention (and naturally one had to make conversation) that she wanted to buy fresh-cut flowers for a party, or pick up Mr. Brinkmeyer's favorite gin so that he would feel at home, she'd say, "Mom, Emily Post runs your whole life."

Usually, Ginny was locked away in her room, reading, emerging only to sink into the sofa and observe Eleanor like some kind of scientist. She'd point out that Eleanor spent three full hours each day in the kitchen, that she read magazines but not actual books, that she hand washed items that could easily go in the machine.

Eleanor thought she'd endure a few years of mild scoffing, after which they'd return to being best friends.

Once, she surprised Ginny with a Hello Kitty doll. "Bunny rabbit, look! Remember how much you used to love this?"

Ginny looked confused. "Thanks, Mom. That's sweet." And she stood on her bed and set the doll on top of her bookcase.

"*The Sound of Music* is on tonight."

"I have homework."

"You work too hard."

"That's a very unparental thing to say."

"Well, you used to beg me to let you stay up and watch the whole thing!"

"I was like nine."

Eleanor could not prevent a long sigh from escaping her. "Ginny, you've changed so much."

"Mom, isn't that what's supposed to happen?"

Sometimes, if Ginny was whispering on the phone in her room, Eleanor had the awful sense her daughter was bad-mouthing her. *Would you believe my mother wants me to watch a musical?* A few years earlier, there had been no friends! It was only the two of them. But with adolescence, Ginny shed her plumpness, her braces came off, and she was becoming an attractive young woman. She no longer needed Eleanor, and the betrayal hurt.

The ache of losing her own mother had been so deep, Eleanor could not fathom the ease with which Ginny dismissed her. Didn't she understand that nothing in life could ever replace a mother?

With high school, their relationship worsened.

At the dinner table, when Ginny talked about classes she would grasp her cheeks in horror if Eleanor accidentally revealed that she did not know the location of the Red Sea or the name of the third president of the United States.

"The electromagnetic force, Mom. It's only what holds everything in the world together. Did you know that Gaby Towers's mother is an astrophysicist?"

"Did you know that Betty Lundberg's daughter never talks down to her mother?"

In college, Ginny would return for the holidays with gift-wrapped books for Eleanor: *The History of the World in 500 Pages; Understanding Politics; The Modern Woman's Guide to Liberation.*

As Eleanor joined the family by the Christmas tree, wearing a new holiday sweater, her hair carefully pinned up, Ginny would say, "Mom, you don't always have to wear makeup. Natural is pretty. You don't have to set your hair every night. It'll fry the ends."

Ginny was nineteen, at the height of her beauty, the age Eleanor had been when she met Gavin. How glittery the world had seemed then. How Eleanor had radiated self-assurance, certain of a blessed future.

So she sat, she listened, she smiled at her daughter's confidence. Because she knew, sadly, it would not last.

DENISE

*W*hat an utterly stupid plan, Denise thought as she unpacked Laura's dolls and stuffed animals in the crowded living room.

Esmerelda at the school had told her that the Spanish phrase for in-laws was *familia politica*—your political family. So you had to play politician.

"Ginny, really," she said, "how great to be here."

"Was traffic bad?" Ginny asked.

For days Denise had been working herself into a state of agitation over the prospect of driving forty-five minutes in heavy traffic to eat her sister-in-law's gelatinous stuffing and runny mashed potatoes that as far as she was concerned, the whole day was already a flop. So clearly had she envisioned the brake lights of the interstate that she had only the vaguest recollection of their uneventful thirty-minute drive from Stamford.

"Bumper-to-bumper," she lied.

"Well, you poor kids," Ginny said to Brian and Brandon, leaning over with outstretched arms to tickle them. "Trapped in that big car!" People without children were always tickling other people's children. It was their sole kid trick. Like rubbing a dog's ears. "Well, you're here now and it's going to be fun, fun, fun."

Denise sat on the couch, relieved and amazed that for once she didn't have any chores. She wondered if the afternoon might actually turn out nicely. After all, in just three months Ginny had bought a house and adopted a child—things no one, not even Douglas (who overlooked her every flaw), would have imagined from her.

"So everything's in the oven?" she asked.

"In a few minutes I'll just put the turkey in . . . Kidding! Fifteen minutes per pound, fifteen minutes per pound. It's my new mantra. That bird has been in since nine thirty this morning."

Denise tried to laugh. "Mantras are good!"

She and Ginny always spoke like local news coanchors making small talk between segments: forced camaraderie.

As far as sisters-in-law went, Denise liked Ginny. Ginny had a good heart and had given a ridiculously long but touching toast at their wedding about the historical significance of marriage. Both times Denise was in labor Ginny had taken off from work and waited at the hospital with Douglas.

But they had little in common.

Denise looked around the room, taking in the cracked ceiling, a rotted windowsill, a buckled oak door frame. The floor was scratched and scarred as though a dozen feral cats had fought there. It had the wrecked feel of a place where she had, in her younger years, spent too many late nights, and the occasional morning: a frat house.

"It's amazing how fast you moved in," Denise said. "Our first house, God, we looked for months, and then it took a millennium to close."

"Who knew preforeclosures move like lightning?"

Denise did. The thought of people falling so far behind on their mortgage payments they had to pack up their home in weeks made her sick.

"Whatever you do, do not let Douglas talk you into flipping this place," she said. "He gets dangerously optimistic." She could hear her husband thudding around in the basement, no doubt measuring spaces to install a kitchenette, built-in bookshelves, track lighting. She'd long wondered if there was a name to describe his affliction: renovation addiction, home investmania. Recently, at Parents' Profession Day, he told the fourth-graders he was a "real-estate mogul."

Which Denise learned secondhand, from her sons, because she was busy working her nutritionist job at Jefferson High School to make their mortgage payments.

"The only thing I ever flip is my finger." Ginny grinned. "To social conservatives."

Denise was a far cry from conservative, but never in a million years would she try a stunt like Ginny's. Having a lousy husband, even a husband who considered himself a real-estate mogul while on the brink of bankruptcy, was better than raising a child solo. And adopting a seven-year-old from India? Denise had seen a *20/20* special on orphans who went years without being held and ended up setting fire to bathroom curtains, dropping hamsters down the disposal. All the noble intentions in the world wouldn't stop a kid like that from taking a paring knife to your throat while you slept.

"Where is the little one?" she asked.

Ginny's head cocked somewhat defensively. "Getting ready. I'd better check on her."

As Ginny disappeared upstairs, Denise watched Brandon and Brian—one donning a feathered headdress, the other a cowboy hat—run around the room in gleeful circles. Brian tapped his fingers to his mouth, Brandon swung a shoelace lasso.

Her sons were identical twins, and even Denise couldn't explain why Brian was obsessed with sailing, scuba diving, Jacques Cousteau, and anything else ocean related, while Brandon had a disturbing passion for tae kwon do, horror films, and slingshots. Nature? Nurture? There were a gazillion variables. After all, Denise was the only member of three generations of her family to escape their blue-collar neighborhood in Pittsburgh.

Laura splayed herself across a rainbow rag rug and flipped through a book called *Images of Colonial Women at Work*. "I want chickens," Laura said with a sigh. "And I want one of these . . ." She pointed to a picture of an old woman hunched over a loom.

"Sweetie, that's toiling. No one should ever want to toil."

Denise knew about toiling. She'd had a dull full-time job for six years. Add to that the exhausting show she had to put on for Douglas's family that everything was fine—it left her with little desire to now feign enthusiasm for Ginny's hosting skills.

Ginny was good at describing how Colonial women made soap from bone marrow, or telling the story of the lost colony of Roanoke. Even her dating anecdotes were amusing. But whipping up a nine-person holiday meal was not within Ginny's skill set. At the previous year's Thanksgiving she'd shown up with a three-hundred-page report on the birth-control methods of indentured servants. She sat reading, her mammoth wool socks propped up on a mahogany butler table, while Eleanor and Denise slaved over the meal. Every few minutes Ginny looked up (oblivious to the platters that needed to be carried out), slid off her purple cat-eye glasses, and said, "Nobody show me a jar of apple-cider vinegar for the next twenty-four hours."

Of course, the new culture of overacceptance forbade anything resembling honesty. Denise wasn't supposed to acknowledge that anyone was bad at anything. She saw it in the schools; children were taught that there was no such thing as losing, that there was no wrong way to do things. Incorrect answers to factual questions were respected: *Well, in some ways, yes, you could say that the South won the Civil War* . . .

At a recent parent-teacher conference, Denise asked the fourth-grade teacher if she would encourage Brian to stop picking his nose.

"His nose picking bothers you?" the teacher asked, scribbling something in her notebook. "Why is that? Do you want him to feel *ashamed* of his behavior?"

"Yes!" Denise couldn't believe the conversation. "Shame, mortification, whatever it takes. Nose picking is not a form of expression, Ms. Persimmon. Neither is ass picking. Why on earth would I want my son to keep picking his nose?"

"Mrs. Olson"—the teacher closed her notebook, uncrossed her

legs, and slid forward in her chair—"is there by any chance a lot of stress in your household right now?"

Denise had had enough. She grabbed her purse, made for the door. "Listen, I don't need my children to be rocket scientists or Nobel Prize winners. But my job as a mother is to make sure they are basically fit for society. I do not want them to be nose pickers. Can you manage at least that?"

Denise accepted that she might lose her house, her savings, her husband—but she would *not* lose her grasp on reality.

She didn't need to pretend Ginny was going to pull off this meal. And in truth, this day had given Denise a point on which to focus her annoyance, an outlet for her anxiety that had permitted her, briefly, to overlook the larger mess she and Douglas were in. For weeks she had been venting to friends and colleagues about having to haul ass in the middle of the day to Mamaroneck to her sister-in-law's for Thanksgiving. In the school cafeteria, she had ranted about the idiotic details of the plan.

Later, when Denise learned who the boys were and where they went to school, she would be forced to admit to the police that someone perhaps had overheard her. She would wonder whether her fierce conviction that the day would be a disaster had, in fact, caused the disaster.

GINNY

*U*pstairs, in the small pink room, Ginny tiptoed toward the sleeping girl.

Asleep. Again.

She'd been to three doctors in the past month, each of whom had run tests of Priya's blood and urine. They all said the same thing: Priya was fit as a fiddle. At first Ginny had thought it was jet lag, then maybe lingering malnutrition. But she'd recently come to accept that, from her own experience, she knew exactly what sleeping all day meant: depression.

"Sweetheart?" She stroked her daughter's shoulder and the girl let out a congested sigh. Wisps of hair clung to her forehead. "You need to get dressed and come downstairs now. Your dress is hanging right over there."

Priya opened her eyes—red, as though she'd been crying again—and looked to the maroon dresser, which Ginny had painted with a border of sunflowers. Above it hung a framed bright blue map of the world. The entire room was the product of dozens of hours of scraping wallpaper, plastering holes, painting walls, and glossing moldings. Ginny had hired someone to lay new carpet—fuchsia with a bathmat-like soft pile—but the rest of decorating she'd done herself.

"Everyone is dying to meet you."

Priya offered a resolute nod, the way she did each morning as Ginny pried her from sleep. She swung her bare legs over the side of the bed, slid on her white slippers, and immediately began straightening the sheets.

"I'll do that," said Ginny, stilling her arm. But as usual, Priya insisted on her morning tidying.

At least they had a routine.

It was hard to believe that only three months earlier they'd been flying back from India. That eternal flight. Ginny's eyelids blinking anxiously against the dry cabin air as she swigged four mini Merlots. Across the aisle a middle-aged woman intently turned the pages of a mass-market thriller beneath her reading lamp, occasionally glancing over at Priya, who carefully tore pictures of perfume bottles from the in-flight magazine while frowning at the flashing wing lights. Ginny had expected Priya to be terrified, flailing at the rumble of the beverage cart, crying during takeoff. Instead it was Ginny who was sickened by nerves, a thick tangle that had amassed when, weeks earlier, she'd stood before an Indian district court and won guardianship of a seven-year-old girl.

In the taxi to Ginny's apartment, Priya's excited breaths left an oval of steam on the window as she gaped at Manhattan, the gleam of towering glass and metal, sharp and spiky, like a forest of cutlery.

Ginny chattered nervously, explaining how it had all once been farmland, that just three hundred years ago it had looked like parts of India.

Finally, with relief, Ginny lifted their bags and stepped into her apartment. Then, like a fugitive, she bolted the door. Priya pattered around the furniture, eyeing paper clips, bookends, letter openers, pens, scissors, thumbtacks. She climbed precariously onto Ginny's elliptical trainer. Oh God, thought Ginny, the place was a death trap. There were no bars on the windows. And what on earth was tucked away in all her drawers? Expired antibiotics, bottles of melatonin, condoms?

She grabbed Priya's hand. "You must be ravenous."

The refrigerator light caught Priya like a paparazzi flashbulb. Slowly, she stuck her hand inside to feel the cool bare shelves. She touched a jar of chutney, and extracted the lone withered carrot Ginny had forgotten to throw out.

"Let's just order Chinese."

After dinner, Ginny bathed her, working the wet washcloth over her spine, the sharp ridges ancient and fishlike. Ginny soaped her shoulders and elbows, her stomach. She gently lathered shampoo in her hair and felt small scabs on her scalp. She slowly combed out all the knots and tangles, wrapped Priya in a thick purple towel.

Ginny pulled out the hair dryer and blew it on her own hair. "See? To dry your hair so you don't catch a cold."

But Priya winced at the hot air.

"God, sorry. We'll let it dry the old-fashioned way."

When Priya finally fell asleep, Ginny phoned her mother. She hadn't told anyone yet about the adoption—or rather, the pending adoption—and as she watched Priya curl up in the stiff white I ♥ NY T-shirt she'd bought at JFK, her chest rising and falling peacefully, she seemed like the most exquisite decision Ginny had ever made.

"Mom?" she whispered. "Did I wake you?"

"Oh, Ginny, I'm glad you called. I was looking at my organizer and I wanted to make sure you sent a present to the twins. It was a shame you weren't at the birthday party. Everybody asked, 'Where's Ginny?' They really couldn't believe you'd want to go to India of all places, and for so long, and then nobody heard from you! Marty Cooper said something about a coworker getting typhoid there. Anyway, a present is important. But not something from India. Not a souvenir, a genuine present."

Ginny walked the cordless over to Priya, to remind herself that she was real: she touched her toes, watching her leg bend reflexively.

"Sure, I'll get them a present."

"Why are you whispering? Ginny, I can hardly hear you. Oh, wait, and this must mean you are back from India! Oh, thank goodness. Is your apartment okay? No trouble with that house sitter, I hope. We just had an awful row with our lawn people, and your father says he's going to mow the lawn himself. Arthritis be damned."

"Everything is fine. I'm tired, though."

"You will remember the present?"

"Good night, Mom."

Ginny climbed into bed with Priya and draped her arm over her. Her bee-stung lips parted and Ginny could smell toothpaste on her warm breath. Traces of strawberry shampoo rose from her scalp. Her long eyelashes fluttered.

Ginny nestled her head against Priya's chest and listened to the thud of her heart.

My daughter.

KIJO

*T*hey were running late, and Kijo was pissed. He'd been standing on the deserted corner of Merrell and Edison almost an hour, his hands cold as ice, when Spider finally pulled up in the Diamond Diagnostics van. Kijo jiggled the familiar rusty door handle and threw his duffel in the back, then squeezed himself into the passenger seat.

"You suddenly forget where the projects are?"

"You gonna sulk all day?"

Kijo had been planning this for weeks. All Spider had to do was show up on time. Kijo had the map, the supplies. Today was their one chance.

"I told you this is big," he said.

"I'm a force of nature, Kij, to be sure. But traffic's traffic."

In the quiet of the blue van they looked each other over. They hadn't discussed what to wear, but Kijo now realized they had both put on special clothing. Spider, who once wore a red leather coat he'd bought at Goodwill for a whole week until he discovered it was for women, was draped in a gray hooded track sweatshirt. Kijo had on a dark turtleneck and black corduroys. Nothing distinctive. Nothing memorable.

Spider gripped the steering wheel with his black leather gloves and hit the gas. In the side mirror Kijo watched the low brick buildings of Vidal Court fade into the distance. Kijo had imagined his departure differently. That morning, he'd felt the urge to tell everyone "I'm a man of action. Nobody messes with me." He wanted people to gather and watch him drive away like townspeople in Westerns did as the cowboy kicked his horse and galloped off. But the stoops had been empty, the parking lot quiet, and his brief vision of heroism was lost in the solitude of the gray morning; as usual, no one much cared what he was doing.

Kijo dangled his arm out the window, the November air bathing his face. The windows were rolled down to clear out the stench of all the blood and piss Uncle Clarence had spent twenty years hauling up the interstate. Spider's uncle Clarence had delivered specimens for Diamond Diagnostics, supplying replacement specimens for a certain price. More times than Kijo cared to remember, hopping a ride to the movies he and Spider heard Uncle Clarence unzip himself in the back, piss rattling into a plastic cup.

But Clarence had died a month earlier and the van now belonged to Spider. From the rearview mirror hung a mop of dirty shoelaces from track races Spider had won. A half-eaten pizza—Spider's "breakfast of champions"—sat on the dashboard. It was an old van, the kind with seats that didn't budge, and Kijo's knees pressed against the glove compartment. He'd never been jealous of Spider, but he now wished he had a van of his own. He'd recently come to understand that for a man to have any peace, he had to command a space: boat captains, pilots, bartenders, gas station owners, fathers—they said how things were done on their turf. Kijo had just turned seventeen.

His birthday had gotten him thinking on the future. Kijo thought it would make sense to someday open a grocery. Put his favorite video games in the back—Mortal Kombat, NBA Jam, the old-school ones, because he believed history gave a place class. He'd set the hours, the rules: no barefeet, no radios, don't even think about coming in here without your shirt, no telling the same dumb-ass long-winded story twice! He'd give kids free Atomic FireBalls so they wouldn't come back waving a gun. He'd call it Kijo's. But to the people working there, he'd be Mr. Jackson.

Kijo wasn't superstitious, especially not about wishes, since he'd swiped so many coins from wishing ponds over the years. But when he'd blown out the candles on the cake Grandma Rose had made and wished for his grocery store, he had a bad feeling in his gut. Like he should have wished for something noble, like Grandma Rose's health, or a safe place for them to live. When he came home from his job at the mall a few nights later and saw her bruised lip, he blamed himself.

Kijo glanced at his watch, tapped the side of the van nervously.

Spider said, "Chill, man, we gonna do this. Your ace is on the case."

They'd been friends since they were five. When Spider's father went to the fed pen. They didn't talk about Spider's father leaving, just as now they didn't talk about Uncle Clarence dying from cancer, or about Grandma Rose getting beaten up. They talked about what was ahead of them. Kijo didn't talk much anyway. For most of his childhood he'd suffered a stutter; when he wanted to speak, his tongue got sticky and his lips tightened. He envied the way words gushed from Puerto Rican kids, like water from hydrants in July. He watched horse races on television because he liked the keyed-up voices of the announcers. But words snagged in Kijo's mouth like a sweater on a nail; they came out long and crooked.

Grandma Rose wrote words on thick rubber bands and stretched them in front of him, reminding him to slow down: BECAUSE, MONDAY, FORGIVE. *B*'s and *m*'s and *f*'s were the toughest. Before supper, she always made him say "The big fat cat sat on the rat." At night, Kijo lay in bed in the dark, reciting:

> *Fresh fried fish,*
> *Fish fresh fried,*
> *Fried fish fresh,*
> *Fish fried fresh.*

He practiced so much that sometimes, without realizing it, he'd walk down the street doing his exercises. Kids would shout, "Hey, big black bastard babbling!" "Whassup, noisy nigger nagging nonsense?" "Good morning, kuh kuh kuh kuh Kijo."

The older boys once told him that if he stuck his tongue to a frozen fence post he'd be cured. Kijo could still recall the taste of blood and metal as he tried to peel his tongue loose, how little Spider Walcott had waited until the boys were gone and poured orange soda over Kijo's mouth until his tongue melted free.

Even at age five, Spider, fast and fidgety, had a mysterious patience for Kijo's stutter. He'd sit with his hands on his knees and watch Kijo's slow lips, examining the jagged syllables Kijo spat out like a child digging for spearheads.

"This is like some nature reserve," said Spider as they drove north of downtown.

Kijo had never seen this part of Stamford but knew folks called it the primeval forest. The roads were kinked; thick trees blocked the sun. Waist-high stone walls lined the road. There were no sidewalks.

Kijo studied the map in his lap. "Take the next right," he said slowly. His stutter was long gone, but years of training had made him careful to pronounce each syllable. His voice was deep, so deep it surprised people. Grandma Rose said he sounded like Paul Robeson, or James Earl Jones. After a few beers, Spider always begged him to do Darth Vader. Kijo would then breath slow through his nose and say, "I am your father, Luke."

In the van's side mirror Kijo studied his face: his lips had thickened, his nose was two thumbs wide, like the Jamaicans', except he wasn't Jamaican, as far as he knew. He didn't know if he was handsome; he was too shy to try his way with girls. Even the girl who worked the Pretzel King counter at the mall, who slipped mustard packets into her purse each night and smiled at him as he lobbed trash bags into his metal cart.

"Nice aim, bag boy," she'd say.

He liked the girl, but didn't like that she called him "boy." Kijo had a boy's face on a man's body. His shoulders were broad and he was tall, taller than any kid he knew. In the past year he'd felt manhood dawn on him: things were opening, pushing, weighing inside him. He understood it was his job to take care of problems.

"Vidal Court," Kijo said. "It's no place for Grandma Rose."

"At least she ain't in a group home."

When Uncle Clarence died, the state sent Spider to a group residence across town. After a lifetime of seeing each other every day, Kijo hadn't seen Spider since the funeral a month earlier. He'd been so distracted by the problems at Vidal Court, he hadn't given much thought to missing his best friend. So Kijo was surprised by the deep happiness he now felt sitting in the van next to him.

"How come you don't just move to Bridgeport?" Spider asked.

"Grandma Rose has forty years' worth of clients at Jojo Jeffersons," Kijo explained, as his grandmother had explained to him each time he suggested they leave town. "She can't just pack up and move."

"What did you tell her you were up to today?"

"Errands," said Kijo. In fact, Kijo had invented an elaborate story for Grandma Rose about going up to Norwalk to help Spider get his van out of a tow lot. He'd added an unnecessary bit about a caseworker who had it in for Spider and had personally impounded the van. But Kijo wasn't a good liar, and Grandma Rose had eyed him with suspicion as he'd left the house that morning with a big duffel bag.

"Can't lock you up for first-degree erranding," said Spider.

"She'll lock us up if we're late for dinner."

"Us?" Spider flashed a smile. "We're the Dukes again, my man."

Spider's all-time favorite show was *The Dukes of Hazzard*. As a kid, he became convinced the show was about black people: "The cousins don't got a father, right? They only got their uncle Jesse. And they're running moonshine, trying to get out from under the foot of that whitey-in-a-white-suit Boss Hogg. The Dukes are just regular black folk trying to raise themselves up selling joy juice!"

Spider was big on uncles. After Spider's father was sent to prison, his uncle Clarence took him in, intending to raise him well so he wouldn't go the way of his father. Clarence once brought Spider all the way to Washington, D.C., to see Minister Farrakhan. Clarence was the only man Kijo had ever known who dyed his hair gray so he would be looked upon more decently. He liked his gin and he liked his dice, but he loved Spider, and Kijo had nothing but respect for the man on account of that.

Kijo once made the mistake of introducing Uncle Clarence to Grandma Rose. This was back when he thought what his grandma needed was a man around the house, before Kijo understood what the aunties who sometimes stayed the night were about. Grandma Rose had said what she said about all men: that she could smell a man who hadn't been to church in years, and Clarence wasn't coming anywhere near her kitchen table. Uncle Clarence ended up finding Lupa, a Uruguayan woman, but they never married.

And when Uncle Clarence's cancer killed him, Spider talked the Diamond Diagnostics people into letting him drive specimens all over Connecticut. Kijo thought he'd have a better sense of direction by now.

"We're going in circles."

Spider took a pull of beer, wiped his nose. "These are back roads, Kijo. They are *made* out of circles. You ever hear of a cul-de-sac? Study that map."

Spider flicked on a bright dome light, and in the glare Kijo noticed that Spider didn't look so good. His braids, usually thick and raised off his scalp like the legs of a spider, were limp. His skin seemed dull and there were dark circles under his eyes. Kijo knew better than to ask.

"I wanna get a GPS," Spider said with a sigh.

"You know how much that'll sink you?" said Kijo.

"I'll just tell the company it's an occupational necessity."

Kijo knew that Spider was broke, and that he didn't have pull with Diamond Diagnostics. They'd told him one strike—even a parking ticket—and he was out. As if he was recalling this, Spider cranked up the radio, singing and shaking along to Jay-Z. Spider shoved a slice of pizza into his mouth, chewing hard and thinking.

"Slow it down," said Kijo.

Spider lightened on the gas, crept along a row of trees, lowered the radio. There wasn't a person in sight.

"There," Kijo said, taking a long look out the window. He felt adrenaline crack through his veins. "That's the one."

DENISE

*D*enise set out the hummus and crackers on the old trunk being used as a coffee table. When hungry, her children were like hyenas. She was not taking chances. She dipped a cracker, took a bite.

"Chow time, kids! You snooze, you lose."

But Laura and the twins were marching along the perimeter of the room, a rash of Eleanor's pink lipstick on their foreheads, Laura at the end dragging her tablecloth.

"We are an exploring party!"

"Hark, I hear a rustling in the forest yonder. Be still, explorers!"

"Who is this strange creature? Does she speak our language?"

The children had paused in front of Eleanor, who was straightening Ginny's antique bric-a-brac on the mantel: a wooden butter churn, two copper candlesticks, a brass compass. She worked a handkerchief over a granite mortar and pestle. A red headband fastened her hair, an attempt at girlishness compromised by her halo of gray roots. She wore her Thanksgiving sweater, an orange wool pullover with a giant red maple leaf in the middle. Denise thought it looked unfortunately like the Canadian flag.

"From where do you hearken, strange woman?" Brandon asked.

"Westport!" Eleanor answered excitedly.

"She is of the Wesportonians," said Brian.

"What is she doing?"

"She is dusting. Note this in the expedition logbook. The Wesportonian is dusting."

"Shall we string her up by her ankles?"

"The Westportonians are known as a peaceful people. They are gardeners and stargazers and drinkers of wine. Let down your weapons, explorers!"

"Oh, my," said Eleanor, touching her heart. "You children were very convincing. I was quite scared."

"Aw, Grandma, we wouldn't hurt you," Brian said, wiggling his index finger up his nose. "We knew it was *you*. Did you know a human being sheds a complete layer of skin every three weeks?"

"How utterly interesting."

"Most dust is dead skin," said Brandon.

"Really!" Eleanor tucked her handkerchief back into her purse. "Well, I am pleased as a peanut you children are here. Denise, how wonderful you prefer to spend the holidays with our family. It's such a treat having everyone together."

"It's nice being with you all." Which was vaguely true. But also, when they visited Denise's family, her mother flirted wildly with Douglas and her father spent an hour asking Douglas for investment tips before insisting he join him on the back porch for a cigar, then pleading for investment capital. It broke Denise's heart. It mortified her. Her father had worked at U.S. Steel until the mill closed and for the past twenty years had picked up odd jobs welding and painting houses. The loan Douglas had given him when they first married—at Denise's urging—to start an auto repair shop, had not been repaid. The shop had never opened. And Denise believed it was a testament to her husband's character that throughout their own financial struggles, Douglas had never once mentioned her father's unpaid debt. Nonetheless, Denise had come to the difficult decision that they would not loan her family money and would not, unless necessary, visit.

"Did I miss the turkey?"

It was Gavin, late as usual, a newspaper wedged under his arm.

Everybody went silent at his entrance; the man had a way of suck-ing the air out of a room.

"Well, look what the cat dragged in." Eleanor snatched his newspa-per and coat and tucked them in the entry closet. "You're not going to read that here. This is family time."

Gavin was nothing like Denise's father. Gavin had worked for the same insurance company for thirty years, but looked more like a mountaineer than a company man. He was broad-shouldered and ruddy-faced and had run marathons until age fifty. He dressed conser-vatively, but almost always wore sneakers, which lent a boyishness to his otherwise solemn demeanor. In the last few years, however, he'd been suffering from arthritis, so Denise watched as he now carefully removed his running shoes, as though every joint and bit of cartilage in his knees was telling him to back off. As he straightened up, he palmed his silver hair into place and gave her a nod. That was Gavin's hello. No hugs, no handshakes. A nod. He wasn't one for gabbing. When Douglas first brought her home to meet his parents, the bulk of her interaction with Gavin had been when he led her out back to look through his old telescope.

"You know any constellations?"

"Zilch," she said.

"Well, neither does Douglas. You two should get along well."

Early on, Douglas had mentioned that his father served in Viet-nam, that he was smart, ambitious even, but had been passed over for jobs because he was a veteran. He'd then been slowed, like many men his age, by the economic swamp of the 1970s and had never quite regained his footing. What struck Denise, though, was the insecurity Gavin elicited in Douglas. Ginny, too, seemed somewhat cowed by her father. Only Eleanor appeared at ease with Gavin's gruffness, and that was because she ignored it. Eleanor treated him more like a defi-ant child than a remote husband. Denise had never minded him—it wasn't in her nature to be intimidated.

"Nobody drink the tap water." Douglas emerged from the basement and brushed off his shirt. "Those pipes look like they're from the Revolutionary War." At the sight of his father, he stiffened. "Hey, Dad."

Douglas often complained about his father's pessimism; he felt his father was too critical of him. After visiting his parents, Douglas, who rarely said much about his feelings, was often unable to sleep. In the dark, he'd whisper to Denise, "It's like he judges the way I breathe." She had at first thought Douglas's compulsive optimism was a rebellion against his father. But over the years she had come to see that Douglas was simply rallying enough confidence in himself to make up for what his father had withheld.

As Douglas and Gavin simultaneously plunked down on the flimsy red couch, the coils whimpered. They looked shockingly like father and son. If Denise had measured each of their jaws, square and chiseled, there might have been only a millimeter's difference. But for two men who looked so much alike, they couldn't have been more different, or more awkward around each other. They triangulated themselves with the platter and reached for the knives.

"The Packers are having a great season," said Douglas, looking at his watch. "An hour till kickoff."

"Did you see today's news about Freddie Mac?"

"I'm taking a news holiday. Today's just food, family, and football."

"A lot of people are going to be taking holidays soon. Mark my words. First the write-downs, then the layoffs."

"You let this stuff psych you out, you make mistakes, miss opportunities. Speaking of. Okay, Dad, if you could go back in time, let's say to the mid-seventies, fiscal crisis, everything's cheap, where would you put your money?"

"We didn't have money then. We had two small children."

"I'm saying hypothetically. You came into an inheritance."

Denise never understood Douglas's bizarre addiction to hypothetical situations. It charmed people the first time they met him—

got conversations going at parties—but after years of marriage, it wore on Denise. *Hypothetically, Doug,* she imagined saying, *if you lost all our money and I were to leave you, what would you do?*

Gavin smeared a cracker with hummus and shoved it into his mouth.

"Or let's say you won the lotto," urged Douglas. "You found a brief-case full of hundreds. Do you put it in GE? IBM? Johnson and Johnson?"

"I report it to the police."

As though she could tell they were all assembled, Ginny slowly came down the stairs, the Indian girl at her side. The barefoot girl wore an ankle-length purple dress, which she carefully lifted off the stairs. Her long, sleek hair was pulled back with two tortoiseshell combs, accentuating her plump cheeks. She smiled shyly, revealing a dimple.

Ginny laughed nervously. "Yikes, this feels like a debutante ball." But she studied her parents' faces, gauging their response.

Well, thought Denise, the girl didn't look like she'd set the curtains on fire. She didn't look disturbed, or even malnourished. She looked Indian, sure. But not like an orphan, not like . . . what was the word Denise once heard? Not like an *untouchable*.

Laura reached for her hair. "Ma! Like Pocahontas!"

"A different kind of Indian, honey," Denise said. "That's your cousin."

Douglas and Gavin set their crackers on the platter and sat up straight. Eleanor clasped her hands. Then an expression came over Ginny's face that Denise had never seen: a shimmering tranquility. Her voice, usually loud and domineering, a lecture-hall voice, softened. "I need to do a few more things in the kitchen before I can kick up my feet and relax with you all." She pet Priya. "You wanna help Mommy?"

Ginny led Priya into the kitchen and they all looked at one another. Denise was speechless. Maybe Ginny adopting a child wasn't so outlandish. Maybe she *could* buy a house and raise a daughter. Maybe she didn't need a husband.

Brian broke the silence: "How did she get here?"

"On an airplane," Douglas said.

"Is an airplane like a stork?" asked Laura.

"A big stork with a big engine," Douglas answered, leaning back in the sofa with a look of delight that suddenly irritated Denise.

"I'll see if Ginny needs help," she announced.

At the far end of the kitchen, Ginny set a piece of gingerroot in Priya's hand. "*Gin-ger,*" said Ginny. "That's also my name."

The girl's mouth hung open and Ginny set the root back on the counter.

Denise felt guilty for her earlier misgivings. "I gotta admit, Ginny, when I heard *orphan* and *India* and *seven years old,* I thought trouble. But she's totally . . ." She stopped herself from saying *normal.* "Totally adorable."

Ginny did not appear as moved by this confession as Denise had hoped, but she smiled graciously. "Thanks."

Ginny looked around the kitchen, at bowls spilling peeled sweet potatoes and peas, the buttered baking pans. She tied on an old apron, and blew hair from her eyes. "I think this is more food than Priya's seen her whole life. All they served in the orphanage were small bowls of watery dal."

"How did you even end up in that place?"

"Research." Ginny guided Priya onto a stepladder, tucked her purple dress beneath her, and had her sit.

Ginny started mixing what appeared to be stuffing, licking her fingers as she worked.

Denise made her way to the dishwasher. "I'll see if I can squeeze in some more and then do a load before we eat. It'll make the cleanup easier later."

"I forgot you're the former caterer!"

Ginny had shoved the dishes in at every angle, the cutlery crisscrossed like pick-up sticks. Flecks of food clung to the plates, crusted tomato sauce and peanut butter, determined flecks that would never, even in the face of scalding water, loosen their grip. Denise removed the dishes one by one, sponged them down (ignoring the brown and livery ancient sponge), and rearranged them.

The kitchen was small, with old oak cupboards and rusted brass handles that needed scrubbing. A Sierra Club calendar hung from a nail, open to the month of June. Her electric oven looked like a stage prop in some 1950s play. But she'd lined the windowsill with clay pots of pothos and aloe and gladiolas. The cheery greenhouse look. For all Ginny's hippie ways, the only thing missing was a nice leafy marijuana plant.

Happy Thanksgiving!

God, it had been years since Denise smoked pot. Growing up in dreary Homestead with three brothers and a mother who spent most nights yelling at her husband to get on *The Price Is Right* so they could put meat on their sandwiches, Denise had found that a little wake and bake out her bedroom window was a good way to start the day. She grew her own in the overrun steel mill yard, occasionally selling to the Homestead High cheerleading squad.

In college, though, it slowed her down. And by then, Denise was starting to realize there were other ways to live, there were things like exercise, studying. If she worked hard, after graduation she might be able to move to New York City or Boston, get away from her family and Homestead. She switched to cigarettes and diet sodas. Sometimes during finals she took NoDoz. The rush from daytime cold medicine wasn't bad either, and left her calm enough to go for a run. A complex regimen of caffeine and exercise got her through thirty job interviews her senior year, perky and well prepared; it landed her a job.

Nowadays she still snuck cigarettes. After three children, it was hard to keep her figure, and smoking subdued her hunger. She kept a pack beneath the seat in her car, and on her way home from work she'd pull into the Minimart parking lot. Leaning against the hood, she'd suck down every last inch of tar and tobacco. She stashed mouthwash in the car. She did a gargle-spit-gargle-spit routine and scrubbed her hands with a baby wipe before heading home.

Douglas would have been surprised. The children, appalled.

But you got married and had kids and that was the end of privacy, the death of anything resembling a solo self, the one that used to, every once in a while, just for kicks, introduce herself as Denise Boeing, heiress. The one who once got so high she made out with Cindy Keegan, the cheerleading captain.

God knew smoking in a parking lot was safer than boffing the history teacher. Which, she proudly reminded herself, she hadn't done.

"Any new men, Ginny?"

"Only if you count my Realtor."

Ginny turned heads when she threw on a dress. But she was high-maintenance and a know-it-all. Every year she spontaneously quizzed the whole family on the states named for Indian tribes.

Okay, guys. Connecticut was named after the Mohegan word Quin-nehtukqut. Who remembers what that word means?

Denise was no expert in Colonial family history or gender relations, but she knew one thing for sure: men liked to teach women trivia, not learn it. Trivia was like a car jack, or a charcoal grill—smart women only let men touch that stuff.

Ginny didn't complain about being single, but Denise had seen, over the years, as Ginny bounced from one dead-end relationship to the next, that it frustrated her.

"Well, men are work," said Denise. "Heavy lifting. Ask my husband."

"What?" Douglas entered, holding a present. "I am a ray of sunshine on a cloudy day."

He put his arm around Ginny, who was haphazardly scraping carrots, peels flying everywhere.

"This is an obscene amount of vegetables," said Douglas. "I hope there's some protein hiding somewhere around here. I had my heart set on a turducken. Suburban homeowner! Mother. I'm still in shock."

"This is how single people have a midlife crisis, Dougie. We abruptly settle down."

"Well, no home is complete without this," he said, waving the box. Douglas loved giving presents. Two months behind on their mortgage and he still arrived home some nights, pale and exhausted, with ribbon-wrapped remote control cars for the boys, stuffed bears for Laura.

"Doug," Denise said, "we're working."

"For months I've been deprived of uncling privileges. I will not be deterred!" He set the box in Priya's lap and she excitedly tore open the wrapping.

"Monopoly?" asked Ginny. "She's *seven*, Dougie."

"I was playing this in diapers."

"You made me miserable forcing me to play that godforsaken game until all hours with you."

"And look at the deal you got on this house! Tell me you don't have my early real-estate mentorship to thank."

Priya opened the box, and examined the pastel-colored money.

"Look at you all! Look at my adorable sweet wonderful grand-daughter!" Eleanor had entered, hands to her cheeks. "Where's my camera? Everybody, get close to Priya."

Suddenly, the enthusiasm Denise had felt for Priya began to dissipate. The girl was a magnet, a curiosity. And while Denise was happy to *meet* her, they didn't need to obsess over her. There were still nine mouths to feed.

"Why don't we get some photos out in the living room?" Denise suggested. "Of *all* the kids?" She set the dishwasher running and tugged Douglas toward the door. "Your sister has plenty of work, leave her be."

But Eleanor was upturning her bucket of a purse. "Camera, camera. Where are you, camera?" Finally, she settled for the extraction of a red-and-white dinner mint, which she handed to Priya.

"Hello, cute little granddaughter."

"Mom, don't give her candy," Ginny said. "I'm trying to get her into good eating habits."

"But grandmothers are supposed to give candy. That's our job. Do you understand English, Priya? Does she understand English?"

"Enough," said Ginny.

"Hello, darling. I'm Granny Eleanor. What is your name?"

"You know her name, Mom."

"Well, I'm just trying to chat with my granddaughter. She's a very quiet girl . . . unusually quiet."

Ginny turned her back to everyone and began studiously arranging a row of carrots on the chopping board. In a soft, matter-of-fact way, and without turning around, she finally said, "Actually, Priya doesn't speak."

KIJO

*K*ijo looked at the house. He had promised his grandmother he'd
never do anything like this, but he'd had enough. Like the day he
was old enough to go to school, old enough to cross the street alone,
strong enough to carry the groceries, or tall enough to answer the
door when someone came knocking at night, Kijo felt something had
changed inside of him. Something he couldn't explain to Grandma
Rose, or even to Spider.

He'd never much liked school, except for history class. He soaked
up the stories about John F. Kennedy and Martin Luther King, Jr. He
knew that history wasn't about how people felt. It was about what
they did.

Sometimes you had to take action.

Spider doubled back a couple blocks and nosed the Diamond
Diagnostics van into the trees. As Kijo climbed out, the door snapped
branches. Spider, on the other side, swatted twigs from his face.

"This is feeling very *Survivor*."

They brushed leaves from their clothing and Spider tugged open
the van's back doors. He rubbed his hands excitedly while Kijo hauled
out their bags of gear.

Spider threw a blanket aside, then pulled out a switchblade and
shoved it into his back pocket.

"You wanna leave the po-pos your phone number, too?" Kijo
pointed at the van's Diamond Diagnostics logo, facing the road.

"Check this." Spider pulled packing tape from their bags, snapped some branches off the trees, and taped them over the words. He did the same to the license plate. "Constitution State, my ass." He pulled the pizza box from the front and held it out. "Now we're just delivering pizza. Arrest me, Officer. It's pepperoni."

Kijo slung the duffel bag over his shoulder and they made for the front door. The house was bigger than he'd imagined, large enough to take up a whole city block. It reminded him of a hotel, or the kind of place they put crazy people and old folks. He expected wheelchairs on the lawn, nurses in white. But there wasn't anyone in sight.

"That's my ride," Spider said, pointing to a tree beside the house.

Spider's real name was Calvin. But no one had called him that since the fifth grade, when he'd climbed a tree outside their school and made his way into the window of the girls' bathroom to surprise Shaquina Nelson on Valentine's Day. He got suspended, but he also got the attention of the track coach. Spider had won blue ribbons in the fifty-meter dash, had once had his picture in the paper, and planned to run the New York City Marathon one day. "You know how much them Kenyans get for winning? A hundred G!"

Spider claimed his people came from Kenya.

Spider was also crazy about the Olympics. "Man, that's so Carl Lewis," he'd say. Or, "That jacket the gold medal." A map hung over his bed with red pins stuck in Sydney, Atlanta, Lake Placid, Athens, Turin, Nagano, Barcelona, Seoul, Calgary—sites of the Olympic games.

Spider got on Kijo's case for not playing hoops. He said the only place a black man could succeed was in the world of athletics. But Kijo had the same trouble with his body as he'd had with speech. He snagged on things—desk corners, curbs. His hands and feet got in his way. It was like his body didn't fit him right or wasn't his.

Spider looked Kijo up and down and smiled. "It's a sad state of affairs when a man dresses like a ninja but can't climb a tree."

"Heights," said Kijo. "You know they make me dizzy."

"One, two, three, I'll be up and through that window. Just hang till I let you in. "

Kijo eyed the entrance for security cameras. Nothing. He pressed his face to the glass and saw an alarm pad inside, but it wasn't armed. He peeled back the doormat. Then he stuck his fingers in the planter box.

Kijo blew soil off the brass key. "Now who's your daddy?"

Spider laughed. "Maybe they left their wallets out here, too."

Kijo slid the key in the lock, but held it still for a moment. He could turn back, he could keep his promise to Grandma Rose.

But then he turned the key and opened the door.

Spider patted Kijo's back. "Now they gonna know you don't mess with Kijo."

ELEANOR

S he's *mute?*" asked Eleanor.

"The doctor says there's no visible damage to her vocal appa-ratus," Ginny explained. Then she rubbed the girl's head, almost proudly. "She just hasn't spoken."

A single mother raising a *mute* seven-year-old from India!

Oh, Eleanor loved her daughter, but what a dung heap of libera-tion her generation had inherited. Ginny cared so much about her *right* to do things, she ignored the difficulties. The girls at Wellesley were reading Betty Friedan. Eleanor went to some meetings, sat quietly in the back during heated discussions about the *movement*. But she didn't fit in, and she didn't think they liked her much. These girls were too brazen, snotty even. She tried. Once, for a week, she stopped wearing a brassiere—though she certainly wasn't going to burn anything for which she had paid good money. In her mind, that was precisely the problem—these girls were burning things, tearing down perfectly good traditions. But they all had fathers and therefore no clue what a house was like without a man around. Well, Eleanor had watched her mother toil alone after her father's death, eating din-ners in a quiet kitchen, chasing mice from the house with a broom when she was frightened. Eleanor was entirely uninterested in statis-tics and laws. She had always wanted a husband.

Eleanor wouldn't have the stomach for hopping from bed to bed, either. After all these years, she wasn't even quite certain she liked sex. Of course, you could never say that. But as far as she was concerned, it was a fraught, sticky endeavor that left wet spots in the bed. She could not understand why her daughter made a sport of it.

What a painful few years it had been watching her beautiful daughter, a daughter she had once been so proud of, approach her midthirties husbandless. Even Mavis Galfrey's daughter, who lost two toes to diabetes, had married. Eleanor couldn't understand it— there was the human-rights lawyer, the veterinarian, the street musician. There were men Ginny referred to as "casual things." Eleanor would encourage her, ask how the relationships were going, ask if she wanted to bring so-and-so for dinner. She was frightened of what would happen to her daughter when she was gone. When Gavin was gone. Who would take care of her?

But Ginny's only reply was: "Mom, don't pry."

The stubbornness! Eleanor couldn't help wondering if Ginny feared her disapproval, if this had set in motion a series of clandestine relationships that, lacking family support, were going kaput. Well, one couldn't sit idly by and watch children wreck their lives.

Ginny had mentioned David Eisenberg worked at the Animal Medical Center in Manhattan. Well, it was a cinch getting Milly Sinclair to bring in her Chihuahuas.

What a son-in-law David Eisenberg would have been! Milly and Eleanor thought he looked like a young Steve McQueen. And how gently he handled little Pierre. Milly said the next best thing to having a doctor in the family was having a veterinarian.

"Dr. Eisenberg," Eleanor said upon leaving, "if there were a special someone in your life, I bet her family would be thrilled to meet you." She gave him a wink.

That night, she called Ginny, easing in with some chitchat about the shockingly high (well, this was true) prices on seedless grapes. "So, Ginny, how are things going with you and that David person?"

"Not now."

"I would like to have this young man over for dinner. In fact, I insist on inviting him for dinner this Friday."

"Do that, Mom. But you should know we broke up last week."

Apparently David didn't listen to Ginny when she talked, although Eleanor had seen him listen with rapt attention to Milly's complaints about Pierre's furniture chewing. Apparently David didn't support her poetry—as if he could be expected to tend to his patients *and* read all her poems. David made her, on some fundamental level, uncomfortable—but how comfortable he had made Pierre!

No man was good enough. If I'd had her attitude, thought Eleanor, I'd be knitting in a rocking chair somewhere right now, beside my cousin Gertrude.

"Your father doesn't always listen," said Eleanor. "He doesn't support every little thing I do."

"Mom, let's not go there."

Then she vanished to India. For two months Ginny didn't reply to e-mails, until one night she called and, in a strange whisper, asked Eleanor if she and Gavin could wire three thousand dollars. Ginny said it was an emergency, that she would pay them back. Eleanor thought she'd been moved to donate to a charity, that she was paying for one of those cleft palate operations, or maybe—she had seen a movie about this—Ginny had been swindled by a handsome young Indian posing as a prince.

She wasn't expecting her to come home with a child!

Who knew what temperament the poor child had inherited. Add to that seven years of sleeping in a crowded, filthy orphanage—what kind of girl would she be? What did the adoption agency know about her? Were there any, well, guarantees? Ginny had been evasive about the details. She was a guardian, the legal adoption was pending, there was paperwork, lots of paperwork. That's all she said.

Eleanor dutifully sent toys and knit sweaters. Gavin set up a college fund, since they didn't know what Ginny had managed to save from teaching.

When they related the news, friends raised eyebrows at the word *India*.

"We thought China was the hot spot for babies. Or Romania."

"Ginny feels connected to India. It's the yoga."

Eleanor had her concerns about Ginny's choice, but they were the concerns of a mother; she certainly wouldn't let other people second-guess her daughter.

"Ginny is a modern woman," she said confidently. "She simply isn't concerned with trends. She is a freethinker, always has been. In ten years, everybody will be living like her."

Gavin nodded.

Above all else, they believed in loyalty.

But now this: *mute* as well? Eleanor couldn't understand how her daughter, who demanded such perfection of men, could accept a child with countless difficulties.

Ginny drew Priya to her stomach, tucking her under one flap of her cardigan as though shielding her from judgment. Eleanor felt the tug of family allegiance. Ginny was her daughter, and Priya was now her granddaughter. It was done.

Eleanor wiped imaginary dirt from her hands. There would be no more dwelling on the negatives.

"I'll get some nice photographs later," she said, moving a strand of hair from Ginny's eye and placing it behind her ear. "Why don't the boys put on the game and leave us ladies to preparing?"

GINNY

*H*er mother had named her for Ginger Rogers, and seemed forever disappointed that Ginny couldn't sing or dance or watch a Ginger Rogers movie without passing out on the couch before the final credits.

Also, her namesake churned through five husbands. Ginny was lagging.

Several years earlier, her mother sat Ginny down: "I want you to know that if you are a lesbian, I am okay with that." This sentiment was undercut by the fact that her mother whispered *lesbian*. "Your father and I accept you no matter who you are."

"Mom, my problem is that I date too many men, not too few." Ginny knew lesbians aplenty, and often thought it would simplify her life if she could rally to the cause. There had been a few halfhearted, clumsy attempts in college; she just didn't have it in her.

"But you never seem able to settle on one, and I have to ask myself, as your mother, what is *wrong*. I wish you could find a man like Douglas."

"Douglas is my *brother*."

"Someone *like* him. Denise says Jodie Foster is a lesbian. She also went to Yale."

"If I go on *Jeopardy!*, I can take Homosexual Oscar Winners for five hundred dollars."

"It's just . . . don't you think it's awkward, teaching what you teach, and . . . Ginny, friends ask me what you are doing, what you are teaching, and when I say family studies, they ask, quite naturally, does she have a family of her own."

"If I taught ancient Egyptian history, would they ask if I was ancient Egyptian?"

"How is a mother supposed to have a serious conversation with her daughter when everything is a clever answer?" When her mother slipped into the third person she was minutes away from tears.

"I've told you a million times, Mom, it wasn't until the fifties that Americans began marrying in their late teens—and only because they were so traumatized by the war. At the turn of the nineteenth century, a single twenty-five-year-old woman was the statistical norm."

Of course, Ginny wasn't exactly twenty-five.

"Oh, none of it even matters to you!"

Which wasn't true. But Ginny believed in putting on a brave face. When she was young her father had told her that it was important not to rub her disappointments in people's faces, and not to ask for pity. The lesson—one of the few her father had ever imparted—resonated. Because she understood, even as a child, why he was saying it. Her mother always seemed so . . . fragile. So Ginny would reveal anger, or annoyance—but not pain. When she was feeling lousy, this was a small act of heroism she could perform. She could at least say, *I protected someone.*

Her mother would simply never understand how things had changed for women Ginny's age. They had the right to work, the right to pursue careers, but they were dating men who had been raised by housewives, women like her mother who sent them off to school each day with neatly packed lunch boxes, each containing a favorite sandwich, a juice box, a bag of yogurt raisins, and a peeled carrot they were told they absolutely must eat if they cared at all about their mothers' wishes or a vitamin A deficiency; mothers who sewed buttons and baked bread and served warm milk with honey before tucking them in; women who, in all matters of finance and business and geography, deferred to their husbands. So even though their girlfriends worked the same hours, slaving away under the same fluorescent lights, staring at the same dull gray cubicle walls, even though their girlfriends, on occasion, made more money, that childhood image of a woman in an apron who offered steaming mashed potatoes and who kissed their earlobes wasn't shaken. Without realizing it, these guys expected their girlfriends to come home from the office, set down their pink laptop bags, slide a meat loaf in the oven, do a quick mop of the kitchen, and serve them scotch and soda after dinner, before giving them a gentle foot rub or, if they were lucky, a blow job.

And these were the *nice* guys.

The ones who would wash dishes if asked, who understood the concept of fabric softener.

These men were caught between two wildly different generations. Ginny imagined them as time travelers, baffled by the wacky women of the future, squinting at their confidence and capability—*Jeez, these girls change tires* and *write books!*—as if the women had lasers streaming from their eyes.

To Ginny, it felt like the Copernican Revolution: men had just learned the sun didn't orbit the earth and weren't taking it well.

Certainly what Ginny had seen of her parents' marriage hadn't sent her sprinting to the altar.

Disputes over napkins versus paper towels. Her mother's lifelong complaint that she could not clean the back deck without moving her father's telescope, which he had forbidden. Her father's glare of disapproval as her mother, upon exiting a restaurant, pawed dinner mints into her purse. The biannual excavation of the refrigerator, her father extracting the half-and-half, the cream cheese, the Zabar's egg salad, incredulously announcing the months-old expiration dates. "September '04! Eleanor, you are trying to poison me."

Her mother would sniff each one, insisting that any vaguely sane person could intuit when the cottage cheese had gone bad. Expiration dates were for the weak and the profligate. They were the work of lawyers, to prevent frivolous food-poisoning lawsuits, and sent perfectly good food down the disposal. *Three hundred years ago, Ginny, did the pioneers churn butter and put a date on it?*

Growing up, Ginny couldn't understand why they'd married. Until she found a photo of their wedding day. Posed on the steps of city hall in Columbus, Georgia, her father clasped one of her mother's hands and braced her back in a mock dip so that the sunlight caught their faces in profile, as though they had no interest in anyone but each other. At twenty and twenty-one they were great physical specimens. Her father's broad shoulders beautifully complemented her mother's elegant neck. They were young, attractive, healthy, horny, and—from the date on the picture—her father was about to go to Vietnam.

Ginny was looking for something that might endure.

And a couple of times, she thought she had found it.

After her book of poetry came out, she was invited to teach in NYU's graduate writing program. Her seminar, Poetic Histories, met in the afternoons every spring, and as the weather got warmer, the first few minutes of class were consumed by the inevitable debate over whether to open the windows and spend the hour discussing poetry to the sound of jackhammers, or to listen unhindered to one another's insightful observations on the poetic process, and die of heatstroke.

Ratu always made his way to the window, either to rattle it open or to bring it thudding closed, the self-appointed climate controller. He was from Fiji, and wrote poems about his fisherman father.

All the girls flirted with him. He wore his long dark hair in a ponytail. He carried exactly four pencils and sharpened them to a lethal point before class and set them beside his notebook. When anyone spoke, he blew on the tip of his pencil and intensely took notes.

He was twenty-three, and it never occurred to Ginny that he might harbor romantic interest in her. But they were seated in her office late one afternoon, the light outside darkening, going over his poem "Bird of an Ancient Land" when the fire alarm blared. She was ready to shrug it off and keep working—the alarms were always being tripped—but Ratu stood and took her hand. "Come, Ginger, it is best to be safe." He led her down seventeen flights of a dark gray stairway, insisting on carrying her tote bag. When was the last time a man had carried her bag?

As the fire trucks appeared, she said, "I have an idea."

At a café on Waverly Place, over herbal tea, Ratu told a story about a terrible fire in his village, Savusavu, started by a French tourist who had fallen asleep smoking in his beach-front rental. The fire burned ten homes, including Ratu's. He said it was the first time he had seen his father weep. He stared at Ginny, his eyes a lustrous mahogany.

The small table and the dim lights of the café unleashed in her a feeling of intimacy.

"You should write about it," she said. "You're quite talented with narratives. And you make great use of Fijian history. You see, in 'Bird of an Ancient Land' . . ." She set his manuscript on the table and slid her chair beside his so they could examine his poem. She glanced around to see who else from the university might be there.

Her students were graduate level, a few of them older than she was, but a classroom triggered certain dynamics, particular boundaries. Whatever maternal urges Ginny had were directed toward her students; she asked endless questions about their dating lives and vacation plans. She brought chips and sodas to class, and always, on a student's birthday, produced a cake with candles.

But with Ratu she had refrained from asking questions, and in the café she realized it was because she had a small crush she'd been keeping in check. Whenever her students turned in poems, she read his first, with an unusual excitement, studying them for clues about what kind of person he was. It did not displease her to see him muscle open the window.

"Your use of juxtaposition is really good, Ratu. Eighty percent of good artistry is knowing what to put next to what." He shifted his leg beneath the table and it came to rest against hers; she found herself afraid of what silence would bring. "There was this famous editing experiment in 1918. Lev Kuleshov, a Russian filmmaker, edited a short film using static images of an actor's face alternated with shots of a plate of soup, a girl at play, and a coffin. After seeing this montage, audience members raved about the actor's varied emotional expressions—pensiveness, happiness, sorrow—when, in fact, the image of the actor was the same in all the shots. Viewers created narratives based merely on the sequence of images, and on their reactions to those images. It's called the Kuleshov Effect."

She began straightening the sugars and the Equals in the dispenser.

"You are an amazing woman, Ginger. Brilliant. When you were my age, you were already published."

His compliment was lost in the thud of the word *age*—she was thirty-three, ten years his senior— and she couldn't stop the blush invading her cheeks. He reached for her hand.

"You're my student," she said, but didn't pull her hand away.

He walked her home that night and came upstairs, and from then on they were inseparable.

Every night, he sat on her bed and slowly brushed his thick hair, smoothing on coconut oil. His chest, tattooed with birds and trees, glowed in her reading lamp. On his right hip, a long, narrow leaf tattoo, feathered with veins, contained the scripted words *Tagane Vuka,* which he said meant "he who can fly." Before sleep, he flossed for a good ten minutes; with an orange rubber tip, he probed the soft arcs of his gums. He rinsed with a bright green fluoride treatment she had last seen as a child. His father and grandfather had lost their teeth at a young age, and Ratu, terrified of decay, avoided sweets and sodas.

In the afternoons Ratu swam three miles in the university pool, furious butterfly and crawl strokes. For the rest of the day, she could smell chlorine on his hair.

He always woke early to make the coffee, and when Ginny showered, he made the bed. By 9:00 a.m., he was off to the library to work on freelance articles, so that his afternoons could be devoted to poetry. He was a man who had never been handed a single thing.

"You work so hard," she said one night while she was reading census data. He sat in the corner, typing away on his laptop, working on an article for *Technology Today*. "You need to give yourself a little time off."

"Ginger, I'm under a lot of pressure from my family." He craned his neck. "To make money, to send money home. The ones who get out, we have responsibility. And with the Internet, oh, I hate the Internet. My uncle came to America years ago, and we would wait to hear from him by mail. Maybe once a month, on birthdays and holidays, he might call. Now my father goes to the Internet café every day to e-mail me. 'Ratu, what are you doing? How much are you earning? Your grandmother's kidney is failing.' That I have chosen to be a poet is not their dream. My father thinks I should drive a taxicab. He's never owned a car and he thinks any job that gives you a car to drive is the jackpot. That is his favorite word: *jackpot*."

"Ratu, I'll give you money. Don't waste your time writing reviews of noise-canceling headphones."

"I couldn't ask that of you, Ginger."

"You didn't ask, I offered."

Sending off the money allowed Ratu to relax. The summer was a delight. Mornings they each went off to write, but by day's end they'd meet at the market and buy fruit and bread and wine and spend the evening sprawled on a blanket in Madison Square Park, reading poetry to each other.

By August, he showed Ginny a one-act play he had written in the voice of his father; she thought it was quite good.

"Good? Not excellent?"

"I'm no expert in plays. Why don't you send it out and see what people say?"

"You say that like it's so easy. If you wrote a play, you're Ginger Olson, people will look at it! You are a respected academic. I don't even have my MFA!"

Ginny showed it to Ari Edleson, a college friend who had spent years directing theater in Japan and London and who had just moved back to New York.

"Gin, it lags in the middle, the end, and the beginning. Fishing is not inherently dramatic, and certainly not to the New York theater crowd."

"He's the voice of Fiji, Ari. The first Fijian poet/playwright. You can *market* him. Fuck, tell people Fijian drama is all about lagging, it'll be authentic lagging, like the long, slow days in the South Pacific."

"You're in love," Ari said.

The play went nowhere, and Ratu began work on a novel about a young Fijian moving to Manhattan. He believed this had market potential. But he confided in Ginny another pressure. Once he got his MFA, his student visa would expire. The only way he could stay in the country was to get an Aliens of Extraordinary Ability visa, nearly impossible for an unpublished writer.

The thought of losing Ratu set off a disturbance deep inside Ginny.

She asked her department chair, Mark Stevens, to write on his behalf; she contacted two writers' organizations. She had made a few poet friends, and asked them to sign a petition to the departments of immigration.

"Ginger, you are doing too much for me."

"I'll hold a goddamned bake sale if I have to. You're not getting kicked out of the country."

"All this help, people will wonder about us."

Actually, she'd successfully kept their relationship private, despite bringing Ratu to a university mixer—Ginny didn't know what she'd been thinking with that. Maybe she was tired of all the gray-haired department secretaries asking her when she was going to settle down. Maybe she was tired of the tenured bores in their tweed jackets wondering if she was a lesbian. Maybe she was embarrassed that she'd shown up with a dud at the last university function, a man who managed to devour an entire platter of smoked salmon while texting

God knew who. But the next day, she overheard Richard Longstretch, in the American Studies department office, refer to Ginger and her Polynesian protégé. No one suspected hanky-panky. Or maybe no one imagined a man like that would ever be interested in a woman her age.

In early May, Ratu's visa was finally approved, and Ginny went to her Tuesday class wearing a yellow sundress and kitten heels, ready to celebrate afterward.

Ratu and Ginny exchanged secretive smiles as she spread out bags of popcorn and a gallon of apple juice. The class went through the usual routine, voting to close the window, which Ratu did, so they could hear everyone read their new poems aloud.

Ginny called on Tracy Manaster, a corn-fed Iowa blonde who was shy about participating in class. Her poems were awkward, suffering from an odd combination of blandness and melodrama. But Ginny was feeling charitable that day, and wanted to send this girl into the world with self-confidence.

Tracy extracted a gray nugget of chewing gum from her mouth and cleared her throat:

> Silent, mysterious.
> I offer him my stare, but he refuses.
> I offer him a book, but he refuses.
> I offer him a candy bar, and he refuses.
> What can I give you?
> You are beautiful, he tells me, offering his smooth shoulder, his
>   warm mouth.
>
> He who can fly.
> A leaf he holds close to his hip.
> Tagane Vuka.
> He offers me——

"Pop quiz!" said Ginny.

"There's more," said Tracy.

"Everybody pull out a sheet of paper," Ginny said as calmly as she could, "and write the first line of six of Shakespeare's sonnets."

Ratu did not take out paper; he had taken down his ponytail and was refastening it, looking determinedly and shamefully out the window. Ginny felt her face prickle with humiliation. She had worn lipstick that day, red, and began to wipe it off with the back of her hand.

Richard Ong, beside her, whispered, "Ms. Olson, you feeling okay?"

"No, I'm sick, Richard. Bad poetry makes me sick." Ginny collected her things. "Leave the quizzes in my mailbox."

She arrived home to the table she'd set earlier with champagne glasses and dropped them in the trash. Then she lost the energy to even leave the kitchen and sat on the tile floor. How many women throughout history had sat on their kitchen floors feeling as pathetic as she did? She was thirty-three, alone, and the crowning act in her epic history of failed relationships was being two-timed by her own student.

After all the nights she'd spent convincing friends how wonderful Ratu was, how perfect they were for one another despite their age and career disparity, how hardworking and kind he was, she was too embarrassed to call anyone. The depth of her stupidity stunned her. Besides, people would expect her to be angry, to scream. *The bastard. The coward.* But she couldn't get to anger because grief was in her way.

Brave face, she told herself.

This was worse than the mess with Dr. Blaise Langley in Africa. She had been twenty-two then and believed, even as she sobbed on the airplane home, that she would meet many men and fall in love again. But Ginny had no such faith this time. It had been twelve years since Blaise Langley broke her heart, and in that time, despite scores of dates and boyfriends, she'd met only two men who she truly cared for. The idea of all the boring first dates and halfhearted relationships that lay ahead filled her with dread.

All around her, she had watched friends and colleagues fall in love, get married, have babies. Ginny had simply assumed it would happen for her, too. It was not that she believed in God, or a fair and ordered universe—studying history had long ago debunked her of that notion—yet she clung to some vague idea that the course of her life, her achievements and setbacks, were, if not regulated, at least *observed,* by something beyond herself. And so for years she had thought: *I am a person who always waits contentedly at the end of the line. It's my nature to let others go first. That must be what's happening, on a cosmic scale.*

Now something had cracked open in her. What if her turn never came?

She took a bath, slowly eating applesauce as the water went luke-warm, until it reminded her of the pool, of Ratu's fierce butterfly strokes—she could see his arms slicing forward—and she lurched out. Hair dripping, she grabbed his books, his dental floss and his silly gum device, his brush and the hair bands—scattered on her night-stand like a Venn diagram. She put them in a Jiffy envelope and sealed it. Then she lost her courage, addressed it to herself.

By the time the envelope returned, Ginny had canceled her last lectures, claiming she had something highly contagious. In fact, she'd been camped out on her bed for a week, surfing the Internet and playing an old version of the Oregon Trail. She recklessly shot rabbits instead of bison and let all members of her party die from snakebites. When finally her favorite announcement came on the screen, *You have died of dysentery,* she called it quits.

She had thought, briefly, of calling Ratu and demanding an expla-nation. But he hadn't lifted a finger to contact her since that day in class. And she knew it wasn't only Ratu she had lost. She had lost the feeling that her life was moving forward, that her life was safe. She had always believed happiness was her due. She was a good person, and had assumed good things would come her way. Suddenly, she was afraid.

Days, years, were churning along and nothing seemed to be progressing. She needed a change of scenery. She needed to do something bold, to strike out. Ginny scrolled through the web listings for international field research. Anthropological surveying in Somalia. A study of Gypsy settlements in Southern France. And then:

Unwanted Girls in India: A Cultural Survey

There are more than 11 million abandoned children in India, about 90 percent female. Last year, only four thousand of those children were adopted, through various governmental and charitable agencies; only a quarter of those placed with families overseas.

Research will be conducted at orphanages in Delhi and Bombay, to document any changes that this new policy may incur. Researcher grants will cover three months of room and board. Sponsor Institutions not required.

Ginny clicked the button: APPLY NOW.

DOUGLAS

*H*e'd overlooked one crucial thing: Ginny didn't *have* a television. His sister delivered this news with such casualness, such cheery indifference, that it was clear to Douglas she'd ignored that every year on Thanksgiving, Dad, the boys, and he watched the game.

"You'll live," she said, chopping the carrots.

"I didn't know *surviving* the day was our goal."

A mute orphaned child, a house without a television, a living room full of plywood furniture. Ginny's obsession with deprivation was like a bizarre medical condition.

"Ginny, where's the nearest Best Buy? I will *buy* you a television."

"Doug, I don't want a television. They tape these things and replay them on ESPN later, right? Or on YouTube? Honestly, it might not be a bad idea to try sitting without your eyes glued to the TV this year."

"Hon, can you stream it on the Internet?" Denise asked.

"All four of you with your noses pressed to my laptop screen?" said Ginny. "Now, that's a Hallmark moment. This is a family holiday, the whole point of which is to be together, to interact. I haven't seen you in five months!"

Douglas knew this was true, and he felt bad about it, but it was also true that the Packers were playing.

"Then watch with us!" he tried.

"Douglas, for God sakes, I'll *play* football if you want. It's a nice day and we can run around. But to dull every neuron in our brains with a virtual experience, somebody else's game, holds zero interest for me. Not to mention it's a ritual reenactment of the source of all violent conflict. Don't you see . . ."

Ginny could talk circles around him and he wasn't going to change her mind. He wished he'd brought his hand-held TV. But this was the first day in months away from the dreary Obervell Construction offices; away from angry calls from site-team captains wondering when they could go back to work; away from the growing pile of threatening letters from the state loan commission; away from neighborhood organizers picketing them to clean up abandoned sites. All season he'd been following the Packers, a powerhouse team, a heroic team, a team of mythic achievement. After two terrible seasons and talk of retirement, Brett Favre had thrown his 421st touchdown pass in a game against the Vikings, setting a new all-time record. Whenever there was an update about the shitty real-estate market, Douglas closed his office door and took a midday break to watch online Favre's eighty-two-yard touchdown pass against the Broncos that October. Favre had made a spectacular comeback and now the Packers were about to wipe the field with the Lions.

". . .well, Doug?"

"Huh?"

"Do you or do you not think that children should be raised with a sense of the collective enemy?"

He was confused. He grinned, and put on his best Arkansas accent. "I did not have sexual relations with that woman."

"Doug!"

"Children," his mother interjected in her hypnotist's voice. "Why don't we all relax in the living room and find an agreeable solution."

Ginny dumped the carrots into a pot, flicked on the ancient burner, and led Priya out. Denise and Douglas followed. Ginny settled into a rocking chair with Priya on her lap, holding her tight.

"Look, this is my home and as guests here, you're going to have to make do with what I've got. Were you all expecting a multiplex?"

"Maybe Aunt Ginny can't afford a television," Laura whispered.

What a considerate and grown-up thought for a five-year-old.

"Aunt Ginny just happens to think the television is the devil," Douglas said.

Laura's eyes widened. "I thought the devil had horns."

"Gin, how do you propose we pass the time while the food is cooking?"

"Ping-Pong!" said Eleanor. His mother, the most unathletic, unco-ordinated, noncompetitive woman he knew, was a whiz at Ping-Pong. When they were growing up, she loved to play against them, until Ginny and Douglas got tired of losing to her and snuck games when she was off buying groceries. Thrifty, bordering on compul-sively cheap, his mother had stunned them all by buying herself a hundred-dollar Ping-Pong paddle for her fortieth birthday. She was always trying to get people to play, channeling what Ginny called "a lifetime of missed adventure and thwarted ambition" into her every swing.

"I don't have a Ping-Pong table," said Ginny. "But I have an idea."

Oh no, here came Trivial Pursuit. Or what had she gone on about the year before? The women who worked as spies during the Civil War? The Boston Massacre resulting in only five casualties? His sister had been teaching too long, mistaking every room for a classroom. Sometimes, a man just needed to stop thinking.

Ginny pulled paper out of her printer and grabbed a fistful of pen-cils. She tore the paper into strips and handed them out.

"Think of a person or a character and write it on that."

His parents both looked stumped, pencils midair as if they were doing a crossword puzzle. The twins folded their papers into minia-ture accordions.

"Anything!" sang Ginny. "Politician, actor, writer, historian. See? This is what happens when you watch too much television, your mind turns to putty."

"Have you heard about this book called *Everything Bad Is Good for You?*" his mother asked.

"You want an activity? I'm going to make it really simple." Ginny pushed up her sweater sleeves. "Dad, give me a name."

"I thought we were supposed to write it secretly on the paper?"

"This is just an example. Any name that springs to mind."

"Jackie Limousine."

"Jackie Limousine?"

"Who's that? I really don't want to play a game that's going to make us all feel stupid," said his mother.

"Jackie Limousine sounds like a stripper," said Denise.

"Dad, it has to be a name of somebody famous, a celebrity," Ginny said.

His mother raised her hand. "Oh, oh, oh. Barbra Streisand!"

"Excellent, Mom. Barbra Streisand. So I look at the paper and start saying, *Funny Girl,* big nose. Maybe I sing. I say, she's married to James Brolin."

"Who's that?" Douglas asked.

"It doesn't matter," said Ginny. "If you don't get the clue, just wait for the next one."

"I thought Diane Lane was married to James Brolin."

"That's Josh Brolin," his mother piped in, to everyone's surprise.

"Do I need to serve Ritalin on the rocks to you people?"

The twins nodded with devilish grins, and Ginny sighed.

"Come on, kids," Douglas said. "We're playing a word game! This will be good for us! We're all going to finally learn to *speaka da inglish*!"

Ginny shot him what he had long ago coined her John Rambo, *First Blood* stare. It was a look that said, I am now your enemy.

"Now, Priya and I need to go back into the kitchen and check on some things, so why don't you all go ahead and enjoy the game."

"Okay," said Douglas. When Ginny was out of earshot, "I propose we do away with the little strips of paper. Just go up there and pluck one from your head."

"I have one!" his mother cried, shuffling in front of the couch and standing perfectly still.

"Mom? We're ready."

She remained still and tightened her lips, but Douglas saw her eyes dart wildly toward the wall, toward a large maroon poster that said LUCINDA WILLIAMS, LIVE AT MADISON SQUARE GARDEN.

"Mom, it's not Lucinda Williams . . ."

She clapped. "Yes!"

"We don't know who Lucinda Williams is," Brian huffed.

"Well, in that case, it wouldn't have mattered. Just follow Grandma's eyes."

The twins moved to Ginny's laptop, their fingers attacking the keyboard to see if they could download World of Warcraft.

"Boys, come on, we're all playing together."

"But this is stupid," Brian whined.

"That may very well be, but we're still all playing."

"I've got one," said Brandon, climbing up onto the sofa. He narrowed his eyes. "I am going to kill you."

Everyone was silent.

"Champ," said Douglas, "this might be a little morbid."

"I am going to kill you in your *sleep*," he continued.

"Stroke!" Eleanor shouted. "Oh, wait. No. Heart attack?"

Brandon twisted his face ghoulishly, wagging his tongue. "I am going to kill *all* of you!"

"Al-Qaeda," said Denise.

"Anthrax!" yelped Eleanor, sliding so far to the edge of her chair, it nearly toppled over.

"I'm going to kill you in your dreams."

"Sleeping-pill overdose."

Brandon shook his head with exasperation. "In your school, down by the pipes . . ."

"Asbestos!" Eleanor yelped.

Douglas could see that Laura was chewing on her tablecloth. "Let's take a time-out, champ."

"Trench-coat mafia," declared Denise.

"Lead-paint poisoning?" his mother asked.

Brandon rumbled out a long, annoyed breath. He pulled one sleeve over his hand and sliced at the air. "I'm your nightmare, on Elm Street," he said, at which point Brian leaped up from the floor.

"Freddy Krueger! Why didn't you say *Nightmare on Elm Street* to begin with?"

"I'm confused," said Eleanor.

"It's a movie," Douglas explained.

"Well, what is that rated?" his mother demanded. "Is that a *horror* movie? Why are the children watching horror movies?"

Laura's eyes were wide. "Daddy, what's anthrax?" Douglas looked at his wife, stumped.

"A city in Nova Scotia," said Gavin.

GAVIN

G avin's father, Alrek Olson, came to the United States at seventeen and worked as a fishmonger. From a cart along Boston Harbor he sold shellfish, cod, flounder, and striped porgy. His palms were like leather from handling the cracked shells of clams and scallops, his fingers blistered from packing the fish in ice. Decades after he stopped working the port, his wife claimed his hands still smelled of fish oil.

He vowed he would never leave the sea, until he took to the air.

During World War II, for three years he flew P-47 Thunderbolts over France and Germany. Alrek received a Medal of Honor and had his photo taken with Dwight D. Eisenhower. For the rest of his life, the photo hung framed on the wall of his office.

During the war, he met Christina Davenport, who, against the wishes of her well-to-do Boston family, served as a nurse in the Italian rear hospital where Alrek had been laid up with a neck injury. When the war ended, they married and returned to the town of Winthrop. With the GI Bill, Alrek attended the University of Massachusetts, finally giving up fishmongering to become an accountant.

Gavin was their only child. "We got everything in our first try!" his mother said, though he later suspected she had wanted more but had been unable to conceive again.

Things came easily to him: blue ribbons in science fairs, first chair in violin. By sophomore year of high school, he was captain of the track team and class president. He graduated Winthrop High as valedictorian and won a full scholarship to Yale. Most important,

Winthrop was a small town, and he was Alrek Olson's only son, which meant he was beloved. The town had lost 111 sons and brothers in the war, and Alrek had not only survived but returned with a medal.

People sought Alrek's advice on investments and wills, on building additions to their homes, on whether to vote for Kennedy or Nixon. He had even saved the marriage of the town tax collector, after talking with the couple for sixteen straight hours in their kitchen. He accompanied Marjorie Plymouth, the town librarian, to visit her estranged father in prison, where he was serving ten years for grand larceny. In 1954, when Hurricane Carol came north, Alrek went house to house helping people board up their windows. That same year, he was elected mayor.

Gavin's father was also a licensed justice of the peace and officiated at thirty-seven marriages. He was godfather to six children, one named Alrek, another Oslo. He taught Gavin to fell a tree, to make snowshoes from twigs and bark, to catch and debone a fish, to skin a deer, to clean a gun. He was a volunteer firefighter, and in 1969, while Gavin was thousands of miles away filling out supply forms on a Smith Corona in a stuffy Saigon office, his father, at age fifty, died pulling Abigail Kentworth, Gavin's eighth-grade teacher, from the second floor of her burning house.

It was Alrek who had first wanted Gavin to fight in the war. Before the political problems were clear, when Gavin was home from college they would watch the news on their small television. "First the Nazis, now the communists," his father said in his thick Norwegian accent. "Good men have to clean up these messes."

So after graduation, while his classmates were driving overpacked station wagons to Canada, or posting applications to medical and law schools, veterinary college, any institution that would keep the draft board at bay, Gavin walked into the naval air program recruiter's office and asked to be a fighter pilot. But because of his vision, they wouldn't take him. The army, however, had different standards.

Eleanor, whom he'd been dating for six months, was crestfallen.

"What if something happens to you? Why do *you* have to go?"

This was 1968. As Gavin later told himself many times, the draft board would have gotten its hands on him soon enough.

Eleanor Haggarty was the daughter of a French Protestant mother and a lapsed Catholic, Irish-American father. She wore short skirts and had a waist Gavin could practically put his hand around. He called her his Little Huguenot.

He met her the summer before her junior year at Wellesley. He had just graduated from Yale, and for one long June weekend, they were both on Cape Cod.

He had noticed her sunning herself on a small raft, dipping her hand in the water every so often to moisten her slender arms. She seemed at first to be with a group of friends, but had floated off on her own, and when she realized how far out she was, slipped off her raft and began swimming somewhat urgently toward the shore. Finally wrestling her raft to the sand, she stood dripping before him, shaking water from her ears. She had a swanlike neck, a delicate and pointed chin, flirtatious lips.

"That was some situation out there," Gavin said.

She thumbed her red gingham swimsuit off her thigh and something plopped onto the sand. "Ick, jellyfish."

"Can't blame them for wanting to get close to you," he said.

"Well, look at you, standing there all amused. What would you have done if I were drowning?"

"Give you the kiss of life."

"Don't you wish, Mr. Shy."

She was a girl who turned heads, and knew it. Her mother, Yvette, kept her on a tight leash. Gavin couldn't take Eleanor out for dinner without first having a glass of apple juice in Yvette's living room and discussing the works of Tolstoy, or Sigmund Freud. Yvette hadn't gone to college, but she loved "talking to big men about big ideas." "And you, mister," she always said to Gavin, "are going places." Yvette had met Eleanor's father at age sixteen when he helped liberate her small village of Gravelotte. She'd been in the United States long enough to shed her accent and all evidence of her Frenchness. Yvette—which she pronounced *I-vet*—was more American than Betsy Ross. On the Fourth of July, Yvette cooked them a five-course meal, pinned small flags on their lapels, and set off her own backyard fireworks.

The Irish-American father was long dead by then, and not much spoken of. When Gavin asked what he died of, Eleanor looked off and said, "Liver trouble."

There had been a sister, too. Simone. A year younger than Eleanor. She had died of polio. Yvette and Eleanor never spoke of her, except once a year on August fifth when they quietly celebrated her birthday. As an adult, long after her mother had died, on that date Eleanor would sit alone in the kitchen at night and blow out three candles on a cupcake.

Yvette was an anxious mother. She wanted to know exactly where Gavin and Eleanor were going, when they'd be back, that they would wear seat belts and stay below the speed limit, that they'd avoid Boston's bad neighborhoods, that they wouldn't fool around with marijuana. Gavin thought it stemmed from the pain of losing her other daughter. Or her childhood under Nazi occupation. Eleanor shrugged off her mother's worries, inventing elaborate stories about puppet shows and choral groups they had seen to cover for the hours they spent making out in Gavin's red Chevrolet.

A month before Gavin shipped off, Eleanor took the bus to Fort Benning to see him. Yvette came as well, nervous about Eleanor traveling, but kept herself tucked away in the Farewell Motel. Eleanor wore a red seersucker dress and yellow high heels and looked so pretty Gavin felt as if he were seeing her for the first time. She had brought scissors and cut off a lock of her hair and tied it with a ribbon.

"Keep this in your pocket all the time. Over your heart. And keep these under your pillow."

From her purse she removed a pair of panties: pale pink with small white flowers and lace trim. She twirled them around with her fingertip, giggling, a blush creeping across her face, before flinging them at his face.

"You're killing me, Ellie."

"Promise me no matter how long they keep you there, you're mine."

"How about I promise in front of a judge?"

His father, his training captain—they both advised him to get hitched. The war could be long, and a wife might be the only sure thing to come home to.

Two days after they married, as Gavin stepped onto the transport plane, he had the deep sense that he was about to prove himself, to define his character in some fundamental way. He imagined becoming a man like his father. Though later he would never admit this to anyone, he was filled with grand visions of heroics, scenarios in which he rescued scores of wounded men, men who, unlike him, had been careless enough to get shot.

But during Gavin's third week in the infantry, while leading a jungle patrol, a piece of shrapnel pierced his knee. And that was that. The three-millimeter sliver of metal, which he would save and occasionally look at his entire life, ended his frontline duty.

He spent his final eighteen months of duty as an REMF—a rear echelon motherfucker. College grads were pressed to work as typists, and Gavin became a clerk in the Administration Company of the 101st Airborne Division. He spent long, hot days writing reports on promotions and demotions, filling out supply requisitions, typing up weather forecasts. He once wrote a report on the plant and insect life of the Ban Me Thuot region, and spoke to a medical-research team about insect-borne illnesses. In eighteen months, those were his most exciting five days.

In the evenings, before dinner, he drafted a letter to his father. Although the war was looking bloodier and more misguided every day, Gavin feared his desk job would disappoint his father. Gavin had written four drafts, but had sent none, when he learned of his father's death.

In 1971, he got his discharge.

A couple of dozen men flew in a military-transport plane to Travis Air Force Base, cheering raucously when they landed. They strolled from the plane to the terminal gulping down the evening air, laughing, and bumping shoulders. To get a half-price standby spot on a commercial airline, they had to arrive in uniform. At the San Francisco airport, the gate attendant told Gavin it would be another hour before she knew if he had a seat to Boston.

He hadn't been in an American bar, hadn't sat on one of those vinyl bar stools, in two years. He was in heaven. He scooped a fistful of salted peanuts into his mouth and ordered a Budweiser.

Down the bar stood a girl with blond hair; a rainbow ribbon fastened a ponytail on each of her shoulders. She looked barely old enough to be drinking. She wore bell-bottom jeans and noisy platform clogs, taking short, heavy steps, as if in leg chains, as she came toward him with her drink. A black beauty mark underscored one eye, and her teeth were perfectly straight and white, the kind of teeth the girls in Vietnam dreamed of. She propped her hand on her hip in that same sassy way Eleanor always did before telling him he'd done something wrong.

"Sorry, I didn't mean to stare," he said. "But you don't know how good you look right now."

"Really?" She leaned close, her ponytails brushing his pants, and whispered, "And how good did all those babies look before you killed them?" Gavin felt the icy liquid on his chest before he saw her emptied glass. "Fucking monster."

He looked around, and through the blur of wet shame he saw the bartender, two stewardesses sharing a martini, a family with small children: they were all staring. Gavin fumbled for his wallet, laid a wad of bills on the bar, and left.

Slowly, dizzily, he made his way to the men's room, where he locked himself in a stall until it was time to board the plane.

In Boston, Eleanor met him at the airport. Gavin said nothing of what had happened. Eleanor had had a difficult couple of years caring for her mother, who had been diagnosed with cancer. They sent letters during his time away, in which she described her literature classes, her professors, and Gavin complained about the food, the weather, or the broken fan in his office. Neither said what was really on their minds, because as soon as Gavin shipped seven thousand miles away, it seemed to have dawned on them both that they didn't know each other that well.

As Yvette was slowly dying, Eleanor was becoming more and more like her mother. She was nervous about where they would live, what job he would find, how they would afford furniture. She was nervous about his mood, which was not, as a matter of course in those days, very good.

His father was dead, the Kent State Massacre had just happened, and war memorials were being doused with tar and urine. In Winthrop, where for years he'd been treated like a prince, people said, "It's such a shame you signed on for that mess."

After Eleanor's mother died, they moved to New York City. Gavin thought it might be easier living in a place where everyone didn't think that for two years he'd been burning villages.

Focused on making good money for a few years to alleviate Eleanor's fears, Gavin interviewed for jobs at Morgan Stanley, Fidelity, Goldman Sachs. But there was no way to hide his war record. The three-year gap on his résumé and his slight limp said it all. After all the gruesome news reports, his interviewers, who had probably once been as enthusiastic about the war as he had been, seemed uneasy with the idea of a veteran down the corridor. Morgan Stanley and Fidelity claimed they didn't have openings. The hiring manager at Goldman Sachs wanted to know if he was undergoing psychiatric treatment.

"I graduated from Yale. With straight A's in economics. I have a recommendation from Franklin Sommerworth. What more do you want?"

"Mr. Olson, try not to let yourself get worked up."

He offered Gavin water, a sugar cookie. No job.

Gavin interviewed for two months before he got an offer.

"I think you'll take to the calm environment here," the man at Reynolds Insurance said.

Gavin was given a small, windowless office on the twenty-ninth floor of the Empire State Building. The walls were blue and hung with framed photographs of roses and irises, powder room decor. Classical music was pumped through a small speaker mounted in the corner. He sold life, fire, car, medical, flood, and umbrella policies. Over the phone he convinced people they could lose everything in the blink of an eye, which he was beginning to believe.

There were ten other office doors, with other nameplates, and occasionally he heard the soft click of doors opening and closing. But they all kept different hours, and submitted their weekly sales sheets to a large oak box marked: PROGRESS. Notes would appear on his desk afterward: *Good work, J. Reynolds*. It wasn't until their first quarterly strategy meeting that Gavin looked around the elliptical glass conference table at a dozen men his age, one with a stump of an arm, another in a wheelchair. Jeremiah Reynolds's only son had been killed flying a Huey over Tay Ninh.

Eleanor was trying to make a life in New York, but Gavin hated the building mixers she arranged. He couldn't bear standing around with law students and hippies, self-righteous draft dodgers who wouldn't have lasted a day in any army.

"You mustn't be so judgmental," Eleanor would complain.

"They judge *me*. Insurance salesman equals idiot. And they're right. It's a dead-end job. If I told them I was a vet, then maybe they'd see what I was up against. But that's a conversation stopper."

"Sweetheart, please don't go about *advertising* it. It makes people uncomfortable."

And this was the beginning of Gavin's realization that for the rest of his life most people, no matter what he said about his Saigon desk job, would still imagine he'd gone on a killing spree in the jungle. Two million men served in the war, only a fraction in ground combat.

The truth was, Gavin had killed two men before his injury. He shot them close enough to see their faces, which he thought of from time to time, and which disturbed him. He wished he'd known their names. It seemed a shameful act to kill a man and not know his name. But none of his feelings resembled those of the disturbed veteran-characters who eventually appeared in the movies.

It seemed to him that the people who had stayed home *wanted* veterans to be tortured. Wanted soldiers to be paying penance for the whole misguided endeavor. Because as long as the men who fought were still dealing with it, everyone else could sweep the war under the rug.

Gavin didn't want veterans neglected—a few Reynolds men kept flasks in their desks, and all day he heard the glide of drawer casters, the loud sigh after a sip of gin—but when the world so firmly expected a person to unravel, it felt like someone tugging the thread.

After six months at Reynolds, Gavin wanted to escape his windowless office. If no one would hire him, he'd go back to school, he'd get so many degrees no firm could pass him over. He decided to apply to law school, studying for the LSATs while he was supposed to be making sales calls. His Reynolds colleagues advised against it: campuses were the hotbeds of antiwar sentiment; hippies were shouting veterans out of classrooms. Gavin also knew that money would be tricky, and he and Eleanor would have to move, but he didn't want to get stuck in sales his whole life, and told Eleanor as much.

"Sweetheart, you can't go back to school. You're going to be a father."

Gavin was stunned. In all the scenarios of his future, parenthood had not entered his mind. And it was the one that changed everything.

In the years after the children were born and they moved to Westport, as Gavin rode the long commuter train home at night with a folder of actuarial reports in his lap, he thought back to high school in Winthrop, where he'd been voted most likely to succeed, to his years at Yale, where he'd once dined with the university president, where, after he took the 800-meter title from Princeton, his teammates carried him over their heads through campus chanting "Ol-son, Ol-son." Sometimes when this memory seized him, Gavin would nearly leap from his train seat and press his palms to the black windows of the doors. He lowered his body in a lunge, one leg thrown back so that his calf muscle tingled in an almost exquisite pain, the seams of his wool suit pulled tight. Through the dark windows lay the towns where all the men seated around him would soon carry their briefcases down silent streets, wipe the bottoms of their polished shoes on a WELCOME mat, greet their aproned wives, kiss their children, and have a conversation about the weather, the grocery bill, new kitchen cabinets.

Sometimes Gavin pushed so hard against the windows that the men around him glanced up from their newspapers. *See? I'm not like you!* But they looked down again quickly, bored and unconvinced, and Gavin eventually lifted his own briefcase in defeat and stood dutifully awaiting his release into the night.

This sense of entrapment produced in Gavin a child's rebellion. In the early years, amid his long days at Reynolds Insurance, he indulged in juvenile deceptions, halfhearted dalliances. But only what he believed fell within the scope of masculine autonomy. Eleanor, who never shed the anxiety she'd inherited from her mother, raised the children, and one day the small giggly creatures who had waved around macaroni artwork, who had stampeded through the house dressed as unicorns and dragons, were, he realized, kindhearted human beings. Miraculously, his house was filled with what he recalled from his own childhood as love. Clumsy, unspoken, harried—nonetheless love. And toward his wife he noticed a growing affection, the familiarity that came with decades of shared breakfasts, whispered postparty astonishment at the misbehavior of other people's children, amusement at drunken neighbors wielding garden hoses at midnight. But this affection was compromised, he believed, by Eleanor having borne witness to what had become of his life, by her memory of who he had been. And he recalled the woman he had imagined his wife would be. From time to time these ghosts, these younger, other selves, tiptoed down from the attic, rattled the windows while he slept. He felt deceived. He woke in the night and looked at Eleanor. Did she feel it as well?

He did not know how to express tenderness to the person who had become the mirror of his disappointments, who had seen his every failure. Eleanor accepted their life, and him, with a cheer that rendered him silent. She suggested after-dinner strolls, picnics at the beach; with a stoniness he did not quite understand, Gavin refused her. The idea that he was punishing her made him sick. It was himself he loathed. And yet in his obligations as a husband, he decided he was fulfilling his duty. He worked hard, paid the bills. He rarely drank, never raised his voice. He was an insurance man now, that was all. She should not expect more. If he had to accept life's disappointments, so would she.

ELEANOR

*O*ne day, several years after they had moved to Westport, Eleanor stood on the back porch cleaning Gavin's telescope; she wiped it down carefully, from the tripod to the lens, with long, slow strokes of a dust rag.

"Oh my, what would Dr. Freud say about this?" A slender, tanned woman stood with a pitcher of lemonade in one hand, a bottle of bourbon in the other.

"My husband is very serious about his telescope," said Eleanor, continuing to dust. "Are you new to the neighborhood?"

"I'm Martha Bixby. We just moved into the Victorian on the corner of Summit and Pleasant."

Which Eleanor already knew because she had spied the woman several times during the day through Gavin's telescope. A habit she had taken up since both children entered school, especially exciting when she saw moving vans.

"Eleanor Olson." She shook hands and resumed her dusting.

"Eleanor, stroke that telescope one more time and it'll have an orgasm. Let's have a cocktail."

Martha was five years younger than Eleanor, and her husband worked as a lawyer for Pan Am. He frequently traveled on business and Martha, lonely, would wander over in the afternoons, light a cigarette, and complain: at 6:00 a.m. he left to take the commuter train, often not returning until 11:00 p.m., too tired to tell her about his day. Pan Am kept a corporate apartment near Grand Central and he often stayed overnight. Martha wanted to know if Eleanor thought he was keeping some floozy.

"Does Gavin ever stay in the city like that? I mean, wouldn't you wonder?"

"Oh, no. Gavin works late about half the week. It's the new corporate culture," she said, repeating a phrase Gavin often used. "Our husbands are just trying to give us a good life."

"*Is* this a good life? This makes you happy?"

"Happiness encompasses many things."

Martha fingered her long, black hair. She had olive-toned skin and always wore a pair of beaded turquoise earrings that fell practically to her shoulders. She said they had once belonged to her great-grandmother, a genuine Navajo.

"I miss when he was a student," Martha said, "when he was in law school and he studied at home while I watched television. I'd throw a bra across the room and tell him to come give me a kiss."

"Gavin used to play violin for me! Can you imagine my husband playing violin?"

"Do you think the war . . ."

"Heavens, no. He's just so busy. You know how many phone calls he makes a day? Two hundred. That's his quota. The company keeps a precise record of every number he dials. Less than two hundred, and it comes out of his paycheck."

"I bet you're a good wife."

"Oh, I really couldn't say," Eleanor lied.

"I'm a lousy wife. I burn toast. I sweep the dirt under the sofa. If we ever move and someone lifts that sofa, I'm done for. I don't know why he married me. All the other Pan Am wives look like they went to wife school. I don't think he knows why he married me. No, wait, I do know. Because I'm a good lay." Martha picked up the pruning shears and slowly snipped the air. "I suppose I could have an affair. But with who? Have you seen the mailman? Denture city."

Such talk! Eleanor told herself not to be judgmental. But she also told herself she was very lucky she wasn't like Martha.

"Martha, I'm sure your husband loves you."

"Hey, let's start a group. For women around here. Consciousness raising."

"We're too late for all that, Martha. You and me, we're a group!"

But things with Martha went downhill. The next time Eleanor saw her, and she lit up a smoke, it wasn't a cigarette.

"Want one, Ellie?"

"The cops could arrest you."

"I wouldn't mind a night in jail." She distractedly fingered one of her turquoise earrings. "A change of scenery."

Then, in early October, Eleanor looked up from weeding the garden and saw Martha with an empty pitcher hooked on her forefinger. She wore bell-bottoms and wedge sandals; her unbrushed hair fell loose at her back. She slumped into a lawn chair and let the pitcher thud onto the lawn.

"Martha, you look purple! What's wrong? Did you have a fight with Richard?"

"I missed my period."

"Martha! Oh, that's wonderful! This could be just the thing to help your marriage!"

"No, Eleanor. I did something stupid. Really dumb, professionally dumb. I don't know what's wrong with me. The baby's not his."

"Oh." Eleanor pulled her chair close, dismay and excitement seizing her at once. This was terrible news—adultery, an illegitimate child—yet Eleanor felt the thrill of secrecy, of her own sudden usefulness. "Look, Martha. You have to go to confession, get it all out, and be done with it. You're not the first woman in history to do something dumb. We've all cut little corners here and there. Just keep this to yourself. You mustn't tell anyone else."

"He'll know, Eleanor." She looked at her belly with confusion, then alarm. "The baby's going to be black."

Eleanor was silent. Ever since freshman year of college, when she and a group of her friends drove thirty miles to see *In the Heat of the Night,* she'd found Sydney Poitier dashingly handsome. She had fleeting daydreams, little romantic scenarios in which Detective Tibbs needed her help with an investigation. But Sydney Poitier was a celebrity. It was a harmless, exciting crush. One didn't just hop into bed with the black housepainter.

"You need to fix this," she said. "Richard will leave you."

"Maybe I wanted an excuse to get out of that massive, lonely house. It's like a tomb in there with all that marble."

"You got curious. You got swept up in some bad ideas. You can deal with it legally and safely now. And if you want someone to go with you . . ." Eleanor imagined the two of them riding the train to the city, Martha leaning gratefully on her shoulder. "I'll go with you."

"How long before I show?"

"Three months."

Martha slipped her feet out of her sandals and toed the grass. She touched her stomach. "I always wanted a baby. Maybe Dexter wants one, too."

"*Dexter?* Martha, have you lost your marbles?"

Eleanor realized there was no helping her. She seemed the sorriest, most doomed creature she'd ever laid eyes on.

"Ellie, swear you won't tell anyone about this."

Eleanor gave her word.

Martha slipped on her sandals, offered a hug. That was the last Eleanor saw of her.

Weeks later, after her husband had gone into the city, Martha left town, taking only a small suitcase. The neighborhood swirled with gossip. Other women said that she had mentioned all sorts of wild escapades. Alice Voddner, who, unbeknownst to Eleanor, also spent quite a few afternoons with Martha, marched into the police station and demanded an investigation. Apparently, Martha had alluded to Richard working for the CIA. Alice was convinced that Martha had gotten close to blowing his cover and been made to disappear by some rogue government agency.

"What would the CIA want with an operative in Westport?" asked Gavin, who found the story of Martha's disappearance melodramatic and irritating. "Alice needs a hobby."

Richard, who quickly put his house on the market, said that his wife had a long history of mental problems, that she had been in and out of hospitals, which was why she was not allowed to work. He thought she would be safe in Westport, that the quiet of the suburbs would soothe her. But maybe, he said, burying his face in his hands (Eleanor insisted on having him over for tea while the Realtor was showing the house), there was only so much you could do to help another person, that sick was sick and love, it seemed, could not conquer all. Martha was an impossible burden. Eleanor studied his expression for artifice.

Who knew what to believe? Maybe everyone had been sworn to a different secret. Maybe Martha had toyed with them all, mocking what she thought of as their suburban imprisonment. Or maybe she was, in fact, crazy. It seemed impossible to Eleanor that there was a black baby, that she was the only one who knew the truth.

Something was *off*, something Eleanor couldn't pinpoint. Whenever Martha's name came up, she felt a knot in her stomach.

Eventually the gossip subsided. Richard sold the house at an outstanding profit, which became a much more popular topic of conversation than the whereabouts of his mysterious wife. Gavin and Eleanor discussed selling. Everybody began reading the real-estate pages. Eventually Eleanor forgot about Martha, until one day, in the mailbox, she found a letter from Indiana.

> *Ellie,*
>
> *God I miss our afternoon talks, lemonade, and bourbon. It's been a rough few years but Jayson is walking and talking now and he's the cutest thing. I wish you could see him. It may have seemed strange to*

you, but it was the right thing I did in leaving Richard. In leaving that town. Anyway, I know you and I know you've kept my secret and for that I'm grateful. It was a confusing time, and I'm sorry for dragging you into it. You were a better friend than I deserved.

Much love,

Martha

Indiana? Eleanor didn't recall Martha having family there. Perhaps she was locked up in some mental hospital, loopy on sedatives. Or maybe she *did* have a baby, but it was Richard's. Again, the thought of Martha left her deeply uncomfortable.

Dear Martha, So nice to hear from you after all this time. Yes, I've kept your secret. Best of luck. Warm regards, Eleanor

Eleanor didn't want to get too friendly. Frankly, she didn't want to hear from Martha again. Eleanor then did something painful but necessary. She dug into the bag of hairpins, where she kept her allowance savings, and took out five one-hundred-dollar bills. She slid them into the envelope and sealed it.

GINNY

Ginny tugged open the oven to baste the turkey, and warmish air, summer sidewalk air, came at her. The bird sat in its roasting pan, plump and pale, its puckered yellow skin thick with olive oil and herbs. A shallow pool of golden broth was topped with a few parabolas of lard.

She looked at the clock—it had been cooking for five hours!

She had seen enough movies, had been to enough Thanksgivings, to know that things were supposed to be browning and crisping, juices were supposed to sizzle and pop. She spun around the roasting pan. She thumbed through the sticky pages of her cookbook to the section on poultry, and cranked the oven up to 475 degrees. She could carve off the burned part. Better than turkey sashimi. She lifted the lid off the carrots and saw that the water wasn't boiling. She jabbed her finger in—bathwater.

"Jesus! Nothing's cooking!"

Shaking off her oven mitts, Ginny looked at the wreckage: mixing bowls and cutting boards, gravy-speckled cookbooks and dented broiler pans. The counter was nowhere to be seen. The small sink hugged a mound of carrot and potato and beet scrapings. The floor was sticky with something—gravy?—and nothing was close to being done.

From the living room came the din of hunger and restlessness. The twins' feet thudding in laps around the sofa. Her mother's high-pitched voice trying to draw everyone into a conversation about E. coli infections. Laura whimpering. Ginny could already hear the impending complaints: Didn't she defrost? Didn't she know turkey took longer to cook than tofu? Couldn't she even cook carrots?

For weeks she had been plagued by a feeling of ineptitude, as if at any moment she might iron a grilled cheese sandwich, or hose down the kitchen. It bothered her that she had a PhD and could not figure out all her dishwasher settings. But Jesus, how many different things could you do with water and detergent?

There was a long comic tradition of the bumbling father— Dagwood Bumstead, Mr. Mom. But nobody laughed at a mother's ineptness. They called child services.

Priya had climbed on a stool and was probing the dirty Cuisinart with a meat thermometer that clicked noisily against the blade.

"Honey, please don't do that."

She slid the thermometer into her mouth.

"Don't do that either." Ginny took the thermometer and lifted her off the stool, her legs tangling in her purple dress so that her foot upended a pitcher of water.

"It's not enough of a sty in here already? Priya, you have to be careful!"

Priya's face reddened in despair. She plucked a potato scrap off the counter and wrapped it tightly around her finger and bared her teeth defiantly.

Oh, no, not again. "Sweetie, I love you. Mommy loves you."

Ginny knelt and papertoweled up the water.

She had desperately wanted the day to be perfect. She wanted her mother to end her second-guessing. She wanted Douglas and Denise to relax. She wanted her father to engage. And she wanted everyone to quit thinking of Priya's adoption as some crazy, impulsive do-gooder gesture that was more than a single woman could handle. But the truth was, and her breath caught in her chest as she realized this, she was starting to think Priya *was* more than she could handle.

What had happened?

Never had Ginny done anything as impulsive or selfless, or risky—they could arrest you for falsifying documents!—as bringing Priya home. But she had believed it was an absolute good.

They had gotten along wonderfully in the orphanage. Once home, Ginny had taken the semester off and had bought a house practically within a month, just as she'd been instructed. She cooked Priya vegetable casseroles and read aloud from *Little Women* each night before sleeping with her arms around her, telling her how wonderful and angelic she was. Maybe she'd hoped, unfairly, that some small word— *hi? Ma? yes?*—would finally escape from Priya. And Ginny now knew for certain that Priya could make sound because Priya often woke crying in the night.

Priya clearly tried hard to pretend that she was happy. She grinned forcefully whenever Ginny entered the room. At the foot of her bed she had neatly arranged all the stuffed animals Eleanor sent, although she never played with them. At the end of every meal, having entirely cleared her plate, she rubbed her stomach in circles.

Sometimes, the degree of Priya's politeness worried Ginny. The way Priya tiptoed around, sat only on the edges of chairs, wiped down the sink after brushing her teeth, and made her bed each morning—Ginny's bed, too, if Ginny forgot—seemed like Priya didn't believe this was her home. As though she was on her best behavior so as not to get sent away.

And every once in a while, when the politeness cracked, Ginnny could see the depths of Priya's frustration. Unaccustomed to such hot water, Priya would shake her fist at the faucets. At the sound of a neighbor's leaf blower, she hid beneath a blanket. She once had trouble turning on the bedside lamp in her room because the bulb had blown, and after flicking the switch a dozen times she tearfully slapped the lamp to the floor.

Priya knew the world of the orphanage well. In her years there she'd learned what every door opened onto, what every cupboard and closet held; she knew the nurses, the cooks, the janitors, the teachers. She was the champion of lunch-hour hopscotch, the queen of jacks. She sat on a dirty wooden floor and shuffled cards like a Vegas dealer. But here, in Ginny's world, she knew nothing.

Like a prisoner released after decades, she missed her regimen, her limitations; sometimes Ginny heard her playing jacks by herself on the bathroom floor. Part of Priya clearly wanted to go back, but she also feared being sent away.

Every night Ginny said, "I love you, sweetie, tell me what to do to make you happy."

It sounded like a dysfunctional marriage.

"You should think about having one," Denise had always said. "They bring you so much meaning."

Ginny had always laughed at *meaning* as a noun. As a verb it worked, a thing could mean something else. But you couldn't stuff the vague concepts of love and happiness and spirituality into one word and expect anyone to take you seriously.

And yet she *had* taken it seriously. She *had* thought motherhood would bring her happiness and contentment. Instead, it brought her exhaustion, confusion, and a deep sense of failure.

Was it all a trick, then? Had all those women in gym locker rooms, those classmates at college reunions flashing pictures of their daughters riding ponies and their sons perched bravely on diving boards—women who for years had made Ginny feel as though her life was inferior—had they all been putting on a show?

In the supermarket, as Ginny watched other women wrestle overflowing aluminum carts down the cereal aisle, children jumping at their sides, she could now see their fatigue. Now she understood the fears that mothers carried, the fear that they might fail their children, that their children would suffer, or that life without children was, frankly, easier. And she recognized the need to convince everyone else you were wonderfully happy, because if others believed it, you might, too.

KIJO

*K*ijo worked the room alone. The walls were dark blue. The carpet was gray and shiny and thick. Four large windows were bright with sun, the thick windowsills made of caramel-colored wood. A large bed had been made up tight, the headboard crowded with bright white pillows stitched with golden anchors and knotted rope. The room looked like a boat.

A wooden desk was topped with a flat-screen monitor, flashing an aquarium-themed screen saver. Beside that, an actual aquarium stood on a pedestal. Goldfish and white fish striped like zebras swam beneath a purple light. A small treasure chest sat on bright blue pebbles, and a fat yellow fish rammed the fake gold coins.

Kijo didn't like fish. Eating them or even looking at them. Something about a creature that never closed its eyes made him uneasy. Even the biggest pit bull on the block had to close his eyes and sleep sometime.

From the closet door hung a small black wet suit—child's size.

A kid's room.

He thought of the room he'd had in the house on Freedom Avenue, half this size with a metal bed. Grandma Rose wouldn't let him have carpet so that she could hear when he was moving around, could make sure he wasn't up to trouble. He hid his prize possession in the bottom drawer of his dresser; underneath his comic books lay five piles of license plates he'd stolen as a kid. Forty-eight. He'd never snagged Hawaii or Alaska, but Kijo told himself if he ever saw those, even now, in broad daylight, he'd get out a screwdriver. A collection wasn't anything unless it was complete.

By the doorway, Kijo saw an empty box: BOSE WAVE SOUND SYSTEM. He thought of Grandma Rose cutting her boxes into bits, throwing out one piece at a time so no one in Vidal Court got the notion she had something new. Window bars wouldn't stop a man with electronics on his mind.

On Mother's Day, things were fine. That was the first of each month, when the assistance checks came. But by week three, everyone was hungry and itching for a fix. Hubcaps, garden hoses, houseplants—the pipers would swipe anything.

It had been the twenty-first of November when someone put a knife to Grandma Rose's back as she set down her groceries to unlock the door. Too indignant not to say her piece, she got a fist to her chin. When Kijo came home, she held a bag of ice cubes to her mouth, working fabric through her sewing machine with her free hand.

"Don'tchu be worrying," she said. "You oughta see the fist."

Beneath her bright sewing light her eyes looked sunken. She wore a short-sleeved housedress and her elbow, bending as she drew her fabric through the machine, seemed small and frail. His whole life his grandmother had intimidated him, and now she looked helpless.

"I shouldn't have let this happen," said Kijo.

"Are you God? You got ways of stopping evil in the world?"

But for days afterward Kijo heard her up all night in the kitchen, arranging spice jars, wiping down the refrigerator. She scrubbed the burners on the stove. She kept all the lights on, the cordless phone in the pocket of her robe.

He understood then that they never should have left Freedom Avenue, that everything had gone wrong since the move.

Kijo finished the room and was on his way to find Spider when a small wooden box caught his eye: beneath the glass lid he could see a red stone knife. The handle was carved with birds and antelope and deer. He slipped it into his back pocket.

He found Spider in a gold-colored bedroom half the size of a basketball court. Spider was splayed on the bed, velvet pillows under his head, a red blanket thrown over his legs. He tapped the remote control nervously against his thigh and stared at parade images on a flat-screen television mounted on the wall.

"Man, those floats are wack."

"We've still got downstairs," said Kijo.

"You said they'd be gone all day. Besides, look at the size of these rooms! We ain't supplied for all this. You seen all this shiggity? They got a fireplace in the bathroom, Kij."

Kijo touched the red blanket, edged with gold stitching. He wondered what a thing like that cost. He eyed the whole room: wooden dressers and tables so shiny they looked drenched in maple syrup. Brass knobs and handles. The ceiling was domed and painted with angels, like something he'd once seen in a museum. Everything there looked huge—like the furniture weighed a thousand pounds. Kijo thought about Grandma Rose's theory of being medium. She'd always said if you had a nothing house with nothing in it, people could snatch it from you in between yawns. If you lived large and glitzy, someone would rob you. To survive in the world, you had to be medium.

Spider rubbed a pillow against his cheek. "It'd take five shovels to buy this pillow."

If there was a decent snowfall, Kijo and Spider would get up early and throw shovels in the back of Uncle Clarence's van. For ten bucks, they'd clear any driveway or sidewalk.

"Quit getting busy with the bedding, Spide."

Spider tossed back the blanket, and something silver slipped from his pocket.

"See? Christmas came early. I asked Santa for the iPod Shuffle."

"Leave it, Spide. We're sending a message." But Kijo remembered the stone knife in his pocket and pulled his shirt down to cover it.

"Message." Spider moved his hands along an imaginary banner.

"'We're too stupid to seize a financial opportunity. Sincerely, Kijo Jackson.'"

No, Kijo knew what the message was. He was going to let them know that actions had consequences. Without retaliation, they'd try to step on you again.

Spider sniffled and wiped his nose with the wrist of his sweatshirt.

"What's with your nose?" asked Kijo.

"The brothers in that group home can't cover their mouths when they sneeze! The state oughta pay for my Robitussin."

Spider's eyes looked pink, and Kijo wondered if Spider was on the pipe. Sooner or later, everyone in Spider's situation went to the pipe. He decided not to ask.

"Let's get to work," said Kijo.

DOUGLAS

*P*ot holders dangled from his sister's hands; there was a smear of gravy on her cheek.

"Dinner's running a bit later than planned, so I hope you can keep yourselves entertained." Ginny marched over to a stereo that looked like it had last been tuned in to Watergate. She put on jazz, flung the pot holders into the corner, and collapsed against the sofa.

"Are you trying to roast an American bald eagle in there, Gin? Want Denise to look?"

"Denise has her hummus to attend to."

"Alert: Ginny's at DEFCON two."

Priya emerged from the kitchen and sat beside Ginny, who slid her arm tightly around the girl.

"This is why I never cook meat, Priya. It doesn't *want* to be cooked."

"I was wondering, Pop, if you maybe brought your telescope. I think Ginny's lucky neighbors are watching the game and I thought maybe we could catch some that way."

"Very funny," said Ginny. "Weren't you the one who was outraged about Janet Jackson's boob a few years ago? Aren't you afraid the game might sneak another bare boob at you?"

"Number one, that was the Super Bowl. Number two, I was outraged because it was *one* boob. As far as I'm concerned, that's just a tease."

"Oh, do you know who has box seats to the Super Bowl?" his

mother interjected. "Roddy Peterson. I saw his mother at the grocery store."

"That's great, Mom."

"What ever happened to Roddy?" asked Ginny. "I always expected to see that guy on *America's Most Wanted.*"

"Oh!" his mother exclaimed. "You didn't hear?"

"More celebrity?" asked Douglas, getting up and collecting the paper scraps.

Roddy Peterson had been his best friend in middle school. Roddy lived three blocks away, and used to carry his lacrosse stick over before dinner so that they could get a game going in Douglas's yard as the sun set. Roddy's father had been in the oil business in Texas and died in a helicopter accident when Roddy was ten. Two years later, Roddy moved to Connecticut when his mother married an accountant, a pale, bald man he referred to as "The Calculator."

As they entered high school, Roddy started getting called in for meetings with the principal. His grades were slipping. He cut class. He quit the lacrosse team, complaining about the rules and regulations; he said he felt boxed in, that the uniforms were stifling him.

"I don't want a number on my back."

Leaving school, Douglas would find Roddy in the parking lot of the 7-Eleven, reading books on particle physics or game theory, smoking a pipe. Roddy's father had smoked a pipe. Roddy said he wanted to start building things: circuit boards and machines.

"I wanna build a machine to take a girl's bra off from across the room."

"You're high, dude."

Which often he was. He had a cousin in Stamford who sold him marijuana. Roddy liked to drive down to Stamford, past the projects; buy his pot; then smoke up at the Westport train station, watching the Metro-North trains go by, the blur of pale, tired faces in the windows. Sometimes, late at night, as the express from New York City rushed by, he pulled down his pants and let a golden arc of piss hit the side of the train.

"Look at all those fucking drones."

"Hey, my dad's one of those drones," said Douglas.

"So is The Calculator. We can't get like that, man. Working for the machine. We might as well cut our balls off."

Roddy's obsession with his testicles soon evolved into what he called his signature move. Roddy believed men were being taught to bury their animal nature. Sometimes, he told Douglas, he just had to let his testicles hang out. He said the air on his balls swinging free triggered a primitive feeling, a communion with his forefathers, his hunter-warrior ancestors. Only when his balls were breathing could he begin to think clearly. "It's like my testicles are claustrophobic." Roddy developed a trick of unzipping his pants, pulling out his balls, then buttoning the waist. He'd sit in chemistry lab, walk into a 7-Eleven, check out books from the public library, all with his bare balls dangling between the teeth of his zipper. Amazingly, no one ever noticed.

"They don't notice because they don't expect us to have balls anymore," said Roddy. "They don't think anything's down there. Surprise, surprise, bureaucratic assholes"—he swung his hips, shouted at the sky—"these aren't going away! You gotta try it, man."

But Douglas had an awful vision of his mother and sister bailing him out of jail for indecent exposure. Or catching a glimpse. In fact, Ginny had once seen Roddy's move.

"Jesuschristalmighty put those things away," said Ginny, running into them in the Minimart parking lot when she was fifteen.

"My sister has eagle eyes," explained Douglas.

"Your sister wants me."

"Don't make me get a BB gun," said Ginny.

Douglas decided to make new friends. When Roddy came over to his house, it was at odd hours; he would rap on the windows after midnight.

"Someone's going to think you're a burglar. I've got a math test at nine tomorrow."

"Three point one four: that's the answer to everything."

They crossed paths a few times during college, when they were both home for the holidays. They'd bring a six-pack out to the West-port station and watch the commuter trains go by, for old times' sake.

"Your dad still working for the machine?"

"He's now a senior sales manager for the machine. Fewer phone calls, more reports. I think he hates it."

"That'll make you old fast. I need to build things, conquer lands."

But Roddy himself looked old, a bit ragged. He still needed to pull his balls out from time to time, in discreet locations, but the signature move no longer seemed funny to Douglas. Roddy was an adult; what if Roddy unzipped around small children? Wound up in jail?

The sight of Roddy grew depressing. When he heard Roddy had dropped out of college in his senior year, Douglas stopped returning his calls. Douglas had lined up a good job in Manhattan, his life was on track.

But a year out of college, Roddy showed up in New York; he called from a pay phone, asking for a place to crash.

He arrived at Douglas's studio with an army backpack and began unpacking notebooks, binders, a tube of blueprints.

"I've got a once-in-a-lifetime proposition for you, dude. You are gonna be grateful you knew me back when." He snapped open a binder and pulled out pages. "Ask me what this is?"

"A love poem."

"This is a United States of America patent application. You see this sketchola? You need a beer to lubricate your mind for the sharpness of the thoughts I'm about to articulate?"

"Roddy, some of us have work in the morning."

"Listen at your own peril, then. This is an inner plate and this is an outer plate and this, oh, I fucking love this, is a slidable drag unit. I am offering you the chance to get in on this now, as partner. Because we are gonna storm the bathroom-lock industry."

"This is a *bathroom* lock?"

"The *mother* of all bathroom locks. It won't go slip-sliding around. Look at the latch unit!"

"Roddy, what do I know about bathroom locks? What do I know about patents? If the patent is any good—"

"It's genius."

"If it's genius, sell it to a bathroom-lock company."

"If you wanna make it big, you gotta be in on the manufacture."

"There's no way in hell you can raise money to get that going. Not to mention marketing a new product, one little lock, when there are probably bathroom-supply companies that already sell doors and locks and toilet-paper dispensers. People like one-stop shopping."

"Doors and dispensers are a breeze."

"Look, I don't have the kind of money you'd need."

"But this is our big break." Roddy's cheeks filled with air and slowly emptied. He stuffed his diagram back into his notebook, his notebook in his backpack. "I just have this gut feeling and it fucking breaks my heart we can't do this together. I mean, you're a cog in the wheel. Pretty soon you're gonna be on that train to the burbs. You're gonna end up like The Calculator, or like your dad, stargazing and depressed."

Douglas got up to brush his teeth. "Don't talk about my dad."

Roddy stayed another two weeks, offering Douglas several more chances to fork over his entire savings, before going to stay with Bruce Fancher, another high school friend who was living in Philly; Roddy thought Bruce had killer financial instincts.

Three years passed before Douglas had any news about Roddy, and that was when he walked in one November day and his mother was waving a magazine called *Entrepreneur* with an article on Roddy.

Douglas had been right, at least, in suggesting Roddy sell the patent to a bathroom-supply manufacturer. Bruce had jumped on the investment opportunity. And when Roddy used the $3.2 million he made on the sale of his patent to start a company called Roderick, which sold padlocks and dead bolts, he made Bruce VP of operations. When the company went public Roddy made over $100 million.

Douglas called to congratulate him, but Roddy's mother explained she wasn't allowed to give out his number. She'd pass along the message.

Eventually, Roddy sent a picture of himself standing before his personal jet, beside his wife and two children. No return address.

On the back he'd written: "Thanks for letting me crash with you." He enclosed a certificate for one thousand shares of his company, and, without thinking, Douglas tore it up.

"Who's that?" asked Denise when she saw him sitting at the kitchen counter staring at the photo.

"Some loser from down the street," he said.

"A loser with a jet?"

ELEANOR

*B*y two o'clock, Eleanor could see that everybody was punchy with hunger. She gave the children mints from her purse, reapplied her lipstick, and to help pass the time, asked Douglas if he had any new projects under way.

"Mom, you've heard about the subprime crisis? No one's building right now."

Well, everything in the news was a crisis of some sort. Long ago, she had urged Douglas to become a Broadway producer. She thought this would be an excellent way to earn a living, as people always liked to go to the theater, and she would have happily used any free tickets, especially to musicals.

"I had lunch with Judith Redmon in Stamford the other day and I made sure we drove by Obervell Tower. *Twice.*" In fact, she only went once, but no one was listening and she hoped this would draw them in. "That tower is so large and, well, *towering,* and I said my Douglas built that. She said how much Stamford had cleaned up in the past decade, and she gave her thanks to you. Her son still lives at home, you know. A painter. Poor woman."

"Large and towering," Douglas said. "With a forty percent occupancy rate."

"Oh, do you know who else drove by the tower and told me how glorious it looked? Margie Peterson. She said she thought it looked just like a big glass rocket. And she said Roddy even remarked—"

"Mom, I don't want to talk about the tower."

What had she said wrong now? She was paying her son a compliment!

Denise set down her wineglass. "Does everyone remember that snowstorm a few weeks ago?"

They'd had a mild snowfall. Gavin had been out that morning throwing salt on the driveway and pulled a tendon.

"Yes!" answered Eleanor.

"Well, they kept the school open," continued Denise. "Anyway, there was no snow day, because it was less than six inches, and so these boys, these black boys they bus in, started calling and complaining. It was over six inches where they lived. And, get this, one of them actually called the house of the school superintendent."

"What does their race have to do with anything?" Ginny asked.

"The point is the superintendent's wife nearly had a heart attack. 'Oh my God, how did they get our number!' She's calling the principal's office, shouting, 'How dare you give out our number.' She had entirely forgotten that their number is listed. She was terrified of these kids."

"Because they were black?" asked Ginny. "Or because they knew how to use the White Pages?"

"Now she thinks because they know where she lives, they're going to break into their home," said Denise. "Or burn it down."

"We had a lovely black girl at Wellesley," Eleanor leapt in. "She was in my British literature class . . ."

"Ginny," said Douglas, "these are boys that call one another"—he whispered for the sake of the children—"the N word. They wear Malcolm X T-shirts. It's not their skin that's black, it's their identity. Hell, it would piss *them* off if you denied them their blackness."

"Besides," said Denise, "if I had said they were white, would you have taken offense?"

"If you are trying, even for a second, to equate the experience of whiteness with blackness in this country," said Ginny, "you've got as much chance of winning this argument as Lee at Appomattox."

Appomattox, Appomattox. Eleanor knew she should know that. But she got all those names confused: Appomattox, Antietam, the Alamo. She disliked when her daughter did this, tossed historical references into casual conversation. Eleanor could only pretend to understand until she could look it up later, at home. She made a mental note to do this and then realized that thinking of Appomattox had cast her entirely out of the debate; it was moving so briskly she couldn't find her footing.

"You *imply* something when you say that they're black," said Ginny.

"I'm just saying, if you saw these kids," Denise added, "forget their race, they look tough, tough talk, have tough angry faces, and all that baggy clothing. It was just so utterly *ironic* that they were so put off by the snow!"

"Ginny," said Douglas. "Fact: some kids have discipline problems. Fact: some of them are black. We're not going to help them if we're too damned politically correct to acknowledge that they have problems. Now, for God sakes, what does a man have to do around here to get a cooked turkey?"

"Fact," said Ginny, pushing herself up and retrieving her pot holders from the corner, "we don't live in a color-blind world." Then she marched off to the kitchen.

In the silence that followed, Eleanor saw her opening; they couldn't ignore a sensible question: "Why do you think these black children thought there was more than six inches of snow?"

"Who knows," said Denise. "I don't think they used rulers."

"Did you ever consider," Ginny hollered from the kitchen, "that those kids don't have proper snow clothes? Waterproof boots?"

It was a fine point, thought Eleanor.

"These kids—white ones, black ones, purple ones—they're always complaining about something," said Denise. As Eleanor watched her daughter-in-law speak with great animation, she noticed something weird about her face. "You should hear them whine about the food," Denise went on. "And I overhauled that whole cafeteria and arranged for some of the best lunches in the state."

Denise looked pretty, as usual, with a hint of a tan, but something looked a little *alien*. Something was missing. Eleanor stared hard, trying to put her finger on it.

"What on earth happened to your eyebrows?"

Denise touched her face. "What?"

"Mom, stop," Douglas cut in.

"Well, what happened? They seem to be . . . falling out."

"Nothing happened," said Douglas, "she looks fine."

"But you can see perfectly well—"

"Mom!"

Well, was there nothing Eleanor was permitted to say? No talking about Douglas's building, no telling Ginny she looked nice, no asking why her daughter-in-law's eyebrows were falling out. They might as well give her a list of what she could say—it wouldn't take up more than a page! Rules for Eleanor! They might as well tape her mouth shut.

Eleanor crouched into her chair, grabbed the armrests, and took a deep breath. She imagined herself a rocket, about to launch.

"Denise," she began, "it occurs to me that every time you talk about the school, you sound entirely miserable. I simply do not understand why on earth you want to work there. Wouldn't you prefer to spend that time with your *own* children?"

Denise's hand dropped from her eyebrows.

"Don't you perhaps think," Eleanor continued, "that Laura's feelings for her tablecloth *might* be a sign she needs more time with her mother?"

Neither Denise nor Douglas stirred.

"A possibility. A little, perhaps?"

"Douglas?" Denise said flatly, utterly uninterested in what Eleanor had courageously suggested. "Explain to your mother why I work at the school."

Douglas briskly rubbed his cheeks, as though to wake himself up.

But at that moment, Ginny reappeared. Pink-faced and shimmering with sweat, she aggressively adjusted the shoulder strap of her black tank top. Her gaze fell on the platter of cracker crumbs and hummus on the coffee table. Eleanor saw a glint of tears behind Ginny's purple glasses.

Eleanor's annoyance with Denise vanished in a fierce rush of maternal protectiveness. It raced like blood to her head, almost made her dizzy. Poor overwhelmed Ginny! Eleanor recalled her own exhaustion the first time she cooked Thanksgiving, the orchestration of vegetables and starches, the fear of failure. She rushed to her daughter.

"Baby, let me give you a hand."

DOUGLAS

*D*ouglas looked over at his wife refastening her ponytail and staring stonily out the window.

"Sorry about that," he called softly.

Denise didn't answer; she didn't even move.

His apologies got nowhere these days. *Doug, we can't put your "sorrys" in the bank.*

The boys, who had been anxiously watching their mother's clash with Eleanor, each wrested a red cushion off the sofa. "The Westportonians have made encroachments into our territory," said Brian. They set the cushions on either side of Denise. "We shall defend you, good woman!"

Laura shook her tablecloth on the floor, lay down, and tried to roll herself into a burrito.

"Daddy, can you seal up my ends?"

"Absolutely, kiddo."

"Hey, Priya, want to play with Laura?" The girl had been examining the hem of her dress since Ginny returned to the kitchen. She looked sad, lonely.

"You can't ask her, Daddy," came Laura's voice from inside her tablecloth. "She has to come on her own."

Denise was still staring out the window.

Douglas shook the Monopoly box. "Come on, Priya, wanna give it a whirl?" Douglas began unpacking the board. "I'll have you playing neighborhood kids and taking their money. Here we have Chance and Community Chest. This game is what America is all about."

The sight of the board and all the pieces seemed to overwhelm her. Priya scratched her calf and looked away.

"Well, this proves you are one hundred percent Ginny's daughter. Anyway, your instincts are good. Definitely steer clear of real estate right now."

He sealed the box and looked around for something else to do. His father had pulled one of Ginny's academic journals off the bookshelf and was thumbing through it. This was his way of conversing with people: examining the things that belonged to them. Douglas pulled his chair across the room, climbed on, and tested the battery on her smoke detector. He then glanced around her desk for the inspection paperwork. All he saw was a messy pile of recipes and grocery receipts, a few bright yellow forms that looked like adoption documents. A butterfly screen saver fluttered across her laptop, and he considered going online to see the game score, but he'd developed a physical aversion to the Internet; all it brought were bad market updates and angry e-mails. The radio, however . . .

"Boys," he whispered, fiddling with the stereo's tuner. But his sons were studiously adding throw pillows to their fort. "Hey, Dad."

His father pulled his chair alongside Douglas's and closed the academic journal in his lap.

The score was 14–7, the Lions ahead, and it wasn't yet halftime.

By the time Ginny and his mother reemerged from the kitchen, Ginny looked ragged. Her hair clung to her neck as though she'd just crawled out of a steam tunnel.

"Everyone, listen up," Eleanor said. "Unfortunately, there is a problem in the kitchen. So we all need to be patient while we make alternate food arrangements."

"The problem is that Ginny looks like she's trying to roast herself."

Ginny flipped him the finger.

"Douglas, stop picking on your sister. The problem is, nothing seems to be *cooking*."

"Not even the carrots?" Denise asked flatly.

His mother closed her eyes and shook her head, too pained to speak of the poor dead carrots.

At worst, he thought Ginny would overcook the turkey. He'd been prepared, out of sibling loyalty, to drench slices of Ginny's holiday char in his mother's gravy and give a heartfelt *yum*. But he'd counted on stuffing, vegetables, dessert. Was this her plan? Deprive them of football and food and teach them some kind of history lesson? *See! This is what Thanksgiving was like for indentured servants in seventeenth-century Virginia!*

"Gin, come on, first you think we shouldn't be watching television, then, mysteriously, there's absolutely no food . . ."

Her attention was caught by the noise from the stereo; she wrapped her lips over her teeth, sealing her mouth.

"Edison invented the lightbulb faster than this, Gin."

"I've been in there all morning getting this meal ready! And I spent the last two days cleaning this house and shopping and"—she looked at her watch—"six grueling hours chopping and mixing!" Priya, in the corner, caught her eye and Ginny lowered her voice. "Look, I'm sorry. But what do you want me to do, Doug?"

"Ginny, what's this?" His father waved the journal.

Ginny's face went even redder. "Nothing, just an academic journal."

"Yes, of the American Historical Society. That much I see. But what's this article? 'The Emasculation of the American Warrior'?"

"It's for tenure, Dad. I have to publish articles for tenure. It's dull academic stuff." She took the journal and slid it back on the shelf. "Look, let's just order pizza."

"By the time we get a pizza here, the turkey will be done," said Douglas.

"The oven is not working anymore, Doug. *No esta funcionando, comprende?* It was good and hot when I put the bird in, but now . . ."

"Did you check the circuit breaker? You probably tripped a breaker, Gin. Your wiring can't handle everything going at once. Go turn off and unplug the oven and shut off everything in the kitchen."

Douglas trudged back down to the basement, a cobwebbed stairway of rotted planks leading to a vintage washer and dryer set. Douglas was generally fond of basements; he associated them with pool and Ping-Pong tables, kegs and bongs. At age seventeen, he'd lost his virginity in Nelly McAllister's basement, on a Ritz-Carlton beach towel laid over her father's weight-lifting bench.

On the shelves sat a row of damp, overflowing boxes marked FUCKHEAD, ASSHOLE, IRISH IDIOT, PROFESSOR PRICK. The last he was certain was Dr. Blaise Langley, the subject of more than two dozen melodramatic aerograms from Africa years earlier. His sister was a pack rat, the adolescent kind—fuckhead?—though surely she had a highbrow name for it: *archiving*. It was sometimes hard to believe Ginny was the intellectual in the family.

The fuse box hung beside a set of shelves. He flipped open the door, but none of the breakers had been tripped.

"It's your *Antiques Roadshow* oven," he called, climbing the last of the creaking stairs. "You probably burned out the bake element."

"Well, fix it, Dougie!"

Behind her, his wife stared dully at him; was she sneering?

Suddenly, the relaxation, the happiness, Douglas felt that morning went bust. Some things could not be fixed! A market implosion could not be fixed! A crappy electric oven from a half century ago could not be fixed! How many times could he apologize? He felt the sour bite of stomach acid at the back of his throat. He was burned out, plain and simple.

Deep breath, he thought. *Do not give into negative thinking, Doug. Focus on positive solutions.*

"You didn't check the oven or the wiring. This whole place is probably wired with knobs and tubes."

"English, please."

"It can't be fixed," he said calmly.

Ginny rubbed her temples, then slowly crossed the room and opened a Yellow Pages. "Pizza Hut or Papa John's?"

DENISE

God, she wanted a cigarette.

The twins had started playing mercy, loudly. Ginny was flipping through the phone book, trying to order pizza. Douglas was hammering away about the electricity, declaring the kitchen a fire hazard—the house could go *kaboom!* any minute—which brought the mercy game to an abrupt end as the boys rushed to carry their sister, wrapped in her tablecloth, behind their pillow fort. Douglas and Ginny stood at opposite sides of the telephone and regressed to a singsong whining, worse than the twins up past midnight. Douglas explained that they needed to leave the house, for safety reasons, and find a restaurant. Ginny planted her hands on her hips and claimed that if they ordered in pizza they could at least eat some of the vegetable dishes, even if they were a bit raw.

This isn't my family, Denise thought.

She slipped into the foyer bathroom, shut the door, and flicked on the light. It was a small half bath with a pedestal sink; the wallpaper, which depicted some kind of bird perched on a branch, peeled from the ceiling, curled strips exposing ancient browned glue. She let down her ponytail and leaned in to examine her face in the mirror. Beneath the dusty fluorescent bulb, she looked tired. All the sheen and sparkle of her makeup had faded. She fingered the makeup-blackened balls of sleep from her inner eyes. She smeared away the loosened bits of mascara. She reapplied her lip liner and stared at her face.

What on earth happened to your eyebrows?

There *was* something wrong with them. Denise could see it. They were thin, too thin, the left one distinctly thinner than the right, throwing her entire face off balance. She ran the water for cover and from her purse pulled her tweezers. She leaned close to the mirror, then paused; something in her told her she shouldn't. But then. She wanted to. She needed to. Just one little hair—pluck!—and it was all better.

Until a moment later, as Denise examined her face, it was not at all better. She could see that the excised hair only brought to light the strange arch of her left brow. It seemed almost . . . pointed, and this made her inexplicably sad. She leaned in again, raised the tweezers, and gripped a lone hair, until the sound of Douglas and Ginny's quarrel brought her back to where she was, to the people on the other side of the door.

She shoved the tweezers into her purse, washed her hands. Slowly, she turned the knob.

As she stepped back into the living room, Douglas looked at her eyebrows, blinked hard.

"Let's go," he said to Ginny. "Now."

"Fine, pick a restaurant," she said.

ELEANOR

*R*estaurant!

"Oh, we'll never get in somewhere," Eleanor interjected. "Reservations on holidays are booked months in advance!"

"We'll call the Hyatt," said Ginny. "It's a twenty-minute ride."

The Hyatt! She could see the bill for nine ravenous mouths ordering off an extra-pricey five-course holiday menu. They'd include the gratuity—20 percent just to write down what you wanted to eat and carry the plate. It was ludicrous. She'd served dinner almost every night of her life, and whoever said, *Eleanor, excellent work getting those plates to the table*? Asking what people wanted to eat and then serving it was child's play. The actual challenge was anticipating what dishes to prepare for hungry mouths that hadn't yet sat down. Because if you forgot someone's broccoli allergy, someone's new diet, if you overlooked someone being kosher, well, at the end of the night you'd be looking at a garbage pail full of waste, waste, waste.

She could see it now, the turkey Ginny had spent good money on, half-cooked and stuffed in the trash can. The potatoes and carrots and parsnips piled on top.

The thought of paying several hundred dollars for what they could cook themselves made her stomach turn.

"The Hyatt?" asked Douglas. "What about the game?"

Never had Eleanor been so grateful that her son wanted to watch football.

"Thanksgiving at a sports bar?" Ginny asked.

"Ginny," Eleanor cut in, "your brother has a point. The men have their traditions. I think we must respect their traditions."

Her daughter looked wounded. Eleanor would never harm her children; she would do anything to protect her daughter. But Eleanor was acting in the interest of thrift. There was, she believed, no greater cause than thrift.

"Where exactly do you suggest we go?" asked Ginny.

"Let's pack up all this food," said Eleanor, "so that it won't go to waste. And we'll just heat it up at another house."

Part II

DENISE

*D*enise stared at her watch. The ride along the Hutch shouldn't have taken more than thirty minutes, but they were stuck in a galaxy of brake lights. Douglas refused to take the interstate because it meant driving through downtown, past Obervell Tower and his office. So the Navigator sat. As the food containers warmed, the smell of gravy seeped into the upholstery, her clothing, her hair.

Denise was hungry and exasperated, but also strangely satisfied at having foreseen, better than anyone else, the mess the day would become.

"Kyee-aaaa!" Brandon kicked at Brian's seat.

"Cut it out," she said.

"Sensei told me to practice for my yellow belt." He whacked again at his brother's seat. "Kyee-yaaa!"

Brian fastened a mask and snorkel on his face and gazed out the window.

Douglas kept his eyes on the road, as usual leaving the scolding to her. Whenever she asked for backup, he'd say, "These things sound softer coming from a mother."

Denise did not think she sounded soft. But when you had two boys, someone had to be firm and, when necessary, scary. If you didn't clarify who was boss, you'd spend your life paying for it. Denise now leveled the threat of all threats: "Act up once more, and you'll regret it. No more *I Shouldn't Be Alive*."

This was her sons' favorite show, their weekly Discovery Channel fix. Every episode charted the near-death drama of hikers lost in the Amazon, honeymooners clinging to capsized yachts. There were dramatic reenactments of shark attacks and kidnappings. Gangrene, frostbite, hypothermia. Disaster porn, Denise had thought the few times she tried watching these so-called survivors narrate how every small decision—*Drinking water? Nah, who needs drinking water? It's only a ten-mile hike up a deserted mountain*—added up to near ruin. They'd hike without a guide, without a map, without rain gear. "Boys," she would announce, "they *shouldn't* be alive. They're morons!"

"But he's got gangrene and they're gonna amputate his foot!"

"He should lose both feet."

"Shssh, Mom."

After her recent tirade against the young couple who, with a half tank of gas, no food, and their newborn in the backseat, drove their truck into a snowstorm, scouring a map for open back roads despite the severe blizzard warning, inspired by five minutes of sunlight to remove their snow chains—Einsteins!—the boys no longer desired the pleasure of her viewing company. They claimed the show made her too emotional. She said stupidity made her emotional.

"We didn't even get to watch the game!" they now whined.

"Call the cops."

"We're *huuuuuuungry*."

"One more kick and we can see if the Discovery Channel wants to do a show on two ten-year-olds surviving alone along the Hutchinson Parkway."

Denise remembered one of Ginny's trivia tidbits, something about Anne Hutchinson and her children having been scalped by Indians. Ginny had called Hutchinson a visionary: an outspoken feminist who, when excommunicated and banished from Massachusetts, packed up and founded the colony of Rhode Island. Denise wondered why all the so-called heroines of history ended up scalped, beheaded, or burned at the stake. Wasn't part of greatness staying *alive*? And whose bright idea was it to present young girls with role models who met brutal ends? Surely there were some smart, slightly less ambitious women to pluck from the encyclopedia, heroines who died of natural causes.

"If we could somehow just shake them before we get to Den Road," Douglas said, glancing in the rearview mirror at the car with Eleanor and Gavin, "I could zip over to the McDonald's drive-through. I should be able to cut into that lane, zigzag through these cars, pop a wheelie. I'd sell my mother for a Big Mac."

Laura, half asleep, mumbled something that sounded like "I'll buy Grandma."

Jokes or presents. Hypothetical situations. Douglas never wanted to do the real work of parenting.

"Douglas, let's just get there."

"There should be a way to order pizza and have it delivered to your car when you're stuck in traffic. Maybe a helicopter that drops pizzas on parachutes. Like those food parcels in Africa. Now, there's a business idea."

"You want to take out a third mortgage and invest in that?" asked Denise.

Douglas's hands clenched the steering wheel. His eyes fixed on the road, he switched on the radio, twisting the volume to high and jabbing at the search button. "Brown Eyed Girl" sliced into a frenetic salsa, hip-hop into something choral and ponderous. He stopped at the game. The twins, sensing the tension, slunk back in their seats and quieted.

How could she be expected to pretend everything was fine?

As they inched through Greenwich and Old Greenwich, the sky turned from blue to gray and Denise laid her head against the cold window, listening to the roar of the crowd, the excited commentator: *Detroit has its back up against the wall. It's third and long, and they are deep in their own territory. If the Packers can hold them here, they have a shot at a solid field position. They're at the line, the Lions in spread formation. The ball is snapped, Kitna rolling to his right. It looks as if he's got a man open . . .*

no. He's tucking the ball and running, Kitna past the thirty, the forty, the fifty. Look at him go. They finally bring him down inside Packer territory. Jim, that's amazing. Incredible. The home team stands strong.

Home, she thought. I just want to get home.

ELEANOR

When her husband drove, he did not like to talk or listen to the radio. He was careful to signal every lane change, to check his blind spot, and to leave a car's-length following distance. The man could give a ten-hour lecture on the subject of following distance. If someone cut into his following distance, he would lift his hand from the wheel and calmly offer his finger.

On the ride from Ginny's house, Eleanor sat quietly, fiddling with the vents, which were assaulting her with arctic air. Then she fiddled with the thermostat and a button that looked, quite reasonably, as if it controlled air circulation. Wiper fluid sprayed the windows.

"What's the problem, Eleanor?"

"I didn't do that."

"What *are* you trying to do?"

"I am simply trying to address the fact that it's warmer outside this car than inside."

"Roll down your window."

"You know very well it took me an hour to set my hair."

"Don't push at dashboard buttons while I'm driving."

"In my car, I have the thermostat set at exactly seventy-three."

"If you want to drive your car, don't polish off every wineglass in sight."

The wipers squeaked across the glass, an arc of sparkling clarity, and she knotted her scarf and buttoned her coat and looked at the other cars—at all the coatless, scarfless, and hatless people luxuriating in interior automotive heating. In the backseats, children ogled mounted screens, thumbed electronic gadgets.

How she missed the days when children, little castaways in the land of backseat boredom, could be counted on to liven up any dull stretch of interstate, pressing their noses to the windows, furiously waving. What delight it gave them when you simply smiled. Yes, I see you. You have made a friend.

Now all the passengers were chattering away on cell phones or nodding resolutely to the music in their earphones. Or sleeping.

Eleanor let out a long yawn. She hadn't slept well. She never slept well.

She couldn't recall when it began, but her friends said it was related to menopause. Take hormones, don't take hormones. Get hot flashes, get a blood clot, go weeks without a proper night's sleep, and in the morning tell the toaster what errands you had planned for the day. You couldn't win.

And why on earth did they call it menopause?

It wasn't a pause; it was a full stop, the end. It wasn't as if you ever went back to being fertile.

These were the things she thought about when lying in bed, unable to sleep. Eyes closed, she saw a hazy kaleidoscope of colors. Like Christmas lights on a foggy night. Or a carousel in the mist. But where did the colors come from? Her eyes were closed, so she shouldn't see *anything*. She wondered if they were blood vessels in her eyelids. But if Eleanor concentrated on the colors, they brightened, changed faster, until finally they bled together into a curtain of black.

Or, the sound of her own breath kept her up.

Sometimes, Gavin would watch television. The History Channel, *Nightline,* or, if he thought she was asleep, something with topless girls splashing around a pool. Through closed eyes, she could see the light flickering on the ceiling. She tried counting sheep. But not sheep; cats, because living in New England, she had only vague sheep images. Past twenty-nine, though, the cats became frightening. Thirty cats was a plague.

Or Gavin would snore into his pillow. A snore that started in his abdomen, nearly shook the bed; a power tool underwater.

Sometimes, while Eleanor was trying to sleep, a headache made camp between her temples; deep in her mind she heard a clanging of tent stakes, felt a tightening of canvas. At which point she took a pill, put on her robe and slippers, and tiptoed downstairs. It was strange, then, the silence of her house. All those years of children's voices and footsteps. The *bap-blip-boom* of Douglas's video games. Ginny pacing the house whispering into the cordless telephone. The bickering.

It was hard to believe there were times, years earlier, when she had thrown down her apron and cried, "Can I please just have a minute of quiet! A moment alone!"

Because in the silence, in the solitude, Eleanor heard things, saw things. When she sat alone at night, the sound of a raccoon wrestling the lid off a trash can tripped her heart. In the distance, dogs barked—but at whom? The headlights of a passing car made her flinch; she brought her hands to her eyes. Away, away.

When had the nights begun to frighten her?

When she was little, her mother had read to her from *Forgotten Civilizations of the World*. Stories of the Inca, the Easter Islanders, the Roman emperors. The final chapter told the story of Pompeii, the city lost under ash and lava for seventeen hundred years.

Her mother said the eruption of Mt. Vesuvius began at five in the morning, while everyone was asleep. The volcano was now at rest, but who knew when it might awaken. Her mother stopped the hands of Eleanor's alarm clock at 4:45 a.m.

"Now five o'clock will never come," she said. "You will always be safe."

When she left Eleanor's room and switched off the light, Eleanor lay in bed, imagining she was a girl in Pompeii, AD 79, the night before the eruption. By flashlight, she wrote notes—*Dear Citizens,*

My name is Eleanor and I am nine years old and I like strawberry ice cream and maraschino cherries and I am very afraid of dogs. This was my room, please keep it clean—which she would then fold and tuck inside one of her Mary Jane shoes, putting the shoe inside her schoolbag, the schoolbag inside a pillowcase, the pillowcase underneath her bed, where it would be spared volcanic ruin.

What would she write now?

Dear Citizens, I am fifty-nine years old. I am a wife and mother. This was my house for three decades. I am still afraid of dogs; I don't know why.

Ginny had gone to Pompeii on an archaeological dig. Eleanor could not understand—such a terrifying place to visit.

"Mom, you've been telling me about Pompeii since I was in diapers."

Had she? Certainly, Eleanor had read to her children from *Forgotten Civilizations*. Ginny returned home with wondrous photographs: Ginny standing tanned and dust-covered, leaning on a shovel; Ginny at a candlelit picnic table drinking wine with archaeologists.

Well, maybe Eleanor could go, too. She left Italy brochures and Fodor's guides on Gavin's desk, but he called ruins one of the world's great practical jokes. That people spent thousands of dollars and flew across oceans to get a firsthand look at where something *used* to be made him grunt with laughter. Gavin would go to museums and look at paintings. He would visit a church or a beautiful courthouse. But ask him to visit something that *was* a church or a courthouse? No, he would not live in the past.

The traffic had come to an almost full stop, and Gavin was fiddling with knobs. She looked at his face—the silver sideburns, the coarse jaw on which she could see every pore, every hair follicle—this sixty-year-old version of the boy she met on the beach in Cape Cod.

"Okay, seventy-three degrees," said Gavin. "Does this please my wife?"

GINNY

As Ginny left Westchester County heading north on I-95, the brightly lettered Connecticut sign welcomed her. She traced the edge of the Long Island Sound, where, even in November, the white sails of weekend yachts shimmered in the sun.

The Siwanoy, Quiripi, Rippowam, and Pequots had once roamed this coast, trading beaver skins and wampum, fishing for oysters and herring. Until first the Dutch, then the Puritans, pulled the deed trick. Someday, Ginny thought she'd write an article on writing, how societies with elaborate languages who didn't have paper had gotten the short end of history's stick. *Saying* the land belonged to you, even living on it, didn't have the oomph of *writing* that it was yours. Or so the early Europeans believed. They waved their deeds, but the Pequots fought. The ensuing Pequot War—the first war between Native Americans and Europeans—bound together the Windsor, Weathersfield, and Hartford settlements, forming the colony of Connecticut to ensure that the Pequots were "blotted out."

Connecticut was good at blotting out. Exiting the interstate, Ginny cut north across downtown Stamford, which looked nothing like the city she'd known growing up, where her mother insisted they roll up the car windows and lock the doors. The areas where you could buy an Italian sub from a store run by an actual Italian, the parts where Salvation Army and Goodwill shops catered to the town's dwindling supply of janitors and home aides, were shrinking. Over the years, HOPE VI money had been thrown at the city.

Homeownership and Opportunity for People Everywhere. Housing projects were torn down, then supposedly rebuilt, cleaned up. The new versions were fancier, sure, but smaller, and filled with white people. Who knew where the low-income black families had ended up? Bridgeport, probably. Bridgeport was the corner where the rest of Connecticut swept its poverty.

Stamford, now a bastion of corporate wealth, had started to look to Ginny like a vast office park. In between the deserted bunker-like buildings, a few sushi bars and tapas lounges were tucked away. She drove past a Bennigan's that had been wedged beside the mall. In the distance, the triangular top of Douglas's Obervell Tower pierced the sky.

Poor Douglas. Four years earlier he'd been happily waving around blueprints; he'd brought a mock-up of the tower to Thanksgiving. But now his big career break had gone bust. He was proud, though, and painstakingly upbeat. When Ginny called to ask how he was doing, he changed the topic, asking about her romantic troubles, barraging her with unsolicited advice. Playing protective big brother made him feel useful. But the way Douglas had harassed her that morning about her oven mishap made Ginny think he was feeling unusually glum.

Ginny drove toward the residential area north of downtown and finally into the wooded area where Douglas and Denise had bought their third house. Deerkill Road. How anyone could want to live on a street with that name was beyond her.

Pulling onto the broad, white-pebble driveway, Ginny saw that she and Priya were the first ones there. At the far end of the vast lawn, the two-story gray house sat like an amusement-park castle, faux stones and fake turrets and a confusion of dormers used to create the illusion of European grandeur. Never had a word so aptly captured cheap elegance: McMansion. The house made her think, when she first saw it, of the JonBenét Ramsey house, gothic and shadowy, a house so large your child could be murdered in one part and you wouldn't hear a sound.

Two massive oak trees, stripped of foliage, framed the house. Already they were winter trees, dark and muscular, with thick branches beseeching the sky, almost human in their nakedness. They must have started shedding weeks ahead of the trees near her house. It was colder up here, damp even. What Ginny fondly thought of as typhoid weather. As she stepped from the car she belted her cardigan.

They lugged their pans of food up the stone walkway, and Priya's eyes took in the gray marble pillars, the massive windows, the towering shrubbery.

"If you learn to play Monopoly really well," said Ginny, "ta-da."

They set down all the food and plunked themselves on the steps.

"Look at all this mess," said Ginny. And Priya began to arrange the pans into a tidy row.

"No, no. It's fine. It's okay to be a kid, sweetie. No one's going to send you away, I promise."

Priya drew her knees to her chest and let out a sharp, frustrated sigh, a sound that Ginny had heard several times before, a sound that made Ginny think Priya wanted to speak.

"Sweetie, you've been a really good sport today. It's a lot of people to take in at once. But you have a great big family who will take care of you now. I love you, you know that? I really love you."

Ginny feared her declarations of love were starting to sound pathological, but the family counselor had said to reassure Priya, in the face of her depression, that she was welcomed. In three months, Ginny had consulted virtually every book and therapist and DVD on the subject of raising an adoptive child; if there was one thing Ginny had mastered, it was research.

"You're more responsible than I am," Ginny said. She rubbed Priya's back and laughed. "Come on, they ought to send *me* away!"

Ginny scanned the yard—easily ten times the size of her parents'.

Maybe that was the source of the strain between Douglas and her father. Who respected paternal authority when fathers no longer had desirable property to pass along?

So much ink—including Ginny's own—had been wasted on the shifts in women's domestic lives that fatherhood had been overlooked. Maybe for her keynote address she could say something about land, patriarchy, geography . . . there were connections to make.

Her paper on the emasculation of the American warrior—God, why had her father thumbed through *that?*—had been a start. The idea, not her own, was that war was still the most rigidly gendered social activity. Tracing the role of the warrior from Native American ceremonies to present day, she argued that post–World War II, the status of the American warrior had been so greatly diminished as to allow the final blurring of gender lines. As far as she was concerned, it was no accident that the Vietnam War coincided with unprecedented advances for feminism. Male power depended upon respect for the warrior, so the shame of Vietnam had completely undermined American masculinity. When the good men were those who *refused* to fight, things went topsy-turvy.

"Good God, did you teleport around that traffic?" Douglas was cradling the turkey, mummified in saran wrap. "I didn't mean to strand you out here. There's a key in the planter."

"We were enjoying your estate." Ginny stood and brushed off her clothes. "But I think it needs a name. You know, something understated. Like Pangaea or Gondwanaland."

"Two point nine acres, Gin. Big enough for three football fields." He craned the turkey behind his head. "Now let's see if academics have any hand-eye coordination."

"Doug, cut it out," said Denise.

Douglas lowered the turkey and looked shamefully at the ground. Ginny recognized the look from when he was a child, when their father would turn his back on Douglas's antics.

"I bet we can get this stuff on the table in under an hour," said Ginny.

Denise marched toward the door, Laura in one arm, a vat of yams in the other. "The cleaning lady doesn't come until Monday," she said dully. "We weren't expecting company."

Denise opened the door, though it would be hard later for Ginny to remember if Denise used her keys. Everyone was talking and carrying things. It would be difficult to say with certainty if the door had been locked.

ELEANOR

Such splendor, such elegance, thought Eleanor as she stepped into the enormous white travertine foyer. A wide, dark-wood staircase laid with a royal blue carpet curved upward to the second floor. To her left spread a large living room with bay windows, to the right, the dining room and kitchen.

This was Douglas's third house. Eleanor had been quite impressed by the first two, but this one practically took her breath away. She even felt a flutter of embarrassment at how minuscule her house now seemed. But she had lived there almost thirty-five years and took great comfort in the familiar. It pleased her that the bottom of the oak banister was still smoothed and bald from where her children had braced their hands for their final leap into the living room. She loved the closet door on which, at every age, she had penciled Douglas's and Ginny's heights. And even though the little palm prints once lining the upstairs hallway had long been painted over, she remembered them, remembered the way her children had touched everything.

Eleanor even maintained a fondness for the small Manhattan apartment she and Gavin had moved into after he returned from Vietnam. They crammed all the furniture from her mother's house into a railroad-style one-bedroom. Their upstairs neighbor, an opera singer, began practicing arias at 7:00 a.m., and at night, couples stumbling out of the Irish pub downstairs squealed with drunken laughter as they whistled down taxis. But it was the first home of Eleanor's own, a space that she could decorate and order, and it made her feel wonderfully adult.

Worried about Gavin's mysterious silences, or the slow clenching of his jaw when she asked about his work, she spent her afternoons preparing mushroom soufflés or crabmeat casseroles, dishes that, although they occasionally suffered from lumpiness or her overexcitement with the salt shaker, showed that she would spare no effort in trying to lift her husband's spirits.

When Gavin arrived home, she lit candles and proudly served dinner on their walnut table. Gavin enjoyed playing cards, so after dessert—peach cobbler or baked apples—he taught Eleanor poker, blackjack, and bridge. He would explain the value of each card, and she would brag about how much money she saved by buying the meat on Fourteenth Street and the vegetables at the corner grocery. In these moments, Eleanor believed Gavin would eventually revert to his former animated self, that time and love would mend whatever wounds the war had left. She believed that fatherhood, too, would reinvigorate him.

Certainly for Eleanor, Douglas's birth marked the beginning of a magical time. Motherhood suited her as nothing else ever had. She adored pushing around Douglas's stroller, describing to him the beautiful stone facade of the American Museum of Natural History, the cars that whizzed by, the oaks and elms of Central Park. They took the bus downtown to gape at the newly built World Trade Center.

They enjoyed three wonderful years in that apartment until she was pregnant with Ginny. By 1973, stories about stagflation and unemployment filled the papers. Wooden planks sealed the entrances of their neighborhood music shops and groceries. Graffiti covered bus stops and storefronts, the sidewalks cracked and crumbled, and one day Eleanor nearly sprained her ankle on a loose chunk of pavement.

The paths of Central Park were strewn with litter, and in the dark underpasses, where she and Douglas had once gleefully listened to their voices echo, men kicked at empty cans and glared menacingly at her swollen belly.

Someone forgot to keep her legs crossed.

Police sirens wailed through the night, punctuated here and there by shattering glass. Remembering how Kitty Genovese had been stabbed to death on the street while more than thirty people listened and watched, Eleanor hugged the phone close. Twice, she called the police: "I heard *something*. No, I don't know exactly where. But you must send help."

Gavin was lost in the loud machinery of his snoring, leaving Eleanor to get out of bed and ensure the windows and doors were locked. Unable to get back to sleep, she brought Douglas to nestle beside her on the sofa.

"We're safe, sweet pea," she whispered as her heart raced.

During the day, she stayed home except for essential errands. With Douglas propped beside her she sat staring at the television news: robberies and shootings and arson; an old woman raped near a grocery store. Eleanor covered his eyes.

People, the newscaster said, were fleeing to the suburbs. Apartment landlords offered three months rent-free to anyone who would brave a lease. Co-ops threw mink coats at potential buyers.

"The Zackners down the hall have gone to Katonah," she told Gavin, "and remember the Connors? Sally and Kevin? Just last week she called to give us their new address. In New Hampshire!"

"Good. He's a pompous ass."

"At least Harold Zackner managed to get his family out."

"You make it sound as if they escaped Nazi-occupied Poland, Ellie. This is the Big Apple. I walk to and from the office every day."

"And come home at bedtime, practically. I sit here, worrying."

After Vietnam, it seemed only a full-fledged war would scare him.

Gavin said historically economies expanded and receded; that this was a brief slump, a phase, and the city would soon snap back. He wanted to take advantage of the discounts in rent.

"This is no time to be frugal!" she said. "Your son has a twitch."

"What?"

"He's doing this thing with his face where he scrunches it up every few minutes. Dr. Robison said it's the nerves."

"What does a two-year-old have to be nervous about?"

"Boarded-up storefronts! Young black men sitting on stoops! Everything is waiting to explode! I can't sleep because I'm too frightened of someone coming in the window." She clutched her belly. "My children can't live like this. This is a sinking ship, Gavin. Women and children must come first!"

"Ellie, suburb equals house, house equals mortgage. We're coming up on kid number two. You don't want me working long hours, but you want to add a train commute? The draft is over and all those MBAs are about to pour into the job market. I'm trying like hell to get out of this dead-end insurance job and into management so I can have some sliver of hope of finding a better job, then maybe doing something with my life. How the hell do I do that if I have to spend an extra three hours a day on sales calls so my commission will pay off a house?"

"Well, we certainly won't need a house when we're dead."

Eleanor had seen a news special about how citizens could protect themselves. She bought two cans of Mace and a pearl-handled pistol and, with five other women, spent Tuesday afternoons in Brooklyn firing at pictures of hooded men, learning to ignore the kickback. She was the best in the class and at the end of the lessons, her instructor, a retired detective named Frank Brodie, gave Eleanor her targets. She folded the large perforated paper and tucked it into her underwear drawer. She walked everywhere with one hand on Douglas, the other on the pistol in her purse.

She considered asking Detective Brodie for a bullet casing from practice, and leaving it in their hallway for Gavin to find. How else could she make Gavin see they couldn't stay? She was furious, but she still carried a vague guilt, a concern that Gavin suspected she had pinpricked her diaphragm.

She was afraid to do anything that would make Gavin feel tricked.

Only when the newspapers reported the city's looming bankruptcy did Gavin wearily lay down his heavy briefcase and say, "You win, Ellie. Pick a suburb."

What relief she felt as they drove their new station wagon to a white one-story colonial in Westport. The sight of manicured lawns and glistening sprinklers delighted her.

Eleanor spent her days watching the children and, while they napped, dusting the bookshelves and nightstands and mantel, scrubbing the floors, scouring the white porcelain tubs. At night, exhausted, she watched *The Waltons* and *All in the Family,* and waited for Gavin.

It was difficult to meet people, so each day she drove to the cool and brightly lit supermarket, where men in red aprons said smiling hellos. She liked to see what other women put into their shopping carts. She enjoyed the classical music that seemed to emanate from between the dewy cantaloupes.

In the spring, she crouched on the grass, raked the earth with her fingers, and planted flowers, tomatoes, and cucumbers, the loamy scent of soil soaking deep into her palms. By summer, her clay pots burst with geraniums and petunias, her vegetables glistened, and as she stood alone in her garden she tingled with pride.

Eventually, Eleanor found other young couples who had fled the city. In their living rooms they reached into crystal bowls of salted cashews, and between sips of scotch swapped stories of stolen cars and snatched purses.

Gavin left the room when these stories began, or he fell silent.

"Sweetheart, I wish you'd try to socialize a little bit more. We're new in town and must try to make friends."

"I'm on the phone selling nine hours a day. That's enough meaningless chatter."

"They'll think you feel superior, that you find them boring. You yawned when Milton McCauley started talking about his work as a prosecutor."

"How on earth would I feel superior?"

Gavin's lack of enthusiasm for their new life concerned her. He seemed to her, even when they sat across the dining table and briefly locked eyes, like a man alone on a sailboat, a man whose return she was awaiting. She wondered if they had been too quick to move, wondered if the commotion of the city would have better distracted him from his unhappiness. Perhaps the city, as Gavin had said, would snap back.

But it did not snap back and this, in fact, worked tremendously to Gavin's benefit. People were frightened and sales of home and car and life insurance skyrocketed. His phone rang off the hook. With his doubled commissions, they put money into the children's college fund and built a small deck where they could set a table and grill. Those were delightful times: the long summer days when Ginny found a pet turtle in the yard, when Gavin built a tree house, when Douglas sold lemonade four Saturdays in a row to buy Eleanor new gardening gloves.

One night, after watching a late-July sunset with the children over a dinner of barbecue chicken, the smell of Eleanor's mint and basil plants swirling in the warm breeze, Gavin and Eleanor settled into bed. As was their custom, they turned on the television and lay close, prepared to exchange opinions, before drifting off, on the various local news reports about animal-shelter spaying policies or proposed helmet laws.

But the screen flashed with apocalyptic images: smashed shopwindows, policemen swinging billy clubs at shirtless men hugging radios, buildings engulfed in flames.

There was a blackout in New York City.

She hugged Gavin tightly, recoiled from the screen.

"You saved us. You got us out of there. And you are a much better man than Harold Zackner."

KIJO

*K*ijo heard a thud and nearly elbowed over a vase as he swung around to find Spider. Another thud. Car doors.

Spider had already dashed for the window; he crouched low. "Thought you said they were occupied elsewhere," he whispered.

"These people got cleaning ladies and stuff."

"Cleaning on Thanksgiving?"

Kijo felt a sudden knot in his stomach; maybe he'd screwed up, got the address wrong, the times.

"What do you see?"

Kijo knew better than to go near the window; he'd knock the glass, or lean into sight.

"Just a Prius out there," Spider said. "No one in it. I can't see through these damned columns. Wait a second, hear that? Some lady sitting and talking to herself."

"She's not coming in?"

"You hear the front door?"

It was too early, thought Kijo. They couldn't be back. The wife had said they'd be gone all day. And just one woman out there? A whole family lived in this house. But he had a sense that something had been bumped; the vision he'd had of the day, the triumph he would feel walking out of that house, went foggy.

"When she leaves," Kijo said, "we scram."

"Kij, when's that gonna be? Maybe she was looking for that key in the planter. Maybe she's calling someone right now, saying the key ain't there. Let's just walk out the door the way we came in."

"The van's too far."

Spider flicked open his switchblade. He opened a dresser drawer and pulled out panty hose. He ripped them in half, and tugged one leg over his head.

Spider's face looked flattened and scary. His lips looked like the lips of a man who'd been hit a hundred times. His hair was trapped like a tangle of worms. He looked like a man Kijo would run from in the night.

Spider handed him the other half of the panty hose. "You, too. Get ready."

Then it was like gunfire—one, two, three car doors slamming. *Boom, boom, boom.*

GAVIN

As Gavin stepped into the living room, the pain in his knee that had been mounting all morning finally struck him like a crowbar. He stopped in his tracks.

"Home, sweet home!" Douglas announced, gesturing the whole family toward two massive leather sectionals facing a flat-screen television.

Gavin braced his hand on the wall and made a show of examining a small touch pad that controlled music; he didn't want to limp across the room. Didn't want questions. He had found that if he could count to twenty, usually the worst of the pain would pass. He clenched his teeth, focused on the numbers, *6-7-8,* and eventually, one slow step at a time, he crossed the room and sank gratefully into one of the sectionals.

Heads of dear and elk hung overhead; a bearskin rug lay in front of the television. The room looked like a hunting lodge, though Douglas had never hunted. Douglas had explained to Gavin on his first visit that their decorator had suggested they do one room in "rustic lodge style."

Gavin thought it odd that he had a daughter who wouldn't eat animals and a son who hung dead ones on his wall.

Gavin had been a runner for most of his life, waking in the last hour of moonlight to experience the unparalleled calm of a long stretch of dark road. He had loved to feel his feet spurn the pavement as his body cut through the cold morning air. His heart racing, his muscles thrumming, he watched the rising sun bring to life trees and mailboxes, parked cars and bright white houses, as though by sheer exertion he had willed the world into being.

Now, at age sixty, Gavin had to think hard about walking a block. Every day he awoke wondering if his knee was going to stab him with sharp pains or hammer him with a throbbing ache. He kept aspirin in his jacket pockets, swallowed them every few hours.

And this knee trouble had brought a new morbidity into Gavin's thinking. As he showered in the morning, letting the water douse his body, he thought: *My body is failing.* The wrinkles, the graying hair, none of that had mattered to him. He found vanity silly. But his knee pain signaled to Gavin that the machinery of his being was breaking down, the nuts and bolts of his flesh coming loose. All those struggles—child rearing and mortgage payments, dumb flirtations and lost promotions—were suddenly supplanted by one basic realization: he was starting to die. It seemed now that there were only two truly terrifying events in a person's life: dying, and understanding you were going to die. For some people, Gavin figured, the latter never happened, or it arrived so close to actual death that the two events became one. But Gavin now carried a certainty of his own death, and it scared him. Mostly it was the decay he feared, the body's slow shutting down. The helplessness.

He'd also studied enough actuarial tables in his line of work to grasp another fact: his body would fail before his wife's. All those years of trying to provide for Eleanor and she would eventually nurse him. He looked across the living room at her, jubilant in her maple leaf sweater, settling into the other leather sectional and reapplying her lipstick. She didn't know what lay ahead. But he understood that for the long married, one spouse's decrepitude became the other's burden. At the thought of this indebtedness, Gavin's throat tightened.

If he died swiftly, though, so much the worse. The idea of leaving his wife alone, and suddenly, disturbed him. Financially she would be fine; he had a good policy with Reynolds and had saved responsibly for their later years. He made sure, from time to time, to show her the necessary file drawers and safety-deposit-box keys. But as much as Gavin had come to covet being alone, Eleanor loathed solitude. When he was gone, she would sit in the house . . . and do what? After all those years of waiting impatiently for him to return home at night, there would be no one to wait for. She would pick cucumbers and tomatoes from her garden, but she would no longer set them in the bib of her apron and stand smiling in the doorway; he wouldn't walk up the front steps and say, "What you got there, salad gal?"

Gavin shook the thought from his mind.

"So what's the addition?" Gavin asked. His son enjoyed a game— guiding them through his maze of a house, then seeing if they could guess what was new. The last time, it had been a set of French doors leading to their sunporch. Gavin meant to beat him to the punch.

"Things are on hold right now."

But the house looked larger, more imposing, than Gavin remembered. It reminded him of a ski lodge in Colorado they had once stayed in; he kept expecting pink-faced strangers to walk in and dust snow off their shoulders.

In the corner was a fireplace that hadn't seen a log in years. The mantel above held a horde of trophies. "Third Place" and "Most Improved" golden plastic towers honoring his grandchildren's bowling and spelling-bee feats.

Douglas sank into a recliner and palmed a nervous drumbeat on the armrests, distractedly looking around.

"That recliner new?"

"Nope."

If this was a newfound humility, it pleased Gavin. The way his son had always shown off his house left him with a bad taste. At age thirty-seven, his son's closet space alone totaled more square feet than the house Gavin had spent three decades paying off. Eleanor would return home and patter around the living room: "Did you see that picture window? And, oh my, the wine cellar. How much do you think a thing like that costs?"

Gavin had assumed the Obervell business was pulling in decent profits. Douglas certainly worked hard enough. Whenever Eleanor called to say hello, Denise said he was at the office. But Gavin never asked Douglas about the details of his work; a man's business was his own. And Gavin got the sense that Douglas thought the details were too complicated for an insurance man to follow. Gavin was surprised when Douglas had called in September and asked for a loan.

"What about that forty-story office tower your company just built? That was supposed to be the Obervell cash cow. Supposed to finance projects all over Fairfield County."

"You don't understand how these things work. There's a natural stagnation postconstruction."

"There is no such thing as a natural postconstruction stagnation. You cowboys all overbuilt, overspeculated."

"The tenants will come."

"Are they at least giving you a promotion? Your mother said that when the project went through you'd be regional manager."

"Look, forget it."

"How much of your own cash is in the company?"

"Dad, forget the loan!"

He sounded wound up. Maybe he had a drug or gambling habit. Maybe after all his wheeling and dealing he was on the verge of bankruptcy. The possibility depressed Gavin and he said he needed to go.

Long ago, Gavin had tried relating to his son. He took him fishing in Massachusetts where he had fished with his own father. But Douglas brought his Walkman. Every few minutes, he shook M&M's into his palm. He didn't like the quiet. If there was no tug on his line, he'd reel it in and pretend the rod was a sword.

His son complained about having to start the day with a cold shower.

Douglas liked hot baths. Towels the size of blankets.

For this softness, Gavin blamed Eleanor; eager for their love, she indulged the children's every desire.

His son enjoyed crime shows and action movies. Arnold Schwarzenegger. A foreigner on steroids with a machine gun. As a boy, Douglas would jump off the deck wearing camouflage and rush the woods with a paint gun.

"I'll be baaak."

He smeared himself with avocado and asked to be called the Hulk.

When Douglas graduated from college, Gavin took him out for a steak dinner in New York, ordered champagne and toasted Douglas's future. Despite their differences, Gavin saw in his son all the prospects the war had denied him. Douglas didn't yet have to support a family; he wasn't looking for work in a bad economy. Knowing that his son would never have to make one hundred sales calls in a day from a windowless office, Gavin felt proud. Douglas might even become a man of consequence. Gavin, who rarely drank, found himself relaxed by the champagne, more talkative than usual, regaling Douglas with stories about his own father. Gavin laid out the idea of law school, becoming a public defender; or medical school. He said there was also great dignity in being a teacher.

"Teach? I barely like to study. Besides, I took a consulting job with Ardor."

"Consulting on what?"

"Whatever they tell me. The pay is crazy. With the bonus, I'll rake in at least a hundred grand."

Gavin went silent. He had never discussed his own salary with his son, but he felt a stiffening shame.

"I don't recall asking you how much you were making."

Douglas looked down at the remnants of his steak. "I thought you'd be pleased."

Gavin let out a gruff laugh.

"Dad, come on. We're here to celebrate."

It seemed to Gavin a sad and bitter irony that after all the knocks and blows he had suffered, his son, who had the great chance to do more with his life than make money, cared only about money.

"It's getting late," Gavin said.

Douglas and his friends wanted to get rich and live well. They read *Fortune* and *Forbes* and never laid hands on a work of literature after graduation. Science and politics were only of interest if they affected the stock market. Within a couple of years, Douglas went from a ruddy-faced athlete to a consultant in a shiny necktie who ordered fancy vodka drinks—instructing waiters in such bewildering detail as to the configuration of his cocktail that Gavin thought his son should get behind the bar and make it himself.

So when Douglas announced he was quitting consulting to go into construction, Gavin was pleased. Helping to rebuild Stamford seemed a respectable undertaking. Gavin imagined libraries, museums, civic centers. Instead, his son spent two years building an office tower that looked like a giant icicle. A tower that now sat virtually empty. And he'd been dumb enough to throw his own money into it.

On their last visit to his house, Douglas showed Gavin and Eleanor his new shower. Spinning on the faucet, he pointed out twenty-two spray nozzles and six preset water temperatures. As Eleanor rolled up her sleeve to feel what Douglas called his "pre-bed shower temperature," Gavin noticed a stretch of the counter crowded with men's lotions and fancy shampoos, stuff you'd see in hotels. Antiwrinkle cream and an electric toothbrush. Built into the blue marble of the shower was a glass case with a CD player; a navy blue terry-cloth robe hung from a silver hook, Douglas's initials embroidered in white. *DGO.* It reminded Gavin of that crap they sold in the airplane-seat pocket catalogs: electric socks and voice-operated teakettles, stuff you were amazed anyone manufactured, let alone bought.

Gavin wondered what his father would have made of Douglas's life, the endless luxury, the shiny bulk of it all.

This thought recalled Gavin to his father's death, to the blow it had struck and the numbness that followed. Later, ashamed of his insurance job, Gavin had even suffered the uncomfortable recognition that he was grateful his father hadn't lived to witness his adulthood. His father still loomed daily in his mind, causing Gavin to wonder how Douglas would feel when *he* died, how his son would remember him.

Gavin slipped Ginny's academic journal under the sectional. He rubbed his knee: *Don't act up*. He looked at Douglas, biting his thumbnail. For a moment he thought he saw—no, it couldn't be—a flash of the facial tic his son had suffered as a child.

"Son, let's see what's left of that game."

DOUGLAS

The Monday before Thanksgiving, Douglas had been sitting in his office when Glenn Mirsky called.

"Doug, you got any bone you can throw me?" Glenn asked. "I'll paint doors on your building if I have to. I'll mop the damned floors."

Glenn had just been let go. Permit problems and sluggish cash flow had brought the Pineway Shopping Center, Glenn's pet project, to a dead stop. He'd already lost his own investment, and now his salary. Glenn and his wife had a newborn.

"My hands are tied." Obervell wasn't putting a cent more into Douglas's tower and he could barely keep himself afloat. "Glenn, try looking at this from the right angle, there—"

"Not the power-of-positive-thinking crap again, Doug. I need a paycheck, not a pep talk." A baby whimpered in the background. "Doug, I gotta go."

Douglas hung up and looked around his desk: a company calendar hung on the wall, November featuring a shiny photo of the forty-story, blue-glass Obervell Tower. Three grueling years to get that building up, two million of his own cash behind it, and now they couldn't find tenants. A brass company paperweight pinned the stack of overdue invoices and legal notices. His screen saver flashed a series of Obervell projects—empty buildings, blueprints that would never see the light of day. Three offices on his floor were now empty: Kevin Henderson, Glenn Mirsky, Ray Sanchez. If they let Douglas go, that was it.

God, if only those homeowners hadn't stalled the project for almost two years. By the time the mayor cut the ribbon that August, the economy was unraveling. If they'd built the tower according to schedule, it might have been filled, and he'd have at least made back his investment.

A photograph of his children stared back at Douglas: he'd taken it last Halloween. Laura, in princess white, stood in front of the house between her Batman and Transformer brothers. Their faces were lit with the excitement from Douglas's announcement that he would build a pool with a waterslide in time for summer.

Douglas rattled his mouse and the screen saver vanished. Up came the MSNBC page, a series of sickening headlines about the losses at Bear Stearns, Countrywide Financial, Bank of America, Barclays, Morgan Stanley. These firms were the financial backbone of the country. If they could crumble, what next? This was worse than the tech bubble seven years earlier. He'd lost money then, but those were new ventures. Everyone knew it was a gold rush. Real estate was supposed to be solid.

Douglas felt the meatball sub he'd had for lunch burn his throat; he shook the Alka-Seltzer bottle sitting on his desk, but it was empty. Who was stealing his goddamned Alka-Seltzer? The ship was sinking *Titanic*-style when coworkers stole your antacids. Douglas pawed around his drawer until he found a box of Gas-X, then he saw— nicked and bent, covered with lint—the photo Roddy Peterson had sent: Roddy grinning beside his wife and children in front of his jet.

Douglas pulled up his Morningstar page and typed in RDRK on the NASDAQ. Shares of Roderick were trading at $98.14. Shares had already split twice since Roddy sent Douglas those thousand shares a decade earlier. By his best calculation, had he not torn them up, or if he had later paid the activation fee, with dividends, they would be worth about half a million. And how much was Roddy's stake worth? A billion? More?

It amazed him. It sickened him with envy.

Douglas had attended his classes, graduated from college, taken a solid job with Ardor, followed all the rules—where was he now? His whole life his father had judged the way he spoke or ate, criticizing what he read or didn't read. But Douglas had shrugged it off. He hadn't let it hold him down. But now his wife couldn't stand the sight of him. He'd let her down too many times. He could see it in her face. She thought he was weak, foolish. And she was right. What kind of man had he become? A man who let people walk off with his Alka-Seltzer?

Roddy said he would storm the bathroom-lock industry and he had. Douglas wasn't storming anything. He was plugging leaks with his fingers. He was hiding, hiding from everyone.

Well, for God sakes, he'd storm things. He was a builder! He cleared wreckage and put up towers that would stand for millennia! A man had to weather adversity, use it to his advantage. Churchill, Edison, Trump. The great men in history had looked failure in the eye and pressed ahead. Roddy was a dropout, a loser, a man who let his testicles hang loose in parking lots, and look what he had done.

Douglas leapt from his chair, walked to the window, stared out at the gray stretch of downtown Stamford. In the distance, above all other buildings, his blue tower glimmered. This was his city; he was building this city. Slowly he unzipped his pants, reached in, and one by one let his testicles loose. He stood still and gazed at the hairy red globes, waiting for the primitive communion Roddy had described. He pictured Neanderthals; he pictured the Aborigines he'd seen on the Discovery Channel; he pictured men with tattooed faces spearing fish and eating them raw, men hunting barefoot through the forest. He puffed up his chest, waited for his pulse to quicken, for a surge of primal confidence, but mainly he felt the cold teeth of the zipper, the scratchy wool of his pants. Suddenly his balls itched. He went to readjust them and found his pubic hairs snagged in his zipper.

Jesus.

So he didn't like having his balls out. Did that mean he wasn't a man? Did that mean he couldn't weather this crisis?

The sound of his office phone startled him. He looked at the caller ID: Denise. God, if she could see him now, what would she think? There was a time she used to finger his balls and put her mouth around them. Those first night in their new house, she'd twirl around the bedroom in negligees. While the children were sleeping she'd make hot chocolate naked. "Baby, I can't belive this is all ours," she'd say. But it had been months, maybe a year, since they'd had sex. She wouldn't touch him. Yes, he'd let her down. Yes, she was working full-time at the school, but didn't she understand what a little affection could do for a man? A little forgiveness?

Douglas felt utterly alone; his family's survival depended on him, but he was out of ideas. He needed help, but who could help him? He found it hard to get out of bed in the morning. He felt himself, day by day, crawling toward, then almost lurching into, a dark gulf of unprecedented self-pity. After all these months, the effort of feigning confidence for his wife and children had drained him of energy, of hope.

Sometimes he imagined packing a suitcase in the night and disappearing to a coastal Mexican town. He could sip tropical drinks and catch up on reading, he could learn to surf and get back into shape. He'd speak Spanish. He'd meet locals and smoke dope and grow his hair long. He'd find some American hippie girl hanging out after college; he'd be mysterious about his past, drop a few strategic clues so that she'd think he was former CIA. She'd be scared, amazed; she'd stroke his balls on a hammock. Eventually, they'd open a little beachfront bar together, start fresh, have more children . . .

No, no, no. He wasn't that kind of man. Douglas loved his children, his wife. Couldn't they see that? Didn't they understand he might be failing, he might be losing money, but he would never leave them?

The phone rang. Denise again.

He would never leave her, but he didn't want to take her call.

He remembered an experiment in which scientists placed a barracuda in a tank with small fish. For weeks the barracuda gorged itself, until the scientists inserted a Plexiglas partition and dumped the small fish on the other side. When the barracuda went for the fish, he bumped his head. Over and over, he rammed that Plexiglas and then, finally, stopped. That's when the scientists took the partition out. Once again, they dumped a bucket of fish in the tank. But the barracuda wouldn't budge.

"Learned helplessness," they called it.

That's what he was feeling. Douglas knew he had to keep ramming that partition. No matter what. He couldn't afford to feel depressed, he couldn't give up. His family was counting on him. He'd fight tooth and nail. He'd talk to Dean Obervell, tell him he needed some new territory to work with. He'd come up with ideas, new lots to assemble. He'd start looking at Bridgeport. He'd make himself essential to the company. He'd show them he had vision and perseverance. And he'd do it before Dean had a chance to think of letting him go. Douglas couldn't end up like Glenn Mirsky. His pulse quickened at the thought; his forehead grew clammy.

Douglas strode quickly down the hallway, past the emptied offices where Glenn and Ray and Kevin had worked for years. Nothing but dusty mouse pads remained on the desks; drawers were open. The leaves on the ficus trees—Jesus, they didn't even water the plants once you were gone?—had shriveled.

He knocked on Dean Obervell's door. "Dean, Dean, listen, you got a sec? I wanted to run some ideas by you. New territories, while the prices are low." Douglas waved a yellow legal pad, but Dean's eyes went straight to Douglas's crotch.

"Olson, Jesus, at least pretend you have some dignity left."

DENISE

As soon as he let the turkey thud into their kitchen sink, her husband had silently trudged off to the living room. Well, let him sulk, she thought. Why should she feel guilty for his gloominess when he had brought it all on himself? Above all else in life she had wanted one thing—not to worry about money   and as though her marriage were a horrible fable, Douglas had wagered everything and lost. His boundless cheer and confidence, the qualities she had once fallen in love with, now terrified her.

"He seems a bit down," said Ginny.

"You know where these go, right?" Denise handed her a stack of plates.

Ginny smiled away the evasion, hugged the plates, called into the living room, "Priya, wanna help Mommy set the table?"

But Denise could see in the distance that Priya was encamped with Douglas and the twins, burrowing her feet into the sectional. Her eyes were locked on the television.

"Priya? Football?" Ginny widened her eyes at Denise, and then shrugged. "Pick my battles, right?"

"Or else you have war."

While Ginny set the table, Denise shoved the turkey into the oven, set the gravy on the stovetop, and slid the carrots into the microwave. She cleared away the plastic bags and containers and wiped down the counter. Order, the day needed some order. If she could narrow her vision to a goal she could accomplish, she could forget for a moment that everything around her was on the brink of vanishing.

"I mean, Douglas is usually Mr. Merry." Ginny had returned; she set her elbows on the counter and leaned toward Denise. "Frankly, I'm worried."

"*You're* worried?" Denise let out a desperate laugh. "Welcome to the party, Ginny."

"He can be very sensitive to criticism, to certain tones of voice."

Denise wondered what Ginny really knew of her brother. Ginny had never put her life in Douglas's hands. She had no idea what it was to lash her fate to a man she loved only to have him plunge off a cliff.

Knowing that to open her mouth would unleash a flood of emotion, Denise continued to wipe down the counter until Eleanor pattered in.

"Shame on me, I left you gals all alone in here! What can I do?"

"Nothing," Ginny and Denise said simultaneously.

"Why don't you play with the grandchildren?" Denise suggested.

"They're watching football." Eleanor sighed. "I asked the boys to play Ping-Pong."

Denise's sons were frightened of their grandmother with a Ping-Pong paddle. She always won, because, she said, *letting* children win was bad for their mental development. She'd probably never been able to beat anyone at anything and couldn't stop herself. Though Denise wondered if she was tipsy enough that the twins might finally claim the family title.

"Did you see that Priya is watching football with the boys?" Eleanor whispered dramatically.

"I'm aware," said Ginny. "They didn't have TV in the orphanage."

And then Denise remembered something that had been bugging her. "So how much time did you spend in that orphanage? I mean, before you adopted Priya." Denise had been amazed at how quickly it had all come together; one day Ginny was off to India, a few months later she had a seven-year-old child. She thought people had to go through mounds of paperwork. A woman she knew spent two years trying to get a child from Vietnam. And Denise worked at a public school. She knew bureaucracy.

"I'm only her guardian," said Ginny. "We still have to go through the legal adoption process here. You want these cranberries in a dish?"

Denise was still puzzled. "So what was the process before you went over?"

Ginny pressed her fingertips to her temples, closed her eyes, and took three deep, noisy breaths. When she opened her eyes, without looking at Eleanor or Denise, she announced that she needed to use the bathroom.

As Ginny left the kitchen, Denise turned to Eleanor.

"Oh, Ginny doesn't like questions about this stuff," Eleanor said. "It's all so mysterious. She acts like she kidnapped the girl!"

GINNY

Ginny did not go to India intending to return with a child. It would have been crazy, and impossible, given the elaborate adoption procedures, procedures no doubt meant to prevent people from doing exactly what she had done: impulse adopting.

She arrived in New Delhi in June, relieved, despite the sweltering heat, to be thousands of miles from New York, from her crammed apartment, from Ratu.

She worked with a team of international researchers: Swedes, Brits, and an Italian couple with Save the Children. During the day, the team separated to conduct interviews at various orphanages, but in the evenings they all dined together. Ginny immediately took to a brother-sister team who worked with CARA (Central Adoption Resource Authority). Ravi and Safia were biological brother and sister who, as infants, had been adopted by a wealthy Bombay family. After learning their own story—while at university in London—they returned to India, making adoption their crusade. Ravi worked with the orphanages, and Safia with the agencies and courts. Ginny had been assigned to the Analisa Home for Girls on the outskirts of Delhi, so in the mornings, alongside Ravi, she compiled data on how long girls had been there and if they had been considered for adoption.

Ginny loved the work. After all those years she'd spent locked away in libraries, digging up demographic data on people who had been dead for centuries, here were living children.

A clear hierarchy dominated the orphanage. The older girls

worked in the kitchen while the younger girls swept, laundered, and dusted. At any given time at least one hundred girls lived at Analisa, and between them, they had few belongings: beautiful pink seashells that Ravi brought each year from his family trips to Goa; pencils; jacks; a faded postcard of the Eiffel Tower that a girl who had been adopted by a French couple once sent, now as soft as cotton from being passed hand to hand.

The girls all wore simple gray frocks, layered with the sweaters and T-shirts that arrived as donations. But on the first day of every month the new girls had their photographs taken in a white dress, of which there were ten in various sizes. Just a few weeks after her arrival Ginny watched as one of the older girls perched at the front of the cafeteria holding a hairbrush and bobby pins. As the new girls lined up, one by one she brushed their hair and carefully pinned it back. She lined their eyes with kohl and smeared it with her thumb. Using a small jar of cooking oil, she moistened their lips.

"Who's the Avon lady?" Ginny asked.

"Priya," Ravi answered. "I'm not supposed to have favorites, but, well, let's just say she has a place in my heart. She's sort of the Queen Bee here."

"And no one has scooped her up?"

"We don't think it's medical, but she doesn't speak. When she was three, and she had just arrived, we tried to place her. But eventually we had to designate her as 'special needs.' Now the years when she had a good shot are over. In a few years, she will go to an adolescent home."

"Then someday open a beauty shop?" Ginny joked.

"Those ones do not fare so well." Ravi looked down. "Prostitutes, mainly."

In the afternoons, Ginny worked at the adoption agencies, watching as couples from London and France arrived with bank statements, home study reports, reference letters, marriage licenses. Orphanages gave babies and infants to Indian couples only, toddlers to Indian citizens living abroad. Children over five were the candidates for foreign adoption, but adoptive couples could not be more than ninety years old in combined age, or individually younger than thirty. They could not be gay. They could not have more than two children, or two divorces.

Every evening, after she had typed up her notes, Ginny returned to the Analisa Home, where she played jacks with the girls, or read aloud from *Goodnight Moon*. When they were herded off for dinner and evening chores, Ginny opened a beer and sat outside on the bench watching the quiet playground, the empty hopscotch board where Priya leapt like a gazelle. The girl, who was assisting Ginny with her interviews, sharpening pencils and filing papers according to Ginny's color-coded tags, was exempt from evening cleanup. At first Priya's silence made it difficult for Ginny to communicate. Ginny was a talker—*Holy moly, how am I going to squeeze in three interviews before a meeting at 11:30?* Or, *The bugs here are like army tanks, I'm under attack!* She had so little experience with children, she rambled on as though Priya were an adult, which Priya seemed to enjoy. Priya listened intently as Ginny spoke. And with graceful indifference, Priya swept the bugs from Ginny's office. When Ginny arrived each morning, Priya was waiting with a steaming cup of tea. And at the end of the day, she tidied Ginny's desk. The girl's industriousness impressed Ginny. And Priya's curiosity—she lifted books from Ginny's shelf, pointing at their titles for an explanation—stirred something in her heart.

Priya used basic signals to communicate. An excellent mime, she could gesture not only eating and sleeping but also listening to the radio or looking for the dustpan; with a simple tightening of her face, she could make it clear which of the other girls at the home she thought were stupid, arrogant, or troublemakers.

Ginny didn't think she'd fare half as well as a mute orphan in a country where beggars lay half-naked on the street, where eleven million other girls awaited a home.

"So I Googled you," Ravi said one night, startling her on her bench. "You specialize in American family studies. And write poetry."

"Uh-oh. Why were you Googling me?"

He opened a soda. "For the very serious official and professional reason of wanting to ask you out."

"Oh, I'm off men for a while."

"Hmnn . . . Sounds like there's a story there."

"Stories. Plural," she said. "You know what they say about American women being slutty? All true."

He laughed. "Lucky me that you are off men. Timing has always been my thing."

"I'd think a man that spends his days crusading for children would be a chick magnet."

"Except that my crusade prevents me from wanting children of my own. I could never manage both. What about you, no children?"

"I still feel like a child myself."

"You are so good with the girls. They adore you. Especially Priya."

At the sound of her name, Priya paused on the hopscotch board and looked over.

"My little wingwoman."

"You know, Ginny, I've seen many people, in many different situations, come here. This place, it is like a mosque, or a church; people come for something they need."

At the end of each day, they sat together on the bench. Sometimes Safia joined them, complaining about the red tape that kept her from doing her job. By July, the monsoons came, and as the rain pounded the corrugated tin roof, Ravi and Safia told Ginny about the day their mother flew to London to tell them, after nineteen years, that they had been adopted.

"We had always known," said Safia. "These things, you know them in your bones before you know them."

One morning, unable to sleep, Ginny arrived early at the orphanage. The sun had not yet risen and as she approached the dark gate she heard a whimper. On the ground lay a cot with three infant girls. Ginny scooped up two of them, who quickly began to wail. In a moment, Priya emerged from the building, rushed to the gate in her nightdress, and lifted the third baby.

In the infirmary, Priya mixed bottles of formula, deftly pinned on diapers, and wrapped each baby in a blanket.

Within two weeks, the infants were processed for adoption, and Ginny watched as Priya, with sad resignation, smeared kohl on the girls' eyes for their photos. Over the years Priya had learned to skillfully communicate every thought and emotion with her face; she did not know how to hide her unhappiness.

"It's not fair," Ginny said.

"If we don't get them adopted now," said Ravi, "they will end up just like Priya."

"Give her a chance! Let a family at least meet her. These rules are moronic."

"It is the bureaucracy," said Safia.

"If someone were to want her, they'd have to go back home, begin the paperwork, the home study, and then what? It would take six months, another year. I could conceive, carry, and give birth to a child of my own faster than it would take for me to adopt her."

Safi and Ravi looked at each other, and Ginny blushed, realizing what she had said.

"It's not just her age," Ravi said. "She doesn't speak. This is a lot for parents to take on."

"*I* understand her."

"Ginny." Safia touched Ginny's hand. "What are you feeling?"

"I go home in three weeks, and I think, well, I think Priya wants me to take her with me."

"And you?"

Ginny thought, *I'm not ready to be a mother*. It was impossible to picture her life in New York with a seven-year-old child. But when she imagined leaving Priya at Analisa, it seemed like abandonment.

"Where would I even begin the paperwork?"

"Ginny, this will take money and time. You must be sure," said Ravi. "But we can contact our subagencies in the States and get the ball rolling."

"Or," said Safia, "maybe we can expedite it."

"How? We need to petition the court with a home study, and we cannot even begin that until Ginny arrives home."

"Ravi, Priya's been with you four years. It's time."

"Fuck, I can't believe I'm saying this. But, Ravi, let me take her home. Now. Please. Don't make her sit in this place another year. Nobody else will want her. You know that. I'll pay whatever fees."

Ravi let his head fall into his hands. "We could lose our accreditation."

"No one will find out," Ginny said. "And you've spent every day for the past two months with me, you've watched me with Priya. What more of a study do you need?"

Safia stood. She was older, and he would always defer to her. Ginny sensed they both feared that if she left without Priya, she might change her mind. "It is decided."

Ginny had to produce $3,500, bank statements, a letter of employment from the university, medical records. Safia changed the name and address on a home study from a San Francisco woman who had applied for adoption the year before. With that, Safia presented Ginny's entire I-600A packet to an Indian district court.

Within an hour, Ginny was granted guardianship.

Ginny applied for Priya's Indian passport, and her immediate-relative visa petition. She would have to wait to initiate official adoption procedures in the United States, after six months of home study. And she would have to relocate quickly, so there would be no questions about the changed details of her paperwork.

The evening before she left for New York, Ginny sat down beside Ravi on the front steps; he was biting his nail.

"I'm nervous, too," she said.

"It's the right thing. I am just one of those people used to following rules."

"Rules are for fools. If that's not already a saying, it should be."

"The rules haven't helped Priya so far."

Ginny dug into her bag and handed him a thousand dollars in cash. "It's not a payoff. It's for the girls. Buy them ice cream, new shoes, something."

He took the money, studied it for a moment, and then slipped it into his pocket. He released a noisy huff of air. "I hate this job. I'm losing two of my favorite girls."

Ginny leaned back on her elbows and looked up at the sky. Dusk was falling; feathered clouds stretched across a purple sky. Tomorrow she would wake up a mother.

"Ravi, did you want me to take her? From the beginning?"

He stood, surveyed the yard, and with his back to her said, "That would be crazy, wouldn't it? Really crazy." Then turned, kissed her forehead. "Send us a postcard of the Empire State Building."

Across the crowded dormitory room, Ginny carried an empty suitcase. Priya sat on her bed playing cards with another girl, but when her eyes fell on the bag, she stopped. Ginny laid the suitcase on the bed and threw it open.

Priya shooed the other girl away and stared at the empty bag. Then, as though trying to remember a list in her mind, she jumped to her feet and began pulling sweaters and skirts from her bedside drawer. First, she set them in the suitcase slowly, carefully, but with each new article of clothing, the reality of her escape began to dawn on her, and she giddily flung her socks and nightshirts into the bag. She held up a blue shirt, shook her head in disgust; it would not do. She held a pair of tights to her waist, and then tossed them to the floor. She flitted and scampered; she rattled drawers, putting on a triumphant show for the room of gape-mouthed girls. She left the hairbrush and bobby pins on her nightstand.

When the suitcase latches were sealed and she had made her good-byes, Priya lifted the bag, held her head high, and slowly stepped forward, as though it were a moment she had rehearsed her whole life. She clasped Ginny's hand, and pulled her along, proudly leading the way, as though she were the one rescuing Ginny.

KIJO

The man who made Kijo was a shadow, a shadow without a name; he was ten names, he was nobody. He was good, or maybe bad. He was a neighbor, a classmate, a man in an alley. The woman who made Kijo was eleven faded pictures locked in a trunk. She was a scuffed pair of tap shoes. An amusement park bracelet. A high school yearbook. She was a name—Arlette—without a voice, without a telephone number, without an address.

Kijo knew it was stupid to miss a person you'd never known, but he did. He wouldn't say it to Grandma Rose or Spider, wouldn't tell them he lay in bed as a child wishing he could talk to his mother. When he stuttered, he'd been certain his mother would have understood him. That's what a mother was, the person who always knew what you were feeling.

So as a child, Kijo learned what he could of his known lineage. *Lineage,* a word he could say. *L*s were easy for him. A man had to know where he'd come from before he could know where he was going.

Just as some kids studied baseball cards, Kijo had studied old photographs. All those years his stutter had made him afraid to speak, he sat quietly at home, on a twin bed beside a gooseneck lamp, flipping through his grandmother's scrapbooks.

He'd traced his family as far back as Elton Washington, his great-grandfather, who'd fought in World War II in a Buffalo division. After Elton had returned from France, he and his wife, Rose, moved north from the Carolinas. There had been a hold on factory walkouts during the war, but once the treaties were signed, workers pulled off their goggles and threw down their helmets and picketed textile mills and auto plants. Since the unions had never let in blacks, Elton had no problem joining an assembly line. That's what he'd told a newspaper reporter, *They ain't let me work beside 'em, I ain't gonna stand beside 'em.* In 1946 he got a job at Yale & Towne, working there until the plant closed. The newspaper had also run a photo of him: a broad-shouldered man with a long beard, standing at the factory gate with a tin lunch pail, ELTON painted on the side.

Elton and Rose rented a small yellow house on Freedom Avenue in Stamford, south of what would be the interstate. They had three children: Franklin, Leroy, and Augusta Rose.

A decent family, Kijo thought. Until another war came.

Franklin and Leroy died fighting in Vietnam, alongside their best friend and sister's husband, Joseph Jackson. Joseph Jackson's father had also worked at Yale & Towne, but when the factory closed, he opened a locksmith shop. As a child, Joseph worked there, picking up the trade so well he became known as Key Joe. The man for whom Kijo would be named. Kijo had a picture of him in a uniform leaning on an army truck. Joseph was smiling, revealing a gold front tooth. That might have been the end of the Jackson line, but Joseph left Augusta Rose with child.

In 1973, with the money from her husband's army life insurance, Augusta Rose made a down payment on her parents' Freedom Avenue house. That same year, in the upstairs bedroom, she gave birth to Arlette Jackson. Eighteen years later, as Grandma Rose would eventually tell Kijo, after both Elton and Rose had passed away, Arlette vanished one night, leaving her newborn on the sofa wrapped in the pink robe Augusta Rose had sewn for Christmas. *Sorry, momma,* the note supposedly said, though Kijo had never seen it. *You better at this.* Augusta Rose said her heart was split in two, snap, like a wishbone. For fifteen years she waited in that house in case her daughter came walking up the porch steps.

231 Freedom Avenue.

Kijo had been made to memorize the address, in case he got lost. On the bottom of his shoes, she wrote it in permanent ink. His grandmother stitched it inside his jacket for when his stutter got him. She showed him how to hold up his fingers: two, three, one.

The house was two stories, with a hot attic crowded with Grandma Rose's sewing forms—armless cotton bodies of every size that terrified the young Kijo. In the damp basement, where Kijo played Battleship on rainy days, was the red trunk that held the things Kijo's mother had left behind. Sometimes, if he couldn't sleep, Kijo would go down there and look through it.

Grandma Rose never spoke of Arlette, but she cared for that house like it was her child. "Aren't you pretty?" she'd say as she hung bright white curtains. Despite her troubled hip, she'd stand on chairs and dust the ceilings using a broom covered with an old pillowcase. In the corner of every room sat a spray bottle of glass cleaner and a folded red rag, in case she noticed a spot while talking on the telephone. The house always smelled of ammonia and mothballs and lemon cleaner. She eyed visitors, even Kijo, as they stepped in, to make sure they wiped their shoes; if anyone trekked mud into her home, if a hot mug was set down without a coaster, her smile would vanish. Grandma Rose once asked Auntie Henrietta to get on her way for putting her feet on the coffee table.

From the decorations around the house, it was hard to tell who Grandma Rose thought more highly of: Jesus or Elvis Presley. Jesus hung in the bathroom, kitchen, living room, and Kijo's room, but not in Grandma's bedroom. A signed photo of Elvis sat propped on her nightstand beside a photo of her late husband. A framed Elvis album hung over her bureau. Kijo figured Jesus probably wouldn't like the lady friends who sometimes stayed the night.

He'd been made to call them aunties. Auntie Evangeline, Auntie Sarah, Auntie Henrietta. When Kijo was young, Auntie Henrietta had come around in the evenings for four years, helping with the cooking, homework, and speech lessons. *She sells seashells, Kijo baby, come on.* She cleaned rooms in the Hilton and always brought wrapped soaps and little bottles of shampoo and bubble bath. After dinner, the women played chess and yawned themselves up the creaking stairs to Grandma Rose's bedroom. Kijo thought she really was his grandmother's sister until he came home one day and Grandma Rose said Henrietta was getting married and wouldn't be coming around again. She spent a week making Henrietta a wedding dress, then tore it up and used the scraps to wipe grease from the stove.

"Grandma, why you crying?"

"Don't you be nosing into my business, boy!"

Spider told Kijo women got lonely in ways men didn't, and did weird things.

Grandma Rose made her living sewing, going down the block once a week to JoJo Jefferson's shoe shop, where she'd measure and pin clothes on neighborhood folks, then carry the clothes home for hemming and mending. She dyed her hair a shade of red that looked pink in the sunlight; she wore it short and curled and pushed it in place with her cracked hands when she was nervous. She walked with a brass-handled St. Christopher cane and Kijo could hear her coming—*click, click, click*—a long time down the street.

When he was young that gave him time to hide his mischief: burning ants or building a potato gun. When his stuttering would frustrate him, Kijo got into trouble pocketing candy from the grocery store, stealing street signs and license plates. He and Spider liked to wander to the white parts of town and put shoe polish on pay-phone receivers. If Grandma Rose caught him, she'd sew a red felt circle onto his shirt so he'd have to tell anyone who asked that he'd been telling mistruths. Doing good deeds was the only way he could get the circles off. Until he was ten, Kijo walked around with so many red spots people called him Pox.

One day he stole a skateboard from a boy across the street. He didn't know why since he was too clumsy to ride it. He fell off trying and the mother, Miss Macy, saw him out her window and marched over to have words with Grandma Rose.

Grandma Rose could do more than sew spots; she took Kijo's earlobe between her knuckles, twisting hard.

"You wanna be a thief? We ain't got enough hoodlums round here, huh? Say you're sorry."

"I'm s-s-s—" Kijo couldn't get the word out.

"He thieve like a man, but speak like a baby," said Miss Macy. "Don't that take the cupcake."

"Don't you think that stutter's gonna make anyone feel sorry for you . . ." said Grandma Rose. "Don't you bring shame on my house!"

"I'm s-s-s—"

"I feel sorry for y'all." Miss Macy turned away with a huff. "He only gonna get worse. We all know where he came from."

Grandma Rose waited until Miss Macy had closed her door, then yanked Kijo close by his ear. "You go bad, I got nothing. You're a good boy, now act like it!"

The next day he asked Spider what Miss Macy had mean by "we all know where he came from."

Spider told him what all the folks in the neighborhood knew. The summer after Kijo was born, his mother fell in love with a man named Sunny who worked at Rye Playland. Sunny ran a small-time drug operation out of the Haunted House. He bought Arlette jewelry and steak dinners, gave her drugs. They drove around town in his red convertible, sometimes with baby Kijo in a car seat, and she told people she was studying be a tap dancer. But Sunny soon broke her heart, and after that, Arlette was only interested in the pipe.

Grandma Rose fought like crazy to keep her daughter decent. This was before they tore down Southfield Village, when dealers still worked the corners of Freedom Avenue, when a man named Lullaby ran the show. Arlette began lying and stealing, whoring herself out in abandoned cars. She came home one night trying to get money from Grandma Rose, waving a knife. Grandma Rose wrestled the knife away—which is how she hurt her hip—and called the cops. She hadn't heard a thing from her daughter since.

Some said Arlette was hooking in Bridgeport, some said she ran off with Kijo's father; there was debate as to who he was. A high school classmate, a man who got rough with her one night. Maybe even Sunny. No one knew exactly when they met. Kijo liked to imagine it was Sunny; it gave him a name, a story.

"We're goners far as the neighborhood's concerned," said Spider, whose father was serving life in the fed pen for cutting up a Mexican outside a bar. "It's like they reserved a cell for us in prison."

Kijo then understood why Spider had become his friend, why he didn't mind his stutter or his clumsiness.

They both had bad blood.

Somehow this new understanding of his parentage allowed Kijo to speak clearly. This knowledge of where he'd come from relaxed his tongue. He stopped stealing candy and street signs, stopped making mischief. He combed his hair, tucked in his shirt, and shined his shoes.

He could now see it in his grandma's eyes, the watery fear that had been there all along: *Where you been, boy? Where you going out to?* When she gripped his shoulders, she shook him like she was shaking out the devil.

She never spoke of his mother or father.

As he grew older, Kijo watched his body change, taking on the shape of a stranger. His hands were thick-fingered and large, his feet long and narrow—they belonged to a man he'd never seen. He felt like clay being shaped by unseen hands. His nose widened, a nose unlike any other in family photographs. He was darker, too. Coffee-bean black. If he passed his father on the street, he wondered, would they know each other?

The mystery of his nature became a sour taste in Kijo's mouth. A loose tooth he couldn't let alone.

As his voice deepened, he imagined hearing his father's voice, a rumbling laugh from some dark corner of a movie theater; *that's him*. Then Kijo could see who the man was, understand what was forming inside him.

How else would you know what might wake up inside you one day?

DOUGLAS

*B*efore he met Denise, Douglas had been dating Sumi Kitamura on and off for six years. They'd met at Duke. She was Japanese-American, and her father was a physics professor at the university. Her father wanted her to be a physicist, and there was no denying Sumi's natural ability with science and math. She won practically every university prize, and the lacrosse coach had arranged for her to tutor players in their weaker subjects. She helped Douglas with physics and chemistry, two subjects she cared little about since her heart was set on being a painter.

She'd appear at their tutoring session hugging a canvas; then she'd set it against the wall and ask him to lift off the sheet.

"Gorgeous," he'd say.

"Be more particular."

In truth, Douglas thought her paintings looked off balance, colorless, depressing. Sickly flowers in cracked vases. "Well, what do the art teachers say? I'm no critic, ask people who really *know* art."

"They're all friends with my father. They'll never encourage me against his wishes."

She told him about how the great women painters of the Renaissance—Lavinia Fontana, Marietta Tintoretto—had, in fact, been trained by their fathers. She gave Douglas paintings, which he hung all over his dorm room and, after graduation, in his New York City apartment. Her father never hung any.

"Hey, why don't you make him a painting of something physics related. E equals MC squared."

"I'm done giving him anything!"

This rebellion against her father was the crux of Sumi's life, making her alternately angry and sulky, prone to fits of crying. They'd be out at a party, giddy and tipsy, and then, on the host's bookshelf, her father's textbooks would catch Sumi's eye. Within seconds her drink was down. "We're leaving."

Douglas's family wasn't much help, either. Whenever he brought Sumi home, his mother, who usually cornered his friends in the living room and excitedly interrogated them about their studies, would feign a dramatic yawn. Before disappearing into her bedroom, she would suggest a few restaurants they might enjoy. His mother said he could date whom he liked, it was no business of hers, but she was quite certain he wouldn't be with Sumi for the long haul.

"Douglas, can't you see how awkward it is for me? I can see what the girl wants, that she's hoping I'll embrace her as a mother-in-law. I simply cannot lead her on."

Who knew where things with Sumi were headed, but he sensed his mother's discomfort stemmed from Sumi's Japanese descent.

"Maybe I can spend the holidays with you this year," Sumi suggested. "I'm sick, sick, sick of my dad. He keeps giving me books on painters who committed suicide."

"The holidays, isn't that family time?"

"You don't want me there?"

"*I* do. It's my mother."

"Well, she probably doesn't think any girl is good enough for you. Remind her I won the Fermi Prize as a freshman."

"I think . . . I think it might be the Japanese thing. My mother's from Massachusetts. She's barely left New England. The big thrill of her week is her gardening club. All her friends are, well, clones of her."

"And you think my father wants me to marry some white boy from Connecticut?"

"Who said marry?"

After that, Sumi insisted they go only to sushi bars and noodle shops. At the movies, she'd pretend to miss lines of dialogue, lean in, and ask him to please explain what was said. She showed up one night wearing a red-silk kimono.

"Sumi, this is ridiculous. What's next, chopsticks in your hair?"

"I won't deny my heritage for you or your mother. I will not play WASP." She tightened her kimono belt in one sharp tug. "You're the first guy in history to date a Japanese girl and turn out to have a Caucasian fetish."

"Sumi, I love you."

"You should," she said. "I'm ten times smarter than you."

He went camping with friends to think things through and when he got home, he told her they were too young to be serious. He started going to parties on his own, asking girls for their numbers. He met Denise at a work conference: Consulting for the New Millenium. Tanned and petite, Denise stood behind a table of sandwiches, directing the flow of food like an air-traffic controller. She wore a red chef's hat that said DISHES.

As Douglas reached for a ham-and-cheese, she said, "Nuh-uh. You look like a foie-gras man. Take this one instead."

"Delicious."

"I made them." She slid her card into his shirt pocket. "If you ever want more."

The catering was just a weekend gig. Her real job was in branding. She made up names for cars, bottled water, bras, and software. She was part of a small team of young women who scoured thesauruses and atlases and encyclopedias of Greek mythology for obscure names that would bait people into buying things. The Cleo Xj2000, Aquamor, Swansol.

In the mornings before work, Denise ran three laps around the reservoir, then she pinned her toes beneath her paint-cracked radiator and huffed out fifty sit-ups.

"Jesus, you make me feel lazy," he said.

"Some people, people who have met with unfortunate ends, have called me high-strung."

"You're industrious. And it's totally hot. You're like the love child of Jessica Rabbit and the Energizer Bunny."

"Well, I'm not a trust-fund kid. Poverty really lights a fire under your ass."

Two years out of college and she'd already set up her own 401(k).

She came from a family of three brothers in Pittsburgh that she didn't like to talk about. Douglas loved her no-nonsense, I'll-arm-wrestle-you-for-it quality. Where Sumi had been angry and despairing, waking in the middle of the night once a week threatening to break up with him, Denise booked airline tickets early and requested bulkhead seats. She read road maps, *accurately*—while rubbing his thigh! She didn't waste time politely refusing telemarketers: *Hi, I'm calling from the* . . . Click, call over. If the maître d' gave them a bad table, if her steak was overcooked, she made her displeasure politely but clearly known.

Once, when a grocery-store bag boy put the eggs at the bottom, she began brusquely repacking it.

"Denise," Douglas whispered, gesturing to the boy, who clearly had Down syndrome.

"I need a big time-out," she said outside. "I feel crazed. I have two jobs. I'm trying to have a relationship. And frankly, I wonder where that's even going. I'm investing a lot of time in you."

"Well, maybe you should ditch the catering gig."

"That, jackass, wasn't the question."

They'd been dating a year, and Douglas had known it was only a matter of time before she started gauging his long-term potential. He was in love, but the idea of settling down made him anxious. His future seemed murky. Ardor Consulting certainly wasn't the right job for him; there was something else he was meant to do, but it hadn't come to him yet. In the meantime, couldn't they enjoy late nights of martinis and karaoke? Smuggling panini into action movies? Bowling and batting cages? Couldn't they be young and carefree? Denise charted her daily runs, planned her lunches on a calendar, laid out outfits the night before. And now he could see it coming—she was going to plan his whole life.

Douglas canceled some dates. He and Sumi had stayed in touch and around that time he called her. One night, in the middle of a storm, she showed up at his apartment grappling with a dripping umbrella. Her face was pink from drinking. She began crying, saying Douglas couldn't let his mother keep them apart.

She spent the night. In the morning he realized she'd stayed awake making a portrait of his face; it looked terrible. She had put on one of his old lacrosse jerseys and she stumbled toward the bathroom in his slippers, hungover. She made a mess of the toothpaste, gargling loudly, and left the cap off the mouthwash. She began to talk once again about the struggle with her father.

Douglas thanked her for the portrait and whisked her out. At the office, he looked around at all the junior partners and vice presidents; he'd met their wives at the annual holiday party and July Fourth picnic. Sharp, practical women. Planners.

"I want to cook you dinner tonight," he told Denise on the phone.

"You don't know how to cook."

"Which makes it all the more romantic, right?"

He boiled spaghetti and oversaw a splattering skillet of tomato sauce as Denise sipped at her wine, looking around his apartment. She plucked a pair of earrings off his nightstand.

"Rhinestones? Tacky."

"Oh, I found them under the bed and assumed they were yours. Maybe they've been here since I moved in."

The water frothed over the pot and he lowered the flame. He lit candles and shook out her napkin for her, waiter-style, and said she looked beautiful. He suggested they get away for a weekend, maybe to the Adirondacks, or to look at old bridges in Connecticut, all the while trying to detect any distrust in her eyes. But Denise twirled her spaghetti, said his cooking wasn't half-bad, and then complained about a coworker who chatted all day on the phone with her sister in Spain.

They went back to spending a couple of nights a week at his apartment.

It couldn't have been more than a couple months later that she called him at work one afternoon.

"We should talk soon," she said. "In person. I have some news."

GINNY

*G*inny had returned to the kitchen and was staring out the window, utterly bored. All the planning and preparing was over; Priya was happily watching television with her cousins. Her mother and Denise were examining a cookbook with the fervor of biblical scholars, muttering about "brilliant substitutions." She wished she'd brought some reading. Standing around the kitchen with women really wasn't her thing.

"I might just sneak upstairs for a quick nap," said Ginny.

"It's the middle of the day!" her mother cried.

"Twenty minutes, just to reboot."

"Have some coffee." Denise gestured toward a restaurant-style espresso machine/coffeemaker.

Figuring she'd caused enough upset for one day, Ginny made her way across the slick burgundy marble floor. She was surprised, given Douglas's alarmist attitude, that they didn't spend their lives worrying they would fall and crack their heads open.

Beside the doorway hung a shiny red fire extinguisher and a defibrillator. Somewhere, undoubtedly, hung a framed plan of the electrical wiring.

Chrome stockpots and kettles gleamed from the stove. Six stools flanked a long island in the center of the kitchen. On it sat two large blocks of Henckels knives and an array of devices for every culinary impulse—garlic press, apple corer, electric can opener, juice machine, electric chopper, lemon zester. All the sharp-edged stuff you were supposed to tuck away in childproof cabinets. But Denise had bypassed the need for ugly childproofing clips by simply dividing the house into child-free zones. She had trained the children as to where, exactly, in that massive house they could and could not go. Whenever she said "training" it reminded Ginny of dogs with electric collars; she was always waiting for one of the twins to walk through the doorway and go *Zaaap!*

Denise had an indisputable frontier toughness, like those eighteenth-century women who ran taverns and brothels. Women who kept revolvers under their petticoats.

"Still liking the job at the school?" Ginny asked.

Denise looked caught off guard, but her face quickly leapt into a cheerleader's grin. She shook her fist. "Gotta keep kids healthy!"

Denise had worked as a nutritionist in the public schools for five years.

"Oh, Ginny, don't make her talk about work on a holiday."

"Some people like work, Mom."

Their voices reverberated off the granite countertops. Denise grabbed a knife and guillotined a Macintosh apple, slicing it with frightening speed. Ginny flipped on the coffeemaker, then stirred the gravy on the stove. On the neighboring burner sat a pot of mashed yams, drizzled with butter and nutmeg.

What tuber, Ginny loved to ask her students on the first day of class, forever changed the lives of women?

Yams! she chided, when no one answered. The source of the birth control pill!

Ginny glanced at Denise, amazed that after all these years, with all her mother's prying, with Denise's constant emphasis on the need for planning and preparation, that no one had brought up the fact that the pill is 99 percent effective. Apparently not so for the unwed Denise. Accident? Sure, Ginny thought when she had heard the news.

But her brother squealed so happily over the phone. He had called her first. "Gin, you'll never believe . . . I'm gonna be a father!"

Maybe Douglas wanted to settle down and needed a woman to trick him. He wouldn't have been the first man in history.

Within a year, he went from being Ginny's big brother to being a husband and father. All his overprotectiveness was channeled elsewhere. Occasionally, when she felt she'd lost him forever, Ginny was tempted to confide her suspicion. But having spent so many years studying the obstacles against women, Ginny just couldn't betray another woman's deception.

"And with Priya?" With one clean sweep of the knife, Denise exiled the apple peels to the trash. "Will you keep up teaching full-time?"

Ginny had spent the bulk of her savings on securing Priya's guardianship and buying the house. There weren't many options.

"Even if it means fewer hours with her per week, I think I'll be a better parent if I'm working. I'll find a nanny or something. I'll need help."

Her mother had been watching her intently while garnishing the cranberry sauce with a band of almond slivers. "Ginny, what do you hear from David Eisenberg these days?"

"David Eisenberg? Mom, we dated for three weeks." Her mother had become fixated on a veterinarian she had dated four years earlier. Ginny was not going to spend the afternoon discussing her romantic life. "A quick catnap would really do me wonders." She feigned a yawn.

"You just had coffee!" exclaimed her mother.

"Mom, listen. I have a daughter now. She's in the next room. I'm not interested in dating."

"Men like children," she said. "And they like women with maternal instincts."

Ginny crossed her arms, trying to contain herself.

"Eleanor, that bowl looks splendid," Denise said, giving Ginny a wink. "Would you mind putting it on the table?"

KIJO

*K*ijo could tell when an auntie was about to leave because late at night Grandma Rose would sit in the kitchen, her fingers punching calculator keys, figuring out how much she could tuck away in another certificate of deposit.

"You know where I been?" she'd say the next day. "At the bank, opening myself another CD." She wore a fancy blue skirt and jacket, sprayed her pink hair into a shiny helmet. "All I need is my CDs, my house. Ain't no one can take that away from you. People come and go, Kijo. But I got this house. And I done near fought a war for it."

This was how his grandmother referred to her fight to save the neighborhood: her *war*. Around the time her parents moved to Freedom Avenue, the state built public-housing towers nearby. Soon the quiet streets where she and her brothers played as children were spotted with young men selling drugs, teenage girls selling tricks. With each year that passed, the area grew more perilous, and by the time Kijo was born, his own mother disappeared into the shadowy danger of the South End. Kijo could remember lying in bed at night watching his wall for the red flash of police cars. When she left the house, Grandma Rose slipped pinking shears into her purse.

Having lost her husband and her daughter, Grandma Rose wasn't going to lose her house. She organized a neighborhood association and held meetings in the local church and at night she and Auntie Henrietta fastened on orange pinnies, took to the streets with bullhorns and flashlights. In dozens of letters to city hall she complained about crime and filth at the housing towers. She included Polaroids. Eventually, the kids who already mocked Kijo for his stutter started calling out, "How's Grandma Rose Hell?"

"Grandma, why you gotta make so much noise about all this?"

"You embarrassed I'm fighting for what's right? I should let these hoodlums take over our street 'cause you don't want me being a nuisance? I never knew I'd raised a yellowbelly."

And she won her war. Eventually the state tore down Southfield Village and in its place built town houses with gardens. White families and Asian families moved in. Streetlights and planter boxes with daffodils appeared.

"Kijo, you think I shoulda just kept quiet?" Grandma Rose asked. "Look around, boy. This here is the reward for working hard and protecting what we got."

Kijo spent his childhood in that house. He knew how the third step whined under the weight of his sneakers; how his bedroom window stayed open only with a phone book propped under it; how the rain sounded best in the kitchen. He knew the location of the jar of pennies he'd buried when he was six. He knew the closet door where Grandma Rose had marked his height until he was fourteen, when at six feet tall he was getting "scary" big, tall enough to quit measuring.

A year after that, the men in gray suits drove up and said the house was a slum, that Kijo and his grandma had to get moving.

They carried stacks of papers. They had photographs of overflowing trash cans, rotten porch planks, wasps' nests in the eaves.

As the neighborhood had improved, property taxes rose, and Grandma Rose began selling off CDs to make the payments. This left little money for upkeep on the house.

"I'm the founder of the neighborhood association," Grandma Rose told the men. "I cleaned up the slum that was here with my very own broom. Four generations of my family have lived in this house. Thank you very much, but we're staying put."

But the men were offering good money. People down the street sold and Kijo didn't understand why she wouldn't budge. She told Kijo that if you let people push you out of their way, it wouldn't ever stop.

Kijo knocked wasps' nests loose. He carried the trash all the way to the dumpster. But then the city itself said they had to move.

"Now it's the government saying so," Kijo tried to soothe her.

"Pontius Pilate," Grandma Rose said. "Just because they're officials, you think that makes it right?"

Grandma Rose put on her bank outfit and dragged Kijo to the office of the Redevelopment Commission. She hugged a scrapbook with family photos and newspaper clippings of her father coming back from the war in Europe. She had an envelope full of receipts from her oil and electric and water bills, showing she'd always paid promptly.

She had sewn Kijo a special suit, which made his legs itch as they sat in the small waiting room for almost three hours. On a table lay all sorts of newspapers, *Time* magazine, *BusinessWeek*. Kijo lifted *Fortune*, flipped through a few pages, but set it back down when he caught the receptionist smiling. Every half hour Grandma Rose jabbed her cane at the woman's desk.

"We didn't come here to breathe up all the air in the waiting room."

The receptionist would then apologize, offer them sodas, and insist that someone would soon be with them. When Kijo got up to use the bathroom, on his way out he saw a group of men standing by the elevator. He recognized one—the man had come by the house to talk with Grandma Rose several times. Kijo knew he should say something, knew that these were the men his grandmother had come to talk to, but he felt awkward in his suit, awkward in the building. One by one, the men turned to look at him. Kijo felt his tongue go thick in his mouth and he looked down at his own feet. When they all filed into the elevator, he heard a voice say, "Clean getaway."

Kijo sat back down beside his grandmother and said nothing. Finally a blond girl no older than Kijo led them into an empty conference room.

Before sitting, Grandma Rose asked, "May I ask your position, miss?"

"The commissioners asked me to take all your statements for our records."

"But you are clearly not on the commission."

"I have twenty minutes. Please."

The girl set a cell phone on the table and throughout the meeting, she flipped it open and closed. As Grandma Rose explained how she bought the house with the army-insurance payout, the girl nodded and took notes, trying hard to look interested, making a sympathetic cluck from time to time. But Kijo could see that she had slipped off her flip-flops and tucked her feet under her skirt. She swung her chair ever so slightly from side to side. Grandma Rose was pleading, and Kijo could see it was going nowhere.

He was angry with himself for his silence by the elevator. Finally, he burst out, "Miss, you got a home of your own?"

He could see her blue eyes take in the blackness of his skin, the bulk of his hands—and now the depth and anger of his voice. She slipped on her flip-flops, sat up straight in her chair, closed her manila folder.

"Thank you both."

"Who else can we talk to?" Grandma Rose asked nervously.

"It's not individuals who make these decisions."

"Who makes them? Dogs? Computers?" Kijo could see Grandma Rose was on the verge of twisting the girl's ear.

"There's a process to these things," the girl said. "Trust in the process."

Kijo, embarrassed, took his grandma's elbow and led her out.

Four months later, the house was condemned.

Kijo hadn't really believed they would be forced to leave. And he hadn't understood that the only place left to go was the West Side. The remaining houses in the city were too expensive, so they made their way to Vidal Court, the last of the government complexes, where all the tenants of Southfield Village had gone years back—all the riffraff Grandma Rose had worked hard to get rid of.

The day Kijo and his grandmother arrived, Lullaby sat in the parking lot in a lawn chair. "I've been waiting on you all."

He was Haitian, light-skinned with blue eyes. A tattoo of a tree covered his back. Kijo could see a knife sticking out of his pocket.

"Does he know us?" Kijo asked Grandma Rose.

"All that man knows is trouble."

They moved into a second-floor unit, and the first day, someone smashed their window. Neighbors said Lullaby was keeping them in line. It was an initiation; he taught everyone who arrived to be afraid.

Kijo stayed up the whole night installing two double-bolt locks.

From the window, Kijo would watch Lullaby sit in his blue lawn chair on the parking lot's edge. He smoked cigars. No one walked in front of him, out of respect, or behind him, for fear Lullaby would think he was being attacked. Lullaby wasn't a large man, but a shield surrounded him. Voices quieted and kids stopped dribbling basketballs as soon as he took up his spot in his plastic throne.

If Grandma Rose saw Kijo watching Lullaby, she'd say, "That boy is the devil."

"That's a *man,* Grandma."

"No man goes around frightening women and children."

"I bet no one ever did him wrong and went on their merry way."

"What's done is done."

Grandma Rose had tried to make her peace with their new home; she hung the curtains from Freedom Avenue, set out her pictures of Elvis and Jesus. But after she got hit, Kijo felt ashamed that he had let them end up in Vidal Court. He replayed the moment by the elevator at the Redevelopment Commission, sickened by the memory of how he had stood silently.

He decided one morning he would talk to Lullaby, but made it only as far as the bottom of the stairwell. It was mid-November, the air was gray and chilly. The parking lot was empty.

"Seems someone tried to redecorate your grandma's face," Lullaby called out, not looking at Kijo. "You from Freedom Avenue. They got you, too. Pretty soon they come for all of us."

Kijo watched Lullaby knot a red scarf around his neck. He'd never had the feeling of both hating and admiring a person.

"And when that time comes"—Lullaby lit a cigar—"it's fight or flight. That, my man, is primitive."

ELEANOR

*A*ll that chatter about work, jobs.

Eleanor remembered when Colleen McKay called. Poof, out of the blue, the phone rang and she wanted to take Eleanor to lunch at the Century Club. It had been forever and a day since Eleanor had had a proper ladies' lunch in the city, let alone lunch with a big-shot magazine editor.

Over the years, she had received phone calls here and there from Wellesley friends. After a fair amount of small talk about children and houses, it usually became clear, through restrained sniffles, that these women had suddenly found themselves at the fat, ugly start of a divorce. Penny Mitchell Davis was about to become Penny Mitchell again, Sue Sanders was phoning from her empty two-story Victorian in Toronto. They needed an ear, a voice from their past, from life before marriage, a reminder that there *had* been a life before the husband who was now off to Machu Picchu with a younger woman.

But Colleen said nothing about a dramatic life change, and it was the first time anyone had suggested a fancy lunch in the city. It seemed, in fact, celebratory. Eleanor let it be known to her gardening club precisely where she was going. She showed Gavin the website, she called Douglas and Denise. "Have you kids been to the Century Club? Oh, no reason, it's just exclusive and I'm meeting my old college friend who's a big-shot editor there . . . The architect Stanford White designed the building."

"Who's Stanford White?" asked Douglas.

"A famous architect!"

"Famous for what?"

"*Other* famous buildings. Listen, I have to go. I don't want to miss my train."

It was Wednesday and she had canceled her usual afternoon Ladies' League tea, noting for the secretary her appointment in the city so that members might get wind of it. She put on her purple tweed suit and tucked a copy of *Good Housekeeping* into her red Liz Claiborne purse—she wanted to appear to be an avid reader of the magazine.

"I'm meeting Colleen McKay for lunch," she announced to the concierge.

As she stepped into the club's vast foyer, the walls rose majestically around her. She was led upstairs past a row of gilt-framed portraits of, no doubt, famous club members.

In a wood-paneled dining room, Colleen sat examining the contents of a large portfolio. Her chair was pushed back from the table, her legs crossed at the ankles, and she wore a slim beige pantsuit with a white silk blouse. When she saw Eleanor, her eyes lit up. Her slim gold watch rattled as she waved. She was a blonde now, though Eleanor was fairly sure that in college she'd been a brunette.

She zipped closed her portfolio. "My God, I've been dropped into a wormhole and am back in 1970!" Her hug was surprisingly muscular and she offered a kiss on each cheek. "Gorgeous, absolutely gorgeous. They must be pumping omega-3s into the suburban tap water. All my girlfriends outside the city have the smoothest skin!"

Eleanor, who religiously lathered her skin each night with cold cream, smiled.

The room was lined with wooden bookcases; marble busts sat atop the shelves. Eleanor had certainly been to fancy restaurants before, but the austere elegance of this space struck her. The nearby tables were filled with men and women who all looked close to her age. They wore business attire, and she sensed in their demeanor a certain gravitas. They weren't just wealthy, they were accomplished, intellectual.

"Look. That's Shirley Hazzard in the corner," Colleen said.

Eleanor didn't recognize the name, but nodded excitedly.

"So is this your usual spot?"

"Oh, you don't have to whisper, hon. It's a little stuffy, I admit. But it's so *easy*. My schedule is so insanely busy that it's great having a place that I can depend on, where I know they'll get me in and out in under an hour. It's frightening how much time you can waste just getting from one appointment to the next if you don't plan well. My office is just a few blocks away."

"Do you have a window?"

Gavin had complained for years about not having a window.

"Ellie, I could fire shots at the Chrysler Building if I wanted to."

"Oh, my," she said, embarrassed that her husband didn't have a window office. "Well, vitamin D is essential to a positive mood."

"I should slip some into the coffeepot at the office. Some of those people are what human resources calls 'attitude challenged.' I call it P-S-Y-C-H-O."

A waiter set down a martini. "Oh, thank you, Jose! Ellie, my dear, sweet Jose knows exactly how I like my martinis. Are you sure you won't have anything? Prosecco? White wine? Very well, then." She clinked her martini glass to Eleanor's water glass. "To old friends!"

She took a long sip. Eleanor noticed she wasn't wearing a wedding ring.

"Tell me all about *vous*!"

Eleanor rummaged in her purse. "My son and his wife just had twins. Brandon and Brian. Aren't they precious?" As she set the photos out, she recalled a vague rumor from thirty years earlier about Colleen having had an affair with a married classics professor and a clandestine late-night drive to Canada to take care of a "situation." Or maybe that was Lydia Siller. So many girls got into trouble in those days. "And this is Douglas and Denise in front of their new house in

Stamford. And I have a daughter, too, who lives here in the city. Ginger. I don't have a picture. She's just been made a professor of . . . history. We're just thrilled her career is going so well. It's only a matter of time before the right man scoops her up."

"Perfect!" Colleen dug a notepad and pencil out of her briefcase. "She'd be a great angle for this project. You see, we're doing this special issue on women of *our* generation, their life choices, how they imagined their lives thirty years ago, what their lives are now. We're wedged between the greatest generation of 1950s postwar, suburban drudgery and the generation of, well, your daughter. We were the first women who actually had to make choices and we all made very different ones. Obviously, among our usual writers, there's a bias. We've got elevators crammed with women who took the professional path to one degree or another; what we need are some women who took the other road, but who can put a noun and verb together in an interesting way. We're looking at a handful of girls from the Wellesley class of 1970, and this will be: 'Thirty Years Later, Where Are They?' I was thinking back to Wellesley and remembered you wrote some good articles for the paper. Good enough to stick in my mind. I went to look you up—I almost thought you'd gone the professional route—but couldn't find your name anywhere. But the alumni office had your married name. Kitty Skyler said she'd seen you at the five-year reunion and you were already on baby number two. I thought, *Perfecto!*"

"Kitty Skyler. Did she ever marry?"

"Twice divorced. But she's working on her third novel, a mystery series, under the name Kate Ashmond. They're a bit slice and dice for my taste, but she has a real following."

"What about Beatrice Cummings? She was in our dorm, right?"

"She's a painter."

"A painter! And Claire? Claire Purcell?"

"Mergers and acquisitions at Pettigrew. God, have I kept up with more classmates than you? Here I always thought I lacked school spirit! Don't tell the alumni fund or they'll have me arranging reunions. Ellie, do you know what you want yet?" Colleen glanced at her watch. "We should order. The Chilean sea bass is fantastic."

She signaled the waiter, and Eleanor excitedly opened the menu. Goodness, the sea bass cost twenty-eight dollars. Did they send someone out on a fishing boat? She was appalled that most of the entrées cost over twenty dollars. For that amount she could prepare dinner for her entire family. She closed the menu and ordered the cauliflower soup, and buttered herself a hulking piece of olive bread. She chewed slowly.

"Anyway, the point is, Ellie, we need your side of it. A lot more of our readers are like you than they are like me. What the hell do *I* know about *Good Housekeeping*? I've had the same Polish cleaning lady for twenty years. I have no earthly idea what Pine-Sol is used for. I live in a loft. I'm on face-lift *numero dos*. But I know how to pick writers. And I think our readers want their lives written about by someone who really gets their choices."

Eleanor perked up. "You'd want me to write about *myself*?"

"Well, yourself, your family, your memories of college, and maybe what it was like to send your daughter to college, to have a careerist daughter. Anything you want, but something that reflects the changes of the last thirty years. I'd be your editor, and we can talk it through as it takes shape. It's personal and creative. We can throw in some statistics at the end if we need to buff it up. And the pay isn't shabby. Look, your kids are grown and out of the house. This could be a nice way to fill some time. And who knows what it could lead to."

"Pay? You mean a salary?"

"We buy the article, a onetime product. At one dollar a word. And we're aiming for at least a thousand words, maybe two, so that's not shabby. And you'd see your byline in print."

"I have to discuss this with my husband."

Colleen let out a small laugh. "Naturally."

Eleanor took a long sip of ice water. Never in all her life had she seen a paycheck with her name on it. And she hadn't seen her name in print since those student-newspaper articles, but, oh, how she had enjoyed carrying her little reporter's notebook! She had a sudden vision of the women in her gardening club, especially Emily Sanders, who went on about her reproductive-rights committee, waving the magazine: "Eleanor's written an article!"

With the last piece of bread she sopped up the remains of her soup. On Colleen's plate lay the forked-over remains of her sea bass and a baked potato. Such waste.

Eleanor imagined hosting a cocktail party, perching on the sofa, and recounting the story of this very moment with Colleen. She'd mention the sea bass because her friends—especially Ruth—would find that a stunning detail. *Well, I really had no idea what she was going to ask me. I thought she was just feeling nostalgic. I thought the poor thing was going through a divorce!* She'd leave copies of the magazine around the house, on her bookcase, just as Ginny did with her poems and articles.

"Of course, I'll have to look at my calendar and see when I might carve out the time. March and April tend to be very busy with my gardening club, but I'll certainly consider it and ring you back soon."

"If you could let me know by the end of next week."

Jose set down the check and Eleanor glanced at the total; those martinis had sent the bill well over seventy dollars. With dismay, and a deep sense of injustice, she lifted her purse.

"Silly, Ellie. This is on my club tab. And Condé Nast will pick it up."

Eleanor wondered how Colleen's company felt about her fancy martinis, and thought: If I were the boss, I'd run a much tighter ship. Then she felt ridiculous. She'd gone from housewife to the boss of Condé Nast in under an hour!

Colleen rushed off to another meeting, and Eleanor stepped into the bustling, sunny street. She smiled at a young woman who looked like Ginny.

In Bryant Park, she sat and fumbled in her purse for something to write on. Ginny always scribbled her ideas in little notebooks. All Eleanor had were a few back pages in her daily planner, mostly filled with the medallion numbers of taxicabs, in case anything should happen to her.

On the one blank page left, she wrote:

Wellesley 1970
Thirty years
Find thesis statement
Make an outline

"Ginny!" she said into her cell phone. "I'm in the city! Remember I told you I was having lunch with an old college classmate? Well, we just wrapped up at the Century Club, and I thought I'd see if you wanted to have tea. I could come by. It won't take me long to get there."

"Mom, I'm in my campus office."

"Well, I could come by there. We wouldn't have to meet for very long!"

"You don't have to shout into the cell phone."

"It's just all very exciting, Ginny."

"Mom, I can't just pop out and meet people in the middle of the day. I have a *job*. I'd love to see you, but just not now. Can we schedule something for when I'm not working?"

"Yes, dear. Of course. We'll look at our calendars later."

Eleanor sat on the bench and once again examined her notes. She added: *Busy and important daughter*. And stared at the words.

Sadness often took hold of Eleanor when she looked at the grown-up Ginny. All the magical moments they had shared were lost in the sea of Ginny's childhood memories, floating between the flotsam of bad playdates and difficult math exams.

Eleanor looked at all the people in the park; student types reading novels, tourists taking photos. She took a deep breath and decided not to sully her spirits. What a day it had been!

She wasn't going to begrudge Ginny her schedule. What child should put aside goals on a mother's account?

She thought about having a one-thousand-dollar paycheck. What would she do with such money? She would buy Gavin something for his telescope. She'd never bought her husband a gift that she hadn't paid for with his money.

The thought made her so happy she treated herself to an ice-cream cone, two scoops with sprinkles, and bought a postcard of Bryant Park so she would remember the day.

She addressed it to herself: *Dear Eleanor, Congratulations on this great opportunity!* She slipped it into her purse and made her way to Grand Central Station.

DENISE

*I*n the beginning, she and Douglas wanted simple things: children, a comfortable house, maybe a lawn large enough to host parties. Perhaps they imagined someday sitting on deck chairs at a yacht club.

Neither of them was intellectual. Denise wasn't going to write a book on American policy in Latin America. Douglas wasn't going to cure cancer. They had no delusions of grandeur, nor did they waste their twenties living on frozen burritos while trying to break into theater or alternative music. As Denise saw it, artists and intellectuals were always demanding respect because they didn't make money. It made them feel superior.

Denise couldn't stand people who felt superior.

And poverty did not impress her.

She had grown up in a family of coupon clippers, in a house where they turned off the heat at night, where one winter, they lined their coats with blanket scraps. Her father, a welder, had been out of work since U.S. Steel closed, but he knew everything about metal, what was valuable. Car batteries. Copper tubing. Bed springs. He once instructed Denise and her brothers to carry a steel post fifteen blocks to collect thirty-five dollars. Her mother ran a beauty shop during the day and worked nights as a nurse; the few hours she was home, she was usually shouting. The family never went hungry, but they never stopped worrying about money.

In high school, Denise worked two jobs: salesgirl at a jewelry store and waitress at Red Lobster. She envied the customers in the jewelry store, and hated the restaurant customers, penny-pinchers who complained there wasn't enough lobster in their eight-dollar seafood pasta, people she feared becoming. She made good grades and played softball and eventually went to Penn State. She held down another two jobs in college and worked for years in New York City until she married Douglas. She'd dated plenty, and there had been what she considered an adventurous yet respectable number of one-night stands, but Douglas was the only man she'd ever considered marrying.

Douglas worked in consulting but had a hobbyist's fascination with real estate. He loved to wander into apartments for sale to see what four hundred thousand or a million dollars could buy. On Sundays at brunch, he'd scour open house listings, and then he and Denise would mosey from showing to showing, inventing stories for the realtors about their impending elopement, Denise's large inheritance, or how Douglas had just been offered a job with AOL.

Denise, who sometimes suffered an uncharacteristic timidity entering these places, admired Douglas's fearlessness. No space was too grand, too imposing, for him. He flung open closet doors, twisted on brass bath faucets. He looked at sweeping views of Central Park, shrugged, and said, "Too bad you have to look at the zoo."

Sunday nights, over tapas and sangria, they ranked the apartments on their cocktail napkins, Douglas's rule being that rank couldn't correlate to price. Amenities had to be valued: doorman service, outdoor space, proximity to Central Park. Wallpaper versus paint. Co-op versus condo. Back at Douglas's small studio apartment, Denise would lie in the dark, envisioning the people who lived in all those lofts and penthouses, wondering if they understood their enormous luck.

And then, in 1998, she and Douglas married, had the twins, and moved to Stamford, where suddenly *they* were living in a house with gleaming parquet floors, a kitchen skylight, walk-in closets. Douglas called the house a financial "stretch"—he'd sold off some Internet stocks for the down payment and worked long hours in New York to cover the mortgage—but Denise loved the house, and there was enough money left over to hire a sitter a few nights a week and eat out. She hired a personal trainer. The boys took music appreciation classes.

For the first time in her life, Denise could stop juggling jobs. Good-bye, fluorescent lights. Farewell, political-correctness seminars. Gone were the pantsuits, the brainstorming sessions with dry-erase boards, the unsolicited midday neck massages from Don Romano, marketing VP. She was delighted that she might go to her grave without fixing another paper jam. She could not, for the life of her, understand women who worried about quitting their jobs to raise children. Were they retiring from NASA? Were they throwing in the towel midway through mapping the human genome? Denise's mother had worked two jobs every day of her life; there was no glory in it. Anyone who thought work was a way to create meaning in life had never been poor.

A distinct misery had hovered over her childhood home. In each room, the strain of their lives could be seen in the frayed and splintered furniture, in the worried look on her mother's face as she set dinner on the table and mentally calculated how much money was about to be devoured. In her father's eyes lurked a constant shame that manifested, at times—if his hamburger was overcooked, if he suspected Denise had spent her paycheck on clothes—as rage.

Douglas, on the other hand, never lost his temper; he rarely complained. He dressed as Santa Claus for Christmas, and when he came home from work, he set down his briefcase, got on all fours, and gave the twins pony rides around the living room. In the first years of their marriage, Denise, who had long used activity as a way to escape discontent, experienced an almost tearful joy in the simple act of being at home.

So when Douglas started talking about flipping their house, claiming that a few modest renovations could turn a 30 to 40 percent profit within a year, Denise was inspired. They put granite countertops in the kitchen, winterized the back patio. They built a sunporch and repointed the brick exterior. Denise didn't ask where the cash for the renovations came from. She'd been under the impression that Douglas, like everybody, was "dabbling" in stocks. At dinner parties, people swapped ticker symbols like recipes. And late at night, he'd disappear into his den and click away at his keyboard. When he climbed into bed, he'd curl up close, stroke her thigh, and whisper, "Baby, I made us a grand today."

Douglas had always given her the feeling of great confidence, and he was not a stupid or reckless man. But a bubble was a bubble. A marketwide implosion was hard to escape from unscathed, if you were in deep.

Douglas had them in ass deep.

Apparently, in order to renovate the house, he'd invested most of their savings in dot-com start-ups: online shoe stores, messaging boards, Brazilian pharmaceuticals. If it was a long shot, he bought. All day long, he'd been checking ticker prices from his computer at the office, dumping one stock, buying another.

He'd practically wiped out the joint account with the money Denise had put away since her waitressing days, and everything they'd saved for the children.

Denise felt sick.

"Everybody got burned," Douglas said one morning as he stared disbelievingly at the financial pages. "I mean, I fucked up. But major financial geniuses. Top players at hedge funds, hon. Everyone was in tech stocks. It wasn't just me."

Denise, clearing his plate, had to stop herself from throwing it across the room. She didn't know at the time that this was just the beginning of their seven-year financial roller coaster.

"Douglas, touch a cent of our money again without consulting me and I'll file for divorce."

There was no getting back what he'd lost. Because of Denise's catering experience, her friend Sally got her a job as nutrition coun-selor for one of the public high schools, replacing a woman who wasn't returning from her maternity leave.

"You don't have to go back to work," said Douglas.

They both knew this was a lie.

Denise started at the end of the spring semester, telling friends that she needed to get out of the house. "I'm bored with baby talk."

In the afternoons Denise left the twins at day care and drove to the gray rectangular slab of Jefferson High. The first few months were dreary; she loved her *own* children, but toward kids in general Denise was indifferent. And these high schoolers didn't even seem like children. All those trashy clothes and foul mouths, the braces and pimples and bored-faced bovine chewing of gum as she tried to explain the food pyramid. The cafeterias reeked of grilled cheese and French fries. The bathrooms smelled of perfume and straw-berry lip gloss and were covered with graffiti detailing which of those lanky, pimply pubescent boys had big cocks. The girls showed so much cleavage even Denise couldn't help staring. The halls were painted pale green and pale blue, asylum colors—not inappropri-ate. Maps and time lines hung in every room, a daily reminder that though she was a college graduate, she couldn't name half the coun-tries in South America. She thought she'd go crazy. Surely there was some other job she could get, a job with more adults and fewer pierced tongues.

But if anyone asked her at dinner or a cocktail party, she professed commitment to public schools and the community. Turning kids around. Combating childhood diabetes.

"Denise, you've gone all *Stand and Deliver!*"

When really she dreamt of torching the place.

Then for the 2001 summer session, a new history teacher arrived. Masood Salam just graduated from Brown and came from a wealthy Jordanian family. God only knew what he was doing teaching at a Stamford public school—a liberal streak, she figured—but he was handsome, dressed fashionably for a teacher, and all the teenage girls had a crush on him.

Within weeks, a bathroom stall read: "Please, Mr. Salam, go down on me."

It was a difficult year for her, losing her savings. Their house, with all its renovations, still had not sold. Denise didn't carry herself like the most happily married woman. When she said "husband" she rolled her eyes. She flirted, even with the high school boys. The truth was, she hadn't worked in two years, hadn't been out of the house, around men, and had forgotten the pleasures of the adult world.

Masood would sit at the luncheon table, where the daily ritual was a competition among the teachers for who had suffered the most outlandishly difficult question in class, and for who had produced the most plausible incorrect answer.

Jorge Velasquez asked me why the Dead Sea was called the Dead Sea.

Derek Freese asked why slaves didn't all just head south to Mexico.

Warren Keating, English teacher of thirty-five years, explained: "Admit ignorance and you lose them altogether. I figure about ten to fifteen percent of the answers we give are jibberish, but that's an acceptable margin of error. These kids need to believe there are people who know."

Denise agreed. As the mother of two children, she understood well the parental obligation, the time-tested maternal mandate, to occasionally make shit up.

Tereza Huzka, the Polish chemistry teacher, had her own solution. "I do not allow questions."

"Google is *killing* us," sighed Angela Nova, who had been outed by a web-savvy student after saying Alaska and Hawaii were the fifty-first and fifty-second states. "I'm an English teacher! I don't teach geography!"

But when Masood arrived, he threw them all for a loop, because he *could* answer every question.

"Of course it was the ancient Greeks who first used bedsprings," he said, cutting into his chicken cutlet. "They fashioned them out of braided leather thongs and hung them between opposite sides of the bed."

Denise thought the school board had sent a mole! Masood wasn't high-school-teacher-smart, he was smart-smart. She'd been told that every few years an Ivy League graduate would arrive, try to teach *War and Peace,* and eventually become depressed by the over-crowded classrooms, the poor lighting, the vague smell of asbes-tos. At the first sight of a switchblade, the new teacher zipped off to law school. But Masood was unflustered by the chaos of the school, and lacked pretension or ambition. While the other teachers forked their salads and sipped their Snapples, Masood like to read aloud the celebrity sightings from Page Six of the *New York Post*. Once, he slid the paper over to Denise and pointed to a picture of Cameron Diaz in a string bikini.

"You could pull off a swimsuit like that," he said.

Since getting married, Denise had become accustomed to what she thought of as window-shopping adultery. As she stood around dreary parties when Douglas went on too loudly with a story she'd heard before or launched into one of his hypothetical situations, her eyes would rove the room, landing on a single tennis pro eating a celery stick or a vascular surgeon checking his pager. She would think: What would *that* be like? And in a flash, the arbitrariness of her life became clear; if she'd sent her assistant to the catering gig where she'd met Douglas, she might be standing at another party with another husband. This thought could, for an hour or so, unhinge Denise's sense of obligation, and even love. But by the time she and Douglas were back home brushing their teeth, critiquing the party's hors d'oeuvres, and by the time she kissed her children good night, the deep comfort of routine took hold. She was happy to curl up beside the man who was, even if by chance, her spouse.

But when Masood caught her smoking in the Minimart park-ing lot and waved his forefinger in a shame-on-you gesture from his car, Denise felt an unprecedented curiosity, one that did not fade by nightfall.

Soon after, he approached her in the teachers' lounge, holding out a pack of Dunhills. "Shall we?"

They smoked behind a dumpster while class was in session—they agreed that the nutrition counselor lighting up would send a bad message. If it rained, they smoked in his car while a strange, mournful Middle Eastern music played from his tape deck. They agreed that mad cow disease was being blown way out of proportion, that the euro would make life easier on tourists; they gossiped about other teachers, wondering whether the track coach and school nurse had something going on, joking about where they might be frolicking; they fell silent as the words *grope* and *quickie* filled the car.

Suddenly Denise's long, dull days were filled with expected and unexpected encounters with Masood. She could breeze through tedious inventory forms knowing she'd see him at lunch and on his break between seventh and eighth periods and at the day's end before he left to coach soccer. Any day he called in sick, the clock hands moved in gel. She wasn't certain if she felt happy or unhappy; she knew only that she felt deeply alive. Longing electrified her. In brief fits of despair, she would suck down a Twinkie in the stairwell, thinking: *This is sugar. This is your brain on sugar.*

By the time she drove home, groggy from her postsugar rush, she was not particularly thrilled to see her husband.

Douglas hadn't taken the financial fiasco well. He didn't dare complain to her, and she knew he wanted her to believe he'd get them out of the jam.

At night he always had a copy of *Forbes* or *Fortune* in his lap. He thumbed through the biographies of Warren Buffet and George Soros. She'd long been aware of the male obsession with the biographies of great men, with trivia about Einstein's napping habits or Lincoln's favorite breakfast foods. On any given morning, the Metro-North trains were filled with pale, tired men in gray suits devouring the lives of presidents and generals. Or athletes. Men who had never swung a bat or thrown a football could wax eloquent about the seasonal stats of Derek Jeter. Men didn't have heroes, they *studied* heroes, as though greatness and masculinity could be transmitted through reading, as though knowing the lyrics to every Mick Jagger song or the names of the E Street Band members got them one step closer to playing Madison Square Garden. A woman, at most, would dress like a woman she admired, maybe slip on some Jackie O. sunglasses, a Princess Di pantsuit, but no woman ever rattled off the title of every Bette Davis film and thought that it made her a femme fatale.

As Douglas devoured countless biographical anecdotes of adversity, Denise wanted to ask: who writes the biographies of men who failed and just kept failing?

Douglas was convinced there was a way for him to ride the recovering economy and make it up to her. Waking up, she'd see him flipping through pamphlets on Chilean copper mines and Dutch wind-power stations; he lifted a small voice recorder to his mouth:

Commodities, Doug, especially soybeans.

Look into foreign currency.

Doug, what can you dig up on Chinese petroleum?

Sure, people talked to themselves, but did they generally use their own names? It sounded like he'd split into two people, and one was a motivational speaker.

And the microrecorder was only one of a host of new gadgets Douglas assembled in service of his financial resurrection. His desk overflowed with MP3 and portable DVD players, a scanner pen, a TiVo machine. If it used batteries and had buttons, he had to have it. Denise came home practically every day to a box from RadioShack or Best Buy on the front stoop.

"What the hell is *this*? Enough! We can't afford all this."

"It's a global positioning system. So you know where you are."

"We're in debt, Doug. That's where we are. Serious fucking debt."

"Denise, I know you're upset," he said. "And you have every right to be. But please understand that I'm trying to see, hands-on, what's going to be the trend of the next ten years. Just a handful of companies are selling these GPSs right now, and it could be a good investment. That digital music player in my office? Soros bought a seven-percent stake in Nomad."

"You are not George Soros."

The daily ritual of returning home to their FOR SALE sign, and to a mailbox stuffed with bills and mortgage statements, began to fill her with dread. She stayed late at work, lingering around the school's abandoned corridors. One night as she wandered out into the dark parking lot, Masood was smoking by his car, sipping a cup of Dunkin' Donuts coffee.

"Come," he said.

They drove about a mile away from the school, to a small parking lot near the old Yale & Towne Manufacturing plant on Canal Street, where weeds and grass fissured what was left of the brick.

He let the engine idle and turned on the radio.

It was late August, but unseasonably cold. Denise was wearing wool slacks and a button-down shirt under a V-neck sweater. It seemed to take forever to elbow her sweater over her head, a move that yanked off one of her earrings and lit up her hair into a halo of static. The charged strands clung to her eyes, through which she saw Masood, shirtless, watching her. He reached to unbutton her shirt and she noticed his musky smell, so different from Douglas. His chest hair was thicker. His arms were hard and muscular and seemed to flash all sorts of veins and tendons as he slowly undid the pearly white buttons of her shirt. He kissed her, his tongue tangy with coffee, his lips working aggressively over hers, lips much fuller than Douglas's.

Good God, was she going to think of *Douglas* the whole time?

She fumbled with her belt. She undid the button at her waist, which seemed to release the slight layer of stomach flab she'd recently developed. Between her stairwell Twinkies and the long days at her desk, no amount of secret squats and buttock squeezes in the staff elevator had stopped the extra pounds. Denise had always taken pride in her figure, and while Douglas, who'd plumped up a bit himself, generously overlooked this corporal addition, she feared it would no doubt disappoint this younger, buffer man who was breathing fiercely as he unclasped what she now realized was one of her ratty beige bras.

What underwear did she even have on?

Suddenly, she couldn't bear to see the look on Masood's face. What if it was disappointment? She'd only feel *less* attractive, which defeated the whole point of this tawdry escapade.

She sucked in her stomach to refasten her pants' button. "I'm a married woman, Masood."

"Please," he said, pressing his warm lips to her neck.

"The cops will come."

"No one is here."

"We'll get arrested for indecent exposure."

"We are alone, Denise."

She fastened her belt buckle and covered it with her hands, as if it might come undone of its own free will. "I have a husband."

"Yes, I have seen your husband."

She stumbled out of the car, looking around at the decaying red brick of the abandoned building. She lit a cigarette, with the full *almostness* of the moment congealing around her. It was seven o'clock, her bra was unhooked, her gold earring somewhere in the filthy carpeting of this man's Mazda Miata, and she was smoking by an decrepit factory.

"What the hell did you mean, you've seen my husband?"

"Denise, you are being childish. Get back in the car."

"Oh, I'll get in, I'll get in so you can drive me back. And for God sakes, please don't roll through the stop signs this time, and try using a turn signal. You shouldn't even have a driver's license!"

At home, Denise tried to still her anger and confusion by preparing an elaborate meal: halibut with sun-dried tomatoes and shiitake mushrooms. She tossed a beet, walnut, and goat cheese salad with cider vinaigrette. She baked an apple pie.

Douglas came in, set his briefcase down, and said, "Oooh, fancy!"

Without pausing from her work, she said, "Doug, I didn't sign on to this marriage to slave away for the goddamned school board. You need to fix this."

DOUGLAS

*E*minent domain. Two words changed his life.

Douglas's father had wanted him to learn a skill. He said a man should be able to make things with his hands. So one summer, Douglas laid foundations and set wall posts and hammered rafters around Fairfield County for J&J Construction, coming home with sawdust on his face, dirty hands, dramatically swinging his utility belt onto the dinner table, hoping for some small word of approval from his father.

When the construction crew wasn't discussing the *Sports Illustrated* swimsuit issue, or which cars had the fastest pickup, they'd talk about F. D. Rich. Anyone who ever lifted a hammer in the state of Connecticut had heard of F. D. Rich.

Rich was a turn-of-the-century Italian immigrant who'd worked in the sandstone quarries of Pennsylvania before setting up shop as a stonemason in Stamford, Connecticut. He built fireplaces, walls, foundations. But after World War I, he set his sights higher. Within decades, the F. D. Rich Company of general contracting had built hotels, libraries, schools, and hospitals across the country.

The company motto was "From Alaska to the Caribbean."

Douglas's ragtag crew had its own motto: "From the front door to the shit can."

In 1960, the Rich Company seized on a major local opportunity. Since Yale & Towne Manufacturing had left Stamford, the city had been crippled by unemployment, poverty, and crime. Collapsing houses and abandoned storefronts were everywhere. The F. D. Rich Company became the city's sole redeveloper, and with federal subsidies it razed more than one hundred acres of downtown slums, then built office towers, shopping malls, and high-rise apartments. Within a decade a dying post-Industrial town had become a midsize metropolis, a city that would eventually lure UBS International from Manhattan, Xerox, GE Capital, and Pitney Bowes.

Signs read: THE CITY THAT WORKS.

Stamford eventually boasted one of the country's highest educated populations: nine out of ten residents were high school graduates, half held bachelor's degrees. It also ranked as one of the safest cities in the country.

So in 2003, after Douglas had managed to flip his second house, when commercial real estate started picking up steam, he recalled F. D. Rich and began thinking about commercial real estate in Stamford. Douglas wasn't going anywhere at Ardor and he disliked commuting. He'd watched his father get stuck at the same company his whole life, spending most of his evenings on a train. Laura had just turned one, the twins five; Douglas wanted to be home for dinner with his children. And after his tech-bubble losses, he wanted his money in old-fashioned brick and mortar.

Douglas phoned his old boss at J&J, who facilitated some introductions. Soon Douglas joined Obervell Construction, a small outfit bidding on downtown Stamford revitalization projects. A lot of people were sniffing around the city then to see what the Rich Company had left undone, what viable lots were left for the taking. The city was offering big loans to anyone with a feasible proposal. Miranda Construction had won a bid on the Canal Street lot for new residential condos. Sanders & Son snatched up the last chunks of Pacific Street for an arts center. Three other developers had their eyes on the waterfront, where the old piano and bicycle factories stood empty.

Douglas wanted in on the action, wanted to carve out a place for himself at Obervell. He remembered the South End from when he was a kid. It was part of town where you'd drive ten minutes out of your way to make sure you didn't ride down the wrong street. But in 1996, the city had razed Southfield Village, the worst of the housing projects, and the neighborhood had been improving. Douglas figured they could assemble a full-block lot there for a bargain, and that its proximity to the interstate and the train station would make it attractive to corporate tenants. He wanted to build an office tower.

Douglas studied the map, driving up and down every street in the South End, an area where mostly blacks and some Latinos lived. The streets were spotted with delis and barbershops and shoe repair stores. A few low-rise condos had been put up since Southfield Village came down. Douglas wanted to find old places that might sell on the cheap. Finally, he homed in on Freedom Avenue. On the block between Hancock Street and Wilson Street stood a Dairy Queen, a U-Haul franchise, a liquor store, a parking lot, and ten row houses from the 1930s.

He brought the idea to Dean Obervell, who gave him the green light. Douglas contracted with a local architect and they wrote up the proposal for an $80 million forty-story office tower with ground-floor retail space. The city redevelopment commission agreed to loan half the capital, offering an additional two-year tax abatement. An urban revitalization grant for one million dollars was issued by the state.

The project proceeded magically. Within weeks, Douglas raised another $30 million—hedge funds were throwing money into real estate; Cooper Realty Loans handed them $10 million. A feverish excitement surrounded the tower; unsolicited investors were calling to get in on the action. Douglas's Obervell colleagues, awed by how swiftly the capital was raised, wanted in. After all those years reading about visionary investors and fearless businessmen, Douglas, too, recognized the chance.

He understood that he had made mistakes before, but those had been with stocks, inherently risky. The tower was a physical asset.

And as soon as the land parcels were combined, the real estate alone would triple in value, not to mention the eventual revenue from the tower. He would never have another opportunity like this, to get in at the start. Douglas took out a second mortgage and pitched in $2 million.

Obervell bought the U-Haul and Dairy Queen quickly. Then the parking lot and liquor store. Six of the row house owners handed over their deeds the same day. But four families held out—parcels 3, 5, 6, and 9a—which Douglas had expected. Surely some of the homeowners would think to angle for a better deal, so Obervell offered another ten thousand dollars.

They said no.

Douglas returned a week later and threw another five thousand into the deal.

At which point one of the homeowners smiled. "That's extremely generous," she said, and handed him an envelope. Douglas, assuming it was a deed, opened it with great excitement.

> Dear Mr. Olson,
>
> It is not a question of money for our homes. We have all lived here many years and our children have grown up in these houses and we are intending for them to have these houses themselves one day. Thank you for your offer.
> Sincerely,
> The families of Freedom Avenue

Douglas panicked. He couldn't build a tower with four houses still standing there. He couldn't get the money back for the land parcels he'd already bought. And he couldn't walk away from the project. This was his big break. Obervell wanted the tower, the city needed the tower. It would provide jobs, tax revenue.

After a few days at his computer, a pot of coffee burning beside him, Douglas dug up a ruling from 1954, *Berman v. Parker,* in which the U.S. Supreme Court ruled that the District of Columbia could lower the wrecking ball on a department store that happened to be sitting smack in the middle of a seventy-six-acre slum that developers wanted to refashion.

Even if a building wasn't a threat to public safety or health, the court said, it could be "an ugly eyesore, a blight on the community, which robs it of charm, which makes it a place from which men turn."

God, those row houses were charmless!

Douglas took Harold Whitehead of the Urban Redevelopment Commission to lunch at the top of the Hilton Stamford, a restaurant that spun slowly so patrons could view the entire city. Douglas spoke passionately about Stamford's rebirth, how it had been pulled from the post-Industrial rubble to become a thriving metropolis. Forty years earlier, he said, Frank Rich razed acres of cheap housing to save Stamford from becoming a slum. Progress took vision, and Obervell was offering to sweep up, pro bono, one of the last messy corners of downtown. Then Douglas pulled out photographs of the Freedom Avenue houses. "This is the Stamford of another era," Douglas said. "And as far as eyesores go, we're talking glaucoma."

He sent the commission cases of scotch, and got Glenn Mirsky to make off-the-record promises about 50 percent discounts on the residential condos Obervell was going to be building on the waterfront.

It would take some paperwork, some time, but the commission said it could condemn the properties and buy them on behalf of Obervell.

But before that could happen, a New York civil-liberties lawyer got wind of the project and warned the homeowners that if the city could prove "blight," their homes might be torn down. One Saturday morning, the lawyer drove up to Freedom Avenue with a truck full of paint, linen curtains, brooms, mops, cans of Raid, a lawn mower. Douglas watched in horror from his car as teenagers, old women, and the lawyer began painting and mowing lawns, pulling up weeds. They planted red begonias.

Douglas thought, *Oh shit*.

Suddenly everybody in the Obervell office was flipping open dictionaries to figure out the definition of *blight*. They called their lawyers. What did *blight* actually mean? Did they have to *prove* blight? Could the homeowners *unblight* these places long enough to shut down the project? Dean Obervell, who was losing sleep and a good amount of hair, suggested they drive by in the middle of the night and hose the places with dirt.

"Or maybe gasoline and a lit match," he said. "I'm not fucking joking."

Douglas visited the homeowners once again and tried to explain about eminent domain, making it clear that if the courts got involved, Obervell would have to pay only market value for the homes: fifty thousand dollars, far less than their original offer. Douglas slapped his checkbook in his palm and offered two hundred and fifty thousand dollars. Parcels 3, 6, and 9a handed over their titles.

The owner of parcel 5, an old woman, refused.

"Look, the law is on my side," Douglas said. "You have to understand eminent domain."

"I understand plenty, Your Eminence," she said, and closed her door.

Fred Bradley at the city council made a call, and garbage trucks stopped picking up on Freedom and Hancock. In a panic one night on his way home from the office, Douglas jumped out of his car and from a pay phone reported a rat infestation. The police made two arrests for open containers and one for drunk and disorderly, and designated the area a high-crime zone.

Finally, the city issued the condemnation notice and filed suit against the remaining homeowner to acquire title by court order. In response, the civil-liberties lawyer filed an injunction for misuse and abuse of the Fifth Amendment. Declaring a "necessity challenge," she said she saw no *need* for the city to redevelop the property.

Douglas was staring down another six months in court, his hands tied on breaking ground, $40 million in investor capital doing zilch. If things didn't start moving, the hedge funds might pull out. Obervell might default on their loans. It suddenly looked like the whole project might go kaput.

But in March 2004, luck hit Douglas like a brick. New London had been knee deep in a similar swamp for five years with waterfront homeowners, led by a woman named Susette Kelo, refusing to budge for Pfizer's proposed $300 million research center. And those weren't even slums. They were middle-class homes sitting on some of the most valuable urban property in northeastern Connecticut. The court ruled that New London had the right to take unblighted property for the purposes of "economic development."

Exactly, thought Douglas.

New London needed Pfizer. When the Naval Undersea Warfare Center had closed in 1996, fifteen hundred people lost their jobs. For a city to survive, somebody needed to build.

He thought about Bridgeport and Hartford. Look what happened when a city lost its industry.

With the March decision, the city of Stamford decided to press forward.

But by summer, Douglas had gotten wind of a terrible omen: in a landmark reversal, the Michigan State Supreme Court decided that the Fifth Amendment's takings clause, which allowed the taking of private property for public use, did not include taking private property for private development, even if the development "contributed to the health of the general economy." The court declared Detroit's history of invoking eminent domain to raze residential communities for GM factories a whopping mistake.

And then another bad omen: the U.S. Supreme Court agreed to hear the New London homeowners' appeal. Not since *Berman v. Parker,* a half century earlier, had the court been willing to reconsider eminent domain and the Fifth Amendment.

While the New London case was being heard, the Stamford courts didn't move an inch on theirs.

Meanwhile the lots Douglas's company had purchased sat vacant. The Dairy Queen and U-Haul stores were boarded up and overrun with weeds. Miranda and Sanders & Son had already mounted the scaffolding for their glistening condo towers and arts center. Nearly a year had passed since Obervell bought the first properties on Freedom Avenue, and the company still couldn't lift a hammer.

The investors called. *Olson, are we looking at another hole?*

"The hole" was a trash-covered, overgrown lot on Tresser Boulevard that had been abandoned for over twenty years, since the Rich Company lost the site after digging the foundation—a terrifying reminder of how a project could tank.

Obervell held a meeting to discuss the financial advantages of declaring bankruptcy. Denise wanted Douglas to pull his money out of the project.

But finally, a year and a half after Douglas drafted the tower proposal, the U.S. Supreme Court decided in New London's favor. Susette Kelo, the Institute for Justice, and the NAACP all went home with their tails between their legs. And the civil-liberties lawyer going after Stamford backed off.

Douglas, who had never been much of a liberal, thought, God bless John Paul Stevens. God bless liberal meddling and its love affair with big government, government that once in a while needed to flex enough muscle to defend economic development.

In the boardroom where for months he had worked until all hours of the morning to keep the project alive, Douglas read aloud Sandra Day O'Connor's dissent. The entire office gathered; Brinkman and Formanek popped open beers. Douglas touched his heart and put on his best old-lady voice: "'The specter of condemnation hangs over all property. Nothing is to prevent the State from replacing any Motel Six with a Ritz-Carlton, any home with a shopping mall, or any farm with a factory. . . .'"

"Exactly! Down with Motel Six! Vive le Ritz-Carlton!"

The project moved quickly after that: demolition permits, asbestos and rodent abatement, utility disconnection.

The day of the demolition, Douglas went to watch the wrecking ball and the hydraulic excavators. Until the last hour, when the police cordoned off the area and handed out hard hats, the final holdout sat on her stoop. Beside her stood a hulking young man, her grandson, glaring at the machinery. The woman jabbed her cane toward a sign:

JUST?

COMPENSATION?

After the city took her title, she had asked for Obervell's original offer. But having lost millions in the almost two-year delay, Obervell paid only the city's appraisal price: $40,000, less than the appraisal when the battle began because the surrounding vacated houses had devalued her plot.

Finally her grandson led her from her house, and the wrecking ball fell.

A newspaper photographer shot Douglas watching the demolition, grinning proudly beneath his hard hat. The photo appeared the next day with the caption: "Project Manager Douglas Olson looks on, after the long fight to demolish the final home."

The excavators dug up the foundations, the fire department hosed down the dust. The arrowheads and clay pots unearthed by the construction crew were sent to the state archaeology department—except for one item, which Douglas, who stayed at the site until dusk, could not believe he glimpsed in the rubble: a polished stone knife, obsidian or granite, carved with small images of deer and antelope. He wrapped it in tissue paper and tied it with a ribbon for his sons, who loved playing Cowboys and Indians.

Once construction on the tower got under way, the Obervell firm never again spoke of the homeowners. As far as Douglas was concerned, they were long gone, on their way to Norwalk or Larchmont or Stamford's West End.

But the civil-liberties lawyer had managed to squeeze one caveat out of the city. Since the uprooted families were all black, the city had to guarantee the children would be bused to public school in their original district if the families so chose.

At the time, the provision seemed meaningless to Douglas.

DENISE

*E*ven if something had happened with Masood, Denise hadn't been imagining an actual affair. Between Douglas and the twins, where was the time? Affairs were for the rich and unemployed. Any woman who had to get groceries and throw a lasagna into the oven after a day at work wasn't going to be lazing around a motel running ice cubes over the history teacher.

Still, she thought about what it would be like to have sex with him. Or what it would be like to be the kind of woman to do that. Denise had always assumed she could be if she wanted to—she was no prude. So she was miffed with herself for what seemed to be, when she thought back on that night in his car, her flat-out fear.

After all, people had slipups, indulgences, and then went on with their cheery suburban lives. Maybe some people could power down the brain's marital lobe, force their neurons to whiz right past the region of spousal sentiment, so they could fondle a new man and not think, *Oh, but he's nothing like my husband!* Maybe they even trained ahead of time, a regimen of sit-ups and leg lifts and lunges, and bought special lace-trimmed adultery panties.

These things took time and planning. She couldn't afford either.

In the cafeteria, as the fall session began, Denise made a point of sitting apart from Masood and staring into her couscous. She left a good five feet between them if they passed each other in the hall, admiring, as though they were museum paintings, the Jay-Z and Snoop Dogg posters plastering the locker doors.

Soon she was grateful she hadn't risked her marriage for a night of tangled sex in a trash-strewn car. After months on the market, their house sold at a shocking profit. "I told you I'd make it up to you," Douglas said. His confidence returned, and with it came flowers and airline tickets to Mexico. Denise felt their life stabilizing, and thought she might even be able to quit her job. They looked for a new house.

One night, well past dinnertime, the phone rang at the house and when she picked up, the line was silent. "Hello? Hello?"

When it rang again ten minutes later, she carried the phone into the bathroom, closing the door.

"Masood?"

Again, the line went dead. Douglas saw her emerge, phone in hand, but said nothing.

The next two days, Masood was not in school, but she feared asking about his whereabouts would draw suspicion.

The third day, early in the morning, after Douglas had taken the train into Manhattan and she was getting the kids ready for day care, the phone rang.

"Turn on the TV right now." It was Douglas, calling from work. "And don't let the kids see."

Over and over again she watched the footage of the airplane hitting the second tower, the buildings crumbling, dazed survivors and sobbing rescue workers wandering the wreckage. She smoked half a pack of cigarettes and drank a glass of bourbon before she pulled herself together enough to call the few people she knew who lived or worked in the city.

By the time Douglas came home that night, his suit thick with dust, she was on her third bourbon.

"Jesus, are you okay?" She licked her thumb and wiped dirt from his cheek. "I couldn't reach you on your cell."

"All the signals froze," he said softly. He looked around the kitchen, somewhat bewildered. "I couldn't reach Ginny so I walked all the way up to her apartment." He almost seemed to be whispering. "You could see all the smoke from there."

"She's okay?"

"She was home when it happened. How are the boys?"

"Sleeping. Oblivious."

He stared hard at her, and then said, "Come here." He enclosed her in his arms, lay his head on her shoulder, and they stood silently like that, in the brightness of the kitchen, for what seemed several minutes. Finally, he began unloading his pockets—keys, coins, Rolaids, phone—and walked in slow circles. "What a mess of logistics everything was." His voice was suddenly louder, gaining in volume with each word. "Cell signals tied up, no trains or buses. We need to be proactive."

He took out a map and designated the north side of the Triboro Bridge as an emergency meeting spot, in case phone lines went dead. He pulled an old duffel bag from the hallway closet and shoved in a first-aid kit, flashlights, batteries, water bottles, umbrellas, Power-Bars.

"Can you get to the mall in the next week and buy gas masks?" He fastened a wad of cash with a rubber band and stuck it into a ziplock bag. "Throw some clothes in there. And we should stock up on canned goods. Soups and stuff like that. I have my old camping stove in the attic. I'll pick up some propane."

In bed that night, Doug fell asleep quickly, exhausted, but Denise lay awake.

Somewhere around her second bourbon she had wondered what Masood was making of all this.

When she finally returned to school a few days later, Carmen Velasquez, the principal's assistant, was holding court by the water-cooler. Nobody ever listened to Carmen, yet she was now sitting on the scoop of her lifetime.

"I mean gone, poof! Just like that!"

After Masood's two days out sick—he had phoned in complaining of the flu—he had not returned to school. In fact, he had not returned to his apartment. All his belongings had been left there, a half-buttered piece of toast on the table, the coffeemaker full, the radio playing. The landlord had called the school.

Colleagues stood around conjecturing that he'd been rounded up in one of the arrest blitzes, whisked off for months of interrogation and sleep deprivation because he was an Arab. Or he was the leader of a Fairfield County Al-Qaeda cell.

"Maybe he was *studying* the school," Carmen suggested, trying to draw out the drama. "Figuring out ways to hurt the children."

Then everyone, Denise included, had to agree that Masood seemed quite nice and normal.

"Did you hear about that Muslim teacher at Jefferson that vanished?" Douglas asked a few nights later. "There was a piece in the paper. He went to Brown, but his family apparently still lives in Jordan. Either the guy is a psycho Arab criminal, or a total victim."

She considered telling him everything. Confession was in the air then. People wanted to come clean, to repent. "We had lunch a few times," she said.

"And he never said anything like 'I hate this satanic, capitalistic American macaroni and cheese'?"

"I'm glad to hear you joking."

They lay in bed. Douglas touched her cheek, his hand warm and clammy. "You and the kids mean everything to me, you know that? My job, the long hours, the commuting, I know I'm not around as much as you'd like, and I know I've screwed some things up. But I'm doing it for us." In the soft glow of the night, she saw his eyes fill with tears. "This, you, it's my whole world."

For months, at the gym, at cocktail parties, all anyone talked about was 9/11. Denise watched the news, listened to the theories and accusations. But no matter how many warnings she heard, no matter how many red alerts she saw flash across the screen, she never felt as afraid as she was supposed to. She didn't buy gas masks. She didn't put a change of clothes into the emergency duffel. Because when she lay in bed at night, looking back on the past year, she realized the loss of all that money and the prospect of her children growing up poor had terrified her more than the ghastly scenarios described on the news. And Douglas seemed more afraid of screwing up their finances again and of her walking out on him than he was of terrorists. And yet they moved into a larger house, they soon conceived Laura, and for a while they stopped speaking about what really terrified them. They'd found a bogeyman.

It was around that time Douglas bought the gun.

ELEANOR

What a moment of absolute delight, thought Eleanor, when the smell of roasting turkey finally drifted into the living room. The light through the windows had faded to black, the football game had ended, and Douglas and Gavin were arguing about some final throw. Their team had lost and they sat frowning at the blank television screen. Douglas finally slapped his thighs and thumbed a remote control that turned on each lamp. Piece by piece, the room came to life with soft yellow cones of light, revealing the twins, exhausted from shouting at the screen, blinking groggily.

"Anyone for Ping-Pong?" she asked.

Laura climbed down from her chair, grabbed a box from the corner, and splayed herself out on the thick white carpet. She began assembling a gray, plastic castlelike house that looked shockingly like her own.

"Well, what a simply delicious smell," Eleanor said. "Has anyone ever smelled anything so scrumptious? Rosemary and tarragon."

"You know, he could have an injury," said Douglas.

"Who has an injury?" she asked.

"The way Favre was running. Something has to explain it."

"Son, sometimes the underdog takes it," said Gavin, retrieving something from beneath the sectional.

She could see Denise stride from the kitchen to the table suspending the platter above her shoulder like a waitress; Ginny trailed cradling two loaves of French bread.

Eleanor rushed to help.

"We've got it, Eleanor," said Denise. "Just go ahead and grab a seat." Normally, Eleanor sat at the table's head, but since it was not her house, she opted for one of the sides.

The silver pitcher steamed with gravy. A pile of golden corncobs glistened with butter. And yet the excitement that had carried her like a wave all day, the anticipation of this very moment—her entire family sitting down together for a meal—was beginning to falter. The sun had set, and soon (she glanced at her watch; how late!) they would load their cars and go their separate ways, driving off into the darkness. Already, she saw the naked corncobs, the emptied gravy pitcher.

No, no, no.

Twenty-seven days until Christmas. Fourteen days until she bought her tree from Mr. Menand at Pinecrest Farms, before she could rescue from the attic the tissue-wrapped glittery orbs she had collected over the years from shops in Newport and Mystic and Cape Cod. Fourteen days before Gavin strung the beautiful white lights along the front porch, and, if she begged him, the front oak tree. How long before she could wear her snowflake sweater? The children mocked it—*Mom, is that an asterisk?*—but she refused to hide her holiday cheer. Masked men could torture her, they could throw her in prison with flesh-eating rats, never would Eleanor renounce her love for the holidays!

Because tomorrow would begin the slow, dull transition to normal. There might be a phone call to Ginny or Denise: compliments and thank-yous. But by Monday, Gavin would return to his office, Douglas would be too harried to take her calls. The days would get shorter, darker. Ginny would whisk Priya back to Mamaroneck. Eleanor would sit alone in her house, as she now sat alone at the table.

She poured herself some wine.

Get outside! Go do something! her family always told her. How easy they made it sound.

She once loved nothing more than to wander in and out of boutiques, rummaging for a nice hat on sale, or to buy herself a cup of tea and sit and read her *Country Gardens* or *Family Circle*. But now she found it unpleasant to leave the house.

When had it begun, her slow exile?

A few years ago, she noticed that the music everywhere had become unbearably loud. In the malls, the angry thud of electric disco seemed to be telling her to stay away. The shops no longer sold her size, or the clothes were manufactured with so much elastic that only a curveless preteen girl could wear them without spilling out indecently.

Her friend Marybeth noticed the same thing: this menopausal cloak of invisibility. They were a forsaken demographic. Too thrifty in their mind-set to be courted by stores or manufacturers. Eleanor and her friends opted for wardrobe staples, plain gray skirts and ivory blouses, and clung, like the drowning, to the sale racks. They refused to exceed their credit limits.

So during the day, after getting the groceries, they would tuck themselves away in the quiet corners of their homes, browsing the Chico's and Talbots catalogs—greatly relieved that when they picked up the phone and asked for a size fourteen there would be no teenage shopgirl to look them over, no slight sway of her long glittery earrings against her slender neck as she swore to herself that she would never let herself get that big.

For the same reasons, Eleanor rarely watched television: most characters were her children's age. Women in their thirties who wore clingy sweaters and dusted for fingerprints. If a woman her age appeared, she was comic background. Or, in the serious dramas, she was dying slowly, usually of Alzheimer's.

"We'll give it a couple of decades," said Marybeth, "and then we can all start watching *The Golden Girls* reruns."

But Eleanor preferred not to watch television at all. Even the ads erased women of her generation. Her friends weren't nervous new mothers trying to decide on baby food; they weren't young men looking to buy cars. They weren't fathers choosing family cell-phone plans. Decades ago, they had settled on the laundry detergent they would use until they died. After all, they were women still married to the men they met at nineteen. They were, by nature, loyal.

But Eleanor did not believe in complaining. She merely sat with Marybeth and other friends in one of their living rooms, reminiscing about the days they wore miniskirts—oh, how Eleanor had loved showing off her legs. The days when waiters promptly appeared at their tables and flirted. When salesgirls eyed their pocketbooks and asked, eagerly, how they could be of help. When they opened magazines and turned on televisions and recognized their beautiful, trim selves.

But Eleanor shook away any regret: she had been a wife, a mother. She had done wonderful and important things. How could she be sad that the world didn't congratulate her for what was a reward in and of itself?

Still, she sometimes wished she had known that a time would come when the world would quietly brush her under the rug, suggest she kindly step out of its way. Perhaps she would have done more, gone more places, while she still felt welcome.

KIJO

Since the bang of all the car doors, they'd been flanking the threshold, listening for footsteps. But they had heard only the faint sounds of a television, which had just been turned off. They sat with their backs against two massive wooden doors, staring at the domed ceiling above them. Now they could smell food.

"They'll be sitting still," whispered Spider. "We gotta bust. Out that window."

Kijo had been staring at the window awhile now; he knew that was what Spider would suggest. He had tried to will himself toward a vision of escape. A vision in which he swung his legs into the night and reached the tree. But the thought of all the empty space below, the weak branches on which he'd clumsily try to brace his feet, made him tremble.

"You know I can't."

"Jesus, Kij! They find two niggers up here, we're dead. They're gonna come up here sooner or later."

But he'd make too much noise trying to climb down; or he'd fall and break his leg, lie there helpless. Either way, they'd come after him. "You go. The police catch you, they'll send you to juvie."

Spider sniffled, wiped his nose with the cuff of his sweatshirt. "I'm not leaving my ace."

Kijo, who didn't, in fact, want to be left alone, said nothing. But in the silence that followed, he could hear Spider's breathing quicken, the nervous pants of a runner. Spider drew his knees to his chest. Spider leaving was the only chance either of them had of escaping.

"Here's what you do," Kijo said. "Go out that window and down that tree, real quiet, and make your way to the van."

"I ain't leaving—"

"Then fast as you can, get back here and create a diversion. Get in that van and start blaring that horn. Drive in circles till they all come pouring onto the lawn. Drive up on the lawn, do figure eights, make like you're crazy. I'm gonna come down the stairs and find a back door. Give me ten minutes after your diversion and I'll find you in the van back in the woods and we ride off. If I don't come in time, I'll meet you back on Merrell Ave."

Spider, who had been steadily rocking while Kijo detailed the plan, came to an abrupt stop. "Kij, what if they get in your way?"

"They're gonna be so worried about the crazy nigger on their lawn, they won't be looking at the stairs."

Spider thought for a minute, then tugged the panty hose back over his head. "Dinner with Grandma Rose, right?"

Kijo fought back his mounting terror, tried to steady his voice. "I'll see you outside."

Spider jumped to his feet and made his way across the room. Beside the dark window, he reached into his pocket and pulled out a vial; he snapped the cap, peeled his panty hose back, and took a sniff.

"You can rip me later."

Spider lifted the window, and then, without another word, Kijo's best friend disappeared into the night.

GAVIN

*T*he game had depressed him. Watching those young players run and tackle made him feel old. Even the fans in the bleachers, jumping at every touchdown in the bitter cold, were half his age. His knee, he had to stop thinking about his damned knee.

Gavin settled back and thumbed through the journal for Ginny's article. "The Emasculation of the American Warrior." Some title. What did his daughter know about warriors, or war?

The print was small—he'd forgotten his glasses—so he leaned close to read:

The hunter theory of human evolution has long been used to explain the societal phenomenon of male aggression and female submission, and modern-day gender roles. Believing that early hominid males hunted animals for food, many have argued that females were forced to stay home and tend the young.

However, paleobiologist Joel Pethica recently proposed that the turning point in hominid evolution came 3 million years ago when climate changes pushed our ancestors out of the trees and into the predator-infested savanna. Pethica argues that it was not the need to hunt that prompted hominid evolution (*Australopithecus afarensis,* he points out, lacked the dental adaptation to eat meat and probably lived primarily off seeds, tubers, and vegetation). Instead, the need to defend against man-eating animals caused the development of the hominid brain.

Primates, and humans especially, lack the sharp teeth of large felines, the tough skin of elephants, the lancing horns of buffalo, the swiftness of antelopes; the great strength of the hominid lies in its gray matter. Menacing predators would have forced hominids to band together, making threatening noises and gestures as modern-day campers will do with a bear. Over time, the need for vigilance would have brought about group living, language, community, kinship, family. Even Darwin argued that if early humans had been tough enough to withstand predators on their own, they might never have evolved as social animals. Safety in numbers.

The family unit, therefore, actually emerged as a means of defense.

It is unlikely in a predator-laden environment that males would have gone off to hunt, leaving women and children alone; more plausible is that the kin network and family unit remained together, with both sexes scavenging for meat and defending the young. In a predator-infested environment, successful mothering would include the ability to repel attackers.

Scientists now recognize that humans were preyed upon almost as soon as they began walking upright 3 million years ago. In fact, 6 to 10 percent of early human fossils show traces of teeth or talon marks. Only three hundred thousand years ago, with the widespread use of controlled fire (sites in Israel, China, and South Africa yield lower Paleolithic evidence of charred wood and seeds), could humans begin to shed their terror of nocturnal menaces. Only fifteen thousand years ago did our ancestors develop effective action-at-distance weapons such as the bow and arrow. And only in the past two thousand years did humans fully eliminate their predators—allowing them to become full-time predators.

Despite the absence of animal predators in the modern human environment, a vestigial fear has lingered. In 1965, a study of urban schoolchildren showed that students were barely concerned with nuclear war or germs, the predominating dangers depicted by the media; 80 percent named wild animals as their greatest fear, mainly lions and tigers and bears.

Darwin himself wondered, when his two-year-old son developed a terror of caged zoo animals: "Might we not suspect that the . . . fears of children, which are quite independent of experience, are the inherited effects of real dangers . . . during savage times?"

But as our predators vanished from the landscape, the weapons we evolved to repel those beasts were turned on other humans. The strong fear and aggression impulses remained.

Thus emerged, Pethica argues, the ritual of war. The first evidence of what looks like war is a rock drawing from the Spanish Levant dating back twelve thousand years, in which a band of stick figures brandish bows and arrows against one another. The rise of war roughly corresponded to the decline of mammoths, bison rhinoceroses, and megafauna in the Northern Hemisphere. In North America, the arrival of the Clovis people 11,500 years ago heralded the extinction of thirty-five mammals, which has been attributed, by many scholars, to "overkill."

Humans had made an unprecedented evolutionary leap up the food chain, but carried the fear of their ancient ancestors.

As hunter-gatherer societies became more sedentary, turning to agriculture, they broke into distinct tribes and communities, eventually erecting permanent shelters to store grain, in case of drought. But where would they have channeled the lingering fear and aggression?

In *Violence and the Sacred,* Rene Girard argues that war

evolved as a means to limit intracommunity violence. By redirecting aggressive energy toward an external entity—the foreign enemy, the *other*—groups could maintain cohesiveness. War became an outlet for human vestigial fear. An enemy would always exist, but the details were irrelevant: a shark, a tiger in the night, a neighboring tribe. Modern humans would always be afraid of *something*.

In these communities, the male, who had once fought off fang-bearing predators, who had once hunted bison and rhinoceroses, became a "warrior." Twelve thousand years ago, this societal role emerged: to re-enact, through violence and aggression, the role of his male ancestors. By doing this, the warrior could assure his community and family of their safety.

If we now examine the American family in the twentieth century, we can see these primitive instincts and rituals at work.

Throughout America's short history, the bonds of the nuclear and extended family have been at their strongest in the face of danger: the original Plymouth pilgrims forged strong family networks during the first brutal New World winter; those ties were only strengthened during the ensuing violence with Native Americans. Only after the slaughter and deportation of most Native American tribes did the colonial family begin to break down.

Contrary to myth, the bonds of the African-American family were strong during slavery. Slaves defied law to marry in secret. Most runaway slaves fled their plantations in order to find relatives, and thirty-five years after the Civil War, the *Richmond Planet* continued to publish the letters of former slaves looking to find their parents, siblings, or children in the column "Do You Know Them?" Early twentieth-century European immigrants, facing discrimination and poverty, housed newly arrived cousins in their crowded tenements, hired nephews; during and immediately after World War II, American men and women married younger, bore more children.

In violent conflict, men have traditionally been asked to make the "ultimate sacrifice" to protect their communities. But the recent American manufacture of "false danger" has poisoned the tradition of sacrifice, and the warrior's status in society.

Both the unethical warrior (Vietnam) and the damaged warrior (beginning with the shell-shocked men of World War I, but fully entering society's consciousness with the traumatized veterans of Vietnam, and, more recently, of Iraq) place great strain on traditional notions of masculine and feminine.

The warrior is the most strictly gendered role left in society; in the face of women obtaining property and voting rights and entering the workforce, the presence of the male warrior has, from the American Revolution to World War II, sustained a societal belief in male "power." As women have become property owners, professors, doctors, lawyers, politicians, the role of physical protector has remained almost exclusively male. Adrian Vergara has argued that the need for warriors permitted men a privileged access to work and wealth because women ceded power millennia ago in exchange for physical protection. This is perhaps why men have sought to maintain a political conversation of danger; it is through physical threat that they derive their social and domestic authority.

But during the Vietnam War, when the American warrior, for the first time ever, lost his standing—his efforts to defend his community were deemed not only unnecessary but also unethical, shameful, and eventually, unsuccessful—American women made unprecedented political and social leaps; since then, the unpopular wars in Iraq and Afghanistan have only solidified women's social and economic gains.

The turn of the millennium may have marked the death rattle of American warriorhood, an obsolete form of manhood that has undermined the very basis of patriarchy.

A pain shot through Gavin's knee. He dropped the journal on the floor and limped to the window.

"Dad, you okay?"

Gavin waved his son away. It was a clear night, the sky black and cloudless; he wanted to get back to Westport. To his telescope.

He dug in his pocket, shook an aspirin from the bottle, and swallowed it.

Unethical, shameful.

Gavin felt suddenly angry. Maybe the country hadn't seen *real* war in fifty years, but his daughter should have known enough history to realize that war had a way of cropping up. What would happen with a nation of men who sat around discussing how they would be judged twenty, thirty years down the line before lifting a finger to defend their country?

Because they didn't want to end up like him—pitied.

Gavin had traveled thousands of miles and killed men and risked his life and all he had received was pity.

The word made him sick. He preferred being spit on.

Long ago he'd made a choice not to pity himself; a man owned his choices, his mistakes. And over time, a mistake of such magnitude hardened like a growth; misshapen flesh on his body that, in the depths of night, roused from sleep, Gavin probed with his fingertips: that is *me*. Over thirty-six years, his anger had amassed, like thickened tissue, around the moment he stepped onto the army-transport plane for Vietnam. That wrong turn—it was *him*. His life was so defined by that choice, how could he say he would have chosen differently? We *were* our mistakes; we breathed them daily. In summer, they seeped from our skin. Gavin understood that he smelled to the world like a man who had taken a bad turn. But was it so much to ask that his own children look to him with some respect? Some recognition of what he had done for them?

Yes, there had been moments—he could see it in the way Ginny looked at him—when he had failed her. Had not known the right thing to say.

But there were the times, too, when he carried her with a bleeding foot to the emergency room. When he took her ice-skating at Rockefeller Center, waited for hours in line with her, and then rubbed her head forgivingly when she was too shy to step onto the ice. These were brief moments, amid many years, but Gavin was proud of them.

To his daughter he wanted to say, I fed you; I clothed you. I made certain you were always safe, never without shelter. I spent my days at a desk, living a life I felt beneath me so that you would never have to do the same. So that you could get a PhD, flaunt your cleverness, gallivant around the world, pursue every fleeting interest, and toss aside any man who bored you, knowing that if you ever stumbled, ever fell, I would catch you.

Was that not being a father? Being a man?

Gavin looked up at the star-blown sky. Its beauty, its familiarity, sometimes tightened his chest. There was Mars glinting in the northeast; Jupiter—the brightest point—getting ready to set for winter; the archer Sagittarius; Castor and Pollux; such radiant and faraway points of light.

At home he would be able to see them closely. Alone on his deck, the cold air on his face, his eye pressed to his Celestron. It was the Cadillac of telescopes: a 1976 C8-SGT Schmidt-Cassegrain. All metal with anodized aluminum, stainless-steel screws. Over the years, he'd used it to see the red spots of Jupiter, dust storms on Mars, binary stars and whirlpool galaxies. He'd pull out his *Cambridge Star Atlas* and peck around the sky, but always ended up looking at one thing: the moon.

As a child, he'd eagerly tracked the progress of Luna 2 and Luna 3.

But in 1969, when Neil Armstrong and Buzz Aldrin finally stepped out from the lunar module, when millions sat glued to their televisions to witness them plant a flag on the moon, Gavin was in a small bar in Cholon, beside a girl he loved and would never see again once he returned home; they held a crackly radio to their ears, trying to imagine what it looked like.

Now, night after night, he'd stare at the East Crater, where Armstrong had left his thirteen-by-six-inch footprint. Night after night, it amazed him.

But when Gavin spoke of Armstrong and Aldrin, his children shrugged. Of course men could walk on the moon. A shuttle launch couldn't hold his grandchildren's attention. It was as though mankind's greatest feat had never happened. As though landing on the moon had made it vanish.

Just after he had accepted a senior sales manager position at Reynolds, recognizing, finally, that he'd spend the rest of his days selling insurance, Gavin wrote Neil Armstrong a letter:

What do you think of the fact that a man could do what no human being has ever done, what the whole world prayed for, and then one day it's forgotten? Are all astonishments eventually meaningless? All accomplishments overlooked?

Armstrong never wrote back. Maybe he thought Gavin was after an autograph to cash in on. Maybe he hadn't read the letter. Or maybe what Gavin said had struck him as true. But Gavin respected a man's need for silence. He knew that silence could be a comfort.

When Gavin looked through the Celestron at night, he sometimes wondered: Was it all darkness and dust out there, particles and nebulas, or was anything looking back at him?

GINNY

Ginny watched her brother carve the turkey, his forearm pumping so vigorously it appeared as though he were punching the bird. She poured the wine, crossed her fingers: *Please let that bird be cooked.*

"Well, look at this splendor!" her mother said, having laid a tidy line of calcium and zinc supplements above her plate. "Who would know that this was thrown together unexpectedly? Such lovely china. And the silverware!" Eleanor admired the tongs of her fork.

Ginny poured Priya some apple juice. As the wine was passed around the table, her mother said, "Oh, no more for me, I really couldn't. Well, maybe just a touch."

Douglas grinned and mouthed *refuse and booze.*

After her mother snapped a series of photographs, the table fell strangely silent. Everyone seemed to be marveling at the steaming food, the elaborate feast they had been awaiting for hours.

"Oh, how about a poem," her mother said.

"Mom, I can't just make up poems on the spot."

"I thought people did that all the time."

"You're thinking of limericks," Ginny said. But she lifted her glass anyway. "Okay, Mom. Since you were so helpful with the kitchen mishap: *There once was a turkey from Perdue, / But being cooked would simply not do. / It sat in my oven, / Demanding some lovin', / A thing only Denise Olson's KitchenAid Electric Master 3.1 could do.*"

Denise raised her glass. "To functioning kitchen appliances!"

Douglas raised his. "To houses with safe wiring!"

"Well, and of course to the newest addition to our family," her mother said. "Dear little Priya."

Priya's face brightened. And as everyone clinked glasses, Ginny felt a long-buried mass of gratitude rush to her skin. Her mother, with all her flaws and her fumbling, would embrace Priya with the same strong loyalty with which she embraced Ginny and everyone she loved. It was the one thing Ginny's mother did perfectly and fiercely: love.

"Now can we please, please eat?" Brandon asked.

"Mangia, everyone!" Douglas speared a slice of turkey.

As the bowls and platters commenced their orbit around the table, the clank of cutlery filled the room.

"So, did you know that on average," Douglas began, "stocks go up the day before a holiday, but dip the day after. Except for . . . drum-roll, please . . . Thanksgiving. It's the only holiday that shows gains both the day before and the day after. Which means tomorrow should be a good day."

"We could go to the movies tomorrow," said Eleanor. "Who wants to go to the movies?"

Tomorrow Ginny would be cleaning up her kitchen, calling an electrician, trying to get her house in order for the home-study.

"Gavin," her mother said. "Let's go to the movies."

Her father sat at the head of the table. He cut a large piece of meat from a drumstick and shoved it into his mouth. He chewed slowly, and seemed to be deep in thought. He sipped his water, eyes darting around the room, then set his glass down with a thump.

"I would like," he began slowly, "my daughter to explain her sources for her extensive article about the—what was the word, Ginny?—*emasculation* of the American warrior."

Ginny froze. After ten years, he decided to read her papers? He barely ever asked about her work. "Dad, it's an academic article. We come up with arguments that haven't been made before, and we write articles. I told you, I need to publish for tenure."

"So you don't believe what you wrote? That's unimpressive."

Then he lifted the massive drumstick and, with a quick tilt of his head, bit into the bulbous thigh. Grease slid across his lips as his teeth churned at the meat. He was breathing noisily, and she could feel his anger across the table; it was frightening, and strangely comforting. It was, finally, emotion.

She didn't want to let it go. "Actually, I completely do."

"What's this article?" asked Douglas uncomfortably.

"It's about how Vietnam killed manhood."

"Jesus, Gin."

Ginny took a deep breath. "Dad, I take it you disagree with the article?"

"Oh, is this for Ginny's keynote address?" Eleanor asked.

Her father looked up from his drumstick and his eyes roved slowly, then deliberately, around the table. As he studied each of their faces, Ginny waited for a flash of rage, for an explanation of what she didn't understand about Vietnam, about him. But he set the drumstick down and rubbed his eye, and for a moment Ginny wasn't certain if she saw a streak of grease on his cheek or a tear. He swallowed deeply, his Adam's apple bulging as though holding back . . . was it pain? Ginny leaned forward, tried to meet his stare, but he turned and smiled at Priya, methodically wiping each of his fingers with his napkin. "Silence is a good thing, Priya. We live in a noisy world."

Her mother, with a lifetime of practiced cheer, said, "Darling, how do you like the cranberries? This year, instead of sugar, I used Splenda."

And her father said, "They're perfect."

The moment vanished; platters were passed. Ginny felt the familiar sorrow of being silenced. As though she were saying good-bye to him, as though every conversation with her father were somehow a good-bye. He popped in from time to time, but within seconds he was grabbing his coat. He could never stay for long.

Brave face, she thought. As though she were reading Ginny's thoughts, Priya touched her arm. Ginny set her hands on the table. She looked again at her father and the memory came, as it often did, in a flash.

Ginny was seven. She had gotten food poisoning, so the school nurse arranged for the music teacher to take her home early.

Her mother was at a flower show in Greenwich. But there was a key under a rock by the front door.

Mrs. Cullman did her best during the walk to convince Ginny to take up an instrument; she thought Ginny had piano fingers. But Ginny's stomach still felt awful and she could muster only a grunt of disagreement.

At her house, the lights were all out. "Now, you know where the spare key is?"

At that moment, the door opened and a woman, a friend of her mother's who lived nearby, stepped out. Her name was Martha Bixby, and Ginny had always thought her very pretty. She was slipping on a long, beaded turquoise earring. Behind Martha stood Ginny's father, wearing an expression of annoyance.

Ginny didn't remember what she saw or what she thought; she remembered clearly that Mrs. Cullman came to a dead stop. She touched Ginny's shoulder and in her opera-singer's voice said, "Dear, you mustn't harp on this," before hurrying off.

Martha cut across the lawn and did not look back. Her father fixed his stare on Ginny. "What's wrong, tiger? Bellyache?"

The look of annoyance was overlaid by a calm, distant smile. He touched Ginny's forehead and he smelled salty, like the ocean. She threw up on his shoes.

It was strange how you could forget things, essential details about people you knew. You remembered, re-remembered, then wanted to forget.

Everyone continued to pass the platters, a tangle of outstretched arms, serving spoons clattering.

"Little Priya here will make a great confidante," her father said, eating contentedly. "Just think how people will trust her. I'm going to whisper all my confessions to her."

"Like confessing that you just took the last hunk of breast meat for yourself?" joked Douglas.

"She'll talk eventually, Dad," Ginny said. "Be careful."

Her father did not look at her.

"Be careful of what?" asked Eleanor.

GAVIN

*T*he girl's name was Nam Hà. Gavin had one picture of her. Seated at a restaurant, her raven hair spilling over her shoulders, her head tilted coquettishly. She'd had her picture taken only twice in her life, and she wouldn't tell him who had taken the other photo, no matter how often he asked.

She knew it would drive him mad. He was pretty sure she wanted to drive him mad.

He'd met her in Saigon in 1968, right after he'd been assigned the desk job. He was bored and restless and everyone had girls in Saigon; Gavin considered it a mark of character that he had just one.

Nam Hà was sixteen.

She had a room in Cholon, next to a tobacco shop. Her grandmother was a great healer and Nam Hà dabbled in herbal medicine, making Gavin teas for strength, for courage, for falling madly in love with her. She kept a parakeet, three cats, a turtle, and what Gavin thought was a lemur. These were animals she had found wounded while she bicycled around the city, and she often arrived to meet him with a bandaged squirrel or crow in her basket, postponing a hello kiss until she had settled the creature into one of the blanket-lined baskets she used as her infirmary.

She questioned him about medicine in America, about the machines that would breathe for a person. She'd also heard they could give you a new kidney, a new liver, a new heart. She said America must be the land of miracles, that in America she could be an actual doctor, that women there wore pants and had robots to wash dishes. She said in America she would have to have a new name, an American name, so joining the name of the president's widow (of whom she had seen many photographs) and the largest automobile she had ever heard of, she decided she would be called Jackie Limousine.

"You know I can't take you," he always said when she spoke of America. It would have been cruel to let her hope for the impossible. Not that Gavin didn't think about it. He once asked his supervisor about the likelihood of getting her papers. The man laughed and said Gavin was the third person that day to ask that question. "You know a war is a real shit storm when love spreads faster than syphilis."

At night Gavin lay beside Nam Hà, her birds and squirrels chirping and scurrying. "You are the queen of the jungle," he'd whisper.

"A queen needs a king."

"I have a wife." He sighed.

"In America, you can speak many languages, practice many religions, drive many cars, but you can have only one wife? This is no fair. When your wife is busy with the robot in the kitchen, who will take care of you?"

She joked about America being the land of one wife, the land of sad men. Until the day Gavin was to ship home. Then the jokes stopped and she cried, "You are the best man I will ever meet. You are smart and you are nice. You listen when I talk. You are good to my animals. What do I do now? Go work in the rice fields?"

Gavin wanted to tell her that she would be fine, that she would meet a nice Vietnamese boy, but most of them were dead. He gave her what money he had. He kissed her and promised to write.

"Maybe I come find you," she said. "Maybe I learn to fly an airplane and come fly over your house. Can wife number one fly an airplane?"

He lifted his bag, her cats meowing fiercely around his legs. As he opened the door onto the noisy street. He felt her hand on his back.

"You don't have to marry me," she whispered. "I will be your mistress. I will clean your house. But please, bring me." She slid her arm tightly around his stomach. "I am begging."

He turned to face her. "I love you."

"Then how come you leave? How come you say good-bye forever?"

"Not forever."

She moved away, scooped a wounded squirrel from a basket, and held it to her chest. Her eyes watered, appearing for a moment in the room's dim light to be the eyes of an old woman. "You lie, Mr. American."

Eleanor once found her picture.

Gavin kept it in the box with his dog tags and his piece of shrapnel and snapshots of his original platoon. On the back of the photo, Nam Hà had left a lipstick kiss, which, over the years, had turned from bright red to brown. It hadn't been easy for her to part with the photo, but Nam Hà's greatest fear was that he would forget her. He hadn't.

"Who is this?" Eleanor asked. "Let me guess, a translator? A special aide to your platoon?"

Gavin had had no communication with Nam Hà in fourteen years. He'd written one letter, just after he returned home from the war. In a fit of frustration one night, during the long tortured months of being turned down for jobs, he wrote that he would come for her and bring her to America, that his life was dead without her.

But he never heard back. He didn't know if Nam Hà had found another man, if she never got the letter, or if she had died. At first, the silence crushed him. In the ensuing years, he tried not to think about her, but sometimes, at night, when he lay beside Eleanor, he recalled the slow spin of Nam Hà's ceiling fan, the warm breeze, the chirping of her pets, the downy insole of her foot where he nestled his toes. They had often chattered late into the night about his parents, about what he planned to do when he returned home. This was before he had decided that if the world would withhold from him, he, too, would withhold.

He had last seen Nam Hà when she was sixteen. In his mind, she was a child still, and when Gavin conjured their time together, so was he.

"God, look at your little fortune cookie!" Eleanor said. "I've heard about those women. Did she walk on your back? Did she wash your feet with her hair? I didn't treat you well enough? I took care of my dying mother and waited for you and you needed something more. Shame on you." She crossed her arms, raised her chin, and basked in a self-righteous silence, until her need to talk got the best of her and she plunged her hand into the box. "What else have you got tucked away?"

She waved the small plastic bag that held his shrapnel.

"That's the little piece of metal that probably saved my life."

"It's disgusting."

"Eleanor, this is all fifteen years old. I was a kid, and it was a war. Let's put the box away."

"It was an *idiotic* war, and you couldn't go to Canada like everyone else. You're the only man from Yale who *wanted* to go to Vietnam. And look what happened!"

What happened? Gavin thought. Nothing had happened to her. She got two children and a house with a yard and a gardening club. And he worked fifty hours a week in a windowless room to give that to her. She had everything she ever wanted.

"Eleanor, you have made a career of self-pity."

She tightened her lips and shook her head; she began pacing, then came to a halt.

"Where are my panties? The ones I gave you before you shipped out. Did you throw them out? Give them to your little friend?"

For the life of him, Gavin couldn't remember what had happened to the pink and white lace panties she'd handed him at Fort Benning.

"You're being ridiculous," he said.

"Give that picture to me. Give me your little fortune cookie."

"Eleanor, she's probably long dead by now. She was a friend during a confusing time. This is all I have of her."

"And to think, when you got back, all your moping and brooding and I thought you'd been through something horrible, that you were suffering some kind of trauma. You were just . . . you were missing her." She began to cry, gulping several deep breaths. "I'm your wife."

He handed her the photo.

"She looks like a prostitute."

"Yes, Eleanor."

Her face was working through some thought. Finally her voice softened and she knuckled the tears from her eyes.

"You couldn't have really loved her, though, because you came back, to me."

"That's right."

"She couldn't have been so wonderful after all."

She looked at the photo one more time, furrowing her brow, and then slowly tore it into pieces. "You're a good man, Gavin. A decent man. And I've always loved you. We will put this behind us."

DENISE

*M*aybe, after all, the day had worked out, thought Denise.
She looked around the room: the twins cheerfully licked
gravy from their forks. Cranberry sauce gleamed on her daughter's
lips. Douglas had pushed back his chair and stretched his legs beneath
the table. His face, no longer twitching, looked tranquil. Denise was
full and groggy, and in her relaxation she let herself, for the first time
in months, see a glimmer of hope.

After all, this table was laid with her wedding china. In the kitchen
beyond, her daughter had first said "Mama." Upstairs was the bedroom where her sons had woken her in the night, flashlights beaming
at their chins, to proudly show their missing teeth. How could they
lose this house?

Denise had always considered nostalgia dishonest. She thought
people lied to themselves about the past, clinging to imagined
beauty, and that they also clad the future in impossible happiness.
Denise had never indulged. She had fled her family in Pittsburgh, not
once looking back. And she had never believed, nor did she now, that
her future held infinite promise. She simply wanted this moment to
endure.

She tried to sear the scene into her mind. Time now seemed like
a monster, devouring each instant—the one monster children were
not afraid of.

The Indian girl stood and straightened her dress.

"Sweetheart," said Ginny, "you've barely touched your yams."

Brian and Brandon jumped from their seats, and Laura, half-tangled in her tablecloth, struggled out of her chair.

"Children," said Eleanor, "the meal is not over."

Denise, who did not want the moment to end, had to force herself to say, "Why don't we let them play while I heat up the pies?"

"Let's teach Priya how to play Mercy!" said Brandon.

"*N-O*," said Ginny.

"Oh, heavens!" said Eleanor.

"I am going to play travel agent with Priya," Laura announced. "She will be my customer and I will arrange for her to go to Disney World." She led Priya into the living room.

But the children's absence changed the air; in the brief silence that followed, Denise recognized a familiar sadness. People always wanted adults-only time, but the moment children left a room, they took some of the joy and the lightness. Everyone at the table suddenly looked very old, very dull.

"It's been good to meet Priya," she said to Ginny.

"I'm glad she's getting to know her cousins. Though I think after seeing this house she might find our place in Mamaroneck a bit shabby."

"Shabby chic," said Douglas.

"She'll be grateful you saved her from the third world," Denise said.

"Well, we'll see," Ginny answered. "In twenty years India's middle class will be 40 percent of its population. By the time Priya's an adult, India will be a world leader and the United States will have gone the way of the Roman Empire. Frankly, she might be pissed off."

Here it came, thought Denise, the moment in the conversation when everyone started to say large and important things. Tried to look well informed.

"I have always wanted to visit Pompeii," said Eleanor. "It is a real window into Roman times."

"Gin, this country has land wealth," said Douglas. "And it has something few other countries have: ambition. *Moral* ambition. Sure, we're idealists who sometimes get it wrong, but at least we're idealists."

"Two words, Douglas, peak oil," Ginny said.

Denise had heard some teachers talking about that. About the fact that half the world's oil had already been pumped from the ground.

"Just look at these houses miles from any train station or supermarket," Ginny continued. "These electric appliances. We spent centuries building a society based on the premise that power was easy to come by. We've already spent our wealth."

Already spent our wealth. The phrase made Denise momentarily dizzy. She announced she was going to prepare the dessert.

"Pies and pear tart! See, we *should* be thankful for this meal," Ginny went on, "because in a few years, I doubt you'll see such abundance."

"Well, we certainly don't need this much," added Eleanor.

"Ginny." Denise paused by her chair; she'd been lured by the game, wanted to score a few intellectual points. "You're always going on about the Trail of Tears, that stuff. But some teachers were talking the other day about how the Native Americans actually raped the land."

"Raped!" cried Eleanor. "What a word!"

"Apparently," Denise went on, "*they* began the whole environmental crisis."

Ginny wiped her mouth, set down her napkin. "It's a matter of time lines. Yes, the Clovis drove most of the megafauna to extinction. About thirteen *thousand* years ago. The Native Americans *we* drove to extinction were living off the land as recently as four hundred years ago. The people who wrote the Bill of Rights? Those bright and shining minds wiped out hundreds of thousands of modern humans. That, Douglas, is your country's moral ambition."

Douglas patted his stomach. "*I* feel like a damned megafauna."

Denise shrugged off her defeat. She'd been raising three children and working full-time; facts and figures would never flow off her tongue. She certainly wasn't going to get into a frenzy over politics.

As she made her way into the kitchen, she could see Laura, in the living room, assembling the final pieces of the elaborate dollhouse Douglas had just bought her.

"You know," Douglas was saying to his father, "I still can't believe the Packers lost."

"Oh, Doug, enough with the game," Denise said over her shoulder. "I hope you didn't put money on it."

GINNY

Ginny rose to help clear the table while Douglas and her father sat once again analyzing their team's defeat.

"A lot of those players use steroids," said Douglas.

Her father had abandoned the issue of her article—the end. And she knew she would not press further. It struck Ginny as a strange yet essential part of her being that she confronted everyone but him.

Denise slid a tart into the oven, and the kitchen began to smell of pears and cinnamon. Ginny started washing dishes, clumsily, and through the vast window, she stared into the eerie blackness. The velvety green lawn, the pristine chinaberrys—the entire yard was now lost in the gloaming, swallowed whole by a dark sky and full moon. In the distance, the soft speck of a single driveway light punctuated the blackness. It amazed her how nightfall narrowed the world to points of light. With the sun's cover gone, civilization glowed with campfires, oil lamps, candles, and chandeliers. Beacons, hazards. After all those years living in the city, she would have been frightened living amidst so much space and silence. She looked away.

"Just hand those to me and I'll shove them into the washer," said Denise.

Ginny had been on her feet for hours, and after all that eating, she felt bloated. She passed along the dripping plates and stifled a yawn behind her dripping rubber glove. Denise caught the yawn, burying hers in her shoulder. Ginny was thankful her family had made no further mention of her oven's failure, of the long drive back to Stamford.

That seemed the gift of family: they knew your mistakes and held none against you.

"Well, here's a funny story," Ginny said, sponging off the plates. "So I happen to know this writer, a novelist named Richard Conway, and he has two novels out. Father-son hunting stuff set in the South. Anyway, his third novel was published about two months ago, to real acclaim, and he's getting nominated for prizes. This is his break-through book. It's getting so much attention that somebody notices that about two full pages of dialogue were lifted from this play. An off-Broadway play that was put on about two years ago. Richard claims he did not plagiarize. He swears it. He says he will take a lie-detector test, demands to take a lie-detector test. He claims, in fact, that the bulk of the dialogue in the book came from the time he spent in coffee shops in the city just eavesdropping on real people. Well, of all things, it turns out that this coffee shop where he used to just sit and listen is the exact same coffee shop where the two actors from the play used to go to rehearse. The scene took place in a coffee shop, so they'd just go there and run lines. Richard thought it was real dialogue; he wrote it all down and put it in his book."

"Does he have to pay a fine?" her mother asked.

"No, no fines or anything like that. Even if it was plagiarism, it's not criminal. The playwright actually forgave him. I mean, why wouldn't he? It's a big compliment to his dialogue and now everyone has heard of his obscure off-Broadway play. It's going up at City Center next spring!"

The rattle of the plates and silverware sliding into the dishwasher filled the kitchen; Ginny sensed they were all drowsy and pretty much talked out. The oven timer beeped and Denise slipped on a quilted red mitt and extracted the pear tart, beautifully browned around the crust.

"Voila!"

As her mother carried the ice cream into the dining room, Ginny followed, balancing a stack of bowls.

"Children! Dessert!"

Ginny set a bowl at every place, and Denise laid the tart in the middle of the table, at which point Brian and Brandon charged into the room.

The television was blaring.

"Laura and Priya!" Denise called. "Please turn off the television and come in here."

The television went silent and Laura pattered in, dragging her tablecloth and rubbing her eyes.

"Priya, honey," Ginny called, setting a spoon beside every bowl.

The twins thumped into their chairs and Laura lifted her spoon, stuck it to her nose.

Ginny sat, every chair occupied but her daughter's, and once more called out: "Priya! Honey?"

"She's at Disney World," said Laura and pointed upstairs.

KIJO

Alone in the closet, Kijo waits. The panty hose flatten his nose so that his nostrils, struggling for air, take in sharp, deep inhalations of cedar, shoe polish, the brine of sweat on his shirt. He thumbs his turtleneck loose from his skin, looks again at the face of his digital watch. Forty-five minutes. He gave up waiting by the doors, scared someone would wander upstairs. But how long can it take for Spider to get down that tree? Make it to the van? They parked two blocks back, but still. Spider's fast.

The idea that Spider took off, that no one is coming for him, feels like a hand shoved down Kijo's throat. He gags, tries to shake the thought from his mind. He swats nervously at a row of cellophaned gowns. Then it occurs to him that the thick carpeting and stacked sweaters may have silenced the honking. Maybe Spider already got them out of the house. Kijo rushes across the room, pushes aside the window's heavy curtains, and gasps. A slit-eyed, misshapen face, the beaten face of a boxer, stares back at him. His.

Panic claws at him. He tells himself to stay calm, to think clearly. He leans forward, slowly, his breath steaming the glass. It's too dark to see anything but the humped shadows of three parked cars, their windows glinting like the eyes of raccoons at night, hungry and alert.

Kijo looks off in the distance for the headlights of the Diamond Diagnostics van. Nothing. But there aren't police lights either, which means no one's had a scare. The yard is empty, silent. If he could just get himself down that tree. But it's a good twenty feet, and what if he gets stuck, trapped? He's seen those pictures of black men hanging from branches.

Come on, Spider.

This room, this house, everything begins to seem horrifically small. Not much space to run or hide. Not much air to breathe.

Kijo inches toward the wooden doors, slowly pulls one open, letting in the sound of faint laughter from downstairs, the smell of gravy, and over that something sweet and cinnamon. Shit, they're nearing dessert and soon enough someone's coming upstairs. And three cars outside? There must be at least half a dozen people down there. Half a dozen people to corner him, chase him out the window, or . . . What would he do if he found a man in his house?

Sweat stings his eyes and Kijo yanks off the panty hose. As the air rushes to his lungs, his chest balloons and he lets out a sharp cough that sounds like a sob.

Please, Spider. Come back.

Looking around at the embroidered blankets, the velvet pillows, the gleaming night tables topped with rainbow-glass lamps, Kijo feels the thought arrive like a blow to his head: coming here has ruined everything. He's going to end up in jail.

He looks up at the domed ceiling, painted with angels, and his mind races with thoughts of what he would still like to do; he mutters the list aloud. He wants to open his grocery, he wants to be called Mr. Jackson, he wants to move Grandma Rose somewhere safe, to take care of her, to make her proud. Someday, he wants to be an old man sitting on a stoop next to Spider, talking about the old times.

When his muttering stops, the silence of the room folds over him. He can see the smallness of himself as though he were standing at a distance, and as the fact of his aloneness seizes him, Kijo's eyes cloud over with tears.

But a circuitry within him switches on; the urge to escape, to live, takes hold.

Kijo sees that he will have to fight. That's what he came here for.

He was done running and hiding. He wasn't a coward. He was here to say, you can push me and shove me and sweep me out of sight, but one day you come home and realize, I'm still here. I'm always watching you.

Pulling the stone knife from his pocket, Kijo sets his bag on his shoulder and stands with his legs apart. He looks again at his watch. He can't wait any longer.

He takes a deep breath, prepares to hurl himself through the threshold, to race down the stairs, when suddenly there's a dark-skinned girl standing before him. For a moment he has the urge to knock her down. He raises his hand, but the flash of alarm on her face stops him.

"I'm just lost up here," he whispers. "I'm not doing no harm."

Her brown eyes roam his duffel bag, stuffed with cans, and she blinks like her eyes are dry. Kijo can't imagine what this dark girl is doing in the house, who she belongs to—a maid? gardener?—or who else might be at the bottom of those stairs.

"How many people down there?"

She tightens her mouth, and then it falls open, in shock, as she catches sight of the stone knife. She turns to run and in one swift move Kijo covers her mouth and lifts her into the room. He pins her to the wall. She is small, fragile. Her heart kicks at his palm.

"I'm gonna uncover your mouth but you aren't gonna scream. You're gonna answer my question so everyone's gonna be fine. How many people are down there?"

He envisions ten, even twenty people downstairs. Too many people to all be drawn outside by Spider's honking. They'll be waiting for him. The pulse in his head grows enormous. "You got guns in the house?"

He puts the knife to her stomach.

"How many people down there? *Hablas español?* Are they all in the dining room?"

She tightens her mouth again, works it like a fish, over and over.

The tendons in her neck stiffen and her chin looks as though it might unhinge.

"Just tell me what I want to know." *Don't make me hurt you,* he thinks. *Don't make it come to this.* "There a back way out?"

Bitterness coats his tongue and he grabs the girl's arm, raises the knife to her neck. Her face goes entirely slack; tears slide from her eyes.

How long before someone comes looking for her?

"You better fucking well talk to me."

Part III

DETECTIVE BILL O'SHEA

*I*n his line of work, observation was key. You observed what people
touched—their pockets, a bracelet, a wedding ring, their hearts—
and how they touched it. You made note of where they looked before
answering questions: eyes up to the right, they were remembering
something; eyes up and left, they were bullshitting. A suspect who
touched his face a lot was trying to hide the truth. Repeating the
question—*You're asking me where I was when the victim entered the building?*—meant stalling for time. Legs crossed, arms crossed were signs
someone was hiding something.

The redheaded woman, Ginny Olson, sat with her arms crossed.
She was bundled in a thick cardigan sweater, belted tight despite the
room being a good ten degrees above comfort level.

He had the Olson family at the station house, still wearing their
blood-splattered holiday clothes. He'd been prepared to separate
them, to ensure they didn't try to coordinate statements, but they
weren't speaking. Their glazed eyes roamed the waiting area; their
mouths hung open, ever so slightly, in the same helpless, unknowing
way of people sleeping upright. No one touched the magazines, or
the turkey buffet Carl Dundee's wife had laid out hours earlier. The
room was eerily silent except for the occasional creak of a plastic
chair, at which they all, instinctively, flinched. Still in shock. And who
could blame them—an invasion, a shooting, two deaths.

O'Shea had been working the holiday overtime when the call
came in. He had spent most of the day organizing his desk and filling

out reports, so this brought him a momentary excitement. Since the station was short on staff, he volunteered to respond, which he hadn't done in years. As he drove north toward Stamford—siren blaring, his red light flashing across the dark, narrow roads—he felt the familiar rush from his days as a patrol officer, a strange renegade vigor that had always made him feel more outlaw than law, an energy that brought, as he neared the house, a slight smile to his face. Until he saw what had happened.

By the time Captain Briggs instructed him to bring the family in for statements, he was relieved to get away from the scene.

"Whatever happens," Captain Briggs told O'Shea before he left, "don't let the press get their fangs in this yet. If anyone calls, be vague. Hopefully, they're all still home eating turkey."

But O'Shea knew that around 10:00 p.m., one of the *Advocate* newspaper crew, Sandra Yumi or Todd Bunson, would phone in for the police-blotter report. They were the rookies stuck with the nightly station-house calls, which usually yielded nothing more than some DUIs and disorderlies, the occasional fistfight outside a West Side bar, a few illegal possessions. Neither Bunson nor Yumi would be expecting much. O'Shea wanted to have a clear story, one that wouldn't rouse suspicion, and one that wouldn't come back to bite him on the ass.

But how the hell were the details not going to rouse suspicion?

Stamford had ranked as one of the country's safest cities three years running. Breaking-and-entering rates were low, and violent stats were negligible, except for the West Side, which had always been a sinkhole as far as O'Shea was concerned. That's where the gangs went at each other over drug turf. Semiautomatics floated around those parts. You saw a few drive-bys. But as long as they were killing only each other, the city's feathers didn't get ruffled. The department knew the precise coordinates of where that mess began and ended. Stillwater, Main, West Broad, and West Avenue. The rectangle of refuse and at the center was Vidal Court. They kept it contained.

Officers got calls to go in there, they kept their hands on their holsters and knew they might see blood.

But North Stamford? Deerkill Road?

A 911 with dead bodies there and O'Shea took note. Everybody took note.

O'Shea was forty-five years old. He'd been with the department twenty years, and he knew this would be a case that got everybody talking.

These just weren't the people you'd expect to have sitting in your station on Thanksgiving Day.

GINNY

*T*hey had begun helping themselves to the pie and ice cream on the
table when Ginny pushed back her chair and went to find Priya.
She suspected her daughter might be camped out in front of the television, or had wandered upstairs to take a nap. As Ginny crossed the
vast dining room she thought about how to explain Priya's fatigue to
her family. Not that they would ask—they'd all done a good job of
keeping any concerns quiet—but it occurred to Ginny they might be
able to help lift Priya's spirits. As she imagined Douglas ballooning his
cheeks, coaxing Priya to squeeze out the air and her mother digging
for candy in her purse, she suddenly saw, at the bottom of the stairs,
a child, a girl she thought she recognized, with her mouth open but
silent, her arm wet and crimson. Ginny stopped.

She almost said, That's not funny. And then, as her mind processed
the image, her neck went stiff with panic. Move toward Priya, Ginny
told herself, but her feet felt leaden. She became aware of a silence
surrounding her, as though she were being plunged underwater. She
looked to brace herself against something when suddenly she realized
that she had, in fact, already rushed to the stairs. She was inches from
Priya when the sound in the room returned in a blast, like a radio
turned off at high volume, then powered on. China clinking, a knife
stabbing a crystal pie platter, and voices, people's voices: "Oh, just a
sliver!" "It's vanilla."

Ginny crouched and touched her daughter's forehead—Ginny
would later remember this, her ineptitude—as though the girl had

a fever. She looked at the blood on Priya's dress, afraid to touch her arm. Priya's eyes, wet with fear, seemed to be pleading with Ginny, then slowly widened as a thud of footsteps sounded from upstairs.

Priya grabbed Ginny's hand, pulled her from the stairs, and released a long, terrified scream: *Maaaaaa.*

ELEANOR

*I*t sounded like a crow cawing, or perhaps like a bell, the high-pitched vibrato that had once filled the halls of her school. Looking up from the perfect triangle of pear tart on her plate, topped with an orb of vanilla ice cream, Eleanor saw Ginny's daughter in the foyer, her dress soiled. Ginny crouched before her. What on earth had happened? What game was the girl playing? *Trouble,* thought Eleanor. The poor girl couldn't even sit for dessert; the tart was cooling, the ice cream would soon puddle on their plates.

Eleanor's head was warm from the wine and she let out a drowsy sigh of disappointment. Then suddenly, Ginny and Priya rushed into the dining room, Priya yanking Ginny's hand. *No running in the house,* Eleanor thought, but then her son threw back his chair and reached for a brass candlestick. Denise jumped from her seat and grabbed Laura, wrestling her to the ground with such force that the girl grabbed hold of the white silk runner and upended the tidy line of platters and pitchers in one strong jerk. Chairs toppled. The smell of coffee filled the air as liquid from spilled cups doused the table. Everybody moved so quickly, Eleanor was confused. The wine, too, much wine; she was becoming dizzy. "Gavin, what's going on?" But he was clutching the other candlestick in a white-knuckled fist and stared past her, into the foyer.

"Boys, get down here," Denise whispered from beneath the table. The twins, who had been seated straight-backed alongside Eleanor at the table, now slid feetfirst from their chairs like rag dolls, vanishing beneath the vast rectangle of lacquered walnut. A strange silence filled the room. Eleanor became aware of a slow, determined thud coming from the foyer, like the sound of a hammer hitting a blanket. But the next thuds were louder. Closer.

"Where's the gun?" Denise whispered.

"Upstairs," Douglas answered, his back to the wall, the candlestick raised like a bat. But it did not sound like her son's voice. It sounded like a single piano note, horribly out of tune.

Ginny had pinned Priya to the side of the tall china cabinet, out of sight from the foyer. Ginny crouched, whispering, "Sweetie, you're going to be okay," as she slowly turned Priya's arm.

"Gavin, I feel sick," Eleanor heard herself say.

From the archway, her husband turned to her. Alone at the empty table, she was surveying the mess.

"For God sakes, Ellie." He hurled her out of her chair by her armpits. "Come on." He clenched her hand so tightly Eleanor could feel her wedding ring press into the bone of the next finger. As he led her from the room, her shoulder socket seemed to unhinge. They were running, out of breath, into the bright, vast kitchen where minutes earlier she had been arranging the dessert, where Ginny and Denise stood washing dishes.

Flinging open a closet, Gavin shoved her in with frightening brusqueness. "Ellie, do not come out. And stay quiet."

She looked at her husband's face, a face she had seen nearly every day for the past thirty-nine years. Sweat had collected in the three parallel furrows of his forehead; his nostrils flared. It was the expression he wore at the end of a run, except in his eyes she saw a flash of something unfamiliar, something like terror.

Then the door shut, and she was stranded in the dark.

DENISE

*D*enise held her children beneath the table, their bodies rigid with fear. She could see only the bottom of Douglas's legs as he positioned himself beside the threshold. As the footsteps thudded down the staircase—one set? two? God, how many people were in the house?—the toe of his gleaming brown shoe tapped nervously on the carpet.

Think clearly, she told herself. *What do you need to do? What if there's a gang? What do they want from us?* She'd seen enough crime shows. Husbands lashed to kitchen chairs with electrical cords while their wives were raped. Gangs of intruders on methamphetamines, beating grandparents with baseball bats.

Never willfully entrap yourself, that was the rule. How many times had she told her children never to get in a strange van? If you were downstairs, you did not go upstairs. You did not get rope for your attacker, or offer more weapons. She flinched at the memory of a story about a young couple and the home intruder who asked the wife to get him a hammer.

People distrusted their spouses, elected officials, but when a stranger waved a knife and said, "Do what I say and I'll let you live"—faith!

There was always a window of time when you had to risk harm for the chance of escape. Slowly, Denise reached up toward the table, groping for the tart knife, aware, suddenly, of the frailty of her fingers, the nakedness of her wrist. At the thump of approaching footsteps she yanked back her hand, retrieving only the ice-cream scoop.

The footsteps stopped and the quick huff of Douglas's breath filled the room. She wished they'd had a moment to speak, to coordinate a strategy. She couldn't even see his face. Someone had to get the gun. But how many intruders were waiting upstairs?

In the shadows beneath the table, Denise kept her hand on Laura's back, feeling the unbridled thump of her daughter's heart. The air around them had steamed over with bodily fear, cut, suddenly, with the ammonia-like scent of urine; Laura had wet herself. Kissing her daughter's head, Denise fought back a vision of the things they could do to children, to girls.

A deep voice broke the silence: "I'm coming down." Its timbre slowly filled the room; like smoke, it crept along the carpet, curled around the doorway, until Denise felt it coming toward her. She breathed it in and felt a sickness.

He was coming. Her knees and elbows locked and as her fingers tightened their grip on Brandon and Brian, her joints became stones. She understood she was bracing herself, but for what? What were they doing under the table? It wasn't an earthquake. They should have dashed for the kitchen and grabbed knives, forks, a rolling pin. They should have called 911. Anguish hit her as she realized her purse and cell phone lay stranded in the living room, that no one was coming to save them.

Denise knew she would have to get out from under the table, but the thought made her suddenly aware of the fragile contours of her skull. She felt as if the air itself might crack her head open. She tucked her chin to her chest. She wanted to stay beneath the table, to stay with her children.

"I'm gonna walk right out of here," the voice said. "I'm not afraid."

Was it the same voice? A different voice?

Wait for the window of opportunity, she thought.

The footsteps resumed, almost thunderously loud, and she saw Douglas's legs spread apart another inch.

Swing hard, she thought. *Straight to the head.*

"I'm gonna—"

Thwap. A body fell. The candlestick rolled across the travertine tile. Grunts and gasps punctuated a long frightening silence of exertion. Through the threshold she saw a tangle of bodies in the foyer, arms swinging, legs kicking at the air. Her husband's brown shoe sailed into the dining room.

Now.

Denise dashed out from the shadows of the table. Barely glancing at wrestling figures, she swiped the knife from the table, leapt over the bodies, and took the stairs two at a time. In the bedroom she rushed to the nightstand and fumbled through the drawer—goddamned magazines, tissues—until she found the gun. Her hands shook as she loaded it. Her fingers had never seemed so enormous, so clumsy. She didn't look up, she didn't look behind her.

It wasn't until she raced from the room that she noticed the walls seemed to be covered with blood, and that the blood had been smeared into symbols, or letters; the same pattern of letters, in fact, over and over again. And she realized that one word had been written across the mirror and over the dresser and closet doors, the bedspread, and headboard:

BLIGHT

ELEANOR

*T*he pitch-black pantry smelled of peanuts; the air was cooler than in the rest of the house and the floor felt like ice against her palms. Eleanor quietly drew her knees to her chest. How long did Gavin mean to leave her in here? She leaned over to press her ear to the door, but when her earring clanged loudly against the wood, she reeled back, terrified.

They accused *her* of worrying, of making too much of things? Well, this hullabaloo was entirely theirs! Shoving her into a closet. She slid off her earring and inched back toward the door. The cold wood sent a shiver from her earlobe down her neck. She heard nothing. The door had sealed her off from the rest of the world.

What if they were already back at the table, eating dessert? What if they were shouting, Come out now! Eleanor, everything is fine!

Fine. Her stomach churned at the word, and the giddiness of her thoughts subsided. She did not believe everything was fine. Beyond the wooden door, something was happening, something frightful. Never had she seen such fear on Gavin's face. Eleanor tried to remain motionless, but the more she tried to still her limbs, the more her bones rattled the cage of her body. As she tightened her grip on her legs, blood rushed painfully to her face.

An explosion of thumping broke the silence. Like horses galloping through the house. She heard a distant whimper, screams. Eleanor scrambled back from the door, toppling a bucket. Her stomach leapt and fell as she lurched forward and vomited; acidic bits of turkey and cranberry caught in her throat, burned her nose.

Her chest was heaving, her eyes watering. She carefully lifted the bucket and placed it over her head; it smelled of bleach. She pressed her handkerchief to her mouth to stifle her moans.

She did not, not, not want to imagine what was going on out there. She would think of anything else. She began to alphabetize the dishes they had served that day: applesauce, carrots, cranberries . . . What else? She forgot.

Her breaths echoed noisily against the steamy bucket. Her kerchief was drenched with saliva.

She thought of her garden, of what she would plant in the spring: marigolds, gladiolas, petunias, impatiens. She remembered how, as a child, Ginny would follow her through the garden, how together they would pluck herbs for dinner. Standing over the stove, Eleanor would watch through the window as Ginny slipped on her thick, quilted gardening gloves and inspected the flower beds. Before she tucked Ginny in at night, they would smell each other's fingertips and name the scents: mint, basil, rosemary.

More screams—sounds that seemed to stretch interminably, sounds with an almost inhuman pitch and decibel. Eleanor scurried to the back of the pantry and shoved her hands beneath the bucket to plug her ears. The muted shrieks seemed to last forever, and then she heard a dry pop. In the silence that followed she knew what it was—a gunshot.

She was too stunned to move, too frightened to call out.

But her children were out there; she had to do something, but what? She felt a tightening, as if something were being carved out of her.

They are fine. They are fine.

A vision came—the bodies of her children, her grandchildren, her husband splayed out helplessly in the dining room. She remembered what each one was wearing: Ginny in her cardigan, Douglas in his blue dress shirt and tie, her husband in his gray wool sweater.

Then Eleanor recalled the sight of her mother when she died, her small bones draped with a hospital sheet. She remembered her baby sister in death, how blue her lips had been, how her fingers wouldn't move when Eleanor clasped them. The cold stillness of death.

Eleanor held the bucket over her head and lay on her side. She would never come out. She would never see her family dead. Better to die in that closet alone.

In the dark silence, Eleanor closed her eyes, and tried to sleep.

GINNY

*B*eside the towering china cabinet, Ginny examined her daughter. The purple dress she had bought Priya earlier that week, which hung from her dresser knob just that morning, was sticky with blood. Ginny didn't understand what happened but she knew she had to block the veins, seal off arteries. Tourniquet—that was the word.

Ginny ripped a strip from her tank top; she gently pushed up Priya's sleeve and pivoted her arm to see where to stanch the bleeding. But her skin was barely scratched. Priya pulled back her arm and shook her head.

"Where are you hurt, sweetie?"

She'd let something terrible happen. And after all those CPR and emergency-child-care classes, she hadn't the foggiest idea what to do with a bleeding child except call an ambulance. Which she hadn't.

Desperation frustrated her attempts to find the wound. Somewhere at the fringes of her perception was a quiet whirl of people dashing, whispering, hiding. She yanked at Priya's collar, lifted the hem of the dress. Ginny couldn't see a single gash. And once again, Priya shook her head.

"I'm gonna walk right out of here." The deep voice of a stranger came from the next room. "I'm not afraid."

Ginny let go of the dress and hugged Priya close, burying her face in the warm valley of her daughter's neck. A sharp odor bit into her nostrils and made her eyes momentarily water—something chemical, like paint. The dress was drenched in red paint.

Ginny nearly let out a laugh of relief. Except now she heard the footsteps. Then the cacophonous collision of bone and brass. The scurry of shoes scraping the floor. Someone tore past her, and she squeezed Priya painfully close. A sound like the air being torn open, like the first burst of thunder in a silent sky, made her think, *Please God, please God. Please.*

DETECTIVE BILL O'SHEA

*T*he dispatcher told him they had a breaking and entering, with violent assault. Later, when the 911 recording was played repeatedly on television and radio, O'Shea would hear it over a dozen times.

There's been a break-in. In our house.

Are the intruders in the house now?

We used our gun.

Do you need an ambulance, ma'am?

It was a home invasion.

Is anyone injured? Do you need an ambulance?

No.

Are you in a safe place?

Just come.

Denise Olson had called. Cool as ice.

As O'Shea pulled into the long driveway and radioed in his arrival, he slowed down to take in the grandeur of the house. At the far end of a blackened yard, it sat like a lone cruise ship on a dark sea, yellow light pouring from every window. As he stepped out of the car, staring up at the dormers and gables, he almost missed the indigo smear against the grass. He pulled his weapon, stepped slowly toward a figure in a hooded gray sweatshirt, hugging the ground. He could see at least one bullet hole, in the left shoulder. The body lay flat and crooked, like a cartoon image of a man run over. On its way down, a body taking bullets broke bones and pulled tendons; when it finally settled, it always looked *wrong*. Arms and wrists lay at odd angles. With his flashlight beam, O'Shea lit the head, thrown back in profile as though howling, bleeding through panty hose where the nose had cracked against the lawn. He checked for a pulse. The boy's hands were empty.

By the time he rang the doorbell, O'Shea's mind was racing with questions. *There's been a break-in.*

A silver-haired man opened the door. He was neatly dressed, his face oddly expressionless. He stepped aside, letting O'Shea enter a vast white foyer, and with a nod indicated a second body on the floor.

This body lay neatly on its back, arms and legs held straight, the face turned to one side like a sunbather's. At a glance, O'Shea calculated the DOA had five rounds in him. But his face was bare, and young. During his twenty years on the force, O'Shea had brought in some of the roughest West Side kids. He knew the car thieves and the crackheads. He couldn't always make the charges stick, but he knew who was making the trouble. He'd never seen this boy before, and he didn't look the type. His clothes, from what O'Shea could make out, were conservative. He wore shoes, not flashy sneakers. His hair was cut short and his hands were empty.

"Are there weapons?" O'Shea asked. The man with the silver hair nodded, this time toward a side table where the gun was laid out—Jesus—on a doily. A Glock semiautomatic. O'Shea slipped on a pair of gloves and checked the magazine—a ten-round clip. It was empty, standard with self-defense. People often pulled the trigger long after the bullets were used. But in general, only one or two bullets find their way into a target. Somehow, almost every bullet in that pistol made its way into the two bodies.

"This licensed?" O'Shea asked.

"To me." The man spoke softly; he had the good looks of a weatherman. "I'm Douglas Olson, this is my . . ." He wiped sweat from his brow with his shirt cuff, smearing blood across his forehead; the buttons of his shirt had been torn.

"Have a seat, Mr. Olson."

O'Shea couldn't figure it. Intruders were career criminals and rarely entered a house teeming with five wide-awake adults; if they did, they came seriously armed. The only weapons the perpetrators had were a couple of knives in their pockets. But they didn't seem to be burglars either. No diamond necklaces dangled from their pockets, no pillowcases stuffed with candlesticks were slung over their shoulders. On the entryway floor sat a duffel bag full of spray-paint cans.

O'Shea pulled a can of red spray paint from the duffel and shook it—empty. He looked around the white floor, the dark-wood walls, the wide stairway curving toward the second floor, but didn't see a trace of paint anywhere. Except on a young Indian girl, lurking in the next room.

"Did they spray these *at* you?" he asked the girl. She shook her head.

O'Shea headed into the massive living room, where the rest of the family had converged. They were circling two leather sectionals, sitting, then bolting up, in what looked like a high-speed game of musical chairs. Their motions were erratic, jerky—adrenaline could stay in the system ten hours. In the past, at crime scenes, O'Shea often got lucky, adrenaline loosening not only tears but also tongues; the right woman could sob out every detail of a crime in a few minutes. But the whole clan had gone stone-cold. Even the children.

The grandmother, Eleanor Olson, crouched on the carpet, taking apart a dollhouse, wiping each piece on her pants before putting it into a cardboard box. "Ma'am, we need to leave everything," O'Shea said. "Until forensics gets here."

Intent on wiping the dollhouse chimney clean, she seemed not to hear him.

"Ellie." Her husband crossed the room and stilled her arms.

She looked up, startled. Damp brown hair clung to her makeup-free face. "It's so god-awfully hot in here," she said, fanning the bosom of a low-cut purple sweater, too tight for a woman her age.

She set the chimney in the box and her eyes roved anxiously toward the foyer.

"Is he still there?" she whispered.

Gavin Olson looked at O'Shea in what would be the first of their silent understandings.

"All right, everyone," said O'Shea. "Captain Briggs is sending backup. Right now I'm gonna get you away from this mess, get the kids away from this. We'll go to the station where we can talk."

GAVIN

Gavin stood in the archway, blood pumping, listening to the foot-steps. His body felt boneless, like a mass of swollen muscle. He felt taut, fierce. He felt as he had forty years earlier, fingertips on the track, lunging at the start of a race.

He thought of Eleanor alone in the pantry. At least he had gotten her to safety. His daughter, across the room, was hiding behind the china cabinet. He could see her red hair, which struck him as it never had before—it made her seem horribly vulnerable.

Across from him stood his son; they locked eyes and in a flash Douglas pivoted into the foyer. Bodies wrestled, fell. Gavin's vision blurred, then returned. He was a six-foot-two current of electricity, the candlestick a part of him. He saw his son pinned on the ground; he struck out.

DETECTIVE BILL O'SHEA

*T*he family stepped out into the night, filing quietly past the body on the lawn. The front walkway lights cast a soft, strangely peaceful glow over the corpse. O'Shea noticed that the adults angled their heads to examine what could be seen of the boy's face. O'Shea, unable to comprehend how a civilian could hit a moving target, remarked, "That's some aim."

Only the sounds of shoes crunching along the white pebble path answered him, until finally, Gavin Olson announced, "Army. Nam. I'm the shooter."

O'Shea had heard of his type—some cops called them *Rice Krispies,* because one day, they went *snap crackle pop* and whipped out a gun as if they had never left the jungle. They thought the checkout boy at the Stop & Shop was Vietcong. The exhaust from a station wagon smelled like napalm. Without family, unable to hold down jobs, these vets crowded shelters and soup kitchens. But Gavin Olson had children and grandchildren; he looked like a man who had held it together. If a burglar hadn't come at him, thought O'Shea, he'd probably have gone on quietly.

The Vietnam vets had gotten a raw deal; most people preferred to forget they'd been sent halfway across the world to do the country's fighting before Americans changed their minds. O'Shea's father had fought in Korea. His father was probably a decade older than Gavin Olson, but O'Shea could imagine him, roused from sleep, unloading a gun into two intruders. The army didn't train you to subdue the

297

enemy, it trained you to kill. Maybe Gavin Olson had crossed legal lines, but these things happened in the thick of fear. O'Shea was certain the race issue would wag everyone's tail and didn't want to see a good man get the raw end of someone's political agenda.

At the squad car, he gestured Gavin Olson into the back. "Why don't you ride with me."

They pulled onto the darkened road, followed by two other cars, and O'Shea radioed his movements into Briggs.

"So when we get to the station, I'm going to have to ask you a lot of questions," O'Shea said, "but right now you shouldn't speak. I'll just fill the time here a little, make the ride go faster. I was watching this show last night, a History Channel thing, about how in the United States we've got a thing called the Castle Doctrine. You know about that?"

Gavin Olson shook his head.

O'Shea continued: "It goes back a few hundred years, right back to the time of the Constitution, actually. It says a man can use force to defend his home . . . but only in certain circumstances." O'Shea stared at the dark road ahead and readjusted his clammy palms on the steering wheel. His first year on the force, at age twenty-five, he'd swiped a hundred-dollar bill from a table at a Greek diner where he'd responded to a stabbing; afterward, he felt so anxious he returned it to an evidence envelope. He'd certainly never coached a statement, and wasn't sure he had the stomach for it. But he'd never before come across a scene where he knew that the victims, if they were sloppy with their words, might be charged as criminals. Overcome by the shock of violation, victims rarely imagined they could end up in trouble, at least not until it was too late. There was a short window of time to help do the right thing.

"The key is," O'Shea continued, "it's different from state to state. Funny little nitpicky things. For instance, in Connecticut, the law gets into the difference between reasonable physical force and deadly force. A whole section of this law specifies that a man has to reasonably believe a trespasser intends to commit a violent crime. So if a trespasser wasn't inside the premises, and wasn't waving a weapon, there would have to be verbal threats of violence. Anyway, it was an interesting show."

They arrived at the station and O'Shea guided the family up the stairs into the waiting room. Their jittery energy had faded, and they quietly settled into the chairs.

He gave Gavin Olson a little while for what he'd explained to sink in, and by the time O'Shea announced, "Now I'll need you to come down the hall and tell me the events at the house. I just need the chronology. I'll be recording it. Understand?" The man nodded.

As O'Shea read him his Miranda rights, his family looked up as if he were being led to slaughter. "This is just so everyone is clear, and everyone is protected. This shouldn't take long."

In just under thirty minutes, O'Shea got the details of the day, beginning with the broken oven in Mamaroneck, leading up to the moment, at the end of dinner, when they heard footsteps upstairs. Gavin Olson did his part describing how the second boy charged the house. He spoke flatly, with little of the embellishment that often accompanied false statements.

"He threatened us verbally," he stated, then cleared his throat. "From the yard, he threatened to kill us. As did the boy inside the house. I felt it my duty to protect my family."

When he led Gavin Olson back into the waiting room, his family looked up anxiously. The youngest child had wrapped herself in a red checkered blanket and was splayed across her father's lap.

"So folks, now I'll need to bring you into the interrogation room one by one, just to go over the sequence of things and to get your statements on record. We need to determine how the perps entered the house, if anyone has a connection to the dead boys. Completely routine. Mrs. Olson, wanna start us off?" he said to the grandmother. She was staring dully at the clipboards hanging on the Most Wanted board; she seemed a pale marble statue of a woman. "Mrs. Olson?"

Finally, the redheaded woman stood: Ginny Olson, the professor from Mamaroneck. She still hadn't uncrossed her arms. "Detective, I think we'll phone a lawyer first."

After all that. Who knew how long it would be before their lawyer showed? Meanwhile, O'Shea was stuck there waiting for the call from Captain Briggs. He fixed himself a cold plate of what was left of the buffet—all the white meat had been picked over, the gravy had turned to gel, and the stuffing had stiffened into globs.

But he had a big appetite. The Olsons turned one by one to watch him eat, with an almost meditative fascination, and O'Shea realized he was chewing with his mouth open, sucking noisily at bits of turkey caught in his teeth. His wife often complained about this, and now he grabbed a dusty napkin from a drawer and quietly wiped his mouth.

Finally the phone rang and it was Briggs. "I'm headed your way soon. What'd you get out of them?"

O'Shea stepped into the next room. "Zilch. First grandpa confesses, I get his statement. Everything's fine. But the rest lawyered up."

"I can see why," Briggs said. "We've got some odd shit here."

DOUGLAS

*A*s soon as Douglas heard the intruder get close, he sprang into
the foyer and swung the candlestick. It caught the man in the
chest—he was tall—and he doubled over long enough for Douglas to
get his arms around his back and wrestle him to the floor. His father,
wielding his own candlestick, struck at the intruder's legs. Across the
slick floor, sliding and flailing, Douglas grappled to get the man in a
Nelson hold and took an elbow to his jaw.

He was aware of his father running along the foyer swinging both
candlesticks, looking to see if other intruders were coming, but he
did not see Denise go past.

Her voice took him by surprise. At first it sounded like *Please*,
until she said it again, louder, insistently, nearly shrieking through the
house as she descended the stairs: "Freeze."

At the sight of the gun in her hand, Douglas jumped off the man.
Denise moved fast down the stairs, charging toward the figure on the
floor. She moved so close Douglas thought the man might grab her
ankles.

"Shoot!" coughed Douglas, scrambling back against the wall.

The intruder slowly raised his hands over his head and began to sit
up. Douglas saw his wife hesitate.

"I'm not—" the man began.

"Denise!"

Denise closed her eyes and the shot rang out. The circle of blood on
the man's black shirt was at first imperceptible. But the sudden curl-

ing of his body signaled to Douglas the bullet had struck. The intruder writhed, releasing an almost childlike whimper, and smeared blood across the white floor as he kicked one leg rhythmically in an attempt to get a foothold. He turned his face frantically from side to side, as though he couldn't quite see, at which point Douglas realized he had some kind of stocking on his face, flattening his nose and lips grotesquely. Saliva bubbled through the mesh of beige fabric.

Douglas stood frozen for a moment as his father set the candlesticks on the floor and removed his belt. His father pinned the flailing intruder beneath his knee and fastened the man's arms, tugging tightly at the belt ends.

Denise had not moved from where she had pulled the trigger; she stood on the bottom stair, the gun still pointed directly at the man.

The children emerged from the dining room, one by one. Behind them, with blank eyes, a disheveled Ginny took in the bound intruder, the blood on the floor. She made a dazed attempt to stop the children, pawing at their shoulders. But of their own accord, the children stopped in their tracks when they saw their mother holding a gun.

Douglas pried the gun from her fingers. "I'm going to check the rest of the house." For a moment, her arm remained raised and he gently set it at her side. "It's okay, his hands are tied."

"Be careful," Denise mumbled.

As he slowly mounted the stairs, they were all silent, until Ginny's voice seemed to bounce off the ceiling.

"Wait, where the hell's Mom?"

DETECTIVE BILL O'SHEA

*B*riggs explained the strange evidentiary details: when forensics dusted the gun, instead of fingerprints they found a perfumed lotion, like from a hand wipe. The coroner, called in for a preliminary exam, determined that the boy inside the house had been shot while lying prone. The boy outside, although struck with two bullets, had been fired at four times.

Briggs had gone through the entire house and determined what the spray paint was about: the word *Blight* covered the upstairs bedrooms. They identified the bodies, and neither boy had priors. One attended Jefferson High, where Denise Olson worked. The other had gone there but transferred a month earlier. Two blocks from the house, a van with a dead engine from a reading light that was left on was recovered in the woods.

O'Shea hung up, uneasy that the gun had been wiped down.

He looked at the family, still waiting on their lawyer. Exhaustion showed on their faces, but was there also some hint of fear? O'Shea decided he'd toss the group a softball to see who might swing. "You don't have to answer, but you might want to churn over if the word *blight* means anything to you all."

Denise Olson was the only one to stir; she turned and glared at her husband. O'Shea could see in her face that the adrenaline was wearing off, that an emotion other than shock had taken hold of her. "It means something to my husband," she said. *The first signs of defection,* thought O'Shea. Someone always broke from the pack.

"Which I will explain when our lawyer is here," her husband answered.

Finally, at about ten past ten, Todd from the *Advocate* called.

"Happy Thanksgiving, William, my man," he said. Todd had just graduated from Princeton and was always trying to win O'Shea's respect with his diligent but awkward use of street lingo. "What're our stats for today, my man?"

O'Shea ran down the disorderlies, the aggravated assaults, and finally said they had a B&E in the North Side with two dead perps.

"Killed?" he asked excitedly. "Licensed or unlicensed weapon?"

"Licensed." O'Shea could hear boredom blowing out of Todd's mouth. The kid had set his career sights higher than the police blotter; he wanted to be covering citywide scandals. He didn't realize he was getting the first whiff of a story that would fill the papers for weeks.

Come on, thought O'Shea, *ask me how many slugs were in the bodies, ask me where the bodies were, ask me who was white and who was black.*

Instead, Todd asked, "You getting off duty soon?"

O'Shea couldn't resist giving a young person a shot at something big. The story was going to break, no matter what.

"As soon as the captain gets back from the scene."

What a bone he threw! The captain at the scene! Wake up, kid!

"Okay, my man. Don't keep the old lady waiting up too late."

"Todd," O'Shea said. "You gotta get yourself a real job."

GINNY

Ginny opened the pantry door and tugged on the light. In the far corner, her mother lay sideways, hugging her knees, a bucket over her head. She lay completely still, as though sleeping, except that from beneath the bucket came a steady, breathy whimper.

"Mom, it's me." Ginny crouched and stroked her mother's hip. "Mom, are you okay?"

From beneath the bucket, in a muted voice that sounded faraway, a voice that sounded like it came through speakers, came one desperate word: "Ginny?"

Her mother unclasped her knees, swung her arms about confusedly, and pushed herself up. Slowly, Ginny lifted the bucket off, revealing a shiny and horrifying version of her mother's face. Rivulets of mascara and blush marbled her cheeks, orange flecks of vomit clung to her chin. Her sweat-flattened hair made her head look small, disturbingly fragile. Her mother closed her eyes firmly in disbelief, then opened them.

"Everybody is fine, Mom. You can come out."

As Ginny began to stand, her mother gripped her wrist and tugged her down with astonishing force. "Oh, Ginny, sit with me." Then she whispered, "Please."

Ginny settled at her side and stroked her shoulder, while her mother wrung her hands through the memory of what had happened, or what had almost happened. As they sat, occasionally her head twitched, or she released a guttural moan. Then, in a rush of affection, she touched

Ginny's chin, fingers tapping Ginny's cheeks like a blind person. Unsure of how to calm her mother, Ginny held still until her mother seemed convinced of her presence, then she tore open a package of cocktail napkins and wiped the edges of her mother's mouth. Ginny finally took her mother's hand and guided her, slowly, into the kitchen. Her mother flinched at the bright lights. Her eyes darted nervously around the stools and the center island as she wobbled across the marble floor. They finally passed into the dining room, where Priya and her cousins, seated at the table, stared blankly at the upturned pitchers and broken plates.

"The poor dears." Her mother looked at the children and pressed her fingers to her lips. "What was done to them?"

Ginny, still exhausted from the shock—whose stomach reeled at the sight of Priya's dress and the memory of the intruder's footsteps—found herself snapping, "Nothing, Mom. Everyone's okay."

But her mother stood still for a moment and began to gnaw her bottom lip; as they finally entered the foyer, she let out a gasp. Blood had begun to pool beneath the bound man. Her mother shook her head, grabbed Ginny's elbow.

"Where's Douglas?"

"He's upstairs, making sure everything is okay."

"Douglas!" she screamed. She bent forward, using her entire torso to harness her voice. "Douglas, where are you? Get down here right this instant!" Her chest heaved almost asthmatically from the exertion, and she gripped the banister. Over her shoulder, she kept her eyes trained on the bleeding man, until Douglas's footfalls on the stairs above summoned her attention.

"Get down here!" she shrieked.

But Douglas descended slowly, his face ashen.

"Was anyone up there?" Ginny asked.

He shook his head, set the gun down on the entryway table, and stared hard at the man he'd been struggling with minutes earlier. He sat on an upholstered bench beside the door, leaning down so that his face was inches from the bleeding man's.

"You *know* me?" Douglas asked.

The man sucked down saliva, wrestling noisily with his own tongue. "I'm not . . . afraid of you."

He spoke like a man with a swollen lip, or a lisp, but something else in the voice struck Ginny as strange. Douglas, too, seemed curious. He kneeled down and reached for the panty hose. Peeling them back, inch by inch, he revealed the neck, the chin, and, eventually, the frightened eyes of a face that looked to be no more than seventeen.

Douglas gripped his own head. "Oh, bloody Jesus."

The boy huffed, holding back tears. His eyes moved around the foyer, from face to face. He tightened his mouth, struggled to get the words out. "I'm not afraid. I'm . . . not," the boy began, but the effort of speaking seemed to set off a spasm of pain. He grunted and his legs bucked, knocking Douglas momentarily off balance.

As Ginny watched Douglas steady himself, she became aware of a sound coming from outside the house, a yelping, high-pitched baying. Douglas, her father, and Denise all fell silent as the distant sounds took on the shape of words.

Whoop, whoop, whoop. Look at me! Whoop, whoop, whoop, see if you can catch me!

Slowly, Ginny opened the front door, where a boy with a stocking over his head zigzagged across the lawn, waving his arms like a drowning man signaling for help. He lunged from side to side, dance-like and frantic, then stiffened his arms into propellers, dipped his head, and sprinted in a vague figure eight.

Whoop, I'm a crazy black mothafucka! Come on out here and look at me!

The boy on the floor thrashed toward the doorway. "Spider, take off!"

Whoop, whoop. Whoop, whoop, look at me. I'm a crazy nigger on your lawn! Come and get me!

Ginny, watching the boy circling closer, was only vaguely aware of someone lifting the pistol off the side table. She recognized her mother's voice, screaming, "Leave us alone! Get away!" but did not see her mother point the gun. She thought nothing until four loud shots thundered through the air. The boy on the lawn spun from the force. His knees buckled and his half-raised arms went limp as he slammed, with a crackling thud, face-first onto the grass.

Stunned, Ginny turned around in time to see the boy in the foyer reel back in fear. Hands bound behind him, he lay on his back, trying to push himself along the floor with his legs. In what she would remember, years later, as the worst moment of that entire night, his eyes caught Ginny's—why hers?—and fastened on her face in a desperate plea for life, as Ginny's mother emptied the chamber into him, *pop, pop, pop,* like she'd been firing guns all her life.

DENISE

Denise had fixed her gaze on her mother-in-law. Her entire vision was consumed by Eleanor's liver-spotted hand squeezing the pistol in steady, deft spasms until the gun offered a hollow, almost mortified click. Bullet casings rolled over the floor, gunpowder thickened the air, and the boy, who moments earlier had crawled across the foyer, now lay hideously still. Through the black scraps of his clothes, patches of bright pink flesh shone obscenely.

Her knees weakened and she sat, noticing that her velour sweatpants were speckled with blood.

The gun clanked to the floor. "Oh, Gavin, what did I do?" Eleanor began to walk in a circle, until it looked as if she might walk straight into the wall.

Gavin led her to the bench.

Her face contorted as though she were in physical pain. "Oh no," she mumbled. She covered her face with her hands, then pulled them back. "Are the children okay?"

"Yes."

"I don't know what . . ."

"Everybody's not okay," Denise heard herself say. "There's a dead body in my foyer and another on my lawn. What the fuck *was* that?"

Douglas moved before her and opened his arms, but she pushed them away, loosening in her own arms a sudden unruly energy. She slapped his knee, his hip, and in one fierce swing her palm landed noisily across his cheek. Motionless, silent, her husband accepted her rage. But almost as quickly as the fit began, Denise's arms went slack with fatigue. She lost the urge to move, to speak. And as her breathing slowed, she discovered that what minutes earlier had been terror, what had been an awful looming possibility, had been replaced by a thick, black certainty of ruin.

They all held perfectly still as the silence of what happened pooled around them. They did not look at one another. Time thickened, molded over, and filled Denise's mouth with sour dread.

Gavin broke the stillness as he crossed the foyer and retrieved the gun from the floor. "We should move quickly," he said, as he began to wipe the gun's handle and trigger with the hem of his undershirt. *Move quickly*. Denise realized what had to happen. Numbly, she stood and from the top drawer of the entryway table pulled a package of disinfectant towelettes. She carefully wiped down her hands, then handed the package to Gavin, who nodded and crouched before Eleanor to clean her fingers one by one. Slowly, Douglas shouldered closed the door. They all moved quietly, senselessly, like sleepwalkers.

"Douglas, untie him," said Gavin, and Douglas, standing over the dead boy, momentarily shook his head before turning him facedown to unfasten the belt binding his hands.

The swift choreography of her husband's motions nauseated Denise.

As she sat there, an image came to her unexpectedly of her parents in Pittsburgh. And her brothers. What were they doing right now? She had an urge to call them and tell them she was all right. To see if they were all right. She rose, rushed for her purse, and dug for her phone.

"Say there's been a break-in," Gavin called out. "Intruders down. But keep it short."

It took a moment for his instructions to register, but then Denise realized what needed to be done, and she began to compose her statement before dialing.

"And Eleanor," Gavin called, "wash your face and take off that sweater."

Eleanor, confused, looked down at her blood-drenched clothes. As though her sweater were on fire, she yanked it over her head, and flung it to the floor.

"The cops will find it," Ginny said distantly, the only one who hadn't moved, still staring at the body on the floor.

The idea came to Denise like the answer to a riddle, and it was almost with pride that she said, "Not if you put it on."

Ginny looked back in horror.

"Under what you're wearing," said Denise, who understood there was no time for niceties or gentleness, who understood they were now all complicit. "That'll get it out of here."

DETECTIVE BILL O'SHEA

*I*t was close to 10:00 p.m. and the lawyer had yet to arrive. O'Shea still needed to interview the other family members individually, which meant a long night of statements. The fluorescent lights had triggered one of his fatigue headaches, usually remedied by activity, though none was in sight. He realized the shock of the scene at the house had taken a toll on him, and what he'd said to Gavin Olson was slowly sinking in, somewhat uncomfortably. As his jaw tingled into a silent yawn, he vigorously rubbed his face. He radioed Captain Briggs to explain the situation.

"Mr. Olson, we have to keep you, for now," he announced. "But the rest of you can come back in the morning."

Gavin Olson nodded with what looked like relief, brushed off his knees, and stood. He turned to his wife and touched her chin.

"Go home with Ginny. Try to get some sleep."

She looked up at him, eyes teary. "I don't want to leave you here."

"I'll be fine."

O'Shea braced for a scene, for screaming, hitting. He'd seen every size and shape of crazy at the station. But she just squeezed her husband's fingertips, then pressed them to her lips.

"You are a good man," she said.

The son stood and stared at his father; they seemed like mirror images but for the father's gray hair. The son set his hand awkwardly on his father's shoulder. They looked to O'Shea like two people who had never before touched.

"We'll come back first thing in the morning, Dad."

Ginny Olson stood, her arms still crossed. Her red hair had come loose from its clip and hung in her face. With his thumb, Gavin Olson shifted it from her eyes.

"Go home," he whispered. "Clean up." Her chin dipped and she nodded.

Denise Olson gathered her sons, but said nothing to Gavin Olson. *The defector,* thought O'Shea. Tomorrow she would be the first to offer up the truth about the fingerprints. "Good night, Detective," she said, and headed for the door. The rest of the family suddenly clustered together, barely an inch between any of them, as though taking shelter together beneath an umbrella, as they made their way out.

O'Shea felt a tinge of pity as they left; he knew none of them would sleep. They'd each lie in bed, replaying the events of the night. As he always did.

O'Shea rattled his keys and led Gavin Olson to a cell. He was tired but wanted a moment with the man. He sat beside him on the cot and poured him a cup of water.

"Sorry I can't offer you anything stronger. It's this or Snapple."

"Water's fine."

"No one ever drowned their sorrows in water."

Gavin sipped his water, swirled it around his mouth, and swallowed. "Can't ever drown them."

O'Shea laughed. "Don't tell the Irish." He twisted the cap back on the bottle. "You know, my father fought in Korea. Fifth Air Force."

"Mine was in the Eighth," Gavin answered. "Over Germany."

"Different times. You Nam guys really got hung out to dry. Just so you know, some of us still give a damn."

O'Shea saw the man open his mouth to speak, then exhale the thought. Instead, he glanced at O'Shea's wedding ring. "Do you have a son?"

"Daughter," said O'Shea. "But I tell you, she'd pick up a weapon and storm the enemy's front line."

"They're tough these days."

"Ballbusters. Still, you want to do everything you can to protect them. Hell, I'd unload a clip to protect my family."

Gavin Olson stared into his cup and seemed to contemplate this. "Parents would do anything to protect their family."

"Was it like a flashback? At the house?"

He threw his head back to take a long, final sip of water, then cleared his throat. "Something like that."

As they sat in the chilly silence of the cell, O'Shea wanted to ask the man why he had wiped the prints off the gun. But he stopped himself—not because he thought he'd overstep boundaries but because, he realized, he didn't want the answer.

Gavin Olson looked down at his knee, gave it a slow, melancholy rub. "I'm tired, Detective."

"Get some shut-eye."

GAVIN

*T*he cell's cement walls had been painted gray. From the bedside table rose an uneven pyramid of distractions that the detective had left for him: car magazines, a Bible, a worn deck of cards.

Gavin carefully removed his shoes and lay back on the bed. He set the cards on his stomach and over and over he cut the deck, shuffled, listening to the soft rhythmic slap of the cards. He wanted to quiet his mind, to block out the evening's events, but kept recalling the look on Eleanor's face in the pantry, an expression of helplessness he had seen before.

Suddenly he remembered—Eleanor's article. An event from seven years earlier that he and Eleanor had never spoken of since.

Eleanor had lunched with a former classmate, a magazine editor who asked if Eleanor wanted to write an article about empty-nest syndrome.

His wife had once been a reporter for the Wellesley newspaper, writing articles about long cafeteria lines or about the plan to renovate the university gymnasium. Once in a while, she'd clip one and send it to him in Saigon. Gavin enjoyed seeing her name in the paper. He liked knowing that life back home, with all its trivial dramas, was chugging along. But he never suffered the slightest regret that she gave it up when he returned home, nor did he think she had.

Which was why he was surprised to come home one night and find their bed strewn with yellow legal pads and a rainbow of three-ring binders. She'd bought ballpoint, rollerball, and felt-tip pens. Post-it pads of all sizes.

"Eleanor, I can get you this crap at the office. We have a supply closet."

"I couldn't wait!" She uncapped one of the pens and tested it on a pad with a dramatic scrawl, like a celebrity signing an autograph.

He could see she'd let her imagination run wild, gotten the idea in her head that this was going to be a breeze. It was going to be fun. Everybody would be talking about the brilliant article by Eleanor Olson, and soon she'd be writing articles regularly. Gavin found something grating in her cheery confidence, something verging on disrespect. He'd worked thirty years at one company, eking out four promotions and five raises, twice forgoing a Christmas bonus when the company was struggling. He'd woken at 5:30 a.m. each day to catch a train into the city so that he could put a roof over their heads and send their children to college. His wife thought a passing invitation to participate in the professional world meant red carpets would be rolled out for her.

"Eleanor, think this through. Magazines have editors, serious editors, and fact-checkers, and they're used to dealing with professionals. This is going to be a lot of work, so don't say you'll do it unless you're really willing to put the hours in. You don't wanna piss people off."

"Well, how many hours do you think it would take? I have oodles of free time."

"You've never done this before. It's going to be hard. You're not a professional writer."

"Colleen believes I can do it. And she's a professional editor." Eleanor settled on a felt-tip and swept the other pens aside. "And frankly, *you've* never done something like this before, so it would be hard for you to estimate the time, right?"

She was treating work as if it were a hairdo she had finally decided to try. Did she have any idea what his days had been like all those years?

"Colleen's trying to talk you into doing this, that's her job. You haven't put a word on a page in almost twenty years. It isn't going to just pour out of you. Eleanor, you hardly manage to finish the books for your book club. You're not goal-oriented. You never have been. These women who write articles and edit magazines—you're not like them. Do this if you want to, I'm not stopping you. But as your husband, it's my job to tell it to you straight. I've never sugarcoated things for you, and I think I should protect you if I see you walking into a brick wall."

"Oh." Her mouth hung open. He could see tears forming in the corners of her eyes. "I thought you'd be excited for me."

"Sweetheart." He sat beside her. "You're a great mother, and you've always taken pride in that, and I've taken pride in that. I just hate the idea of you thinking that's not enough. I hate to see you set up to feel lousy about yourself."

"Well, it was nice to be asked," she said, dabbing her eyes. "I think that's certainly very flattering. Don't you?"

"Being asked is what's important."

He had thought that was the end of it. Life went on as normal; she ran her errands. She kept busy with her gardening club, planted a whole row of petunias and begonias in the backyard.

But then he came home one day, months later, and found her in the bedroom at six o'clock in the afternoon, sitting at her vanity table, her face naked and shiny with cold cream, staring dully at her own reflection. At first he worried something had happened to the kids, and he tried to think of where they were—Douglas at work, Ginny teaching. Then he noticed the pencil behind one of her ears, the pen behind the other. The bed was littered with crumpled pages, along with an open thesaurus and dictionary.

"I just thought I'd try a few pages, nothing that would take up too much time, and that maybe once Colleen gave me some encouragement . . ."

"You don't need this kind of stress. She'll understand if you back out. It happens all the time in the working world."

"But I already sent it!" She whirled around and plucked one of the balled-up pages from the bed. "Look! I wrote seven of these and sent them along. Oh, I felt so happy! So proud of myself! I thought . . ." She had to swallow hard to continue. "I thought they were *quite good*. Then Colleen phoned ten minutes later. She took one look, for *ten* measly minutes, and that was that. My prose style isn't for their magazine, but thank you for putting in so much effort. I said I could try a different approach but she said, 'Oh, don't worry,' and practically *hung* up on me. That's it! No second chances! When is something like this ever going to come my way again?"

"Eleanor, try to calm down."

"I can't be expected to read minds! How could I have known what she wanted? I could have done it differently. Taken a different approach. I'm good with feedback, you know that. I don't take criticism to heart. The editors at the Wellesley paper said I was a pleasure to work with!"

What could he do to make her feel better? "Ellie, sweetie, lie down for a while."

He led her to the bed and she curled up on her side. Then she bolted upright. "You won't tell Ginny, will you? Please, please, please don't tell her. I should have listened to you. I wish I'd never wasted any time on this stupid thing. Now all I feel is awful, awful, awful."

"No one will know."

She took a sleeping pill and poured herself a glass of scotch. She took a long sip, wiped her mouth dry, and pressed her face to the pillow.

"You shouldn't drink with pills, Eleanor."

But she had grown calm, tranquil. "Please, take them away. I don't ever want to see those pages again."

He collected the crumpled pages, put them into a plastic bag, and carried the bag downstairs. In the kitchen, he made a cheese sandwich, opened a beer, and thought about how she'd been working in secret. It seemed strange to think of his wife doing anything secretive. He took one of the pages out of the plastic bag and flattened it.

Long after a mother provides milk for her children, she provides the metaphorical milk, the emotional nourishment, like adult milk combined with a vitamin of love. She gives of herself without asking; she becomes like a psychic, someone with extrasensory perception, anticipating the needs and wants of her family.

Her husband is like the captain of the ship. Sometimes, it may seem as though he is far away, aloof. But it is his duty to stand on deck and watch for storms, to steer the family clearly toward safe waters, and a wife must never nag and ask him to leave his watch.

He set his dish in the sink, threw out the rest of the pages, and, repentant, went upstairs to lie beside her.

DETECTIVE BILL O'SHEA

*A*s O'Shea expected, the case got the entire city talking.
Diana Velasquez was the *Advocate* reporter who finally realized that five white adults plus two dead, unarmed black kids equaled one major story. Having worked at the paper for a decade, she knew to double-check the police blotter every night in the hopes that the cub reporters missed something. She knew that a shooting in the North End would sell papers. When word got out about the stone knife in Kijo Jackson's pocket, a Siwanoy Indian relic, Diana dubbed the incident the Thanksgiving Day Massacre.

In the week following Thanksgiving, parents and children, even gang members and drug dealers from the city's West Side, gathered outside the police department jabbing picket signs into the cold gray air, shouting, "Justice for Kijo and Spider." News about the hand wipes used to clean the gun prompted signs that read: YOU CAN'T WIPE US AWAY. Television reporters filmed the protestors, whose breath steamed in infuriated clouds. The occasional egg landed on a squad car. Still, the district attorney wouldn't prosecute Gavin Olson.

At sunset, candles were lit before photographs of the dead boys. As the crowds went home, the empty parking lot remained a galaxy of sad remembrance, at the center of which sat an old woman.

For days, Kijo Jackson's grandmother presided over a milk crate across from the police station, accepting brown-bagged sandwiches and thermoses of soup from the other protestors. She spoke extensively to the reporters about how Kijo had always taken care of her, how he'd never raised a hand to anyone. O'Shea could see her from his window. She spoke with an almost violent animation, jabbing her cane in the air. But when she fell silent, when she sat looking at the photos of her grandson, the life seemed to drain from her body.

One night, as O'Shea was leaving the station, she called out to him from her perch.

"My boy didn't deserve what them folks done," she said. Her voice sounded weak and the candlelight danced slowly across her face. "Nobody deserves five bullets just for stepping in a house. You don't like what someone's doing, you point a gun and you say 'freeze.' Just like the police. You give a boy a chance."

O'Shea should have slipped into his car, but he paused. He had seen her grandson's body, had helped to protect the man who had shot him; he felt he owed the woman some peace of mind.

"In situations like that," he said, "it's all chaos, confusion—"

"Five bullets. You imagine what that felt like?"

O'Shea was silent. He had, in fact, never been shot.

"You give a child a chance," she cut in, her voice going hoarse. "A chance. You don't kill a child for using spray paint. That man took our house. Kijo did wrong, but he was trying to do right."

O'Shea found it a sad irony that even with all the news stories about how Kijo and his grandmother had been dislocated by Obervell Tower, about the designation of blight, the protests actually spurred talk of tearing down Vidal Court. The station got word to arrest for any disorderly conduct in that area and O'Shea suspected the mayor was hoping a protest would get out of hand, that a small riot would make the case for cleaning up the city's last project, the final bastion of drugs and crime.

Whenever he took a seat at a bar, O'Shea told of his small part in the case; it got people's attention, brought out heated opinions about everything from handguns to eminent domain. Everybody had a theory of what he would have done in the same situation, as did O'Shea. He was certain he would have unloaded his weapon, yet he never told anyone, not even his wife, how he had explained the Castle Doctrine to Gavin Olson. He never spoke about the fact that he could tell Ginny Olson was hiding something.

Afterward, however, he wondered about it. Wondered if he had missed some piece of the puzzle. Whenever he heard the 911 recording, his mind always tripped on the phrase *We used our gun.*

He often recalled how, after the Olson family had gone home, after he had locked up Gavin Olson's cell, he returned to his desk to finally call his wife.

"Bill, for God sakes, it's after ten o'clock at night!" Brenda cried.

As they always did when he had to work a holiday, they argued that morning about the nature of his job. As he left, she grumbled about the hours, the fact that he did little more than sit at his desk and read the sports pages. Now, on the phone, he was eager to tell Brenda about the incident on Deerkill Road. He whispered, the way he would if they were lying in bed in the dark.

"I was the first one on the scene."

"My God, Bill. That could have been dangerous."

"I was prepared."

"What on earth were those kids doing there?"

"Spray painting, it seems. But you know, the economy's taking a dip. We might start seeing all sorts of crime coming back."

"Did the family seem weird? Rich-people weird?"

"They seemed like perfectly nice folks with a dead body in their house."

He could hear her pacing the living room, pictured her settling, barefoot, into her favorite reading chair. "I didn't know you were out on a call," she said. "I'm sorry, sweetheart." He loved the sound in her voice—and he could detect every slight change in his wife's tone—when she thought he was doing something important.

"I just have to write up a few more notes, then I'll be on my way." It would be a long ride home, though, a good thirty minutes to Port Chester. It was as close to the station as they could afford.

"Oh, Bill. The food is all cold," she moaned. "I took it out of the oven two hours ago."

"Don't worry." He couldn't tell her he'd already eaten the food Carl Dundee's wife had brought to the station; it would break her heart. "I'll make myself a turkey sandwich."

"It's not the same."

"Don't worry, hon. Look, let me wrap up and get on my way."

"I love you," she said, as she always said when he'd had a brush with danger.

"I love you, too."

The station was virtually empty. He wrote up a few more notes and made his way out into the parking lot. As he walked, he was thinking of the dead boys, who were just about his daughter's age, and the Olsons, the way they had huddled together in the station, folding in on one another, as though any physical distance might separate them forever.

When something like this happened, he had to wonder: Was this an aberration? Or was he looking at the beginning of something bigger, that first little crack that eventually opens up the ground?

The parking lot was quiet. He was tired and he was happy to finally be making his way back to his family. And then, he wasn't sure why, he looked over his shoulder, with the strangest sensation that something, unnamed, was coming.

EPILOGUE

*I*t was March, and Ginny sat beneath the fluorescent lights in the vast auditorium. Beside her sat Douglas, tapping a rolled magazine nervously on his thigh. Those days, he always kept something in his hands—a noisy box of Tic Tacs, his cell phone, which rarely rang, or the keys to Ginny's house in Mamaroneck, having moved there after Denise filed for divorce.

For Christmas, Denise had taken the children to Pittsburgh, returning alone with a trunk full of empty boxes. On a bitter cold day just shy of the New Year, she carried her belongings from the house while Ginny watched quietly from the stoop. Denise had asked Ginny to come help, not to carry things, but to keep Douglas calm. So Ginny watched as a ghostly version of her sister-in-law—Denise's tan had faded to an unsettling shade of white—hoisted each box with her hip into the trunk of her car.

Douglas had been relegated to the kitchen, but every few minutes he rushed to the front steps and tried to help Denise carry things. She refused, but once, he wrestled a box from her and planted his feet on the ground.

"Don't go," he said.

For a moment it looked as though Denise might slap him. Then she said flatly, "Keep it," returning inside for another load.

He stood alone on the lawn, hugging the box, staring up at the house. His shoulders shook as he fought back sobs. Ginny gently pried the box loose, and he whispered, "I never want to see this place again."

A FOR SALE sign was, in fact, already pitched on the lawn, since Denise made it clear that in addition to petitioning for sole custody of the children, she wanted the proceeds from the house. She told Douglas that if he contested either, she'd stand in court and belt out the details of what happened on Thanksgiving, even if it meant admitting she fired the first shot and went along with the cover-up.

What Ginny remembered most about the day Denise left, the last day Ginny saw the house on Deerkill Road, was that they never once spoke of what happened there. And yet, with all the carrying of boxes, the walking inside and out, she, Douglas, and Denise deftly avoided stepping in the areas where the boys had lain.

Their father was not charged and the protests eventually faded, but the media kept the case alive by putting the entire family under the microscope. Having exhausted insinuations about excessive violence, the newspapers began portraying the family as victims; they became the innocent "every family" whose lives could, in an instant, be torn apart. Her mother's Wellesley yearbook photos were printed, as were excerpts from Ginny's poems. Photographs of the house on Deerkill Road appeared with sidebars detailing the size of the sunporch and wine cellar. But a well-intended profile on Ginny's adoption of a special-needs child prompted a journalist to contact the home-study agency for information. When it became clear there had never been a home study, Ginny was accused, in print, of "buying a child."

Ginny and Priya were eating breakfast when a child-services official arrived to remand Priya to the state until the matter could be settled in India. Priya, who seemed to immediately grasp the situation, ate her oatmeal in slow, deliberate spoonfuls while Ginny tried desperately to explain to the woman—a plump woman whose teeth were large and white, like piano keys—that she had worked in the orphanage where Priya had been, that leaving her behind would have been neglectful. Ginny's pleas were met with bureaucratic silence, and she was instructed to pack Priya's clothes or risk immediate arrest.

For a moment Ginny thought she would risk arrest. She even glanced through the kitchen window to see if the official had blocked her car—which she had. The large-toothed woman seemed familiar, almost bored, with Ginny's desperation. She soon offered what was surely the perfect, and no doubt practiced, falsehood that brought all such heartrending moments to a calm conclusion:

"I'm certain you can sort out any misunderstandings and get her back. But right now I have to take her."

This lie helped to steady Ginny's hands as she packed the suitcase she had once helped Priya carry from the orphanage. As Ginny lugged the heavy bag down the stairs, she stilled her panicked heart by telling herself this was temporary. She set the bag beside Priya, who had not budged from her seat at the breakfast table.

"Priya," she said.

The bowl of oatmeal was almost empty, but Priya quietly scraped her spoon around the edges, refusing to look up.

"Priya."

The toothy woman reached for the bag, and in an instant Priya grasped the handle. Priya looked at Ginny, who recognized for the second time the look of someone pleading for life. Ginny held Priya's stare—it was like holding the hand of a person dangling from a ledge. Slowly the weight overcame Ginny and her gaze slipped helplessly to the floor.

"For now," the woman said.

Priya pushed back her chair and lifted the suitcase. Her face settled into a blank expression that made her look, for a moment, like an entirely different person. In a trick of light, Ginny was suddenly certain that Priya's face belonged to another child. It was not until Priya stepped through the door, not until Priya stood outside carrying her suitcase, glancing back at Ginny for the last time ever, that Ginny felt the full and stunning force of losing her daughter.

An odd assortment of people—her entire department, former students, even Ratu—leapt to Ginny's defense. Petitions were circulated. The possibility loomed that another person or family could apply for guardianship, but Priya was a mute seven-year-old who witnessed the Thanksgiving Day Massacre. Ginny kept her room ready, should the Indian courts decide it was best to return her to the only mother she had ever known. But it became clear that Priya would likely end up right back in the same orphanage.

But not with Ravi.

Ravi and Safia had been dismissed for doctoring Ginny's 1-600A form.

Amid Ginny's sadness, Douglas's companionship provided a merciful distraction. That winter, the two spent many late nights sitting on her couch, drinking wine, trying to trace the origins of everything that happened. Neither of them was sleeping well, so sometimes until 2:00 a.m., Douglas would explain his work at Obervell, the eminent domain issues, and what he knew of Kijo Jackson. At moments they had to pause in their conversations, recognizing the silent boomeranging of blame. Ginny pitied her brother for all that had been taken from him (he kept an array of photographs of his children on his nightstand, and each day he e-mailed Denise, begging her to return), but also felt, at times, that his greed had brought the disaster upon them, upon those boys. He, in turn, believed that if she had just served the meal as planned, everyone would have been fine. At times, they each blamed themselves. But they were entirely unable to speak of what their mother had done. Their silence about her actions drew them even closer, as did the painful knowledge that since Thanksgiving, she had sealed herself away in Westport, withdrawing from the world. If Ginny called, it was her father, now, who answered the phone. They weren't sure if Eleanor would ever return to her former self. So Ginny and Douglas were desperate, as they had never been before, even as children, for each other's love and for acceptance of each other's mistakes. They stood together in the dark truth of what happened that night. Before turning in, they always shared a fierce and silent hug.

By March, when Ginny had to attend the West Coast conference, Douglas said he was concerned about her flying across the country by herself; he didn't want her stranded alone at some stuffy academic gathering. In fact, she suspected it was he who feared solitude. The Thanksgiving Day events had triggered a barrage of attacks on Obervell Construction, which finally let Douglas go. For the first time in years, his days were empty.

Ginny was not giving the keynote address that day. In light of everything, she decided not to call undue attention to herself.

In the auditorium, people took their seats, silencing their cell phones and settling their bags on the floor; the auditorium was crowded, but the mood was somewhat grim. Near the coffee-and-donut table, a television playing CNN reminded them that it was the fifth anniversary of the Iraq War, reporting the casualty statistics and offering a montage of grisly images from Baghdad.

Now the conference organizer stood at the podium and welcomed everyone to the Fourth Annual Feminist Geography Conference.

And then, from behind a blue curtain, a young Indian woman walked onto the stage. She looked to be twenty-three or twenty-four and approached the podium with her shoulders held like a ballerina's. As Ginny watched the woman slide the paper clip off her speaking notes and survey the auditorium, her heart tripped. She was convinced this was precisely the woman Priya would have grown into. Ginny realized Douglas must have had the same feeling, because suddenly his hand was touching her elbow.

Ginny glanced at her program, flipping through to the biographies. Beena Sengupta, a PhD candidate at Harvard, had immigrated to the United States at age eighteen. As Beena adjusted her microphone, her eyes met Ginny's, triggering the awful memory of Priya's final, pleading stare. Except this woman wore an expression that seemed strangely like an accusation. As Ginny often did in those months after the incident, she imagined strangers knew the story, had read the details in the paper.

"Hello, and thank you," Beena said.

She had only a trace of an accent. Her hair was thick and brilliantly shiny, her eyes large and walnut colored. She was beautiful and poised; Ginny could hardly look at her.

"I was asked today, as the youngest speaker at the conference, to say a few words in my keynote address about American youth, as pertains to trends in women in the shifting urban landscape of the United States. But I want, instead, in light of today's anniversary, to speak about the youth of America . . . that is, America the child."

Beena turned her page, rattling the gold bangles on her thin wrist. Her nails, painted maroon, splintered the overhead light.

"The United States is but a mere two hundred and thirty years old, the baby of the world. Too young to remember crusades and plagues . . ."

The words flowed from Beena's mouth and Ginny was mesmerized by the gentle smile that accompanied her fierce indictments. As Beena calmly flipped through her notes, Ginny grew certain that this girl, this woman, would succeed. And Ginny tried to imagine that this was the path her daughter would take, that Priya would leave the orphanage; that she would be loved and fed and clothed; that she would be whisked off to Bombay as Ravi and Safia had been; that she would learn to speak and read and go to London for college. She would fall in love and whisper stories late at night to her boyfriend of how she was taken to America by a woman who had broken many rules, but meant only to love her. How one day, she would find this American woman, would ring Ginny's doorbell, and over tea she would explain what she had seen of the world. And she would tell Ginny that despite Ginny's mistakes, everything had worked out all right, that Ginny was forgiven.

"We must stop and we must repent," Beena said, her voice intensifying. "The mistakes, the offenses. Only then will America repair itself . . . We must mourn the fallen, the slain, the sacrificial lambs who suffered at our hands."

Douglas leaned close and Ginny turned to look at him. Life had worn on him; loss had carved papery lines along the edges of his eyes. But she clasped his hand and felt a deep warmth in it, a familiar strength. His palms were callused from his recent work—he was building new doors for her house, sanding the floors, stripping away the rotted windowsills and thresholds, and mounting thick new cedar planks.

Together, now, they slid forward in their seats, remembering, regretting, awaiting the return of hope.

ACKNOWLEDGMENTS

In researching this novel, the following texts were of great assistance: *Streetwise* and *A Place on the Corner* by Elijah Anderson, *The Way We Never Were* and *The Social Origins of Private Life: A History of American Families, 1600–1900* by Stephanie Coontz, *Past, Present, and Personal* by John Demos, *Blood Rites* by Barbara Ehrenreich, *Homecoming: When the Soldiers Returned from Vietnam* by Bob Greene, *Man the Hunted: Primates, Predators, and Human Evolution* by Donna Hart and Robert W. Sussman, *Cities in a Race With Time* by Jeanne R. Lowe, and *Bulldozed: "Kelo," Eminent Domain, and the American Lust for Land* by Carla T. Main.

For answering my endless questions, I'm grateful to Detective Bob and the men of Vidal Court.

For their invaluable feedback on this book, I would like to thank Eric Bennett, Alex Berenson, Stuart Blumberg, Sarah Shun-lien Bynum, Justin Cronin, Sarah Funke, Olivia Gentile, Steve Kistulentz, Daniel Mason, Dan Pope, Timberwolf, Josh Weil, and my parents. A special thanks to the brilliant Kurt Gutjahr.

This novel would not exist without the generosity of the following institutions: the Corporation of Yaddo, the MacDowell Colony, the Virginia Center for the Creative Arts, Ledig House International, the Guggenheim Foundation, the Dorothy and Lewis B. Cullman Center for Scholars and Writers, and the Stamford Historical Society.

Two extraordinary guardians have been watching over this book: my agent, Dorian Karchmar, who helped bring it to life and find it a home; and my editor, Alexis Gargagliano, who gave me the perfect guidance and encouragement.

The entire Scribner family has been wonderful. Thank you to Rex Bonomelli and Stephanie Evans for their patience and perfectionism, and to Nan Graham and Susan Moldow for their support.

An interesting aside regarding the *Kelo v. New London* Supreme Court decision mentioned in this novel: in November 2009, Pfizer announced it was closing its New London research facility; the land on which Susette Kelo's home once stood remains an undeveloped lot.

ABOUT THE AUTHOR

Jennifer Vanderbes is a graduate of the Iowa Writers' Workshop and the recipient of numerous awards, including a Guggenheim Fellowship and a New York Public Library Cullman Fellowship. Her debut novel, *Easter Island*, was translated into sixteen languages and named one of the best books of the year by *The Washington Post* and *The Christian Science Monitor*. Her essays and reviews appear in *The New York Times* and *The Washington Post*. She lives in New York City. Visit her website at www.jennifervanderbes.com.